D1253813

Books by JEROME WEIDMAN

A FAMILY FORTUNE

Jerome Weidman

SIMON AND SCHUSTER

New York

1 2 3 4 5 6 7 8 9 10

LIBRARY OF CONGRESS CATALOGING IN PUBLICATION DATA

WEIDMAN, JEROME, DATE.
A FAMILY FORTUNE.

I. TITLE.
PZ3.W4257FAM [PS3545.E449]   813'.5'2   77-26922
ISBN 0-671-24106-0

FOR
CAROL AND PAVY

Pas si fou.
Family crest, the Dukes of Dorset

PART I
1976

1

"One thing I have learned," Max Lessing once said. "Never work for two spoilers."

He was seventy-two when he said it. Now that she herself had passed seventy-two, Ida Lessing wondered why at this moment her husband's remark had come back to her, in the middle of an unexpected telephone call from Joe Catalini up in New York.

"Joe, you're not making sense," she said into the phone. "Nobody is landing at Miami International in forty minutes. Not even Henry Kissinger. The field is shut down."

Ida was annoyed with herself for the way her voice had risen. An American citizen for fifty years. With her own telephone in her own house for more than forty. When would she get over the foolish notion that on the long-distance wire talking louder made you sound clearer to the person at the other end?

"Henry Kissinger's pilot is not on the Lessing family payroll," Joe Catalini said. "Abe Shantz is."

"Abe Shantz is paid to fly our family jets," Ida Lessing said. "Not control the weather."

"Abe doesn't worry about things we don't pay him for," Joe said. "One of those things is controlling the weather. Abe is paid to get that Lear through to you with whatever it's carrying no matter where you are, whenever I order him to get there."

"If you ordered him to get here in this weather," Ida said, "you did something that for you is very unusual, Joe. You made a mistake."

"Mrs. L.," Joe Catalini said. "For damn near half a century I have been getting paid by the Lessing family not to make mistakes. I have never yet not earned my money. I am not beginning now, Mrs. L."

Inside Ida's head the seasoned old security guard snapped to attention. Joe called her Mrs. L only when the words that had crossed his mind meant bad news.

"You're calling from New York," Ida said. "It's not exactly a mistake for you not to know up there what we all know down here because we can see it and you can't. Down here in Florida, Joe, we've all of a sudden got a hurricane heading our way."

"Mrs. L.," Joe said. "What's heading your way at this moment could make a hurricane a cheerful experience."

Suddenly Ida could see him clearly. All the way up there in New York, Ida Lessing could see Joe Catalini in his big office on top of the Lessing Tower, staring down Park Avenue toward Grand Central. Over his head the framed membership scroll from the Minneapolis Second Ward High School National Honor Society. On his desk the silver-framed picture of the fat wife with the name Ida could never remember. On the wall to the right the framed diploma from Harvard Law School. On his face that intelligent, sad look.

"All right, Joe," Ida said. In her normal voice. "Tell me."

For some things, at certain times, even a foolish old woman remembered that on the long-distance wire what carried clearest was a whisper.

"Abe Shantz will be landing at Miami International in forty minutes," Joe Catalini said. "By my watch it's now ten minutes after midnight. Almost eleven. The field is shut down, of course, for regular traffic. Not for Abe Shantz. He

14

will touch down ten minutes to one this morning. Nine minutes at most. Add to that the fifty minutes it takes to reach The Frontenac."

"Not in this weather," Ida Lessing said. "We're getting TV reports every fifteen minutes, Joe. Here in Florida things are falling down. Palm trees. Power lines. Statistics on hurricane frequency. Everything. Nobody can get here to The Frontenac from Miami International in fifty minutes, Joe."

"Chick Rosen will be driving," Joe Catalini said. "He's waiting with the car on the Miami airstrip right now. He'll have Abe Shantz in your living room at twenty minutes to two. No later. Tell Shotzie please to have a cup of hot coffee ready for both of them."

Inside Ida Lessing's head her other plans for the next few hours slid away into a "hold" drawer. The drawer clicked shut. The contents would have to wait. Everything would have to wait. Joe Catalini had rung the fire bell.

Ida said, "Joe."

"Yes, Mrs. L?"

All the way up there on Park Avenue, in the middle of the night, she heard the change in sound for which she had not realized she was waiting. Ida Lessing responded the way a Dalmatian responds to a fire bell. The way she had been taught to respond. The way she had been responding for half a century.

"Abe Shantz and Chick Rosen," Ida said. "Will they want something with their coffee?"

"For Abe a piece of *lekach* with almonds," Joe said. "If you can manage."

The change was not in his voice. Joe Catalini's voice never changed. It was in the spaces between the words. After half a century of listening, Ida Lessing knew how to read the things Joe had taught her long ago were better not spoken. Even on private-private-private-three-times-private family wires.

"Shotzie just baked a fresh loaf this afternoon," she said. "I can manage."

15

Joe said, "Good."

One word. No room for spaces. Except up front before the word was spoken. And then after it was spoken, when he knew the word was safely lodged in Ida's ear. It told her what she wanted to know. She was back in Joe's good graces.

"Anything else?" Ida said.

"Yes, please," Joe said. "For Chick Rosen, a slice without almonds. If that's possible, Ida?"

The old reliable security guard inside Ida's head had snapped to attention. Now it sounded the alert.

"If you want it," Ida said, "it's possible."

Joe Catalini said, "Good girl."

Scratch the annoyance about talking louder on the long-distance wire. Ida Lessing had a more important question. When would she get over the embarrassment of feeling herself light up inside like the seven-branched silver candlestick on the table in the dining room on Friday night? Just because he used those two quiet words. The words that only she and Joe Catalini knew were meant for her as a medal? A woman of seventy-three? And a man of sixty-eight? A man she had known since he was a Boy Scout in Minneapolis wearing khaki knickers and a royal blue neckerchief?

"Good girl." She was that, all right. And she was proud of it. As long as Joe Catalini said so, Ida Lessing would never be less than that.

"Anything else, Joe?"

"Not till I talk to you again," the voice from Park Avenue said. "Take care, Ida."

As though she would do anything else. Or could.

2

Taking care was her job. It had been her job for almost six decades. She did it well. Nobody knew this better than her husband. The knowledge kept Max Lessing alive.

"Ida," he said.

Nobody heard him. Not even Miss Farragut, who sat beside the bed, eyes pasted to the TV screen like Band-Aids. The hand of the nurse rested lightly on the folded *Wall Street Journal* at Max's elbow. She had brought it with her, as she did every day, when she came on duty a few minutes before midnight.

Miss Farragut was new. She had not been on the job long enough to demonstrate many talents. One of these, however, was getting a copy of *The Wall Street Journal* from the Pompano Beach News Dealers to the bedside of her patient. As nurses went, this was not bad. Two years of immobilization in an orthopedic bed had taught Max Lessing to appreciate small gifts.

The 8:00 A.M. to 4:00 P.M. nurse brought *The New York Times*. She picked it up at the Fort Lauderdale airport on her way to work. She lived just off A-1-A. The girl on the 4:00 P.M. to midnight shift brought the *Boca Raton Clarion*. She lived at Lighthouse Point. Miss Farragut brought *The Wall Street Journal*. The Pompano Beach News Dealers, just around the corner from her home, had on their racks almost all the New York papers only a few hours after the city editions hit the New York newsstands.

"Ida," Max Lessing said again.

Miss Farragut continued to stare at the TV screen. She did not hear him. Max Lessing did not expect her to. A television comic was laughing his head off. Max Lessing did not hear the comic. He did not expect to hear anybody. Max Lessing's hearing had vanished two years ago along with his speech.

For almost a week after the stroke came down on him like a rockslide, Max had been unaware that he had been cut off from sound. During those first days of disaster, he had been totally preoccupied with the problem of adjusting to the knowledge that he could no longer use his vocal cords, both legs, and his right arm. It was a big piece of knowledge to absorb. Max Lessing fought it.

When the struggle ended, when Max knew he had lost the fight, he knew also he had nothing left with which to take on the battle for his hearing. This was the sobering bit of knowledge. In Joe Catalini's phrase: the bottom line. Max Lessing had never lost a battle in his life.

The new experience took him by surprise. Astonished, he watched his mind fill with jostling images of people he had forgotten long ago. Men who had lost all sorts of battles because Max Lessing, who could no longer remember what the fights were about, had won them. It was not easy to grasp that every one of those men must once have felt the way Max Lessing felt now. It was not easy, but Max worked at it.

Working at it now, under these strange new conditions, Max wondered why these forgotten men were in such a desperate rush to pluck at his lapels and call themselves to his attention.

Examining them with interest, Max found he missed something in their performance. It was as though they had come hurling themselves into his presence so rapidly, courtiers seeking to establish the authenticity of lineal descent from a dying monarch, that they had neglected to bring along some of their identifying documents. Max Lessing concentrated, using parts of his mind he had never known he possessed. The results of the concentration were a source of further astonishment.

What he had missed was a sound. A familiar noise. The sound of bleating. What Max had not realized until now was that one of the great satisfactions of achieving success, which for half a century had been as natural to him as breathing, was hearing the whine of the victim from whom the triumph had been wrested. The new knowledge embarrassed him. Max Lessing had always thought of himself as a decent human being.

"Ida," he said once more.

He did not expect her to hear him. Max did, however, expect her to respond. She always had. From that day in 1919, when he had stopped at the barn door of the farmhouse outside Klein Berezna to beg something to eat. At the sound of his voice the blond girl had turned and risen from the milking stool and come toward him. That had been more than fifty-six years ago. Fifty-seven, come December. Ida Lessing was still doing it. Even though Max Lessing no longer had a voice with which to summon her.

"Ida," he repeated.

The sound was made inside his head. Only there. Nowhere else. Inside his head, where everything was still brilliantly clear. Clearer than it had ever been.

It was a clarity that had added a new dimension to what was left of his life. As though on the edge of death Max Lessing had been granted—for a price, of course, because everything had a price—the opportunity to see it all. The whole enchilada, as Joe Catalini would put it. The whole ball of wax. Especially the things Max Lessing had never had time to look at.

The price was confinement to an orthopedic bed. Built by a firm in Zurich under the meticulous supervision of Dr.

Herbert Zlotkin of the Rusk Clinic. In it Max Lessing was the prisoner of a round-the-clock squad of white-uniformed attendants. They moved him and fed him and drained him at will, unaware that the expensive vegetable in their care was anything more.

Ida's vision went beyond the eyes of hired nurses. Ida knew when Max wanted his wife.

He said again, "Ida."

Ida Lessing came into a room as though from the moment she opened the door anybody inside who had up to then thought he or she owned the place would be well advised to consult an attorney at once and have him check out the title.

"Miss Farragut," Ida said.

The nurse lurched up out of her absorption in Johnny Carson. She looked frightened. "Everything is okay," Miss Farragut said hastily. "Nothing wrong, Mrs. Lessing."

Max Lessing did not, of course, hear the exchange. In the angled mirror hanging from the ceiling over the bed, however, he had a clear view of the two women. From their faces he could read the meaning of the words they had spoken as plainly as though they had been uttered in the soundproof chamber of his mind.

What Max read was funny. So funny that his mind abandoned for a delicious moment the reason he had summoned Ida into the room. In the life to which two years ago he had been reduced, laughs were few. Max gave himself over to the rare pleasure of an inaudible chuckle.

Miss Farragut was new on the job. All Max Lessing's nurses were new on the job. Between what Herb Zlotkin demanded for him and what Ida saw to it that her husband got, Florence Nightingale herself would not have lasted very long in the master suite of The Frontenac's penthouse.

"Miss Farragut," Ida Lessing said gently. "In the whole state of Florida at this moment nobody is okay."

As though Ida's arrival had tripped some sort of trigger,

the comic was suddenly wiped off the screen, smirk and all. He was replaced instantly by the newscaster with the pudgy face whose name Max could never remember.

"As of midnight," the man said without even so much as an introductory Hello, folks, "which is five—no, seven—as of seven minutes ago, Hurricane Carla was still moving steadily across the Caribbean on her course west-northwest, heading straight for Cuba. The latest coordinates are—get your pencils, please—"

Miss Farragut exploded from the chair. In the wrong direction, unfortunately. Ida Lessing picked up the pencil from the table beside Max's bed. With a kind smile she pointed the pencil in the right direction.

"Sorry," Miss Farragut mumbled through a nervous giggle.

She took the pencil from Ida in a snatching lunge. She turned herself in the right direction and trotted to the hurricane-tracking map. It had been clipped from yesterday's *Boca Raton Clarion*. The scrap of newsprint was Scotch Taped to the lower edge of a picture frame. It contained the Margaret Bourke-White shot from *Life* showing F.D.R. in the Oval Office three months after Pearl Harbor swearing in Max Lessing as Deputy Chairman of the War Production Board.

"—latitude eighteen point nine north," the newscaster said from the TV screen; "longitude seventy-six point five west."

"Gee," Miss Farragut said, pinpointing the appropriate marks on the map. "The darn thing sure seems to be heading our way."

Soothingly, Ida Lessing said, "Let's hope it changes its mind."

Inside his head, Max Lessing retreated from the scene he could not hear. He had never liked Florida to begin with. This dislike had grown more intense when he began to grasp, shortly after he was hit, what Ida and Joe Catalini had planned for him.

Buying a great big piece of beach as private as the lump of sand owned by that Rainier kid over there in Monaco. Building on it a fifteen-story apartment house with a penthouse top floor that was practically a private Lenox Hill and Mt. Sinai rolled into one, including the Klingenstein Pavilion. It was enough to turn a man's stomach.

Not because of the twelve million the structure had cost. The way Joe Catalini cooked books, Max was sure the I.R.S., as usual, had probably paid for most of it anyway. What turned Max Lessing's stomach was the fact that for the first time in his life he had no more control over his destiny than he had over his bladder.

The doctors had told Ida to take him to Florida, and Joe Catalini had said it was the only way. Anything Joe said, Ida did. So here Max was in Florida.

The only people Max had ever known who had a good word to say for the place had been Al Capone and Joe Kennedy. And what Max Lessing thought of those two characters had been placed on the record long before the man Rex Reed and Suzy called the Head of the Lessing Empire had lost the power of speech.

What Max Lessing had not lost was the power of his mind. He had decided two years ago not to waste any of that on working up a head of steam about anything that happened in Florida, including hurricanes. Max moved his mind back to something important: the reason he had summoned Ida into his bedroom.

From the corner of his left eye Max Lessing saw Ida's beautifully netted head of blue-white hair turn toward Miss Farragut.

"In the kitchen, please," Ida said. "Wait."

"Wait?" Miss Farragut said.

"Yes, please," Ida said.

Miss Farragut, wondering why, said, "Yes, Mrs. Lessing." She left the room.

"I'm not sure about this new nurse," Ida said.

Just as casually. Sending the words into the air over the bed with no more emphasis than the normal expulsion of breath to be expected from a still girlishly slender, always beautifully tended body dropping easily into a chair beside a bed.

"I hope I'm wrong," Ida said, "in the feeling I get that she's more interested in Johnny Carson than in her patient."

She said it without rancor. Or even inflection. Dismissing a janitor who had come from the agency with high recommendations as a broom pusher and, all too soon, had proved what Ida and Max had learned long before they got to The Frontenac—way back in Minneapolis, half a century ago, when they were newlyweds, when they were just beginning to be astonished by the fact that things were working out well enough over here in America for them to be able to afford servants. What they had begun to learn then was that there are no good broom pushers. If they were good, Max had pointed out long ago with a philosophical shrug, they would not be broom pushers.

"I'll call Fennell-Schwartz in the morning," Ida said. "If they can't send over somebody better, I'll tell Shotzie to call Herb Zlotkin in New York and get his office to line up a new employment agency for us down here."

As the words emerged, Ida's glance slid from the TV screen to the angled mirror overhead.

Two years ago, when she had brought Max down here, Herb Zlotkin had taken two days off from his Rusk Clinic practice to come along in the ambulance plane. Herb wanted to make sure Max's room was fixed up properly for the therapy program he had laid out.

The angled mirror was important not only to make it possible for Max to watch TV. More important, Herb Zlotkin had pointed out, was the constant inducement it provided for Max to try to move his head. The hope for poststroke therapy, Dr. Zlotkin had explained to Ida, rested not only on what was left of the victim's musculature.

23

More important was what remained of his psychological structure.

During his years as Max Lessing's doctor, Herb Zlotkin had learned one thing about his patient's psychological structure: Max Lessing, in appearance, voice, and manner a gentle, slow-moving giant, was driven inwardly by a curiosity so insatiable that it had kept him for decades on the edge of nervous exhaustion. In fact, Herb felt sure this tension had contributed a good deal to the severity of the stroke that had almost destroyed his richest and most famous patient.

One of the principles of Herb's success in this field of rehabilitation was his insistence on the necessity to divert the patient's unconscious destructive drives into constructive channels. A man who had never in his life been able to avoid turning nervously toward an opening door might be able to learn how to do it again if the capacity were placed within, or almost within, his reach.

The angled mirror had been fixed, therefore, in such a way that a man immobilized on his back in the bed under it could, or just might if he made the effort, catch more than the TV screen. He could, or just might, pick up a glimpse of the door.

Soon after Herb returned to his practice in New York, Ida had had a small change made in the way Dr. Zlotkin had arranged the room. She ordered Mr. Ohmstetter, The Frontenac's building manager, to shift the angle of the mirror over Max's bed.

As a result, when Ida sat in the chair near Max's good hand, she could by glancing in the overhead mirror catch a glimpse of Max's eyes. Max had no way of knowing she was catching this glimpse, so he had no way of knowing what Ida did not want him to know: it was her only way of coming close to charting the movements of a mind that for half a century she had known as intimately as she knew her own. A mind that now, for two years, had been as closed off to her as those huge white spaces on the maps she remembered seeing back in Minneapolis in her son Norman's school geography book. The spaces had been marked UNCHARTED.

"Joe called a few minutes ago," Ida said. "He was still in the office. My God, how that man works. Sunday night, it's after twelve, the rest of the world is home in bed, but Joe Catalini is still at his desk up there on Park Avenue making telephone calls to London and Beirut and Mexico City and God alone knows where else. He'll kill himself, that man, he really will."

Rattling on casually, Ida watched Max's eyes up on the mirror. She watched and she wondered. What was getting through to him?

The doctors said: absolutely nothing. The doctors said Max could no longer hear sounds. Ida did not argue. She was not a doctor. She had never had a day of formal schooling. But Ida Lessing knew things you didn't learn in schoolrooms. She knew things the doctors didn't know. Things you learned only by living with someone for fifty-six years, night and day, seven days a week. No doctor could do that with any patient. Not even Herb Zlotkin.

"Joe said Abe Shantz is flying down," she said. "He didn't explain why, but Joe said Chick Rosen is meeting the plane at the airport and he'll drive Abe up here from Miami."

Ida glanced at her wristwatch.

"Joe said they'll be here at twenty minutes to two. Almost an hour yet. Joe said I should see Shotzie has coffee for both of them. As though I wouldn't, but then Joe said it would be nice if I had for Abe a piece of *lekach* with almonds. So I knew whatever it was Joe was calling about, he didn't want to talk about it on the phone, but he wanted me to come in here and tell you right away."

Ida's heart jumped. In the angled mirror she had seen something. Max's eyes. They had moved.

They did it again. This time the hand moved, too. The good hand on the bed humped itself up like a diver gathering his body at the end of the board. The bunched knuckles inched forward, toward the electric typewriter. The machine

25

sat on the shelf built into the bed. Herb Zlotkin had arranged the angle in such a way that it brought the keyboard directly under the crawling hand. Only one finger on it was strong enough to do the job.

Ida watched the pinky come down the turned-back bed sheet toward the keyboard. She leaned over and clicked the ON button. The motor began to whirr. Max's pinky crawled slowly, dragging itself from key to key like a tiny bird with a broken leg.

Ida waited as she always waited when Max's good hand surfaced with something from the walled-off, airtight, soundproof hole in which he was living out what was left of his life. She waited with her mouth slightly open, so that the air would move more easily into and out of her lungs. Max must never be aware that at such moments her heart always tried to hammer its way out of her body.

What she had told him about Joe Catalini's call had got through to him. No matter what the doctors said, even if they could prove Max Lessing was deaf, Ida could prove he was not deaf to her. Max was telling her what Joe's telephone call meant. He was deciphering the special code that it had taken all of their lives together, from Klein Berezna to Fifth Avenue, to construct. Max was explaining as he had explained to her for fifty-six years what she had to do, what her next move must be in the private world she and Max Lessing had put together with his brains and her devotion in this extraordinary country from which, when they were a couple of frightened kids, they had expected nothing but temporary safety from pursuit.

For the last two years the command post of that private world had been Max Lessing's walled-off, airtight, soundproof hole. From it was coming now what the doctors said was impossible: Ida Lessing's periodic, expected, explicit instructions from the only man from whom she had ever taken orders.

Inside the walled-off, airtight, soundproof hole, the mind that was all that was left of Max Lessing's life was busily at work. It had turned from the temporary amusement of watching Ida skillfully set Miss Farragut straight.

Slowly, in erratic little spasms, single letter by single letter, Max Lessing's orders to his wife began to appear on the sheet of paper in the electric typewriter.

3

"Next time out," Chick Rosen said, "I'm going into an honest business."

Abe Shantz, on the seat beside Chick, stared straight ahead, scowling at the night beyond the streaming windshield. He was unaware that the man at the wheel had spoken. Then, through the roar of the weather, something came back to him. An echo. A shift in the pattern of sound. It reminded Abe that a new sound had appeared inside the speeding Cadillac. A sound that had nothing to do with the tunnel of whipping foliage and lashing rain through which they were roaring toward The Frontenac at seventy miles an hour. Abe Shantz turned from the windshield. He looked at the driver with displeasure. Abe roared, "What the hell are you talking about?"

"What I'm doing right now," Chick Rosen bellowed.

The big black car lurched. Abe grabbed at the buckle of the safety belt. It was flopping wildly over his head. At the Miami airport Abe had disdained Chick's suggestion that he strap himself into it. Doing it now, Abe grunted, then added a number of other not dissimilar sounds. The few moments of wild rocking settled back into the bumping, jolting discomfort through which they had been riding for almost half an hour.

"What goes on down there?" Abe said.

"A hurricane," Chick said in the sudden silence.

His voice, geared to the roar, boomed foolishly in the now quiet enclosed space.

"If I was in an honest business," Chick said, "I'd be home in bed now."

Rudely, without warning, the roar of the wind returned. It came in a slicing chop, hurling the silence back out of the car.

"I can't hear a word you're saying," Abe yelled. "Save your juice for when you get back to bed."

These Miami jerks were all the same. Especially the wise-guy college sons of the old creeps who had made it. On the take, these little bastards could find their way blindfolded to the gravy boat. But when it came to gratitude, it was just another word in the dictionary. This Chick Rosen was typical.

If it hadn't been for the Lessing family, this kid's old man would still be just another tubercular slob coughing out his lungs trying to pay the rent by pushing a hack on the streets of New York. The old man, though, had been lucky. He used to ride Mr. Max once in a while back in the early days right after Prohibition was knocked out of the box, when in 1934 the Lessings had first come east out of Minneapolis.

Mr. Max liked Mr. Rosen. When the old man had got too sick to work, Mr. Max had staked Rosen to the front money for setting up a limousine service in Miami. The old man had not only got better. He had also got rich. How could he avoid it? When the Lessings let you play in the family ball park, you couldn't stay poor if you worked at it. The poop up in the New York office was that the Rosen family had almost thirty 1976 Cadillacs working the Gold Coast out of Miami, every one of them one hundred percent family-owned, grinding out an annual gross somewhere around the two-million mark.

"When you get to Exit 31, make a left," Abe said.

Chick said, "That's not the way to The Frontenac."

Abe Shantz said, "You Yale or Harvard?"

"Penn State," Chick Rosen said. ·

"When I get back to New York," Abe said, "I'll tell Joe Catalini to call the dean and tell him the Lessing family is sending over a brand-new football stadium. A token of gratitude for turning out a limo driver smart enough to know when you hang a Louis at Exit 31 it's not the way to The Frontenac."

"Listen, Mr. Shantz," Chick said.

Abe said, "You do the listening, son."

When Joe Catalini had hired Abe Shantz, after the boys in Washington had picked up their marbles in Korea, to take over the Lessing family's jet fleet, Abe was wearing a gold leaf on the shoulder of his Air Force tunic. He retired one rank higher, lieutenant colonel, and "Colonel" was what he was entitled to be called, even by kids from Penn State. And when Abe Shantz started on the Lessing payroll it was for thirty big ones a year plus. At a time when a big one was a big one.

Abe Shantz had gone on from there, because in the Lessing organization you didn't stand still. You went on, or you went out. Abe Shantz knew who he was, and he knew where he stood in the Lessing organization. Where Abe Shantz stood he did not take shit from Penn State slobs whose fathers owned limousine services in Miami that had been handed to them by Mr. Max like a tip to a waiter.

Chick said, "All I'm trying to say, my orders from Mr. Catalini in New York, he spoke to me personally on the telephone just before midnight, he said I should get to Miami International immediately and I should pick you up and I should take you to The Frontenac. That's what Mr. Catalini told me."

"I know what Mr. Catalini told you," Abe said. "I was on the blower listening to him while he told it to you. Now I'm telling you the rest of it. Ready?"

"Yes," Chick said, and then, after the faintest moment of hesitation, he did something that might very well have saved his father's business from going down the drain. The young man said, "sir."

"When you get to Exit 31," Abe Shantz said, "you make a left."

Chick Rosen said, "Why?"

Abe said, "We're not going to The Frontenac."

4

"The Frontenac," wrote Larry Conyers, Real Estate Editor of *The Miami Herald,* in the 1976 Annual Home & Design Section, "enjoys two distinctions on the Florida Gold Coast. It is probably the most eye-catching structure ever built south of the Mason-Dixon line, and it is the only high-rise between Key West and Palm Beach on which Lloyd's of London is willing to write hurricane insurance."

This made easier the task faced by Ida Lessing and Joe Catalini. They knew it was impossible to keep from the world the fact that Max Lessing had suffered a stroke. Equally obvious was the fact that it was essential to the continued smooth functioning of the Lessing organization that the world remain unaware of the extent of the damage. Ida Lessing and Joe Catalini knew better than to attempt to handle this with P.R. denials. Instead, they leaked a steady flow of tidbits to the media. This plethora of misinformation was stuffed with colorful detail, most of it fanciful, some of it just conceivably true, all of it printable.

Through the cloud of gaudy internationally circulated fantasy, the theme Ida and Joe had set as the cornerstone of the campaign began to emerge clearly.

Stroke? Yes. Fatal? Nonsense. Damage? Minimal. Recovery? A matter of months. Meantime?

Meantime Mr. Max's son, Norman, remained at the helm of the family dreadnought. Norman Lessing had been there for years, anyway. And Mr. Max, his temporary physical incapacity in no way diminishing his mental acuity, would remain on the bridge, keeping his sharp eye on the helmsman. The cover story was complete.

To make the cover story work it was important that Mr. Max's true condition remain totally blacked out. In a clinic, however private, this was impossible. Nurses and attendants talked. Especially about famous patients. Hospitals, even sealed-off wings of hospitals, were no better. Foreign sanitariums, no matter how remotely perched, were worst of all. There were no more magic mountains. The trick was to keep the world from beginning to wonder, and then starting to ask, if Max Lessing was in fact dead.

"To do this," Ida said to Joe Catalini, "I think I've come up with a solution."

She said it one night a few days after Herb Zlotkin had given her and Joe a picture of Max's condition, and the subject of Florida had entered the discussion.

"Tell me," Joe said.

Ida said, "I think we should build ourselves an apartment house on the beach. A co-op, not a condominium, because with a condominium the people who buy the apartments run the building and they stick their noses into everything, and we don't want anybody sticking their noses into anything because no matter how you look at it, Joe, what we're doing is going into hiding with Max. If we do it in a place where people expect people to hide, every reporter will be scheming to stick his nose inside the door. If we do it in a place where people don't expect people to hide, it won't cross anybody's mind there's anything to stick their nose into. In an apartment house, if we build it ourselves, we can control the kind of minds we allow to buy apartments in our building."

Joe Catalini said, "Good girl."

He gave her a few moments in which to enjoy the glow

that came with the medal. Then he added, "You'll need help."

"I know where to get it," Ida said.

"You will," Joe said.

She did. With the result that now, two years after Herb Zlotkin had supervised Mr. Max's installation in the orthopedic bed on the penthouse floor, the other fourteen floors of The Frontenac were occupied by a group of people who had never met one another before they moved into the building.

They had come from many parts of the world and all walks—"In some cases runs," Joe Catalini said—of life. None of them was poor. The cover of the real estate broker's brochure for The Frontenac said $100,000 AND UP! It would never have occurred to any of them that aside from affluence, they all had only one thing in common.

Before he or she had been allowed to purchase an apartment in The Frontenac, every buyer had been passed by a secret screening committee. It consisted of Ida Lessing and Joe Catalini. Their acceptances and rejections had been based on reports from the Lessing legal department and the Lessing intelligence network.

The same rigorous selection process had produced the staff. From Paavo Ohmstetter, the building manager, to Kevin Cooley, the newest of the four porters, every examinable inch of their recorded lives had been gone over with greater care than Henry VIII ever devoted to a prospective wife.

What staff members had in common with the owners, who had purchased their interests from something called The Frontenac Real Estate Company, Inc., was the imprint at the top of their weekly paychecks: THE FRONTENAC REAL ESTATE COMPANY, INC.

Behind this corporate anonymity Ida Lessing was able to run her world. She ran it as effortlessly as, long ago, she had run her world from the tenement flat in Minneapolis and later, until Max was stricken, from the town house on Fifth

Avenue. This capacity to function was the core of her existence. She found many satisfactions in being able to function at seventy-three as efficiently as she had functioned at seventeen. Not the least of these satisfactions centered in the area of security. From her wrist, day and night, swung an elegantly unobtrusive carryall that contained, among a number of things not as a rule found in a woman's handbag, a Smith & Wesson .38 Chief's Special.

Ida Lessing had lived with the problem of security for fifty-six years. It had begun in Minneapolis at a time when she had never heard the word, certainly not in English. On a day in 1920 when Max had came home at dusk. He parked the pushcart downstairs in the yard behind the tenement and came upstairs for their evening meal.

Max said, "Things are going to change."

Ida turned from the stove. When Max came home, the first thing she did was clean up the soup. Max was not fussy. He never complained. He ate anything. But Ida knew he hated the layer of gluey fat that accumulated at the top of the pot during the long hours she had to keep it on the boil. It was the only way she knew how to make edible the lumps of tough meat that were all they could afford. She had to make each lump get them through at least three meals. On the seventh day, when the week's money usually ran low, sometimes out, they became vegetarians.

Turning with the wooden spoon, Ida saw that Max was still at the sink. His head was under the tap. He took a long time scrubbing away the filth that had accumulated during his day with the pushcart. America was turning out to be a surprisingly dirty place. Max pulled his head out from under the tap and turned off the water. He took down from the nail over the sink a piece of the Hecker's flour sacking Ida had learned to convert into towels.

"Change how?" she said.

"Those things I sell from the pushcart," Max said.

His head disappeared under the piece of Hecker's flour

sacking. Those things Max sold from the pushcart were razor blades, needles and thread, toothpaste, shoe polish, thimbles, buttons, kits for mending frying pans, plugs of chewing tobacco, boxes of wooden matches, toothache drops, pocket combs, castor oil: the things these people in America used all the time and yet always seemed to forget to buy when they came downtown on their regular shopping trips to Anoka Avenue. Things Max learned he could pick up cheap in the wholesale houses down on River Street early in the morning and sell for a few pennies more at the back doors of the houses in Sunningdale and Columbia Heights.

Plus one thing Max refused to identify for Ida. He said please not to ask him. It was not a nice thing for a husband to talk about with his wife. It was a big seller, however, and Max made a larger profit on each package than he made on razor blades or shoe polish.

As he made his awkward explanation, Max's face got red, the way it had got red that day almost three months before, in 1919, when Ida was in the barn and a voice called to her. Ida had got up from the milking stool and gone to the door. Standing in it was this tall, handsome boy with hair that looked like one of her mother's freshly polished copper pots. He asked if she could give him a cup of milk. He was on his way to Klein Berezna, he said, where he hoped to find work. He had no money, the boy said, and he had not put anything into his stomach since the night before.

Their eyes met, and the blood came running up into his face from his neck, and Ida's heart turned over.

Three months later, in Minneapolis, in 1920, she did not ask what those things were that Max sold from the pushcart but felt it was wrong for him to discuss with her. Even though she loved the way the blood came rushing up out of his neck into his face, Ida had learned in the time they had been together how angry it made her husband to feel his face grow red. But Ida didn't have to ask. She knew what those things were.

Mrs. Schiff, downstairs on the third floor, had told her.

Fat little Shotzie Schiff was only twenty-one, a little more than four years older than Ida, but she was already sewing for her third baby. The reason? The man she called her dopey husband was so religious he refused to use those things Max Lessing sold from the pushcart. Shotzie Schiff was outraged by her husband's stupidity. She felt Ida should learn from her neighbor's unfortunate experience. Seventeen was too young to have babies. Especially with never enough money in the house to know if, when this piece of meat was worn out, there would be enough to buy another piece for the next three meals.

"How are things going to change?" Ida said.

Max stepped away from the sink, still toweling his copper hair, so that Ida could bring over the soup pot to spoon off the fat.

"I'm going to sell something new," he said. "Something I think I can make more money out of than I make from toothpaste and shoe polish."

Ida said, "More than from those other things, too?"

Max's head came up out of the piece of Hecker's flour sack. His face looked hot.

"Don't talk like that," he snapped.

Ida laughed and said, "Then you talk. What's this new thing you're going to sell?"

"Wine," Max said.

Ida said, "Wine?"

"For Passover," Max said.

"Here in America people buy wine for Passover?"

The surprise in Ida's voice drove the blood down out of Max's freshly scrubbed face. She had given him a chance to explain something to her. Max liked that. Not those things he sold from the pushcart, of course. But there were other things, things he learned in the streets during the day, new things about America. Those things it did not make Max Lessing's face red to explain to Ida. It made him feel good. It made him feel on top of things. He laughed.

"It's not like at home," Max said. "Here in America

people don't make their own wine for Passover. Here in America they have to buy it."

"I'm glad," Ida said. "Then you can stop selling those things that Shotzie Schiff's husband is too stupid to use."

The blood went shooting up into Max's face. Ida laughed again. For a moment Max looked angry, but then he also started to laugh. He bunched up the piece of Hecker's flour sack and hurled it at the sink. Then he grabbed her, and he wrapped his arms around her in that way of his that made Ida feel he was trying to squeeze her like a piece of lemon into a glass of tea.

They laughed together for a while, the way they always did, and then all at once they stopped laughing, the way they always did, and Max picked her up and he carried her to the other side of the room, to the corner that was their bedroom.

Later, when Ida was back at the stove, reheating the soup, Max came up beside her.

"There's one thing," he said.

Ida Lessing stopped skimming the ugly fat from the top of the pot. She turned to look at her handsome husband. There was that thing in his voice, the funny little sound that she had learned meant his mind was full of something he didn't think it was right for her to hear.

Ida said, "What thing?"

"The wine," Max said.

"What about the wine?"

"You mustn't tell anybody I'm selling it from the pushcart."

"Why not?" Ida said.

Max said, "Not even Mrs. Schiff."

"Why not?" Ida said again.

Max said, "It's one of those things it's better a man doesn't tell his wife."

"Could a wife ask something else?"

"What?" Max said.

"This wine that you're going to sell," Ida said. "You have

to buy it somewhere before you can sell it. The way you buy those other things on River Street. Am I right?"

"How could you be wrong?" Max said. "Do I know how to make wine?"

"No," Ida said. "But I do."

The way Max stared at her made Ida laugh again.

"At home in Klein Berezna," she said, "I always helped my father make the Passover wine. Every year we did it together. It's very easy. If you find out where in this country you can buy grapes, the way you buy razor blades and shoelaces on River Street, you won't have to buy somebody else's wine on River Street. You'll be able to take out on the pushcart the wine I make here. That way you'll make more money on each bottle."

She expected him to react with excitement and gratitude. Instead, Max stared at her with a thoughtful frown.

"That doesn't change it," he said finally.

"Change what?" Ida said.

"Telling anybody I'm selling wine from the pushcart," Max said. "Whether I sell wine you make or it's wine I get somewhere else, you mustn't tell anybody I'm selling it, not even Mrs. Schiff, and don't ask me why. It's one of those things it's better a man doesn't tell his wife."

He didn't have to. Ida found out about Prohibition soon enough. Just as she had found out about those other things Max sold from the pushcart. Shotzie Schiff told her. Soon Ida found out something else. She found out that Max didn't mind her finding out. What he minded was being the one through whom the information came to her. He couldn't bring himself to tell her certain things. So long as Ida didn't tell him how she found out, however, Max was glad she knew. It gave him a broader platform on which to stand when the time came to make a decision based on the information. Max didn't like partners. What he liked was the assurance that came from having a partner. Ida made it possible for him to have it both ways.

The system worked. Ida Lessing never told her husband

how she found out the things he wanted her to know, and Max Lessing never asked. He merely depended on her knowing everything he wanted her to know.

Now, fifty-six years later, in 1976, in the Swiss orthopedic bed on the top floor of The Frontenac, Max couldn't ask, but that didn't matter. After half a century Ida knew her job. She knew it, and she enjoyed doing it. Tonight, even with hurricane Carla rattling the windows, Ida was not surprised to feel a special edge of pleasure in her enjoyment. It was a feeling she always had after a telephone talk with Joe Catalini.

When Ida came into the kitchen, Miss Farragut said, "The front bell just rang. Should I go?"

"No," Ida said. "I'll go."

As she moved down the hall Ida ran through in her mind what Joe had told her on the phone, settling from the choices available to her on how she would greet Chick Rosen and what she would say to Abe Shantz. Whatever it was Joe had sent them to tell her, it was big. Bigger than usual. Joe never used the *lekach* code unless he was dealing with something out of the ordinary.

When Chick Rosen and Abe Shantz finished telling her whatever it was Joe had sent them to tell her, Abe would fly back to New York and report her response to Joe. Ida felt the small, familiar tingle of pleasure. She wanted Abe to report it right.

Ida Lessing reached the door. With her forefinger she touched the proper buttons. The red light went out. The green light came on. The door slid open. She started putting together the pieces of the smile she had found worked best with messengers like Abe Shantz and Chick Rosen. She could feel the pieces of the smile stop gathering on her face. There was only one man at the other side of the door.

"Hello, Ida," Joe Catalini said.

5

They were both silent as she led him to her sitting room at the north end of the penthouse. It was next to Max's private suite. Ida waited until Joe was settled in the chair he always occupied when he flew down from New York. Then Ida took the chair she always occupied during these visits: facing him across the enormous jigsaw puzzle spread out on the low table between them.

"You don't look comfortable," Ida Lessing said.

Joe nodded, as though in agreement, but he continued to stare down at the puzzle. It was one of many that were made up for Ida by a Russian woman who lived in Hong Kong. Joe Catalini's intelligence network had found the lady shortly after Mr. Max was moved down from New York into The Frontenac. What F. A. O. Schwarz had always been able to offer Ida during her years in New York had proved inadequate for the new demands that living with an invalid were apparently making on her piano-wire nerves in Florida.

"I'm sorry if I don't look comfortable," Joe said. "That's probably because I feel uncomfortable."

He said it to the puzzle. The box cover showed a picture of "The Bridge at Argenteuil Under Attack by Caesar's Fifth Legion." What gave their special quality to the puzzles created by the Russian lady in Hong Kong was her unfettered imagination.

"Why do you feel uncomfortable?" Ida said.

"I don't seem to be very welcome," Joe Catalini said.

"Here?" Ida Lessing said. "In this house?"

The astonishment in her voice was, of course, spurious. They both knew it. So Joe knew something else. She would not be hurried. He would have to touch all the bases.

"I've been coming to your house for so many years," Joe Catalini said, "I can feel it in my bones when you're opening the door for me without sending up a cheer."

Ida said, "When you called me a couple of hours ago and you said you were flying Abe Shantz down from New York in the middle of the night, and Chick Rosen would be meeting him at the airport and driving him up here in the middle of a hurricane, I didn't get the feeling from your voice on the phone that what they were coming to tell me was something you expected me to send up a cheer about."

Joe blew out his breath in that tired way Ida had always found oddly attractive. He had a heavy look. Not fat, not fat at all, but solid. As though, it had occurred to Ida long ago, he were sitting on money. His wavy hair was clipped close to the skull. His short, slightly tilted nose was well positioned in relation to the good, strong jaw. And he had the sort of straight white teeth that Ida remembered thinking, the first time she saw Joe Catalini, made him resemble the boy in the Steeplechase ads. When Ida Lessing came to America in early 1920, people who had the sort of face Joe had were called he-men.

"You're right," he said. "I didn't expect you to send up any cheers, but I didn't expect you to be all this angry because instead of the promised Abe Shantz and Chick Rosen, who shows up is me."

"Angry?" Ida Lessing said. "Me?"

Again he blew out his breath in the small, patient, tired sigh.

42

"Yes, you," Joe said. "And yes, angry, and I don't blame you, because I've never lied to you in fifty years—"

"Fifty-four," Ida said.

"—but tonight I had to start, and I'd like to ask do you think I am the sort of person who would make such a start without knowing what I'm doing?"

Ida Lessing's face changed exactly as he had expected it to change. As though inside her head the focusing ring on a pair of binoculars had been given a short twist. The tense feeling in Joe Catalini's stomach eased slightly. He knew what was happening. She was facing the fact that in her eagerness to prove her anger was justified, it was just possible she had missed something. Maybe she had spoken too quickly. She was retracing her steps, scanning the maps more carefully for possible overlooked checkpoints.

Finally she said, "What was the last thing you said to me on the phone?"

Joe nodded. This was better.

"What you said, you asked if there was anything else, and I said Not till I talk to you again."

Ida nodded, and Joe Catalini understood that, too. When she realized she was not running the act, she always broke into a sprint to catch up and get into it.

Ida Lessing said, "You said Not till I call you back."

"No," Joe said. "I said, and I quote, I said Not till I talk to you again."

Another nod from Ida. She was back in the act. Joe knew what would be coming up next.

"And here you are," Ida said. "Talking to me again."

On schedule, the smile slid into place. It did things to Ida Lessing's face. Things that smiles rarely do to the faces of seventy-three-year-old women. Of course, Joe Catalini pointed out to his favorite audience—himself—not many seventy-three-year-old women had what Ida Lessing had before she started smiling.

"Yes," he said. "Here I am."

43

"When you called me a little after twelve," Ida said, "you were not calling me from your office in New York, of course."

"Of course not," Joe said.

"You just wanted me to think that."

"You and anybody else who might be listening," Joe Catalini said.

"I see," Ida said, which is not a major achievement in any conversation, a fact that Ida Lessing clearly understood, because she added at once, "Where were you calling from?"

"Palm Beach," Joe said. "A phone booth in the airport."

What he got now from Ida was another careful look. Again Joe Catalini waited. After a few moments, on the map inside her head, Ida Lessing had clearly found what she was looking for.

She said, "This anybody else who might have been listening. You wanted them to think, if in addition to listening they were also watching, you wanted them to think you were sending the Lear down to Miami empty."

"Which I was," Joe said.

"And when it got to Miami," Ida said, "if they were watching they would see Chick Rosen pick up only the Lessing pilot Abe Shantz."

"And follow him," Joe said. "If they were in a following mood."

"Follow him where?" Ida said.

"To wherever the Lessing pilot was going in a limo that belongs to the Rosen Miami fleet. Which anybody who was interested in following a Lessing pilot would know is a limo fleet that is part of the Lessing organization."

"And where Chick Rosen and Abe Shantz were going was not here to The Frontenac."

"If anybody was following them," Joe Catalini said, "the follower would think Abe Shantz and Chick Rosen are a couple of hardworking members of the Lessing organization who have a night off and are on their way to spend it with a couple of girlfriends in a bowling alley somewhere up in Deerfield."

"Leaving you free with nobody to watch while you come down from Palm Beach here to The Frontenac."

"When Abe Shantz took off in the Lear from Kennedy," Joe Catalini said, "I was taking off from La Guardia on Delta for Palm Beach."

"Which nobody expects you to do because you always use one of the family jets," Ida said. "So you were free to come down from Palm Beach in a taxi."

"Unfollowed," Joe said.

"You're sure."

"I'd better be," Joe Catalini said.

He could almost hear Ida Lessing's heart skip. Joe knew why. She had never heard that strange little note in his voice before. Neither had Joe. Something happened to Ida's face. Not much. But it did not have to be much to convey the message Joe Catalini had been waiting for. He had made his point.

"It's bad?" she said.

"Very bad," Joe said.

Ida Lessing leaned back in her chair. Away from the jig-saw puzzle that when completed would show "The Bridge at Argenteuil Under Attack by Caesar's Fifth Legion." It was as though she were clearing the space between herself and her visitor so that no obstacles would interfere with his news reaching her as clearly as he uttered it.

Ida Lessing said, "All right, Joe."

Joe said, "It's Stevie."

The sound of her grandson's name narrowed the distance between Ida Lessing and Joe Catalini. Not by much, and only for a moment. Almost immediately she leaned back again.

"Stevie is in school," Ida Lessing said firmly. "In Harvard College. In Cambridge, Massachusetts. Stevie is this minute sleeping in his rooms at Leverett House. On the fourth floor. Four-D."

"No," Joe Catalini said.

45

For once the tired voice was just right. Just right, and absolutely terrifying.

"Where is he?" Ida said.

"I don't know," Joe said.

"Joe," Ida Lessing said. "Tell me what you *do* know."

Joe Catalini said, "Stevie has been kidnapped."

6

Ida Lessing seemed to lose track of the next few moments. When she caught up with Joe Catalini's voice, what he was saying made no sense to her. Then she realized she must have said something to which he way replying. She made an effort and concentrated.

"Money," Joe was saying. "That's the first thing all you Jewish women think of.

The missing moments came back to her.

"When a member of the family gets kidnapped," Ida said, "what do Italian women think of?"

"The Pope," Joe Catalini said. "Wops always go to the top."

"Is that why you flew down here tonight?"

Joe said, "Don't do that, Ida."

"You're treating me like an old woman," Ida said.

"I've told you all I know," Joe said.

"Except why you had to come down here in person to tell it."

"You think I could let you hear a thing like that on the TV?" Joe Catalini said. "Or learn it from seeing it in the papers? You think I'm capable of doing a thing like that?"

"You are capable of doing anything," Ida Lessing said. "I've seen you do all of it."

"Not this," Joe said.

"Why not?"

"This is not an ordinary kidnapping," Joe Catalini said. "The trouble is, all the things you learn in a lifetime, there's always still something you never had a chance to learn. Ida, I don't know very much about kidnappings."

"How can you say that?" Ida said. "After the war? That Spanish man with the two names? There was a hyphen in between? Mr. Max put him in charge of those mines at the beginning. In Bolivia?"

"Yes," Joe said. "I know."

"And the first Nixon campaign?" Ida Lessing said. "Just before the election? The wife of that Italian man? Mr. Max was backing him in Chicago because of the Armour meat people?"

"Yes," Joe said. "I know."

"Then those two very fast?" Ida said. "One right after the other? In Canada? During the trouble on the Teamsters' contracts for the pipeline? When Norman said he had a deal with that Senator? The funny name? Like 'his blister'?"

"Isbister," Joe said.

"That's the one," Ida said. "He and Norman made the arrangement for us."

"Ida," Joe said. "You don't understand."

"What don't I understand?" Ida Lessing said.

"Those kidnappings," Joe Catalini said. "They were not important. They were ordinary things. Part of the cost of doing business. Like paying for fire insurance, or printing stationery, or heating bills, or buying office furniture. Those kidnappings, Ida, they were just money."

"Everything is just money," Ida Lessing said.

"You don't see what I'm saying," Joe Catalini said.

"Not yet," Ida said. In the voice that meant *Tell me, I'm ready to hear*.

"Whoever they are," Joe said, "we don't know why they took Stevie."

Ida Lessing frowned. Watching her face was for Joe like watching the face of the French clock on the marble mantel over the fireplace in the big drawing room. It was all glass. Joe could almost see the wheels inside her head going around, working their way through the problem.

She said finally, "They haven't asked for money." It was not a question.

"They haven't asked for anything," Joe Catalini said. "All they did was let me know by phone they had Stevie, and said I should wait for further instructions. I tried to trace the call. Nothing. I called Harvard. Stevie's roommate said Stevie was out. He wasn't sure when Stevie would be back. The boy didn't seem upset. I had the feeling it was better not to upset him. I said Just tell Stevie I called, it's nothing important, and when he gets back he might call me if he gets the chance.

"I'm not going to get that call, Ida. I don't know why I know that. I know only that at this moment it's better for Stevie if we don't upset anybody. If you think back on all those examples you just mentioned, Ida, you'll remember the one thing that stands out is that we never really knew anything about the kidnappers before they started to give us information. All our guesses were wrong. In this case, with Stevie's life on the line, I don't think we should do any guessing. I think we've just got to wait until the kidnappers make their next move. I'm sure that move will be what they said it would be, namely, a call to me. That's why, as of now, nobody knows Stevie has been kidnapped."

"You know," Ida Lessing said.

"Because they made sure I would know," Joe Catalini said. "I'm the only one who does know."

"I know," Ida said.

"Because I just flew down and told you," Joe said.

"Aside from the kidnappers, then," Ida said, "we're the only two people who do know."

"Only you and me," Joe said.

49

"Norman?" Ida said.

"Luckily," Joe said, "Norman is in Stockholm for the King's wedding."

"With Claire?" Ida said.

"Claire does not let Norman go alone to the weddings of kings."

"The police?"

"Not yet," Joe Catalini said.

"You're sure?" Ida said.

"I haven't called them," Joe said.

"A mistake," Ida Lessing said.

"Usually, yes," Joe Catalini said. "Not now."

"Joe," Ida said. "The police always know."

"Not in this case."

"They'll find out," Ida said.

"When I get ready to call them," Joe said.

"The way I remember it," Ida said, "kidnapping is hard work."

"And dangerous," Joe said.

"That kind of work, that kind of danger," Ida said. "I can't believe the people who do it do it for anything but money."

"Usually," Joe said.

"Usually?" Ida said. "Or always?"

"Always," Joe said. "Always up to now."

"But these people who took Stevie?" Ida said. "You say they don't want money?"

"That's my guess," Joe Catalini said. "What I say is they haven't asked for money."

"Not yet," Ida said.

"Not yet."

"You think maybe they won't?" Ida said.

"What we have to think," Joe Catalini said, "I think the real danger we have to think about is that there's a chance they *won't* ask for money."

"Then what they'll ask for," Ida said, "what they want, the reason they took on this hard work, the reason they went into something as dangerous as this, whoever they are, the reason they took Stevie—"

Ida Lessing paused, as though the process of thinking aloud had led her to a surprising conclusion.

"What they want, Joe," she said finally, "it's going to be something more important than money."

"More important to them," Joe said.

"Then what's important to us is to find out who they are."

"And what they want," Joe said.

"If we find out who they are," Ida said, "we'll know what they want."

"Good girl," Joe Catalini said.

7

Whenever Joe Catalini flew down for a meeting in the Lessing penthouse, the building manager, Paavo Ohmstetter, knew he was coming to The Frontenac before Joe set foot in the building. The fourth or fifth secretary in Joe's office took care of that. When the meeting was over, Paavo always met Joe in the lobby to speed the visitor on his way. The elevator panel took care of that. Tonight, when Joe Catalini stepped out of the elevator, Paavo Ohmstetter was wearing oilskins.

"It's wet out there," Paavo said. "I was just checking your cab and driver."

"He still afloat?" Joe said.

"When you went upstairs I told him to run the car down into the garage," Paavo said. "I just had him come back up. He's waiting out front, and he's dry enough to ride."

"Thanks," Joe Catalini said. "What's the weather report?"

"Not much change," Paavo said. "I just had it from Liv on the TV she heard the thing is hanging round over Cuba, trying to make up its mind which way to go. We may get it, we may not. Right now there's no immediate danger to this area."

"Then I have time to make a phone call?"

"Plenty of time," Paavo Ohmstetter said.

He led the way across the lobby toward his apartment. He opened the door with his key. He held the door for Joe, then closed it behind them. Joe walked into the living room. He put his raincoat on the couch and sat down next to it. The telephone was on the coffee table in front of the couch. The button panel was more complex than the one supplied by Southern Bell for ordinary home instruments. Joe Catalini took the receiver from the hook. The dial tone seeped into the silent room. Joe stopped the sound with a forefinger.

Paavo Ohmstetter accepted the signal. He said, "I'll be in the bedroom with Liv until you want me."

"Thanks," Joe Catalini said.

He waited until the bedroom door clicked shut. Then Joe took his forefinger from the instrument. The dial tone came alive again, filling the room with the whining, nervous, insistent hum.

Joe tipped his head, as though the hum contained a coded message he was trying to decipher. Actually, what was going on inside his head had nothing to do with codes. It was Ida Lessing's voice saying, "You can do anything. I've seen you do all of it."

Joe Catalini sighed. It was his normal, slightly weary expulsion of breath. On the surface, anyway. Actually, there was something more in this particular sigh. Something Joe wished was not there. Wishing, however, was a waste of time. He had learned that long ago, on Minnehaha Avenue. Ida Lessing was right. He could do anything. What Ida didn't know was the bad times, the times when Joe Catalini wished he did not know he could do anything. In a tired voice he said, "Okay."

To nobody in particular. Then his forefinger began to tap the buttons on the telephone panel.

"What number are you calling?"

Joe Catalini came out of his thoughts and repeated the number to the operator.

53

"Is that Boston, sir?"

"Yes," Joe said.

"The correct area code for Boston is 617," the operator said. "Would you try it again, sir?"

"Thanks," Joe said.

He tried it again. A woman's voice came on the wire.

"Hello?"

Joe Catalini said, "Is this the home of Mr. Louis Mangan?"

"It is," the woman said. "Who is this, please?"

Joe said, "Is this Mrs. Mangan?"

"Yes," the woman said. "Who's calling, please?"

"I apologize for calling at this hour," Joe Catalini said. "Could I talk with Mr. Mangan, please?"

"Who is this calling?" the woman said.

"Tell Mr. Mangan it's his friend from Park Avenue in New York," Joe said. "He'll understand."

"His friend from Park Avenue in New York," the woman said.

"Yes," Joe said. "And would you hurry, please? It's very important."

8

"Nobody comes into this room until I call them," Ida Lessing said. "You know that, Max."

She did not like the sharp note in her voice. It told her something she had not grasped a few minutes ago when she said goodbye to Joe in the foyer. She grasped it now. It shook her. Ida had not realized she was scared.

She said, "I mean, Max, you don't have to worry."

This time she was able to say it casually. The way for two years she had made it a point to say everything when she was sitting beside Max's bed. She did a lot of that, pretending to share his absorption in the garbage that poured down into the room from the tilted TV screen on the ceiling.

"This new nurse," Ida said, "she's out in the kitchen having coffee."

Now that she was making this effort to be casual, Ida wondered if she was succeeding. Being scared was nothing new. It was an emotion with which, during the half century between Minnehaha Avenue and The Frontenac, she had grown familiar. What was unfamiliar was the apparent depth of this present fear.

"This Miss Farragut, Max. She won't come in here until I send for her," Ida Lessing said.

Never before, never once in the two years since Max had been stricken, had she allowed herself to forget the difference between Herb Zlotkin's attitude toward her husband's condition and the attitude of Ida Lessing.

Herb spoke for all doctors. Max, they said, was finished. He was a vegetable. They were very fond of that word. It was what Susie Shale, when she was Ida's old English teacher in Minneapolis, used to call a euphemism. A way of saying something nasty without actually saying the nasty word. The doctors didn't want to say the best thing to do with Max was shoot him and get the whole thing over with. So they said he was a vegetable. There was no way to get through to him.

Ida said nothing. She spoke only to herself, and she spoke firmly. Max was far from finished. Max was not a vegetable. Max understood everything that was happening around him. Speaking only to herself, Ida did not have to fool around with euphemisms. The doctors, she said to herself, could go their way. She would go hers.

There was, of course, the big problem. To handle it she had schooled herself in casualness. Max Lessing was not a man you took pity on. Not unless you were inviting his wrath. It was an invitation Ida had learned long ago to avoid. She knew that Max must never know from her attitude that she thought there was anything unusual in his condition. Ida Lessing had not realized until this moment how much of her attitude depended on how she sounded.

"So there's no chance Miss Farragut heard a word about what I've just been telling you," Ida said. "And there's no chance she'll hear anything you want to tell me now, Max."

Ida paused, and she waited. She was trying to be casual in the hope of getting Max to instruct her, as he had been instructing her all of their lives together. This time, however, she was seeking his instructions in an area about which it was impossible for either one of them to be casual. They had faced many things. Never anything like this.

"Joe didn't say Stevie is in any danger," Ida said. "What

Joe said, he repeated it over and over again, he wanted both of us to have it clear, Max. What Joe said was the situation right now is this: the kidnappers have not yet told us what they want. Until they do, Joe says, Stevie is perfectly safe. Joe says there's no point in worrying about things like—"

Ida's voice stopped. Not because, by keeping a flow of soothing words going, she had brought herself inadvertently to the edge of stating the boundary of her terror. Ida Lessing's voice stopped because in the angled mirror from which her glance never moved she had seen Max's eyes suddenly come alive.

A moment later the good hand did the same. It humped up in the familiar movement, a diver pulling himself together at the end of the board for takeoff. The bunched knuckles inched forward, across the bedsheet, toward the electric typewriter sitting on the shelf built into the bed.

Ida reached across and pressed the on button. The motor began to hum. Max's pinky crawled slowly, dragging itself from key to key.

Ida waited, as she always waited when Max's good hand surfaced with something from the walled-off, airtight, sound-proof hole in which he was living what was left of his life. Slowly, in those erratic little spasms that it hurt her to watch, single letter by single letter, on the sheet of paper in the electric typewriter, his wife watched the slow appearance of Max Lessing's orders for saving the life of their grandson:

```
1 thng hav lernd nvr work 4 2 spoilers
```

9

"I'm a friend of your roommate's family," Lou Mangan said. "I have a message for him."

"Now?" the boy in the doorway said. "It's three o'clock in the morning."

"It's also drafty, and I'm susceptible to head colds," Lou Mangan said. "I don't like to stand around in hallways."

The boy said, "You can stop that by getting the hell out of here."

He started to shove the door shut. Mangan caught it with his palm and shoved back. The boy staggered, tripped on something, and fell. The big man came in, kicked the door shut behind him, and kept on moving. Mangan carried his heavy body around what looked like a distorted Christmas tree with a bad lean. The branches were lengths of gun-metal-colored cast-iron pipe. From these hung the thick red and green glass faces of old-fashioned traffic lights. They were marked STOP and GO. Perhaps there were too many of them. On one side, anyway. The thing certainly looked as though it were about to tip over. Or perhaps the lean was part of the design.

Lou Mangan, in swift motion, couldn't pause to check out that particular impression. He did notice, however, that the arrangement was set in a three-foot base of lacquered tree stump. It seemed solid enough. It was obviously some sort of decoration. A retired Boston cop, especially if he used to work the Cambridge area, did not waste much time registering surprise at the things with which Harvard students decorated their living quarters.

"What the hell do you think you're doing?" the boy said.

The voice went with the face. Sharp but not quite dangerous. Like a blade with its cutting edge folded into the slot of a pocketknife. If you handled it with care, there was no reason why you should get hurt. The face went with everything Lou Mangan had hated about working in a city that contained a place like Harvard College. In the days when he was still on the force, even the penniless jerks from Midwestern slums who were in for a free ride on scholarships, they never missed a chance to ram it home that they knew they were in the presence of a dim-witted, flat-footed, potbellied slob. An Irish harp with mainly oatmeal between his ears plus just enough functioning gray matter to keep his snout firmly fixed in the public trough until pension time rolled around.

"Stand up," Lou Mangan said.

"Wha-aht?" the boy said.

Former Inspector Mangan reached down, hand stiff, as though he were offering it for a glove fitting, palm in vertical position. Two short whipping motions. First the flat of the hand, left. Then the knuckles, right. The long hair flew, left and right, like a couple of outflung handfuls of sand. In between, the slapped face came clear. The startled expression was decorated with acne scars.

Lou Mangan's hand kept moving. It bored in and became a fistful of crimson T-shirt. The flat-footed, potbellied Irish-harp body stopped moving forward. The hard Cat's-Paw rubber heels sank into the yellow shag carpet. Two hundred and ten pounds of retired Boston police force heaved backward. One hundred and ten pounds of Harvard undergraduate came lunging forward.

The boy grunted. The toothpick body came up on his

dirty bare feet. He managed to say, "Hey!" In a small boy's startled squeak.

For the hard shove that followed, former Inspector Mangan brought his thus far unemployed left hand into position for an assist. Both hands went to work. The boy went over on his ass. Right smack into the middle of the couch from which he had risen to answer the door.

"Don't do that again," Lou Mangan said.

To steady himself, Idwal Lurie bounced up and down on the excellent springs of the couch. It was much better constructed than the Filene's number from which Lou Mangan's wife and the five Mangan offspring watched the antibusing riots on TV in their modest but mortgage-paid-off South Boston rumpus room.

"Jesus," the boy said.

The excellent springs stopped bouncing. The long hair settled back around the sharp, pimply face like the wings of a football helmet.

"Boy," said the one-hundred-and-ten pound occupant of Leverett House's 4-D. "All I did was answer the door. I didn't know I was admitting Efrem Zimbalist, Jr."

"He's been canceled," Lou Mangan said. "I'm Lou Mangan, friend of your roommate's family."

"You told me that," the boy said.

"You forgot it," former Inspector Mangan said. "So I'm starting all over again."

"Would it arouse your passion to pummel if I asked you to sit?" the boy said. "You're rather on the large side."

"Pick the place," Lou Mangan said. "When I talk, I want to see all of you."

One of the boy's bare feet snaked out to the right of the iron-pipe Christmas tree. When it came back into view, the foot had hooked to its toes a ladder-back mahogany chair.

"Try this," the boy said. "It's stronger than it looks."

Mangan set the chair with its back to the wide picture window. He had nothing against picture windows. This one, however, seemed part of the plan laid out by the unknown designer who had thought up the Christmas tree. Lou Mangan had not come to Leverett House in the middle of the night to catch the spectacular view of the Charles River being washed white in the sort of full moon he was more accustomed to seeing on stage during one of those pre–New York tryouts at the Shubert Theatre.

"Okay," former Inspector Mangan said.

He sat down.

"Okay," the boy said.

He smiled. The smile took Mangan by surprise. He was not prepared for the sudden appearance of all those snow-white, clearly healthy toothpaste-commercial teeth, all bunched up in the middle of that pasty, pimple-spotted face. A startling thought moved into the former policeman's mind. Could it be this one was not the usual Harvard prick? Lou Mangan allowed the thought to keep right on moving. He had work to do.

"Your name is Idwal Lurie," he said.

"That's right," the boy said.

"Your roommate here is Stephen Lessing?"

"That's right," Idwal Lurie said.

"Where is he?"

"I don't know," Idwal said.

"Why not?" Mangan said.

"What kind of question is that?"

"One you better answer," Mangan said.

"Steve walked out of here about midnight," Idwal said. "He told me he was going over to the *Crimson* office."

"The paper?" Mangan said.

"Steve's on the staff," Idwal said. "He's got a limerick coming up in the Wednesday issue. It goes to the printer in the morning, that's now this morning, and Steve just thought of a way to fix the end. So as I said, he went over to the *Crimson*. That's all I know."

Lou Mangan said, "Steve Lessing's family thinks you know more."

"I don't know Steve Lessing's family," Idwal Lurie said. "I don't know you either."

"You don't have to know me," Mangan said. "But you have to know Steve Lessing's family."

"Why?"

"The same reason everybody knows Gerald Ford's family," Mangan said. "Where is he?"

"Ask Ron Nessen," Lurie said.

"Don't start that again."

"Then why don't you listen?" Idwal Lurie said. "I told you Steve Lessing went down to the *Crimson* to fix his limerick."

"Limericks have five lines," Lou Mangan said. "In three hours he could have hacked out all five of them on a slab of marble and been back here safely tucked away in bed."

"He sleeps in the room just behind you," Idwal said. "Go look."

Mangan moved in the opposite direction. This time, when he came up out of the rocking chair, he took the fistful of crimson T-shirt with his left hand.

"Take a harp's advice, young man," Lou Mangan said. "When a question is put to you by one of your elders, answer it."

"Okay, okay," Idwal Lurie said in a tired voice. "I don't know where Steve Lessing is. But he could be in Florida."

"What makes you think that?"

"These last few weeks he's been flying down to Miami as regularly as a carrier pigeon," Idwal said.

"In the middle of the night?" Mangan said.

"The Lessings don't go standby," Idwal Lurie said. "When they get the urge to move, they summon one of the family jets."

The sound of the boy's voice signaled what felt to Lou Mangan like a message.

"Without telling their roommates they're going?" he said.

Idwal said, "Especially without telling their roommates."

The bitterness nailed the message into place.

"He's got a new girlfriend down there?" Lou Mangan said.

"If she's a girl," Idwal Lurie said savagely, "it will be a first for both of them."

PART II
1919

10

For Mr. Max the first was a place called Fürstenfeld. A
garrison town one hundred and eleven miles southeast of
Vienna.

The crucial area was the enlisted men's barracks of the
First Bohemian Imperial Dragoons. At a time when Max
was not quite eighteen. A time when the Imperial Dragoons
were not quite a military unit. Not anymore. The Allies had
won the war.

Everybody knew that. Nobody, however, had yet got
around to telling the commander of the Fürstenfeld garrison
what to do about it.

What Colonel Eyquardt did not know he could not pass
on to his subordinates. Numbered among these were about
two hundred men of whose existence Colonel Eyquardt had
never been more than dimly aware. Even in the days when it
looked to him and his superiors as though the Central Powers
were poised at last to give the British and French high com-
mands a long overdue lesson about the facts of military life.
Now that the opportunity for passing on this crucial lesson
had vanished, Colonel Eyquardt's dim awareness of the existence of these two hundred men who were still technically
under his command had grown dimmer. Many of these men
were boys. During the third year of the war, the Emperor's

conscription machinery had exhausted the lists of men who were, arithmetically speaking, men.

When Max was called up, he had just parted with his last wisdom tooth. He made the painful discovery that it was impacted when he chewed down hard on one of the Pfefferkuchen his mother had baked for his seventeenth-birthday party.

Max carried the uneaten Pfefferkuchen with him in a paper sack when he went up to Fürstenfeld for his induction. Oberfeldwebel Sauerlich, to whom he reported, placed Max under his wing and the Pfefferkuchen into his tuck box.

"The war is over," Oberfeldwebel Sauerlich said. "None of us is in any danger. All we have to do is use our heads while the big shots decide what to do with their armies. Stick with me, kid, and you'll go home to your family in one piece. You got any more of these cookies?"

"No," Max said, "but I could write to my mother."

"Here's a pencil and a piece of paper," Oberfeldwebel Sauerlich said. "I'll address the envelope for you. I write a very clear script. The post office is not what it used to be. And oh, yes, there's one more thing."

"Yes, sir?" Max said.

"Fuck Colonel Eyquardt," Oberfeldwebel Sauerlich said.

"Yes, sir," Max said.

"He hates Jews," Oberfeldwebel Sauerlich said.

"Yes, sir," Max said.

"We Jews we got to stick together," Oberfeldwebel Sauerlich said.

"Yes, sir," Max said.

"We" proved to be Oberfeldwebel Sauerlich and his lackey, Gefreiter Schildwachter.

He is a very nice man just like Oberfeldwebel Sauerlich, Max wrote to his mother in Vetzprem. *He says could you use less cinnamon in the next batch of Pfefferkuchen. Cinnamon gives him heartburn. Please do not worry about me. Being in the army is not so bad as I thought it would be. This is because of my two friends Oberfeldwebel Sauerlich and*

Gefreiter Schildwachter. They say we Jews must stick to-gether.

They did, in many ways. All these ways were helpful. Some were ingenious. At least one was astonishing. To a seventeen-year-old boy from a remote farm district like Vetzprem, anyway. This was the punchboard. Max had never seen one. Indeed, until he came to Fürstenfeld he had never heard about the existence of such a device.

"All soldiers are gamblers," Oberfeldwebel Sauerlich said. "All soldiers are also *shmucks*. Especially the *goyim*. So all you do is get yourself one of these punchboards, and you're on your way to fame and fortune."

He held up the interesting-looking square of pressed card-board. At the top, in bold type, appeared three words: WIN A FORTUNE! Below, the main area of the device was covered with small colored dots. When poked with a key that looked like the piece of metal used for opening a can of sardines, each one of these dots yielded, from the back of the card-board square, a tightly rolled scrap of colored paper. On it was printed a number. Max guessed there must be at least a hundred of these dots on the device Oberfeldwebel Sauer-lich was showing him. Later, when he had an opportunity to examine the device, Max counted twenty rows across by ten rows down. Two hundred dots.

"Each one of these dots gives a *shmuck* a crack at the prize," Oberfeldwebel Sauerlich said. "You charge ten Pfennig a crack, you sell out the whole board, you've got a take of two thousand Pfennig. The *shmuck* who wins the lucky number, his prize is five hundred Pfennig. That leaves fifteen hundred Pfennig for the smart-asses who are running the show."

"The Oberfeldwebel, me, and the third man," Gefreiter Schildwachter said. "That's you, Max."

Max was flattered. Aside from his being a Jew, he saw no reason why these two experienced older men should have become his counselors and benefactors. Max was, however, pleased and grateful. Max was also cautious. He wrote his mother about the pleasure Oberfeldwebel Sauerlich and Gefreiter Schildwachter took in her Pfefferkuchen, but Max did not mention the punchboard.

Max was nobody's fool. A punchboard was a gambling device, and he knew how his mother felt about gambling. This knowledge caused him for the first time in his short lifetime to tell her a lie.

Here is a little present from Oberfeldwebel Sauerlich and Gefreiter Schildwachter, Max wrote to his mother in the note that accompanied the beaded coin purse he sent her out of his share of the profits from the first punchboard for which he had acted as the team collector.

They asked me to tell you it is a small sign of their appreciation for the Pfefferkuchen you have been sending us. Gefreiter Schildwachter has asked me to make a special point of mentioning the cinnamon. You have got it just right at last, Mama. Gefreiter Schildwachter eats them now with no heartburn. Without these good friends of mine, I think my life here in the army would not be as pleasant as it is. They don't like Jews here, but because of Oberfeldwebel Sauerlich and Gefreiter Schildwachter I have had no trouble. Oberfeldwebel Sauerlich says Jews never have any trouble if they stick together. He is right. We stick together, the three of us, and nobody bothers us. Oberfeldwebel Sauerlich says I should tell you he thinks I will not have to serve my full three years. He thinks what the peace conference says, it says the big shots on the other side don't want to leave an organized Austrian army sitting around with nothing to do any more than they want to leave an organized German army sitting around and sort of waiting, so they will disband all of us and send us home. I certainly hope so. Meantime, now that the wisdom tooth no longer bothers me and my gum has healed, I really have nothing to complain about, thanks to my friends Oberfeldwebel Sauerlich and Gefreiter Schildwachter. You would like them very much. They are like a couple of big brothers to me.

Max was an only child. As an accurately observed yardstick, therefore, the big-brother comparison may have lacked something. There was no doubt, however, about its sincerity. This was demonstrated by the way Oberfeldwebel Sauerlich and Gefreiter Schildwachter treated Max on the Christmas jackpot project.

It was based on a calculation made by Oberfeldwebel Sauerlich, approved by Gefreiter Schildwachter, and turned over to Max for what they both called implementation. The idea was to shift from garnering chicken feed to making a killing.

"The smart-asses who are running the show" had been Oberfeldwebel Sauerlich's description of the triumvirate that had invented the Fürstenfeld barracks punchboard operation. They had been fleecing their fellows with great success for almost a year. Nobody could predict how long this happy state would continue. Before too long, the conscripts marking time in Fürstenfeld would probably be dispersed. It would be disgraceful if "the smart-asses who are running the show" allowed this point in time to be reached without cashing in on the goodwill they had established among the *shmucks* they had been fleecing.

"It's coming up Christmas," Oberfeldwebel Sauerlich said. "A time of year when even *goyim* who are not *shmucks* can be made without much sweat to act like *shmucks*. Here's what we will do."

Oberfeldwebel Sauerlich and Gefreiter Schildwachter did it. Max was sent in on the morning of the Saviour's birthday to, as Oberfeldwebel Sauerlich put it, "pick up our present from under the frigging Christmas tree."

This consisted of showing up in the orderly room at 4:30 A.M., a half hour before reveille, to collect the loot. Max showed up. Gefreiter Poushental, on duty, had been expecting him.

"One thing about you Jew-boys," Gefreiter Poushental said. "You're prompt."

"Yes, sir," Max said.

Oberfeldwebel Sauerlich had assured him he did not

have to say "sir" to an NCO, "especially he's a fucking *goy*"; but Max had been prepared for army life by his mother on the farm in Vetzprem.

"When in doubt, always say 'sir,' " she had told her son when she sent him off to Fürstenfeld with a paper sack full of Pfefferkuchen. Max's mother had learned about army life from her husband. He had been killed in a training exercise two months before Max was born. "To put a 'sir' into the pot doesn't cost a Groschen," his mother had said. "If you leave it out, it could cost you an arm and a leg."

Gefreiter Poushental came out from behind the duty officer's desk in the orderly room.

"The Rabbi said you'll need twenty minutes," he said.

The Rabbi was the barracks nickname for Oberfeldwebel Sauerlich.

"Yes, sir," Max said.

"I'll give you a half hour," Gefreiter Poushental said.

Max said, "That will be fine, sir."

It almost was. Oberfeldwebel Sauerlich had worked it out that the collections would take no more than fifteen minutes. To be on the safe side he had allotted twenty. It took exactly fourteen minutes for every one of the seventeen men on Max's list to report, turn over his money, and get out unobserved.

He was making a final count, aware that he still had six minutes before Gefreiter Poushental came back to resume his post as duty officer, when Max became aware that he was not alone in the orderly room. He looked up from the desk.

"Gefreiter Poushental?"

Even if it had occurred to the suddenly terrified Max that a possible way out of this unforeseen complication was to lie and say Yes, sir, he would have been unable to utter the words. For one thing, the plan, as Oberfeldwebel Sauerlich had explained it, was foolproof. He had made no provision for unforeseen complications, because for Oberfeldwebel Sauerlich, in dealing with *shmucks* there was no such thing as an unforeseen complication. For another, it was perfectly clear even to the terrified Max that the man who had asked if Max was Gefreiter Poushental did not expect an affirmative answer. And third, if Max were stupid enough to give such an answer, the man would probably not hesitate to have the liar dragged in front of a firing squad in a matter of minutes. The man was Colonel Eyquardt.

"No, Herr Oberst," Max said.

Colonel Eyquardt said, "Where is Gefreiter Poushental?"

"In the latrine, Herr Oberst," Max said.

"Doing what?" Colonel Eyquardt said.

The fact that the Colonel had asked this question indicated to Max at once that there was a flaw in Oberfeldwebel Sauerlich's theory that all *goyim* were *shmucks*. In fact, the one facing Max at the moment sounded like a wise guy.

"I don't know, Excellenz," Max said.

It occurred to him in a stab of panic that he had left something out. The same thought had obviously occurred to Colonel Eyquardt.

He said, "Do you not recognize your commanding officer when you see him?"

Max came to his feet as though he had been kicked out of his chair. The situation might have worked out better if he had waited until he was actually on his feet before he attempted his next move: a snappy salute. As it happeened, Max did not wait. With the result that his series of hasty movements, not thought out, totally uncoordinated, was too much for his normally resilient, perfectly healthy young body. It toppled. Or started to.

Max clawed at the desk to save himself from falling. He managed that, all right, but in the process he illustrated unwittingly the truth of Robert Burns's celebrated observation about the best-laid plans of mice and men, even when they are laid by Oberfeldweebel Sauerlich. Three objects went skittering across the shaken desk.

One, the small canvas bag in which Max had deposited the money he had taken from the seventeen men who had reported to him during the past fourteen—now probably fifteen or sixteen—minutes. Two, the list on which he had checked off the names of these men. And three, the pencil with which Max had done the checking.

The pencil bounced once or twice on the stone floor and then rolled off into some dark corner of the room. The list fluttered, swayed back and forth on several small indecisive air currents, then ducked out of sight under the desk. The canvas bag landed with a solid clunk at the feet of Colonel Eyquardt.

He dipped down, swooped up the bag, and pulled the drawstring wide. He poked a hand through the opening and ran his fingers around the contents. He seemed to be confirming by touch a thought that had already taken clear shape in his mind. So clear that it had brought his tight, hard, ugly little features into something that was clearly a characteristically nasty imitation of what on most human faces would have been described as a smile.

"As usual," Colonel Eyquardt said, "I see you kikes are making a financially good thing out of our sacred celebration."

What happened next never came clear in Max's mind. Not for half a century. Even though he rarely in all that time ever stopped for very long working it over in his head, reliving each moment, trying to puzzle out why he had done what he did. Max never got any closer to an answer than the word Colonel Eyquardt had used. At not-quite-eighteen, Max had never yet been called a kike.

He reached out and grabbed Colonel Eyquardt by the hair. The colonel had a lot of it for a military man. Then Max ripped the canvas bag from the C.O.'s hand. And finally, in a sweeping, savage thrust that ended in a wet, egg-splattering sound, Max smashed the head of Colonel Eyquardt down on the stone floor in the orderly room.

Later, Max realized there was a fourth thing he did. Carrying the small canvas bag, he moved out of the orderly room and across the flagstone yard, and in the just-beginning glow of dawn Max walked away from the Fürstenfeld barracks area.

11

The way led east, toward Budapest. To keep himself on the way, Max fell instinctively into the first act of the military fugitive. He shed his uniform. From a clothesline on the outskirts of Fürstenfeld he stole a frayed pair of corduroy pants and a faded flannel shirt. Both were several sizes too big even for his big body. The floppiness, however, helped with the identity Max had chosen. A farm kid on the prowl for work, wearing an older brother's hand-me-downs.

Max did not realize he had moved out of Austria into Hungary until he saw the Klein Berezna road sign. The place name used to thread through Oberfeldwebel Sauerlich's boastful accounts of his sexual exploits. These accounts always turned on the comic fact that while Oberfeldwebel Sauerlich spoke only German and Yiddish, the girls involved spoke only Hungarian. Max began to feel a little easier. As a result, he also began to feel a lot hungrier. During the long furtive hike away from Fürstenfeld, food had been the big problem.

Max had never before been on the run. Common sense, however, supplied some of the precautions experience had not yet had an opportunity to provide. Instinctively Max knew it was important to avoid leaving anything in the way of a trail behind him. He had avoided thinking about his hunger by avoiding food shops.

Now that he was in Hungarian-speaking terrain, Max grasped that his problem had changed. The canvas sack he had filled in the Fürstenfeld orderly room was tied safely around his waist under the stolen pants. Unfortunately, however, the sack contained only Austrian currency.

In his not-quite-eighteen years Max had never been very far from the farm in Vetzprem. He had never set foot on Hungarian soil. He did not know that, as part of the Empire, Hungary had long accepted Austrian currency as freely as its own. The same common sense that had kept him out of food shops while he was in German-speaking terrain now reminded him that he was hungry, yes, but he was also uncaught. It seemed stupid to do anything that might change that.

Max cut away from the marked road, heading cross country in the direction indicated by the arrow on the road sign lettered KLEIN BEREZNA.

Moving out of German-speaking terrain seemed to have cleared away whatever fears he had carried with him out of the Fürstenfeld orderly room. In spite of his growling stomach, Max realized he was enjoying himself. He had not realized until he left it behind how much he had hated the constriction of barracks life.

He swung along the unpaved lanes with a feeling of confidence. Whatever turned up in Klein Berezna he had not the slightest doubt that he could handle it.

It was a feeling with which Ida Wawrth was familiar. That was why she did not hesitate when, through the barn door, she saw Rabbi Jobsky's skinny figure coming across the south pasture toward the big house on the hill. Ida had been watching for him.

She jumped up from the milking stool and ran out of the barn. She cut across the vegetable garden, knowing her footprints among the tomato vines would later make her father furious. At the edge of the apple orchard, Ida came face

76

to face with the skinny old man wearing the shiny alpaca ankle-length coat and the broad-brimmed *shtrahmel.*

She said, "Good morning, Rabbi Jobsky."

"Good morning, good morning," the old man said impatiently. "I'm late."

He moved to step around her. Ida stepped with him.

"No," Ida said.

She planted her feet firmly in front of the bearded old man and crossed her arms. She scowled up into his nearsighted eyes.

"Not until you talk to me," Ida said.

"About what?" Rabbi Jobsky said.

"My education," Ida Wawrth said.

Astonished, the angry old man said, "Your what?"

"My ed-yew-kay-shun," Ida said, twisting her lips with each mocking syllable.

"But you're a girl," Rabbi Jobsky said.

It was obvious that in his mind the statement was a definitive reply.

"That's why I want you to talk to my father for me," Ida said. "My father doesn't listen to girls."

"Look, child," Rabbi Jobsky said impatiently. "Don't talk in riddles. Just tell me what you want."

"What my brothers are getting," Ida Wawrth said. "What you're teaching them. To read and write."

"That's what you want me to tell your father?" Rabbi Jobsky said.

"Yes," Ida Wawrth said. "Because he won't listen to me. All he says is he never heard of girls' being taught how to read and write, and he's not going to do something nobody else ever did. But my father respects you. If you tell him I should learn to read and write the same as my brothers, my father will do it, and it will be good for you too, because he'll pay you extra for teaching me."

"You believe that?" Rabbi Jobsky said.

"Yes," Ida Wawrth said.

"Why?"

"Because he's my father," Ida said. "He's a decent man."

"Your father is also a sensible man," Rabbi Jobsky said. "He hired me to teach your brothers to read and write because your father believes I too am a sensible man. If I go to him with this nonsense, if I tell him he should allow me to teach you as well as your brothers, I will not earn more money. I will stop earning any money. From your father, anyway. He will tell me to get out of his house and never come back. And now shall I tell you something, my girl?"

"What?" Ida Wawrth said.

"Your father will be absolutely right," Rabbi Jobsky said. "Get out of my way, please."

Ida didn't, but she didn't move, either. So the rabbi was able to step around her and hurry away up the hill to the house. More slowly, Ida moved back to the barn.

She did not know how long she had been sitting there, her forehead resting against the flank of the cow, sobbing like the fool she always felt herself to be when she sobbed, but helpless to stop herself. Then she heard a voice calling to her from the doorway. Ida had a feeling the voice had called twice. Perhaps three times. She pushed herself away from the cow and looked up.

Peering in at her was a tall, broad-shouldered young man. He wore frayed corduroy work pants and a faded gray flannel shirt. Both were too big for him. He looked shy and a little afraid. As though whatever it was he wanted, he knew it would be refused, but he was desperate and could not stop himself from asking. A farm boy on the prowl for work, Ida guessed, wearing the hand-me-downs of an older brother who had probably been taken away into the army.

She brushed the tears dry with the bottom of her apron and she rose from the milking stool. Coming across to the barn door, Ida saw the boy's hair in the afternoon sunlight. It was the color of one of her mother's copper pots immediately after it had been freshly polished.

"Yes?" Ida Wawrth said.

78

"Excuse me," the boy said. "I wonder could I please have perhaps a cup of milk? I am on my way to Klein Berezna, where I heard there is work to be had. I have no money, and I have put nothing into my stomach since yesterday."

12

During the next two days, Max put as much into his stomach as the blond girl was able to sneak out of the house on the hill and carry to his hiding place in the barn. This proved to be quite a lot. Max ate all of it. Between meals he answered her questions with a caution she seemed to consider proper under the circumstances. She even seemed to believe what he told her. She seemed to think everything Max said was proper. Even his suggestion, when he felt he should be moving on, that she move with him.

Max remained hidden in the barn while she made all the arrangements. These clearly did not include obtaining permission from her parents, but Max thought it best not to mention this. Making a mental note of it, he felt, was enough. They left Klein Berezna in the middle of the night. It took them two weeks to reach Amsterdam. Max ate all the way.

By the time the S.S. *Friesland* cleared Amsterdam Harbor, the corduroy pants and flannel shirt he had stolen on the outskirts of Fürstenfeld looked almost as though they and Max had been made for each other. This could not be said of sea travel and Ida Wawrth.

She started to retch while the ship was still slogging its way out of the Zuyder Zee. It took two days for the just barely seaworthy old tub to make it into the North Sea, where without much conviction the vessel headed west for the English Channel. Two days after that, when the *Friesland* steamed out into the open Atlantic, Ida was still retching. So were most of the other women in steerage. Quite a few male passengers were similarly afflicted. Not Max.

Max seemed to thrive on what he was fed. In fact, because so many of these passengers, including Ida, were incapable of facing their daily ration, Max every day put away more than his share.

When he was not eating, Max tried to do what he could for Ida. He soon realized, however, that his attempts to soothe her misery were not having their intended effect.

Out of the cask bolted to the planking in the middle of the steerage hold, Max had dipped up a cupful of water. It was warm and slightly greasy and tasted of herring, but it was the only beverage the owners of the *Friesland* provided for steerage passengers who were thirsty. Max brought it to Ida. He knelt beside the pallet on which she was lying and put the cup to her lips.

"Take a sip," he said.

"No," she moaned.

On the soiled, straw-filled canvas sack she rolled her head away from him.

"It will make you feel better," Max said.

The statement was preposterous, and Max knew it, so he did not blame Ida for her reaction. With a surge of fury of which he would not have thought her capable, the slender girl smashed the tin cup out of his hand. It bounced away with a clatter on the planking.

Moving out into the aisle to retrieve the cup, Max heard two women talking on the pallets near Ida. These women were not at the moment specimens of radiant health, but they were not quite as sick as Ida. As a result they were able to keep flowing the prime lubricant of the female metabolism: chatter. Picking up the tin cup, Max also picked up the word "Passover."

"At home," one of the women was saying, "they're talking about what my mother will put on the table for the *seder* when Passover comes, and me, when Passover comes this year, where will I be, in what country? And will I even be at a *seder*?"

"Make them shut up," Ida groaned.

She was, of course, asking the impossible. Max knew that. He also knew, however, that this girl had been very good to him. Less than a month had elapsed since that day in Klein Berezna when he had stopped in the barn doorway and asked for a cup of milk. In that time Max had come far on the road to safety. Farther than he could possibly have come alone. Nobody knew better than Max that without Ida Wawrth's help, he might not have come away at all. If she survived this voyage, this girl might be useful to him again.

"All right," Max said.

He stood up and went across to the two women.

"Please," he said. "Stop talking about food."

"Not with *tzimiss*," the first woman said. "White sugar my mother uses only for Eierkuchen. For *tzimiss* never anything but brown sugar."

"By our seder we don't have *tzimiss*," the second woman said. "Mama always makes for our seder applesauce with cinnamon."

"If you don't shut your mouths," Max said in a low voice, "I will knock your stupid heads together."

"What's wrong with cold applesauce with hot chicken?" the first woman said.

Max turned and headed in the opposite direction. This was not easy. The floor space of the steerage hold was dotted with pallets the way a pox victim is dotted with spots. Max worked his way cautiously around the sprawled bodies toward the exit to the deck. He knew the deck was not going to be much of an improvement, but he'd had all the retching he cared to see for a while. The reason the deck could not be much of an improvement was that it was a well deck.

From it the passenger did not look down into the sea. When a passenger was on that deck the sea looked down on him.

The angry ocean was pitching the *Friesland* around like a splinter in a whirlpool. The ocean was doing this pitching right under the noses of half a dozen men who, like Max, had staggered out of the steerage hold for a breath of fresh air. They were clinging desperately to the heaving rail with both hands and trying to steady themselves with braced legs. Max joined them. Just as he managed to get a good grip on the rail, the angry sea slammed a big one against the plates directly under Max's chin. The icy salt water sprayed up and hit him in the face like a shower of needles.

"Christ," Max muttered.

"You can say that again."

Holding tight to the rail, Max turned to the voice. It belonged to a neat-looking little man in a black leather jacket. This was obviously not the jacket's first sea voyage. The leather was cracked and stained and crusted with dried salt.

"It stinks inside," Max said. "You come outside in what's supposed to be fresh air, it stinks worse."

The little man said, "I know a place where it doesn't stink so bad."

His upper lip was decorated by a neat little dab of black hair.

"Where?" Max said.

"Follow me," the man said.

He shoved himself away from the rail and moved aft. Max managed to stagger along behind the black leather jacket without falling. At the far end of the well deck, the black leather jacket disappeared behind an ugly capstan from which most of the paint had rusted away. When Max reached the capstan he grabbed at the drumhead with one hand and, with the other, at a bar hole. Standing steady for a moment, he was surprised to find the little man at his feet, squatting tidily behind the capstan on the pawl ring at the base. He slapped the scooped metal beside him.

Max eased himself down on the few inches of sloping iron. The metal was wet. The corduroy pants were not waterproof. Max's head, however, was now below the level of the rail. He did not mind the wet pants. It was as though he had followed the little man out of the storm into a snug little cave.

"Not bad," Max said.

"It's better, anyway," the little man said. "The smell of herring and people puking, it could wear out a man's nose."

"You can say that again," Max said.

The man laughed. He said, "I figured right away you weren't one of these deadheads like the rest of those *shmucks* back there."

Max had figured pretty much the same thing about the owner of the black leather jacket. That was why he had sent the man's words back at him. It was the trial-balloon trick Max had learned from watching Oberfeldwebel Sauerlich operate among the *goyim* at Fürstenfeld. Max decided to send up another one.

"The guys who own these ships," he said. "They don't give you much for your money."

"No," the little man said, "but sometimes they give you a chance to pick up as much of the stuff on your own as you can lift."

It was the sort of remark that carried a message. Max got it. He was not making an acquaintance. He had made a contact. He had no doubt that he would soon find out with whom and about what. All he had to do was watch for his cues.

"I wouldn't mind that," Max said.

"My name is Sumeg," the little man said. "Saul Sumeg. What's yours?"

"Max," Max said.

The leather shoulder wrinkled against Max's gray flannel shoulder. Saul Sumeg's head had turned for a look at the man squatting beside him on the pawl ring. Max was pretty sure he knew what the next question would be.

"Where you heading?" Saul Sumeg said.

It was not the question Max had expected. He had expected to be asked for his last name. Some of Max's certainty about the little man faded. For almost a month things had been going smoothly. More smoothly than Max had expected. Maybe it had made him cocky. A little caution wouldn't hurt.

"Same place everybody else on this ship is heading," Max said. "Halifax."

"I'm not," Saul Sumeg said.

"How come?"

"Ever been there?" Saul Sumeg said.

"No," Max said.

"If you had been you wouldn't ask," Saul Sumeg said. "Nobody goes to Halifax except somebody is holding a gun on him."

"I didn't mean that," Max said. "I mean you're on a ship, it's not like you're on a train. On a ship you go from where you start to where it says on your ticket the ship stops. Amsterdam to Halifax."

"This your first time on a ship?" Saul Sumeg said.

"Yeah," Max said.

"Next time around you'll maybe know you don't always have to go where it says on your ticket," Saul Sumeg said.

"Where else can you go?" Max said.

"Where you can pick up some money."

Max stared at the railing in front of him. All at once the snug little cave between the capstan and the rail didn't seem so snug anymore. Max was not sure he liked the cues he was picking up.

"You and this girl you're traveling with," Saul Sumeg said. "You got papers?"

"We're here on the ship," Max said.

"It's a big ship."

"People don't get on ships without papers," Max said.

"It's been done," Saul Sumeg said.

"How do they get off?"

"There's ways," Saul Sumeg said.

Max gave some more attention to the railing in front of him. He was not very happy about his papers. They were the best he had been able to get under the circumstances. He was not, however, going to tell that to a stranger. If there was any way to improve Max's papers, and Max knew the room for improvement was vast, the information would have to be volunteered by the stranger. It seemed to Max that that was the way this Saul Sumeg had set it up. The next move would have to come from the neat little man in the leather jacket.

"I wouldn't want to go all the way back to Amsterdam," Max said.

"Then you'd better get off this ship before they turn her around."

"Doesn't sound easy," Max said.

"Maybe I can help you," Saul Sumeg said.

"I'd appreciate that."

"Appreciation," Saul Sumeg said. "You go try taking that down to the bank and make a deposit with it, my friend."

"I've got some money," Max said.

"I don't need money," Saul Sumeg said.

Max didn't know where this thing was going, but he had a feeling the direction was right. Saul Sumeg smelled to him the way Oberfeldwebel Sauerlich had smelled. A vicious little bastard who thought he was twisting around his finger a rube Jew-boy who didn't know which end was up. Quite obviously what Saul Sumeg wanted from this rube was not a steady supply of homemade Pfefferkuchen. Whatever it was Saul Sumeg wanted, however, it was clear he thought he could get it from Max free, or at least dirt cheap.

"If you don't need money," Max said, "I don't know how I can pay you for your help."

"I'll explain it," Saul Sumeg said.

13

The explanation was thorough. As a result, the night before the S.S. *Friesland* was scheduled to dock at Halifax, Max and Ida Wawrth were squatting on the pawl ring of the rusted capstan where Saul Sumeg had made his explanation. Ida was still not feeling her best.

"Mr. Sumeg said we shouldn't make any noise," Max whispered.

He did not know whom or what they were waiting for. In this sort of plan, Saul Sumeg had said, it was better not to know things like that until the moment of meeting.

"Max?"

He turned toward the voice. Or where he thought the voice had come from. Max saw nothing. The fog sat on the ocean and the ship like a dirty gray blanket.

"Max?"

He swung sharply the other way, ramming into Ida's hunched shoulders. She shivered.

"I heard something," she said.

The voice came in again: "I told you to listen for me, didn't I?"

It was the voice of Saul Sumeg.

"Where are you?" Max said.

Something tugged at his corduroy pants. Max looked down. A hand was clutching his right cuff.

"Saul?" Max said.

"Whom did you expect? Lloyd George?"

The voice seemed to be coming up out of the sea at Max's feet. He said, "What should I do?"

"The girl first," the voice said.

"First where?" Max said.

The answer came in the form of a thin screeching sound. The fog was boiling around them slowly, like lumps of smoke from a wet wood fire. The screeching seemed to cause some of the smoke to roll over and made an opening at Max's feet. In it he saw the face of Saul Sumeg. The hand that had tugged Max's pants shifted to the lower part of the railing. The screeching grew louder. It was caused, Max saw, by rusted hinges. The lower part of the railing opened like a gate.

"Push her through," Saul Sumeg said.

"You're sure?" Max said.

"Quit worrying," Saul Sumeg said. "Just give her a good hard shove."

Max put his arm around Ida's shoulders.

"No," she said, cringing back against the capstan.

"Come on," Max said.

"No."

"For Christ's sake," Saul Sumeg said. "Shut her up."

Max put his hand over Ida's mouth. Her teeth sank deep. Max made a sharp gasping noise.

"You crazy up there?" Saul Sumeg hissed.

Behind the capstan heavy footsteps came toward them from the left. Moving fast, Max pulled the flannel shirt out of his pants and dragged Ida's head down. He shoved the shirttail into her mouth and hauled her forward, off the pawl ring, toward the gap in the rail. She made a small choking sound. Max did not stop. Just before he released her he had a moment of astonishment. It was like holding a doll.

Then, with a hard thrust, he pushed her through the gap in the rail, into the slowly boiling lumps of fog, toward the place where he had seen Saul Sumeg's face.

As Ida fell, the shirttail came loose. Her mouth was free, but she did not scream. She disappeared into the fog. A moment later Max heard what could have been a scream. It was followed by a grunt and then a muffled thump. Max held his breath. Behind the capstan, on the deck, the heavy footsteps moved away, to the right. Max's breath eased out of him slowly.

"Okay, now you."

Sumeg's face reappeared between Max's shoes.

"Which way?" Max said.

"Come down backward," Saul Sumeg said. "Like a ladder."

As he came down backward, Max's probing foot found a soft place. It proved to be a shoulder. Hands came up and took Max around the waist. A moment later he was thumped down on what felt like a plank. His hand slapped down to steady his toppling body. The plank was covered with some sort of rough matting. A flashlight beam hit him in the face. Max winced away.

"You all right?" Saul Sumeg's voice again.

"Yeah," Max said.

"So is she," Saul Sumeg said.

The flashlight beam vanished. In the total darkness Max heard muttering. It sounded peculiar. A couple of moments later he realized why. The muttering was the product of more than one voice. Another noise took over. Max recognized it. In the enlisted men's barracks of the First Bohemian Imperial Dragoons he had grown accustomed to the sound of badly worn motors struggling to come alive.

This one clearly controlled the life of the boat into which Max had just jumped. The motor went from coughing to growling. The boat throbbed, then jumped and swerved to the right. Max's body whipped to the left. Whatever it was he was squatting on slid swiftly from under him. He hit wood with a thump that sent a sharp stab clear up his spine. Then he toppled against something soft. He grabbed at it for support. Ida grunted. Max held her tight.

"It's okay," he said. "We're in the same boat."

Max felt something crawling around his feet. The flashlight beam exploded. Saul Sumeg was holding the light on his mustache. For identification purposes, obviously. After a while the light was smothered by the fog.

"We'll be riding without lights," Saul Sumeg said. "For a while, anyway."

"Riding where?" Max said.

"The names won't mean anything to you," Saul Sumeg said.

Max said, "It will make her feel better to hear them."

The bundle of bones squirmed gently in his arms. For a moment the light came alive.

"She looks pretty worn out," Saul Sumeg said.

The light disappeared.

"There's nothing wrong with my ears," Ida said.

Saul Sumeg laughed.

"Once they get away from that herring," he said, "they all feel better."

Max said, "As soon as we got off the ship you said you'd tell us where we're going."

"We're heading toward Yarmouth," Saul Sumeg said. "For the run across the Bay of Fundy. That make her feel better?"

Ida said, "Why don't you ask me?" She pushed herself out of Max's arms.

"Okay, I will," Saul Sumeg said. "We're heading toward Yarmouth to make our run across the Bay of Fundy. That make you feel better?"

"Yarmouth is Canada," Ida said. "Across the Bay of Fundy that's America."

"How did you know that?" Saul Sumeg said.

"On the pier in Amsterdam," Ida said out of the darkness. "When we were waiting to go on the ship. On the wall. There was a map."

90

Saul Sumeg said, "Max told me you'd never learned how to read."

"I asked a woman near me to explain it," Ida said. "Besides, you don't have to know how to read to look at pictures."

Max had never thought of maps as pictures. Thinking about them now, he remembered the wall in the waiting room on the pier at Amsterdam.

His concern at the time had been neither with pictures nor with walls. What had Max worried was would he and Ida be allowed to board the *Friesland*. Tucked safely in his shirt were the two steerage-passage tickets for which he had paid. Also the documents Ida, who spoke Hungarian, had helped him purchase from the best forger in Klein Berezna.

Max was aware there were people who would have questions about these documents. People cut from the same bolt of cloth as Oberfeldwebel Sauerlich, for example, or Gefreiter Schildwachter. Such people, however, could be handled the way the forger in Klein Berezna had been handled. With some of the contents of the sack Max had carried away with him from the orderly room of the Fürstenfeld barracks. Police, however, were another matter. A matter with which Max had never had any experience.

He was not quite sure of the condition in which he had left Colonel Eyquardt on the stone floor of the Fürstenfeld orderly room. Max was certain, however, that as a result of that encounter, forces would be set in motion. Thus far, with the help of Ida's knowledge of Hungarian, Max had managed to avoid those forces. Their last chance to catch up with Max, assuming they were heading in the right direction, was the Amsterdam pier. They had not caught up. They had not even been sighted.

Now, twelve days later, Max was squatting beside Ida in the bottom of a motorboat crawling away from the *Friesland* in the fog-sealed night toward a part of the world about which Max knew absolutely nothing beyond what Ida had just said: "Yarmouth is Canada. Across the Bay of Fundy that's America."

Max concentrated.

He knew the outlines of the European continent from the military maps he had seen on the walls of the orderly room in Fürstenfeld. He knew also that America was off somewhere to the left. Following the longest red line that ran left from Europe, his eye reached a long fat island. It was colored orange, but it was shaped like a slightly smashed banana standing upright: Nova Scotia. In the middle of Nova Scotia was the place to which the *Friesland* would be carrying him and Ida: Halifax.

Except that Max's meeting with Saul Sumeg had changed that. So now he and Ida were squatting in the bottom of a motorboat, poking along through total darkness toward something Saul Sumeg had called Yarmouth.

"When we get there," Saul Sumeg's voice said out of the darkness, "I'll tell you what to do."

Max did not know how long it took them to get there. He did not own a watch. If he had had one, he would not have been able to read it. Out here, wherever they were, there was something strange about the way it was dark. As though the absence of light had been smeared on his eyes with a spatula.

Then, gradually, the thickness began to thin out. As though whatever it was that had been smeared on his eyes, somebody was scraping some of it away. Black became gray. Gray seemed to make the fog lighter. It pulled away slowly. What had been a dirty blanket in which the whole world had been wrapped now became a dirty blanket sitting just a few feet overhead.

Light began to filter down through the blanket. The sea across which the boat was crawling had lost the anger that for twelve days had tossed the *Friesland* around. The water was the color of the rifle barrels in the racks on the walls of the orderly room in Fürstenfeld. The motor was noisy—noisier than the motors of the old lorries in Fürstenfeld, noisier even than what must have been the huge engines of the *Friesland*—but the noise did not seem to bother Ida. She slept quietly, breathing easily, her head resting against Max's shoulder.

He saw for the first time that they were squatting at the front of the boat. In back, at the wheel, his back to Max and Ida, stood a bearded man in a leather jacket and a blue stocking cap. The jacket looked exactly like the one worn by Saul Sumeg. The two men stood side by side, talking quietly. The space between Max and Ida and the men at the wheel was piled solid with wooden cases. They were wrapped in some sort of dirty brown sacking. Max realized that this was what he had landed on when he had jumped down from the *Friesland*.

"Look."

Max looked before he realized it was Ida who had told him to do it. What he saw was a long, narrow wooden platform. It seemed to be floating in the fog like a kite. Max looked down at Ida.

"You awake?" he said.

"No," she said, "I'm talking in my sleep." She was feeling better, all right.

"I meant a little while ago you were sick," Max said.

"I'm better," Ida said. She certainly looked better.

"What's that thing?" Max said.

"If I knew," Ida said, "would I tell you to look?"

The answer was yes, but Max thought it wise not to say so. She was not only better. She was in a good mood. When she was in a good mood, Max had learned during the past month, it was better for him.

"I never saw anything like it," he said.

"The motor," Ida said.

"What about it?"

"Listen."

He did, and became aware of the silence.

"I guess we're there," Max said.

"Where's there?" Ida said.

93

"Sumeg said he'd tell us when we reach it."

"Here he comes," Ida said.

Saul Sumeg came toward them, clambering across the wooden cases like a monkey, using his hands as well as his feet. Max wondered if the little man had gone to the back that way in the total darkness, while the boat was heaving its way across the blue part of the map toward Yarmouth.

"So okay," Saul Sumeg said.

It was as though he had addressed the blanket of fog, telling it sharply he'd had enough. It separated. In the opening the long narrow platform emerged as a pier. It stuck out into the sea across a skinny ribbon of beach that stretched away and disappeared into the fog on both sides. At the far end, where the pier was fastened to the higher ground above the sand, an automobile was parked.

Max became aware that the man at the back had left the wheel. Just before the boat touched the side of the pier, he scooped up the end of a rope and jumped out onto the pier. He whipped the rope around an iron mooring butterfly and yanked it tight. He reached down, grabbed the end of another rope Saul Sumeg was holding up to him from the boat, and whipped the second rope around another mooring butterfly.

"Let's go," Saul Sumeg said.

"Where?" Ida said.

Saul Sumeg jumped up onto the pier. "The suitcase first, " he said.

Max handed it up. Then Sumeg helped Ida up to the pier.

"You see that machine up there?" Saul Sumeg said.

"What about it?" Ida said.

"Go sit in it and wait."

"Why?" Ida said.

"So you won't be in the way," Saul Sumeg said.

Ida took the suitcase. She went up the pier and climbed into the automobile. Saul Sumeg jumped back into the boat. "Start unloading," he said.

Max watched Sumeg grab one of the stacked wooden

boxes and heave it up onto the pier. Max grabbed a box and did the same. The man on the pier pulled the boxes away from the edge. Saul Sumeg grabbed another box and heaved it up onto the pier. So did Max. The man on the pier dragged the boxes across toward the first two. He did this as fast as Max and Saul Sumeg hoisted the boxes up from the boat.

It was heavy work. When they had emptied the boat and the boxes were stacked neatly in the middle of the pier, Max's shoulder muscles were sore. Saul Sumeg didn't even seem winded.

"Wait in the machine," he said.

Max walked up the pier to the automobile.

"What are they talking about?" Ida said.

Max looked back. Saul Sumeg and the man from the boat had their heads together.

"I don't know," Max said.

Finally, the two men shook hands. The man who had stood behind the wheel all the way from the *Friesland* now knelt, untied the rope from the rear mooring butterfly, and jumped back into the boat. Saul Sumeg went to the other end of the boat, knelt, untied the rope from the front butterfly, and tossed the loose end down into the empty boat. The motor coughed, then took hold. The boat backed away from the pier, turned, and circled in a long, lazy arc. The man at the wheel waved. Saul Sumeg waved back. He stood on the pier, watching, until the boat disappeared into the fog. Then Saul Sumeg turned and walked up the pier toward the automobile.

"Move over," he said.

Max and Ida moved over. Saul Sumeg came around the front of the car and climbed in behind the wheel. He started the motor. The car pulled away from the pier.

"What about those boxes?" Max said.

"They won't be there long," Saul Sumeg said.

That was all he said for quite a while. The car moved along dirt roads. Several times it cut across paved roads.

95

Looking out the window Max saw very little. The fog was still thick. Once in a while he thought he smelled pine trees. Finally, Saul Sumeg stopped the car at the side of the road. He did not stop the motor.

"You see up there?" he said.

Sumeg nodded toward the windshield.

"Where?" Max said.

"The telegraph pole," Saul Sumeg said.

It was planted at the top of a low rise, perhaps a hundred yards up ahead of the car, in the bushes at the right of the road.

"What about it?" Max said.

"I'm going to drop you here," Saul Sumeg said. "When you get up there, just over the hill, there's a nice little town. It's very small, just one street. In the middle there's a nice little rooming house. It's owned by a woman named Perlmutter. She's a very nice lady. She speaks Yiddish. Don't mention my name. Don't say where you came from. Don't explain how you got here. Mrs. Perlmutter won't ask. You just tell her you've come here looking for work and you want a room."

Saul Sumeg took an envelope from his pocket.

"Here's your money," he said. "It's enough to keep you till you find work. You won't have any trouble. There's lots of work around here. They're looking for people. Mrs. Perlmutter will get you started learning English. You'll be all right."

"Where are we?" Max said.

"America," Saul Sumeg said.

"I don't have papers for America," Max said.

Saul Sumeg smiled and nodded, as though Max had said something that a teacher who believed in but had not yet seen a demonstration of his ability had been waiting to hear. Sumeg took another envelope from his pocket and handed it over. "You have now," he said.

He did something to the automobile. The purring motor erupted in a coughing roar. Saul Sumeg reached across Max and Ida and twisted the door handle. The door swung open.

"Get going," Saul Sumeg said. "It's better nobody should see us together."

Max got out. He reached in for Ida's yellow straw suitcase, then helped her out of the car. He did it slowly. Max was trying to think what to say. He had a feeling something important had been omitted. The words, however, would not come. This puzzled him. He rarely had this sort of trouble. Max always knew what to say.

"That's all?" he said finally.

It didn't seem enough. Saul Sumeg, however, apparently found the question helpful. It seemed to get him going again.

He said, "Well, yes, there's this."

"What?" Max said.

"With these new papers you're perfectly safe," Saul Sumeg said. "So long as you remember one thing."

"What's that?" Max said.

"From now on your name is Lessing."

14

In 1920, on Mrs. Perlmutter's telephone in South St. Stephen, Maine, there were no buttons. There were no instructions, either. If there had been, they would have been useless to Max Lessing.

During the few hours that had elapsed since Saul Sumeg had dropped him and Ida and his new identity on the outskirts of the tiny town, Max had managed to pick up half a dozen English words. These did not include any that involved the use of a wall telephone.

It was a neat little golden oak box with a black metal crank protruding from one side. The box hung on the wall under the stairs of the ground floor in Mrs. Perlmutter's rooming house. Answering it required no knowledge of English. Max had seen and heard Mrs. Perlmutter do it several times. She made of it a small, unhurried ritual.

When the bell at the bottom of the box started its tinny tinkling, Mrs. Perlmutter appeared from the kitchen and stood in the open doorway. The tinkling was not always the same. There were different combinations of short rings and long rings. It became clear to Max soon enough that only one combination held any interest for Mrs. Perlmutter.

When the landlady heard the combination that suited her, she came out of the kitchen doorway into the hall and moved under the stairs. She took down the receiver from the golden oak box, put it against her ear, and yelled into the mouthpiece, "Hello?" An English word.

Everything else Mrs. Perlmutter said was in Yiddish. Leaning over the banister, listening carefully, Max tried to find a pattern in the Yiddish words the landlady hurled into the gooseneck mouthpiece.

These words were few. Most of her time at the box under the stairs Mrs. Perlmutter spent in listening. Her Yiddish replies were variations of "Yes" or "All right" or "Sure" or "Okay" or "I understand." Max Lessing had a feeling he needed more than that.

"Hello?"

He could not see Mrs. Perlmutter barking the English word into the phone. He was hanging over the railing on the floor above. But Max had seen the landlady appear and stand in the kitchen doorway while she listened to the bell and wiped her hands on the flowered yellow apron. When the bell made the appropriate combination of sounds she had come forward and disappeared under the stairs.

"All right!" Mrs. Perlmutter shouted. "Yes! Okay! Sure! I understand!"

Thus she apparently exhausted her talents for coming up with variations of vigorous verbal affirmation. Or perhaps whoever it was at the other end had exhausted the orders he or she was hurling at Mrs. Perlmutter. The only thing about which Max was certain was that he heard the receiver go back on the hook. Mrs. Perlmutter reappeared at once from under the stairs. Taking a few finishing swipes at her hands with the flowered apron, the landlady went back up the hall and disappeared into the kitchen.

Moving swiftly, on his toes, Max Lessing came down from the second floor. He made a sharp right turn and ducked into the alcove under the stairs. He had never handled a telephone. From watching and listening for the last couple of hours, however, Max knew what he wanted. He took down the receiver from the golden oak box and put it to his ear.

With his free hand Max cranked the black metal handle furiously.

"Hello?" he roared into the gooseneck mouthpiece.

He added to his roars more vigorous crankings of the handle. Every turn of the black metal drew a string of tinny tinkles from the bell. Getting what he wanted at this end, Max wondered what he was stirring up at the other end. He wondered, but he did not worry. It was this end that counted.

"Yes?" he screamed into the mouthpiece. "All right! Fine! Don't worry! I'll be there!"

Behind him he heard the kitchen door open. Max slammed the receiver back on the hook. He turned. Mrs. Perlmutter was standing in the kitchen doorway, working on her wet hands with the flowered apron.

"What are you doing?" she said.

"I finished," Max said.

"Finished what?"

"Talking to my uncle," Max said.

"Nobody told me you have an uncle in America," the landlady said.

"Nobody," it seemed to Max, was obviously the voice at the other end of the telephone to whose orders Mrs. Perlmutter at regular intervals kept bellowing her variations of "Okay."

"I forgot to tell you," Max said.

It seemed wise not to indicate he was aware she had registered surprise.

"You talked to him on the telephone?" Mrs. Perlmutter said.

She made it sound like an accomplishment previously included among the Labors of Hercules. For Max the achievement would not have been dissimilar. He had no uncles.

"My uncle wrote me the minute I arrived in America I should call him on the telephone," Max said smoothly.

It was not difficult, in view of the obvious mental capacities of his listener, to make certain that only he was aware of the smoothness.

"My uncle has a job waiting for me," Max said. "He wants me to come right over."

"Over where?" Mrs. Perlmutter said.

"I don't know if I'm saying it right," Max said. "In Yiddish, I mean. Cherryfield Beach?"

"It's not far from here," the landlady said.

"That's what my uncle said," Max said. He started for the stairs.

"Where you going?" the landlady said.

"To see my uncle," Max said.

"How?" Mrs. Perlmutter said.

Max said, "How does a poor man go to a place that's not far?"

The creases in her face started to rearrange themselves. It was obvious that this time the process was painful. Mrs. Perlmutter was trying to think.

"It's too far to walk," she said.

Max liked the pace at which Mrs. Perlmutter did her thinking: a slow crawl.

"If it's too far to walk," he said, "maybe you'll lend me your automobile?"

Since just after dawn that morning, when he and Ida had paid Mrs. Perlmutter two dollars for a week's rent and moved into the room on the second floor, Max had spent most of his time hanging over the banister, studying the relationship between Mrs. Perlmutter and her telephone. Most of his time, but not all of it. Max had managed to work in a few productive minutes out back with the small black Ford.

It was not as large as the automobile in which Saul Sumeg had driven Max and Ida from the pier on the beach to the foot of the hill outside South St. Stephen. The driving mechanism, however, was not dissimilar. Also, the lorries at the First Bohemian Imperial Dragoons depot in Fürstenfeld had been built by the same company.

"You know how to drive an automobile?" Mrs. Perlmutter said.

She was groping her way toward something that was waiting for her in a corner of her mind. The creases in the Pfefferkuchen face indicated that Mrs. Perlmutter was doing it on her hands and knees.

"In the army back home," Max said, "that's all I did."

It was also all he said. Max knew where Mrs. Perlmutter's thinking was bound to lead her. Mentally speaking, she was not a breaker of new ground. The landlady did not yet know what she was going to do, but Max did. Mrs. Perlmutter clearly had only two speeds on her gear box: forward and reverse. It was important, therefore, for Max to do two things. One, get out of the landlady's way so she would be free to do the inevitable, and two, get out of her house before she finished doing it.

This took a bit of fleet footwork, but Max had always been fast on his feet. He managed.

For one thing, he had not allowed Ida to unpack the yellow straw suitcase. For another, he had instructed her to move down the back stairs with the suitcase as soon as she heard him go down the front stairs and start shouting into the telephone. And finally, Max had learned during the month since she had brought him that first cup of milk at the barn door in Klein Berezna that when it came to executing her share of a carefully worked-out plan, it would be hard to find someone who could beat Ida Wawrth. The girl was a born accomplice.

"All right," she said when Max had got the Ford under way. "Now."

The unprepossessing but efficient little automobile had without difficulty carried them and the yellow straw suitcase the few hundred yards down the town's one street. This was the only requirement that had to be met by anybody eager to shake the dust of South St. Stephen, Maine, successfully from his or her feet.

"Now what's next?" Ida said.

"Keep your eye on that map," Max said.

He was hunched over the steering wheel. It seemed to be leading a life of its own. The thing clearly resented being held captive by human hands.

"Where we're going," Max said, "it's called North St. Stephen."

"Here it is," Ida said.

She put her finger on a piece of the map Max had stolen from Mrs. Perlmutter's second-floor room. It had been tacked to the wall over the dresser.

"I can't look," Max said. "This thing jumps."

He kept his eyes on the road ahead. It was unpaved, like the roads along which Saul Sumeg had driven them early that morning.

"What do you want to know about it?" Ida said.

"The color," Max said.

"Red."

"You're sure?" Max said.

"When I see something red," Ida said, "I'm sure it's red. Now ask something that makes sense."

"Where we just came from?" Max said. "What color is that?"

"Yellow," Ida said.

"Then we're all right," Max said.

"Why?"

"Yellow is America," Max said. "Red is Canada."

"You always said you wanted to go to America," Ida said. "Now we are in America you say you want to go to Canada."

"We couldn't get papers for America," Max said. "That's why in Klein Berezna we bought papers for this place next to America. Canada."

"Before he left us this morning," Ida said, "this Saul Sumeg gave you papers for America."

"That's the trouble," Max said.

"What trouble?"

"We got the papers from Saul Sumeg," Max said.

He couldn't risk a look at her face. He was afraid to take

his eyes from the road. But from the corner of one eye Max could see the blond hair dip down over the map. Ida was silent for a few moments. Finally she said, "It's safer for us to be in the place for which we bought our own papers?"

Max nodded. A bit of self-congratulation. Max was giving himself a good mark for this further display of a talent he had long known he possessed. The ability to separate the smart from the stupid. In this girl he had picked a smart one.

"South St. Stephen, where it's yellow," Max said, "that's where Saul Sumeg wants us to be. What Saul Sumeg wants I don't think is what we want."

Ida tapped her finger on the map. "Here, this North St. Stephen, where it's red," she said. "This is what we want."

"Yes," Max said. "Until we have time to sit down and figure out which way we want to go."

15

The process of figuring out which way they wanted to go did not take long.

When they took off from Mrs. Perlmutter's rooming house Max had not thought about the fact that getting from South St. Stephen to North St. Stephen involved crossing a border between two sovereign states. There had been too many other things on his mind. Fortunately, the omission was brought to Max's attention when he and Ida and Mrs. Perlmutter's Ford were still some distance from the international boundary.

Max had learned on the hike from Fürstenfeld to Klein Berezna that it is not necessary to know a foreign language to grasp that it is foreign. When the language is used on road signs, anyway. When he became aware of the signs on the road from South St. Stephen to North St. Stephen, Max stopped the automobile.

"What's the matter?" Ida said.

"The signs," Max said.

He pointed. Ida turned to look. "You're right," she said.

"About what?"

He was teasing, and she knew it. He was also dead serious. Ida knew that too.

"They're written in two languages," she said.

Ida tapped the map on her knees.

"Which means," she said, "we're now coming to a place where they stop talking what they talk on this side, where here on the map it's yellow, and they start talking what they talk on the other side, where here on the map it's red."

He gave her a grin. Praise, if cautiously rationed, is a useful cement for binding the pupil's loyalty to the teacher. From the writings of Oberfeldwebel Sauerlich.

"Neither one of which we talk," Max said.

"You know what I think we ought to do?" Ida said.

"Tell me."

She did, and to the grin he added a small chuck under the chin. He got a bit of his own back. Her grin made him look at her more closely. While he had been hanging over the banister on the second floor of Mrs. Perlmutter's rooming house, studying the landlady's relationship with her telephone, Ida Wawrth had washed and combed her hair. She smelled the way she had smelled on that first day in Klein Berezna.

"Not now," she said, slapping his hand away. "First we have to get rid of this stupid automobile."

Max did that by running the Ford off the road into the bushes.

"How about now?" he said.

"Why not?" she said.

They both laughed.

Later, Ida said, "Which way?"

Max said, "The way that when Saul Sumeg and his friends start looking for Mrs. Perlmutter's automobile they won't think it went that way."

"So we should go this way," Ida said.

She started across the field, heading west.

"Hey," Max said.

Ida stopped and turned. "Hey what?" she said.

Max said, "You forgot something." He tapped the yellow straw suitcase with his toe.

Ida said, "You carry it for a while."

She didn't say what she meant by for a while. Max didn't mind sweating. Moving cross country, he expected that. But eventually, enough was enough. He was not a mule. He was about to point that out when Ida spoke up.

"I'll take that for a while," she said.

Max gave her the yellow straw suitcase and an uneasy glance. This was not the first time it had occurred to him that this girl, who possessed many skills, seemed to possess one that Max could have done without. He did not like people reading his mind.

"Wait," Ida said. She stopped.

Max came up beside her.

"For what?" he said.

"Listen."

He did. Max heard a familiar sound.

"An automobile," he said.

The sound stopped. Ida pointed to the low rise up ahead. It was topped by a thick mass of trees and shrubs.

"There must be a road," she said.

"Yellow or red?"

"Take this," Ida said. She shoved the straw suitcase at him.

"Where you going?" Max said.

Ida said, "To find out if we're still in yellow, or if we're over on the other side in red."

"You keep this," Max said. "Things like that I'll find out." He pushed the suitcase back at her and started up to the massed foliage.

"How will you know?" Ida called after him.

Max stopped and turned. He said, "The way we knew back there."

He waved over her head, in the direction where hours before they had abandoned Mrs. Perlmutter's automobile.

Ida said, "Suppose here on this road there's no signs?"

Max was annoyed by the way she put the question. Not, however, by the question. He should have put it to himself.

"What would you do?" he said.

107

"At the bottom of Mrs. Perlmutter's automobile," Ida said. "In the front and in the back. Hanging down between the wheels there were numbers."

Into Max's head came a picture of the front and the back of Mrs. Perlmutter's automobile.

"Signs made of tin," he said.

"Not words, though," Ida said.

"Numbers," Max said.

"The numbers were black," Ida said. "But the tin the numbers were painted on, the tin was yellow."

"Like the map," Max said.

"Like the map," Ida said. "I asked Mrs. Perlmutter. She said in Canada the tin they paint the numbers on is red, also like the map."

Max thought maybe there had been nothing annoying in the way she had put the question. Maybe it was only that she was tense and worried, the way he was.

"Good girl," Max said.

During the past month he had said many things to her. Never that. The two words made a sound in her ears that was new to Ida Wawrth. She wondered how the words would sound in English.

"Be careful," she said.

Max stepped back and reached down. He took the straw suitcase from her and, with his other hand, grabbed Ida's elbow. "Come on," he said.

He pulled her up beside him and led her to the trees and bushes. Using the suitcase as a shield for their heads, he shoved a path through the foliage. It was not as dense as it had looked from the field below.

"Okay," Max said finally.

He dropped the suitcase and signaled for her to sit on it. Then Max dropped to his knees beside her. Carefully he parted the bushes. Through the gap they looked out on a stretch of dirt road not unlike the road on which at noon they had left South St. Stephen. There was one difference. The road out of South St. Stephen had been deserted. On this road, at the other side, to the right, perhaps twenty feet from the hole in the bushes, an automobile was standing in the shade of a huge maple tree. The automobile was almost exactly like the one Max had borrowed from Mrs. Perlmutter. Almost like, but not quite. This automobile was different in two respects.

The black tin hood of this automobile was open at one side, and a man was standing beside the automobile peering into it. The man was making movements with his hands in a way that seemed to indicate he was trying to do something to the motor. Max had seen Oberfeldwebel Sauerlich and Gefreiter Schildwachter make similar movements when they were bent over the hoods of uncooperative lorries behind the stables in the Fürstenfeld barracks.

"Look," Ida said.

"At what?"

"The numbers," Ida said.

From the back of the automobile, between the wheels, hung a tin sign on which were painted black numbers. The tin on which the numbers were painted was colored red.

"We're in Canada," Max said.

Ida didn't answer. Max had learned that her silences were not always due to an inability to think of something to say. Sometimes she was silent because she had not yet piled up enough worth saying. Max suspected why she was not yet ready now.

"What do you think?" he said.

"I think he's a rabbi," Ida said.

A month ago Max would have uttered a derisive comment or he would have made a joke. Now he looked more closely. The man bent over the automobile hood was wearing a long black alpaca coat. His flat fur-trimmed hat was so obviously a rabbi's *shtrahmel* that the long side curls hanging down beside his ears seemed inevitable.

"I'll go talk to him," Max said.

"Don't talk too much," Ida said.

There were times when Max wished she wouldn't.

"Wait here," he said.

He climbed out onto the road and walked down to the automobile.

"You got trouble?" Max said in Yiddish.

The man's head came up. He looked younger than any rabbi Max had ever seen, but Max had never seen a rabbi in Canada.

"You know about automobiles?" the young man said.

"Let me take a look," Max said.

The young man stepped aside. Max poked his head under the black tin hood. What was wrong was obvious. It had been pointed out to Max during Oberfeldwebel Sauerlich's first lesson behind the stables at Fürstenfeld. Max slid the tiny forked brass end of the loose wire against the battery post and twisted down the loose screwhead.

"Get into the car," Max said.

The young man in the *shtrahmel* climbed in behind the wheel. Max went around to the front, dipped down into position, and took a good tight grip on the crank.

"Okay," Max called.

The young man at the wheel fed gasoline. Max whirled the crank. On the third twist the motor caught.

"Keep it running," Max yelled.

The young man in the *shtrahmel* made the adjustment, then climbed down out of the shivering automobile.

"You'll be all right now," Max said.

He put down the side of the black tin hood and snapped the catches into place.

"Thanks very much," the man in the *shtrahmel* said.

He examined Max with great care, as though he were trying to guess his address. Max didn't think there was anything about his appearance from which even an excessively cautious man could draw suspicious conclusions. He was still wearing the faded flannel shirt and the corduroy trousers.

"Where are you going?" said the young man in the *shtrahmel*.

"Anyplace you're going," Max said.

The young man pursed his lips. He turned and looked up the empty road, then turned back and looked in the other direction.

"I'm going to Rivière du Cojot," he said.

The name sounded odd in Yiddish.

"Is that in Canada?" Max said.

The man in the *shtrahmel* hesitated. Max didn't blame him. He would have done the same if a stranger had asked him the question. That was why Max had asked it.

"You don't know where you are?" said the young man.

"If I did," Max said, "would I ask you if I'm in Canada?"

The young man's eyes narrowed, as though he had suddenly received a signal reminding him that he was staring into the sun. There was no sun. It had disappeared behind the trees and bushes in which Ida was hiding.

"You have papers?" the man said.

"Money, too," Max said.

"What kind?"

"Canadian papers," Max said. "American money."

It sounded like the right combination.

"I can give you a lift," the man said.

It was the right combination.

"There are two of us," Max said.

"That will cost double," said the young man in the *shtrahmel*.

"All right."

"Go get her," the young man said.

Max could feel his eyes flick.

"How do you know it's a her?" he said.

The young man smiled. Not what Max would have called a good smile. Under the circumstances, however, better than none.

"It's always a her," said the young man in the *shtrahmel*. He looked up at the sky. "Gets dark here fast after the sun goes down," he said. "We better go."

16

They went for what Max guessed was about four or five hours. Without a watch he had only one way to measure the passage of time. His stomach. It ached.

Several times during the long ride he was tempted to say something about it. He didn't because Ida said nothing about it. Ida's stomach must have been in the same condition.

The last food they had put into their stomachs was Mrs. Perlmutter's breakfast. Substantial, true. By now, however, no more than a historical reference point. Ancient history, at that. The sun had just come up over South St. Stephen when Max had dipped up his first spoonful of Mrs. Perlmutter's oatmeal. From the way his stomach felt now, that was like maybe a couple of centuries ago. Yet Ida sat in silence on the front seat of the automobile, between the young man in the *shtrahmel* at the wheel and Max at the far end against the door.

"Don't talk too much," she had said to Max.

Who was this sixteen-year-old kid from a Hungarian farm to tell him he talked too much?

"Where do you want me to drop you?" asked the young man in the *shtrahmel*.

"What do you mean?" Max said.

"We're coming into Rivière du Cojot," said the young man at the wheel. "Where do you want to go?"

"Where are you going?" Max said.

He added a totally unplanned "Oof!" It was the result of an invisible but sharply felt stab of pain in his rib cage. Max winced away from Ida's elbow.

She said, "Do you think we could stay for one night in the synagogue?"

"What synagogue?" the young man said.

"Excuse me," Ida said. "I thought from your clothes you're a rabbi."

"My father is a rabbi," the young man said. "I'm a student."

"Someday you too will be a rabbi," Ida said.

"I hope so," the young man said.

"Then someday you will have a synagogue of your own," Ida said. "Tonight it would be very nice if you talked to your father and asked him if we could stay overnight in his synagogue. Just until morning, when we will locate my aunt and uncle. For staying the night we will pay, of course."

"You have an aunt and an uncle in Rivière du Cojot?" the young man said.

"I think so," Ida said. "We're not sure. It's too late at night now to find out. We'll have to try in the morning. All we need until then is a place to stay overnight. My mother always told me in a new city it's always better for Jews to stay with Jews."

"I'll ask my father," the young man said.

He did it in a narrow, three-story brownstone house on a small street in what to Max did not look like a very prosperous part of town. It was possible, of course, that the street was as prosperous as any other part of town. When they came into Rivière du Cojot, however, it was very late, and the street lighting was not much better than the street lighting had been in Fürstenfeld.

The young man's father, on the other hand, looked very

prosperous indeed. Rabbi Fruchter's dark suit was made from the same kind of very good broadcloth out of which Max's mother had made the skirt she wore to synagogue in Vetzprem on the High Holy Days. Furthermore, around the edges of his vest Rabbi Fruchter had a narrow band of white silk piping. Max had never seen that before. He had never seen such courtesy, either.

"First to eat," Rabbi Fruchter said when his son brought Max and Ida into the house. "Then to talk."

They ate in a basement kitchen while Rabbi Fruchter sat at one side and watched in silence. The rabbi's son brought the bread and milk and cheese to the table. He led Max and Ida in the appropriate prayer and then ate with them. There was no sign of a Mrs. Fruchter. The rabbi and his son seemed to be alone in the house.

"Now to talk," Rabbi Fruchter said.

He led the way back up to the room on the street floor in which his son had introduced Max and Ida to the rabbi and had explained how they met. Rabbi Fruchter settled Ida in a stuffed chair at one side of a small black cast-iron fireplace. The mantelpiece was a slab of white marble. In the empty coal grate sat a neatly folded fan made from a sheet of newspaper. It was, Max noted, a Yiddish newspaper.

"Jacob," the rabbi said when Ida was seated. "Take our guest upstairs and show him the guest room. I want to talk to the young lady alone."

Max did not like that. Not because he did not trust Ida. Nor was it because on a full stomach he was still annoyed with her for telling him not to talk too much. Max did not like leaving Ida with Rabbi Fruchter because Max had not been alone with her since he had parted the bushes and they had first sighted the young man in the *shtrahmel* bent over his disabled automobile. Max had not yet had time to work out all the details of a plausible story to tell Rabbi Fruchter. Once she opened her mouth, God alone knew what this girl, unbriefed by Max, would say.

"You go up and look at the room," Max said to Ida. "I'll talk to the rabbi."

Not much of Rabbi Fruchter's face was visible to the casual observer. The lower part was covered with a thick fan-shaped black beard that glistened as though groomed with some sort of oily dressing. The area above the beard disappeared into a handsome and clearly expensive black homburg hat with a gleaming satin edge. In between the beard and the hat were the eyes.

They were large and brown and sharp in a way that evoked in Max's mind a recollection of the tiny dancing flames on the seven-branched silver candlestick that his mother lighted every Friday night for the sabbath meal. It was clear to Max that unaided by words these eyes were capable of accomplishing whatever tasks Rabbi Fruchter set them. This time the rabbi brought to his assistance a few edged words.

"This is my house," Rabbi Fruchter said. "If you want to spend the night in it you will now go upstairs with my son, Jacob, to inspect the guest room."

Max had learned at Fürstenfeld the difference in sound between a suggestion and a direct order. He went.

The inspection did not take long. The guest room was hardly that. A sort of closet on the top floor with a slanted ceiling and a narrow cot. Rabbi Fruchter's son, Jacob, opened the door and waited while Max peered in. When Jacob felt Max had seen enough, he motioned to Max to step aside. Jacob closed the door and went back downstairs. Max followed.

When Max and Jacob came back into the room, Ida was sitting quietly in the stuffed chair. Her hands were folded in her lap. She examined her knuckles with concentrated attention while Rabbi Fruchter talked. He talked as though he were dictating a set of army orders.

"Here is how it will be," the rabbi said. "In the morning my son, Jacob, will put you both on a train for Winnipeg. In Winnipeg you will be met in the station by my brother

Jekuthiel. My brother Jekuthiel will take care of you in Winnipeg until he is ready to put you on a train that will take you across into America to the city of Minneapolis. In Minneapolis you will be met in the railroad station by my brother Zalman. From then on you will have only two things with which to concern yourselves."

"What are they?" Max said.

"To be good Jews," Rabbi Fruchter said, "and to become good Americans."

"Yes, sir," Max said.

The way, even though he had been told he did not have to say "sir" to an N.C.O., Max used to say it to Oberfeldwebel Sauerlich.

"Anything else?" Rabbi Fruchter said.

"No, sir," Max said.

"I have something else."

"Yes, sir?" Max said.

"The young lady will sleep tonight upstairs in the guest room," Rabbi Fruchter said. "You will sleep down here on this couch."

In the morning Max found out why.

"I will go with you to the station," Rabbi Fruchter said. "On the way we will stop for a few minutes in the Town Hall."

"What for?" Max said.

"On the telephone last night when I talked to my brother Jekuthiel in Winnipeg," Rabbi Fruchter said, "I told him I was sending him to take care of a young married couple named Mr. and Mrs. Max Lessing. To my brother Jekuthiel I do not tell lies. You will please hurry. In Rivière du Cojot the director of the marriage-license bureau is a Frenchman. At eleven o'clock sharp he closes his office because it is apéritif time. We must get there before he goes for his vermouth cassis, or you will miss the train to Winnipeg."

17

They did not miss the train. On it they spent their two-day honeymoon.

The first day Max devoted to nursing his fury. It was bad enough to be betrayed by a person you had befriended. For that person, however, to be a sixteen-year-old hick from a Hungarian farm was insupportable.

By the time the train crossed from Quebec into Ontario, Max was beginning to support it. But he was still not speaking to his brand-new wife. Ida did not seem to mind. She kept her nose in the English phrase book Jacob Fruchter had given her as a wedding present, studying the letters as if somehow their meaning would communicate itself to her. Rabbi Fruchter's wedding present was the ticket for a private drawing room. There was no other place on that train in which the newlyweds could sleep except together.

On the second night, when the train crossed from Ontario into Winnipeg, Max lost his fury. In the morning their relationship was back where it had started a month earlier in Klein Berezna. Just before the train pulled into the Winnipeg railroad station, Ida made a statement.

"When you asked me to go away with you from Klein Berezna," she said, "I said yes. You never asked me why. So

I didn't tell you. Now that you're my husband I feel I should tell you."

"I'm listening," Max said.

"I didn't like being a girl in Klein Berezna," Ida said. "It was like being a pet dog. You were fed and nobody kicked you, but that was all. My brothers they taught to read and write. Not me. The day you came to Klein Berezna I knew from Rabbi Jobsky it would never change."

"Who is he?" Max said.

"The man my father was paying to teach my brothers to read and write," Ida said. "On that day I talked with Rabbi Jobsky, but he said no, he would not ask my father to let him teach me, because nobody taught girls, only boys. I was in the barn, making up my mind to run away from Klein Berezna, to a place, any place, where girls were not treated that way, when you came to the barn door and you asked for something to eat."

She paused, frowning, as though she were rechecking what she had just said to make sure she had said it right. Max filled the pause by pretending to himself that he was not trying desperately to straighten out his nose. It had just been put out of joint. From his experience with women in Vetzprem and Fürstenfeld, he had assumed that what had caused this girl to leave Klein Berezna with him was the way his muscles rippled when he moved and the way his teeth flashed when he smiled and the way the light bounced off his copper hair in the sun.

"I didn't realize when we left Klein Berezna that we would meet someone who could force us to get married," Ida said finally. "So you might as well know that if you don't like being married to me, I'm not going to like it either. When we're safe in that American city, this Minneapolis, if you want a divorce, you just open your mouth and say so."

To himself what Max said was, Not yet seventeen, remember.

Aloud he said, "In this family the one who talks too much, I don't think it's me."

At odd moments during the crowded days that followed, he did a lot of thinking about what Ida could have told Rabbi Fruchter in that street-floor room in Rivière du Cojot while Max was upstairs with Jacob Fruchter inspecting the guest quarters. That, however, was all Max did. Think. He avoided reference to that blank space in their lives. He avoided it in Winnipeg, anyway. There was no time. Jekuthiel Fruchter made that clear at once.

"There is no time," he said as soon as he introduced himself to Max and Ida in the railroad station. "Things have happened."

Jekuthiel Fruchter did not say what those things were. It was impossible for Max to tell from the man's face if the things that had happened were good or bad. The only inference Max felt it was safe to draw from Jekuthiel Fruchter's appearance was that he was not a rabbi.

On his tall, powerful body he wore a sailor's navy blue double-breasted pea jacket. It was buttoned up to a chin that had clearly been modeled on the prow of an Arctic ice-breaker. His legs were tucked into knee-high hunting boots laced tightly with yellow leather thongs. Slung across one shoulder he carried what looked like a not very clean canvas laundry bag, but it could just as easily have contained the carcass of a just-bagged caribou. On his head a checked red-and-black hunting cap with a duckbill visor sat like a mallard that had paused for rest in its annual migratory flight south.

Rabbi Fruchter in Rivière du Cojot had looked as though he were ready at the drop of a *shtrahmel* to consign a defector from the laws of the Talmud to the fiery furnace. His brother in Winnipeg looked as though he were ready at the first faint peep of a pitch pipe to burst into a rousing chorus of "Frère Jacques." He was precisely what Max, when he learned it later, always felt was meant by the word "lumberjack."

"Come quick," Jekuthiel Fruchter said.

He scooped up Ida's yellow straw suitcase as though it

were a postage stamp he was about to slap down on an envelope. With the suitcase at the end of it, he cupped the same arm around Ida's shoulders. With his other hand he grabbed Max's biceps. Taking off like a skier poling himself from a standing position out onto the slope, Jekuthiel Fruchter swooped his charges from the train platform, through the crowd, to a bench at the far side of the waiting room. He sat them down as though he were sinking tent pegs, leaving a wide space between the two, then dropped himself into the slot.

"The papers," he said.

"What papers?" Max said.

He knew what papers. He knew also, however, that he had better slow down this whirlwind. Max had assumed from the way Rabbi Fruchter had outlined the plan three days ago in Rivière du Cojot that their movements would be more or less clandestine, but Jekuthiel Fruchter was acting as though he were trying to assemble a street crowd as an audience for a political speech.

"The papers," Jekuthiel Fruchter said. "My brother said on the telephone you had two sets of papers. For Canada and also for America."

That cleared up in Max's mind at least one of the things Ida had told Rabbi Fruchter when they were alone in the downstairs room of the Fruchter house in Rivière du Cojot.

"That's right," Max said.

"Of course it's right," Jekuthiel Fruchter said. "Would my brother call me on the long-distance and tell me you have papers if you didn't have papers? Stop wasting time. We have to move fast. Let's see the papers."

Max pulled out the small sack tied to the belt inside his shirt. He handed over the papers. The knots of muscle at the corners of Jekuthiel Fruchter's mouth tightened into stubble-covered walnuts as he studied the two sheets Max had purchased a month ago from the forger in Klein Berezna. Then the lumberjack examined the two sheets Max had received from Saul Sumeg four days ago at the foot of the hill leading up into South St. Stephen.

When he looked up from Max's papers, Jekuthiel Fruchter's eyes could have been staring out of the head of Francisco Pizarro when the Conqueror of Peru looked up from the east-to-west line he had drawn in the sand with the tip of his sword and said to his tiny band of sick, exhausted, starving followers, "Choose, each man, what best becomes a brave Castilian. For my part, I go to the south."

It was the direction Max knew he and Ida would have to take if they were to get to America. What Max had not known was that they were going to take off for their destination like a couple of pebbles out of a slingshot.

"Come," Jekuthiel Fruchter said.

"Where?" Max said.

"The train."

The Paul Bunyan of the Fruchter family came to his feet like Jack Dempsey, the Manassa Mauler, coming out of his corner to dethrone Jess Willard, He pointed to the huge clock on the wall of the railroad station.

"Six minutes we got to make it," he said.

They made it mainly because Jekuthiel Fruchter practically carried Ida as well as her suitcase all the way out to the train platform and into a drawing room. It was exactly like the one with which his brother had provided the newly-weds for the journey from Rivière du Cojot to Winnipeg.

He brushed the conductor aside with a few muttered words Max did not understand but which the trainman apparently found impressive. Then Jekuthiel Fruchter hustled Max and Ida into the drawing room at the end of the car, followed them in, and slammed the door shut.

"Here is how it will be," he said. "You will stay here in this room for the entire trip. Your ticket is paid. The conductor won't bother you. He won't let anybody else bother you. Don't come out for anything. You don't have to leave this room. You know already what this thing is. A toilet. And this."

He dumped the canvas sack onto the lower berth.

"This is enough to eat until you arrive in Minneapolis," he said. "It will be tomorrow night when the train gets there. My brother Zalman will come on the train here to this room. From then on you will be in Zalman's hands, and better hands to be in you won't find anywhere, so don't worry."

Oddly enough, Max didn't. Neither, so far as he could see, did Ida. She seemed relaxed enough after Jekuthiel left. Max, however, did some wondering.

Since the morning of their departure from Rivière du Cojot when he had found himself unexpectedly in the local marriage-license bureau, Max had realized that this girl was not to be taken for granted. This girl? Correction. This wife. A lot more went on inside that beautiful blond head to which he was now married than Max had suspected when, five weeks ago, he had stopped at that barn door to ask for a cup of milk.

Ida had the English phrase book open now and was pointing to a line of type. "What does this say?" she asked him.

" 'Where is the grocery store?' " Max said in Yiddish.

"Now say it in English," Ida said.

" 'Where is the grocery store?' " Max read in English.

"Where is the grocery store?" she repeated. "And this?"

" 'How much does this cost?' " Max said in Yiddish.

"Now say it in English," Ida said.

" 'How much does this cost?' " Max read in English.

"That's what I'd like to know," Ida said in Yiddish.

"You want me to say that in English?" Max said.

"No," Ida said. "I want you to answer it in Yiddish."

"Answer what?" Max said.

"Three days ago?" Ida said. "When we found Rabbi Fruchter's son on the road with his broken automobile?"

"What about it?" Max said.

He knew what about it. He had been thinking about it since they had left Rivière du Cojot. It wouldn't hurt to see if this smart girl who was now his wife had been thinking about the same thing.

"When he agreed to take you in the automobile and you told him there were two of you?" Ida said. "What did Rabbi Fruchter's son say to you?"

"He said, 'That will cost double,' " Max said.

"Has it?" Ida said.

"No," Max said.

"Not even single," Ida said.

"No," Max said.

"Not even a Pfennig," Ida said.

"We have to learn English," Max said. "You mean not even a penny."

"I mean why hasn't it cost a Pfennig or a penny?" Ida said. "Sleeping overnight in the rabbi's house. The train tickets to Winnipeg. The special room on the train. The train tickets on this train. This special room. All paid for. Everything. Why?"

"Maybe they're waiting till we get to this place Minneapolis," Max said. "Then they'll hit us on the head with a bill for the whole thing."

"You think so?" Ida said.

"What else is there to think?"

"How do they know we have enough American money to pay their bill for the whole thing?" Ida said.

"On the road, when we met him," Max said, "I told Rabbi Fruchter's son I had money."

"Did he ask to see your money?" Ida said.

"No."

"So?" Ida said.

"So what?" Max said.

"So why are they spending all this money on us?" Ida said. "We're not relatives. We're not friends. They never heard of us before. We never heard of them. We're total strangers."

"What do you think?" Max said.

"I think they want something from us," Ida said.

So did Max. This girl who was now his wife had as good a head on her shoulders as he had suspected she had when the thought of marriage had never yet entered his own head.

"What do you think they want from us?" Max said.

"That's what's worrying me," Ida said. "I can't think of anything these people haven't got already that they can get from a couple of greenhorns like us."

"Let me have that book," Max said.

Ida handed over the phrase book. Max leafed through the pages, scanning the columns of Yiddish words until he found what he wanted.

" 'Please do not worry,' " he read in English.

"What does that mean?" Ida said in Yiddish.

Max repeated it in Yiddish.

"Why should I not worry?" Ida said.

"Because that giant in Winnipeg," Max said, "the one who put us on this train, Jekuthiel Fruchter, he said we should not worry."

"You have that wrong," Ida said. "What this Jekuthiel Fruchter said was when we get to Minneapolis we will be in his brother Zalman's hands, his brother Zalman has the best hands, and that's why we should not worry."

"Then the only thing we can do," Max said, "I think we'll just have to wait until we take a look at this Zalman's hands."

They were not as large and rough as the hands of his Winnipeg brother, or as soft and white as the hands of his Rivière du Cojot brother. Perhaps because Zalman Fruchter was neither lumberjack nor rabbi.

"I'm an honest man," he said when he boarded the train in the Minneapolis railroad station. "I work for a living."

He did not enlarge on the statement, so Max had no idea what kind of work Zalman Fruchter did for a living. The way he made the statement, however, gave him an instant identity in Max's eyes. Zalman was the only member of the Fruchter family who had smiled at Max and Ida when he talked to them.

"If my brothers didn't tell it to you already," he said as

he guided Max and Ida out of the railroad station into an automobile that looked exactly like the one responsible for their introduction to the Fruchter family, "I'll tell it to you now. You are in good hands."

"First I'll take you where you're going to live," Zalman Fruchter said.

This proved to be one room on the fifth floor of a tenement on a street called Minnehaha Avenue. It contained an iron sink, a coal stove, and a double bed in one corner.

"The toilet is downstairs in the yard," Zalman Fruchter said. "It's not Count Itufski's palace, but for a young couple starting out fresh in a new country like America, it's not bad. My wife and I we started with a lot worse, believe me."

Max didn't. Not because he could not conceive of a place that was a lot worse than this room on Minnehaha Avenue. The Fürstenfeld barracks, for example, had been much worse. Max did not believe Zalman Fruchter for the same reason he had never believed Oberfeldwebel Sauerlich or Gefreiter Schildwachter or Saul Sumeg or Mrs. Perlmutter. All of them had two things in common. They all smiled a lot, and their smiles were totally devoid of conviction.

"The bed I put in for you myself," Zalman Fruchter said. "My wife said a young couple, just married, if they have a bed the rest will come along soon enough."

The smile flowered into a laugh. Max felt no inclination to join the merriment. Neither, he saw, did Ida. Zalman Fruchter did not seem to be aware that his enthusiasm for his own humor was not shared by his audience.

"To eat you'll get a visit in a few minutes from your neighbor downstairs on the third floor Mrs. Schiff," Zalman Fruchter said. "She's a very nice person and a very good friend of mine. I told her all about you."

The phrase nicked a note for itself in Max's mind. It joined the list of other notes that had been accumulating there since Saul Sumeg had first spoken to him at the rail of the well deck on the *Friesland*. The list had an odd touch of uniformity. All the notes on it ended with question marks.

"I'll leave you alone now so you can rest from the trip," Zalman Fruchter said. "In the morning I'll come early and take you out to show you how you can start earning a living here in America."

Early in America proved to be earlier than early in the Fürstenfeld barracks: 4:00 A.M. Earning a living in America involved the acquisition of a pushcart and picking up a working knowledge of the wholesale houses on River Street. Zalman Fruchter provided both. The effort seemed to exhaust him.

Late in the morning he suggested they stop in a River Street bakery for a refreshing bagel and cup of coffee. Max decided to enlarge the menu with a trial balloon.

"By now," he said, "I must owe you and your family a lot of money."

"Don't worry about it," Zalman Fruchter said.

"My mother taught me that when it comes to reasons for worrying," Max said, "I'll never find a better one than owing money."

"When the time comes to prove your mother is right," Zalman Fruchter said, "I'll give you the message."

18

The message was delivered almost two months after Max and Ida moved into their tenement room on Minnehaha Avenue, three weeks after Max started selling Ida's home-made wine from his pushcart. The message was delivered in Krasner's Bakery on River Street. Max had stopped in for his midmorning bagel and coffee.

"Hey, my friend, you're really living!"

Max looked up. Zalman Fruchter had appeared beside the table. Zalman Fruchter and his smile.

"Hello," Max said.

"A man who has cream cheese and lox on his bagel at eleven o'clock in the morning," Zalman Fruchter said, "to such a man the whole world knows America is giving a happy welcoming smile."

He had said a mouthful. Max wished Zalman Fruchter had said it in some other place at some other time. Max had been looking forward to this treat. He did not want it spoiled by this oily bastard.

For weeks Max had watched the more successful peddlers pick up from Krasner's counter the bagels smeared with cream cheese and spread with lox and carry them with their coffee to the tables along the walls. Max had watched, and lusted. He had watched, and lusted, and counted his pennies.

Biding his time was not a phrase with which Max Lessing was familiar, but he knew how to do it.

During his first weeks on the Minneapolis sidewalks with his pushcart, Max had acquired a yardstick. He could tell whether or not he was going to have a good day if, when he came into Krasner's at eleven o'clock, his profits added up to eighty cents or over. In the beginning they rarely did. The yardstick never failed. If by eleven o'clock he had not picked up at least eighty cents of what Ida in Hungarian called "the soft," Max knew it was going to be a bad day. The best pushcart hours were from six in the morning to eleven.

If by eleven o'clock Max had accumulated eighty cents of "the soft," he knew he could count on a dollar to a dollar ten by the end of the day. On that, multiplied by six days a week, he and Ida could manage. Managing meant that on a dollar ten a day Ida could pay the rent and buy their food and, in addition, Max could afford the penny bagel and the penny cup of coffee at eleven. On a dollar ten a day, however, Max could not afford the cream-cheese-and-lox bagel. In Krasner's this delicacy cost three cents.

Max lusted, but he did not succumb. What Max did was wait. He waited with confidence. He could tell from the response he was getting from housewives at the back doors in Sunningdale and Columbia Heights that he was moving steadily uphill. Without pushing. The women liked him. At first, somewhat uncertain about the way things worked in this new country, Max had taken at their word the women who said no, they didn't need anything today. Max soon learned to pretend he had not heard. He learned to give these housewives another few moments for· soaking up the presence of the tall young man with the copper hair to whom they were saying no. The soaking process always worked.

Not once in a while. Not on the average. Always. It worked every single time. Max began to have a very special feeling about this new country. He had always been successful with women. Even in Vetzprem, where the number available was small, and in Fürstenfeld, where what was available cost money he did not have. Here in America, Max learned that his capacity to get along easily with women was more than a useful skill that made pleasant the disposal of leisure time. At the back doors of Sunningdale and Columbia Heights Max learned that what he possessed was a commercial talent.

He took it in hand. He polished it. He tailored it. Above all, he honed it. The cutting edge made an immediate difference in two areas: the size of the daily "soft," and the dimensions of Max's confidence in his new country. Both took marked leaps upward. As a result, Max set himself a series of marks to shoot at. The first involved his daily stop at Krasner's.

Max decided that as soon as his eleven-o'clock count of "the soft" added up to a dollar and twenty-five cents or over, he would celebrate by carrying from Krasner's counter to one of the wall tables his first cream-cheese-and-lox bagel.

On this morning, after he chained his locked pushcart to the iron railing in the vacant lot back of the bakery, Max counted his "soft." One dollar and thirty-one cents.

Max did not realize that when he picked up the plate on which sat the long-coveted delicacy, the beating of his heart was not unlike the turmoil inside the chest of Alexander Graham Bell when the inventor picked up the crude instrument on which he had been working for so long and said into the mouthpiece, "Mr. Watson, come here, I want you."

The last thing Max wanted was to share his moment of triumph. He had not even told Ida he was contemplating it. He had other things to tell Ida, things that would please her. This, however, was a moment with which Max wanted to be alone. Zalman Fruchter had ruined that. Zalman Fruchter and his smile.

"I didn't have anything to eat when I left the house this morning," Max said.

That was not true. Every morning, when he got out of bed at four o'clock and went to the sink to wash, Ida already had waiting for him on the table Max's cup of coffee and two slices of buttered bread. Ida did not believe it was healthy for him to start trundling his pushcart down to River Street on an empty stomach.

"In this country," Zalman Fruchter said, "a man who eats alone in a restaurant gets a reputation for being stuck up."

"I wouldn't want that to happen to a friend," Max said. "Sit down."

Zalman laughed and sat down at Max's table. Rabbi Fruchter in Rivière du Cojot had filled Max with a sense of awe. Jekuthiel Fruchter in Winnipeg had given him a feeling of strength. Zalman Fruchter in Minneapolis gave Max a pain in the ass.

Max had not yet taken the first bite of his bagel. Already he knew that the treat to which he had looked forward so long had lost some of its glow. Not Zalman Fruchter's smile.

"Max, what I like about you," he said, "not only you're a hard worker, you're also a good joker."

"Three cents for a bagel with a smear of cream cheese and a scratch of lox," Max said. "If a man couldn't laugh, the tears would keep him from enjoying what he's paying for."

"In this country you'll never cry," Zalman Fruchter said. "This country was made for Max Lessing."

"Out of your mouth into God's ear," Max said.

"He's listening," Zalman Fruchter said. "Last night I told that to my brother on the long-distance in Rivière du Cojot."

Max's gut tightened. "Rabbi Fruchter?" he said.

"How many brothers does a man have in places like Rivière du Cojot?" Zalman Fruchter said.

"You talked to your brother on the long-distance last night?"

"A man's brother calls on the long-distance," Zalman Fruchter said, "I should *not* talk to him?"

"Something is wrong?" Max said.

"That's why my brother called," Zalman Fruchter said. "He wanted to know if you and your wife you're all right."

"He called about me and Ida?" Max said.

"Why not?"

"I don't know why not," Max said. "I'm just surprised."

"My brother worries about you," Zalman Fruchter said.

"In Rivière du Cojot?"

"What other places does my brother have to worry in?" Zalman Fruchter said.

"What does he worry about?" Max said.

"He worries if you're making a living."

"I guess I am," Max said.

"A man who at eleven o'clock he eats bagels with lox and cream cheese," Zalman Fruchter said, "such a man has to guess?"

"Do you think I'm making a living?" Max said.

"I know you are," Zalman Fruchter said.

"How do you know that?"

"You're selling wine," Zalman Fruchter said.

Max did not ask how Zalman Fruchter knew he was selling wine. Max knew Zalman Fruchter would not have answered the question. The way it would have remained unanswered if Max had put the question to Oberfeldwebel Sauerlich or Gefreiter Schildwachter or Saul Sumeg or Mrs. Perlmutter. Or even to Rabbi Fruchter or his brother Jekuthiel in Winnipeg. Sources of information were like fuses. You could ignite them. Once they were ignited, all you could do was follow their sputtering progress up to a certain point. At that point either they sputtered out, or they detonated the charge to which they were connected. Until you had made arrangements to handle the consequences of the detonation, it was best to let them sputter out.

"I'm not starving," Max said.

"That's what I told my brother on the long-distance last night in Rivière du Cojot," Zalman Fruchter said.

"What was his answer?" Max said.

"In that case, my brother told me, maybe it would be all right now if we asked the young man to pay what he owes us," Zalman Fruchter said.

Max took his first bite of the lox-and-cream-cheese bagel

to which he had looked forward for so long. He was not surprised to discover that the flavor was not what he had expected. He had not, of course, expected to take that first bite in the presence of Zalman Fruchter and his smile. It was important to bear that in mind for the future. There would be other bagels with lox and cream cheese.

"How much do I owe you?" Max said.

"Not me," Zalman Fruchter said. "Our family."

"How much do I owe your family?"

"Five thousand dollars," Zalman Fruchter said.

It was not the size of the sum that caused Max to set the bagel back on the plate. It was his instant grasp of what the size of the sum meant. The distinction had been nailed down in Max's mind in the Fürstenfeld barracks when Ober-feldwebel Sauerlich was explaining how an NCO with brains and a ten-Pfennig punchboard could pick up a young fortune if he knew how to handle *shmucks*. Here at a table in Krasner's on Minneapolis' River Street, the only surprise for Max Lessing was that it should have taken him so long to grasp that to the Fruchter family Max Lessing was just another *shmuck*.

"I don't have five thousand dollars," Max said.

"You will have," Zalman Fruchter said.

Max did not doubt it. Neither did he intend to turn it over to Zalman Fruchter. Not all *shmucks*, it might come as a surprising discovery to the Fruchter family, were *shmucks*.

A week later, while Max was having his eleven-o'clock coffee, the Minneapolis branch of the Fruchter family again appeared at Max's table. Smile and all.

Zalman Fruchter said, "Today you're not eating cream cheese and lox on your bagel?"

"I'm saving my money," Max said.

"For what?"

"To pay the five thousand dollars I owe your family," Max said.

"How much have you saved?" Zalman Fruchter said.

"A dollar and seventy-five cents."

"Working so hard a whole full week?" Zalman Fruchter said. "Only a dollar and seventy-five cents?"

"Your brother up in Rivière du Cojot, he told me when I got to Minneapolis one of the two things he expected me to devote myself to, it's to be a good Jew," Max said. "Even to pay off a debt to your family I don't think your brother the rabbi would want a good Jew to work on the sabbath."

Zalman Fruchter said, "What was the second thing my brother told you when you got to Minneapolis he expected you to devote yourself to?"

"To be a good American," Max said.

"A good American," Zalman Fruchter said, "when he owes somebody five thousand dollars he doesn't pay it off a dollar seventy-five a week. That's almost three thousand weeks."

"Two thousand eight hundred fifty point seven one weeks," Max said. "A little more if you carry it out beyond two decimal places."

"A person who waits that long somebody should pay him five thousand dollars," Zalman Fruchter said, "he could get carried out long before he gets the money, and the place he could get carried to, it won't be a decimal point."

"That's the best I can do," Max said.

"My brothers and I," Zalman Fruchter said, "we think you can do better."

"How?"

"We think a man who sells wine," Zalman Fruchter said, "we think such a man can afford to pay fifty dollars a week."

Max said, "Where am I going to get fifty dollars a week?"

"The same place you got the dollar seventy-five," Zalman Fruchter said. "I'll take that now."

"I haven't got it with me," Max said.

"Where is it?"

"In the Minneapolis Savings Bank," Max said. "On Anoka Avenue."

"A dollar and seventy-five cents you put in the savings bank?" Zalman Fruchter said.

"In my pocket it's a dollar and seventy-five cents," Max

said. "In the savings bank it's a dollar and seventy-five cents with every day they add on a little bit. It's called interest."

"Where did you learn about interest?" Zalman Fruchter said.

"Your brother the rabbi in Rivière du Cojot, he told me to become a good American," Max said. "I asked one of my customers in Columbia Heights how a good American makes his small money grow so he can pay people like rabbis the big sums he owes them. She told me."

Zalman Fruchter's smile did not change. It merely shifted slightly. Like a mask on the face of a Mardi Gras reveler who is jostled by the crowd.

"Rabbis are not rich," he said. "Especially in places like Rivière du Cojot. My brother needs his five thousand dollars. Next week you bring me the dollar seventy-five you put in the savings bank, and you add to it the fifty dollars you will be giving me every week from now on. I will be here at eleven o'clock."

He was. Max was not.

The morning after that, when Max went down to the backyard at 4:00 A.M. to start the day's work, his pushcart was not there. He did not go back up to the fifth floor to tell Ida. After she made his breakfast coffee and buttered his bread, Ida went to work with her wine press on the fermented grapes in the tubs under their bed. It took her all day to fill enough bottles for Max to take out on the pushcart the next morning. Max did not want to disturb her work. He walked over to River Street. Mr. Marawitz, at the north end of the long block, opened his pushcart stable every morning before the wholesalers took down their iron shutters.

"I don't know if you remember me," Max said to the asthmatic owner. "Two months ago? I bought a pushcart from you?"

"I never forget a pushcart," Mr. Marawitz said. "Wait."

He closed his eyes. He rubbed his nose. His chest heaved and rumbled like a churning lava bed. He opened his eyes.

"With blue wheels?" Mr. Marawitz said.

"That's right," Max said.

"Lessing?" Mr. Marawitz said. "Max Lessing?"

"That's right," Max said.

"Mr. Fruchter brought you in here?" Mr. Marawitz said. "Zalman Fruchter?"

"That's right," Max said.

"It's something wrong with the pushcart?" Mr. Marawitz said.

"Somebody stole it."

"America," Mr. Marawitz said. "Even a peddler he's not safe from those crooks in Washington."

"I don't think Washington has anything to do with this," Max said.

"Because you're still a greenhorn," Mr. Marawitz said. "You'll learn, young man, you'll learn. In this country, no matter what happens, even to a pushcart peddler, it's always Washington. You don't believe me, you wait till you get to the police station, you just watch the way they'll treat you."

"I'm not going to the police station," Max said.

"See?" Mr. Marawitz said. "Already you're learning. A poor man goes to the police station to tell them somebody stole his pushcart, they'll just stand there and laugh their heads off, that's what they'll do."

"That won't help me," Max said. "I have to put bread on my family's table. I need another pushcart."

"Don't I understand that?" Mr. Marawitz said. "A peddler without a pushcart it's like a baker without flour."

"That's why I came to you," Max said.

"What kind of pushcart you want?" Mr. Marawitz said.

"Whatever you can let me have on credit."

"Credit?" Mr. Marawitz said.

"I'll pay you as soon as I can," Max said.

"You read English?"

"A little," Max said.

135

"Read that," Mr. Marawitz said.

He pointed to a neatly framed placard on the wall.

IN GOD WE TRUST, it read. ALL OTHERS PAY CASH.

"I have no cash," Max said.

"Then another thing you don't have is a pushcart," Mr. Marawitz said.

What Max did have was six and a half hours to kill. It was only four-thirty in the morning. He walked to the south end of River Street and climbed down to the sloping turf that edged into the muddy river. Max pulled a couple of discarded vegetable crates into a crude couch and stretched out with his hands folded behind his head.

He watched the produce boats come in. He saw the first vegetables being unloaded. He saw the peddlers push their way into River Street and stop to make their purchases for the day. He watched the sun rise. He turned things over in his mind. He dozed a bit. Mainly, however, what Max did was turn things over in his mind. It was not easy.

The things he turned over revealed other things underneath. Things that surprised him. Things Max Lessing did not want to see. No. That wasn't exactly right. They were things he had not expected to see. Not in America. In Fürstenfeld, yes. Anyplace after a war, surrounded by people like Oberfeldwebel Sauerlich and Gefreiter Schildwachter, you could expect to see things like that. You saw them and you learned how to handle them. It wasn't much to learn. It didn't take much in the way of brains to handle people like Oberfeldwebel Sauerlich or Gefreiter Schildwachter or, in the end, Colonel Eyquardt.

The trouble was that Max had never dreamed he would have to handle people like that in America. It worried him. He wondered if he should go back to Minnehaha Avenue and discuss it with Ida, but Max Lessing did not wonder about that very long. He knew he could not discuss this with Ida. To discuss it with Ida would be to upset their relationship. What made this girl useful to Max was that he did not have to ask her anything. What he had to do was tell her. She took it from there. Where Ida took it Max did not know. But she always came back with an answer. To get the answer, he had to earn it. He would have to earn it now.

When Max saw the peddlers start coming back into River Street, shoving their pushcarts up toward Krasner's, Max figured there wasn't much more he could do with the things he had been turning over in his mind. He rose from the vegetable crates and he climbed back up from the sloping turf to the pavement of River Street. He did it the way he had finally gone to the dentist in Vetzprem with his aching wisdom tooth. Not exactly happily, but not unhappily either. A decision had been reached. It was going to hurt. Nobody got a tooth pulled without pain. But nothing was going to hurt as much as the pain of indecision. Max slapped the dirt from his pants. He walked up to the bakery, aware in an uneasy way that this was not just another decision. He was not moving toward a dentist's chair. He was heading toward a whole new way of life.

Embedded in this uneasiness, however, was a sense of excitement. Not the excitement he had felt about coming to America. That excitement, Max saw now, was the excitement of a boy going to a new place. Any new place. This excitement, however, this new feeling he had as he walked up River Street to Krasner's, was the excitement of self-discovery. Max Lessing had learned how to make this new place his. The way other men had learned to make it theirs. Men like Zalman Fruchter.

Max waited on the river side of the street until he saw Zalman Fruchter go into the bakery. Max followed. Zalman Fruchter was sitting at his usual table with his cup of coffee and his bagel and his smile. Max walked up to the table.

He said, "I need the pushcart."

"You got the money?" Zalman Fruchter said.

Max said, "I can get it."

"When?"

"You tell me," Max said.

137

Zalman Fruchter took a bite of bagel. He dissolved it in his mouth with a sip of coffee. He gave himself over to making a calculation in his head. He did it all without disturbing the smile.

"Six o'clock," he said finally.

"You'll have the pushcart?" Max said.

"Where do you want it?"

"Where I left it last night," Max said.

"That means your own backyard."

"That's right," Max said.

"Not for handing over money," Zalman Fruchter said. "People look out of windows."

"When my wife looks out she knows I'm away working," Max said. "When I come home and she looks out I don't want her to know the pushcart is missing."

Zalman Fruchter took another bite of bagel and another sip of coffee.

"For you I'll take a bath," he said finally.

"What time?" Max said.

Zalman Fruchter said, "I'll meet you at six o'clock upstairs."

19

Upstairs was the kitchen of a three-room flat on the top floor of the tenement on Minnehaha Avenue.

The tenement was owned by a Minnesota corporation. The name was an unpronounceable acronym of letters from "Jacob," "Jekuthiel," and "Zalman." The tenants were unaware of this. The tenants were aware of only two things. The man to whom they paid their rent, and the inadequacies of the building as a structure intended to shelter human beings.

The man who collected the rent was the corporation's part-time employee, the barber on the street floor, Mr. Angelo Catalini.

The inadequacies of the building were many. The sources of most of the complaints fielded by Mr. Catalini were two. The toilet that was downstairs in the backyard, and the bathrooms that did not exist. Some of the tenants had learned that homes in America had bathrooms, and they wanted them. There was nothing Mr. Catalini could do about moving the toilet to a location more convenient for the tenants. He was able to do something about the bathrooms. He did it by suggesting an experiment to one of the major stockholders.

"That three-room flat on the top floor," Mr. Catalini said

one day to Zalman Fruchter. "It's been empty over six months. People they come and they look but they don't rent. They say you're asking too much, Mr. Fruchter. It's no different they say from every other three-roomer here on Minnehaha Avenue. Why so much rent for this place?"

"What do you think we should do?" Zalman Fruchter said. He had learned to value the barber's opinions.

"Make it different," Angelo Catalini said.

"How?" Zalman Fruchter said.

"Tear out the cement washtub in the kitchen," Angelo Catalini said. "Put in a white bathtub."

"In the kitchen?"

"Why not?" Angelo Catalini staid. "They look nice. Nicer than those dirty old cement washtubs we got up there now. And they're pretty cheap. I priced them over on Anoka Avenue. You put one of them white tubs in that top-floor flat and you'll be able to say you're renting the only flat with a private bath on Minnehaha Avenue."

Zalman Fruchter was able to say it, and he did, but he was still unable to rent the top-floor three-roomer. Perhaps to turn away some of Zalman's smiling wrath, the barber came up with another suggestion. Many of his customers were local politicians.

"If we can't rent the flat," he said, "why don't we rent the bathtub?"

"How much?" Zalman Fruchter said.

"A dime a shot."

"Nobody on Minnehaha Avenue cares that much to get clean," Zalman Fruchter said. "Make it a nickel and it could maybe work."

It didn't. Angelo Catalini came up with another suggestion. They dropped the price to four cents. Several tenants tried it, but none repeated. Angelo Catalini's final suggestion worked. A drop to three cents did the trick.

By the time Max and Ida Lessing moved into the building, a great many of their neighbors were paying three cents for the right to spend a half hour in the kitchen of the untenanted top-floor flat. The customers supplied their own towels and their own soap. Angelo Catalini collected the money, handed over the key, and kept track of the time. If a customer did not reappear in the barbershop and return the key within the allotted half hour, Angelo Catalini sent his eleven-year-old son upstairs to hammer on the door.

Max Lessing did not tell Ida about his six-o'clock appointment on the top floor with Zalman Fruchter. Max did not want Ida to know the pushcart had been stolen. When he got it back she would know as she always did what he wanted her to know, and then what he had done to get it back would be all right.

Max stayed away from Minnehaha Avenue for the rest of the day. When he came into the flat at the usual hour, Ida would have no reason to believe he had not been shoving the pushcart around the streets of Sunningdale and Columbia Heights since he had left that morning. Max did not plan to come into the flat until after his meeting with Zalman Fruchter, by which time the pushcart would be chained as usual to the iron fence in the backyard. Max wanted to be sure that Ida remained unaware of the unpleasant aspects of the incident. All that would do would be impair her usefulness to him. What mattered was to keep her uninterruptedly at work producing the wine he sold from the pushcart. She was, after all, a very young girl. It was important for him to spare her any unnecessary anguish.

At five o'clock Max slipped into the backyard from Edina Street. Twilight had come down on the neighborhood. Max was sure nobody saw him. He waited in the downstairs hall until he was equally sure he could hear nothing on the back stairs. Then he ran up swiftly, two steps at a time, to the top floor. On the door of the untenanted flat he gave the prearranged knock. The bolt clicked back at once. The door opened. Max stepped in.

At ten minutes to six Mrs. Berlfein, fourth floor back, came into the barbershop to pick up the key. The day before, Mrs. Berlfein had put her name down on Mr.

Catalini's list for a six-o'clock bath on Friday. Mr. Catalini went to the rack on the barbershop wall. The key was missing.

"Must be somebody up there," he said to Mrs. Berlfein.

The barber consulted the list. Mrs. Schiff had paid her three cents and picked up the key at four o'clock. She had returned the key at four-thirty. So far as Mr. Catalini could remember, nobody had used the key from four-thirty to five. A few minutes before five o'clock, Mr. Zalman Fruchter had come in, taken the key, and gone upstairs.

Mr. Zalman Fruchter did not pay three cents for a bath. Mr. Catalini saw nothing wrong in that. If you and your family owned something, you had a right to charge others for using what you owned, and you had a right to use it yourself free of charge.

"Wait a minute, please," the barber said to Mrs. Berlfein. "We've got a slow soaper up there."

The barber turned to his son. The boy was wearing his Scout uniform and working on a customer's shoes. Joe helped out in the barbershop every day after school. On Fridays, when he came home from school and before he went down to work in the shop, Joe changed into his uniform. On Fridays, Minneapolis Troop 24 held its weekly meeting in the basement of the public library around the corner on Edina Street. Joe was senior patrol leader. If, after his father closed the barbershop at six o'clock, he did not have to run upstairs to change into his uniform, he would not, the boy knew, be late for the meeting. He had never been late for a Troop 24 meeting. It was one of the reasons for Joe's high standing in the estimation of Mr. Shale, the troop scoutmaster. There were other reasons.

"Joe," his father said, "run upstairs to the top floor and knock on the door. Tell Mr. Fruchter we got a customer waiting."

"You bet," Joe Catalini said.

The boy ran out of the barbershop and up the stairs. When

142

Mr. Zalman Fruchter was in the building, Joe Catalini always ran. He knocked on the door. No answer.

"Yoo-hoo!" the boy called.

No answer.

"Hey, Mr. Fruchter!" Joe yelled.

Still no answer. Joe Catalini tried the doorknob. It turned. The door squeaked open. The boy walked in. He stopped, stared, then started across the kitchen to the bathtub. The boy moved slowly. Joe Catalini had never before seen a drowned man, so he had not yet grasped the fact that Mr. Fruchter was dead. The boy's mind was busy with something else. Coming across the room, Joe was trying to work out the answer to a puzzling question.

Why was his father's boss lying in the tub full of soapy water with all his clothes on?

20

The next day Mr. Marawitz said, "You know what I'd like to know?"

"What?" Max said.

"What a man like Zalman Fruchter was doing there lying in a bathtub full of soapy water with all his clothes on."

"He was?" Max said.

"That's what it said in the paper this morning," Mr. Marawitz said. "You didn't read it?" He pulled a folded newspaper from the back pocket of his overalls. "Here," he said.

Max took the newspaper. With a groaning expulsion of breath Mr. Marawitz eased himself down on his knees beside the pushcart Max had just wheeled into the shop.

"I never have a chance to read the paper till I get home at night," Max said.

His glance moved quickly across the headline, down the paragraphs of densely packed Yiddish type, and paused on Mr. Marawitz' kneeling figure. The fingers of the proprietor of the pushcart garage explored the jagged holes in the side of the pushcart where the chain hasps had torn away.

"How did you get it back?" Mr. Marawitz said.

Max said, "Yesterday, when I went to the police station to report it was stolen, they said I should come in again tomorrow. That's today. Maybe somebody would report they found a pushcart somewhere on the street with no owner. This morning, when I came downstairs, I took a look in my backyard, and I didn't have to go again to the police station. The pushcart was standing there in the yard where it belonged."

Still on his knees, Mr. Marawitz said, "You mean the crooks they stole it the night before, then they brought it back last night?"

"I don't know who brought it back," Max said. "Whoever it was that took it, though, they must have torn away the chain from the iron fence in my backyard where I lock it every night."

Mr. Marawitz placed both palms flat on the cement floor, hauled air into his asthmatic chest, and shoved down hard. He came up onto his feet coughing fiercely. When he could utter intelligible sounds, Mr. Marawitz gasped, "They cleaned you out?"

"That's the crazy thing," Max said. "They didn't take anything. The way it looks, all they did they tore away the chain, then they took the pushcart some place I don't know where or for what, maybe it was just kids fooling around, and then it could be they got scared maybe, so they brought it back without the chain with these holes in the side."

Another coughing fit sent Mr. Marawitz' head forward. Bent over the pushcart, supporting his heavy body with one hand on the wooden top, he used the other to pull open one of the pushcart's two side doors. He swung the door back and forth as though he felt he should test the hinges in order properly to assess the extent of the damage to the whole structure.

"You can fix it?" Max said.

"Something good you can always fix," Mr. Marawitz said. "When that Zalman Fruchter he brought you in here a few months ago to buy a pushcart, I didn't sell you a piece of junk. I sold you what I sell everybody who comes in here. A good pushcart."

He gave the wooden top a proud slap and, for emphasis, added a blast of the deep, croupy cough.

"How much will it cost?" Max said.

"You're making jokes?" Mr. Marawitz said. "Yesterday you didn't have any money."

"Yesterday I didn't have my pushcart," Max said. "How much will it cost to fix?"

Mr. Marawitz tapped the pushcart door.

"Those bottles in there," he said. "Wine?"

"Homemade," Max said.

"Kosher?"

"My wife makes it the way she used to help her father make it back home every year for Passover," Max said.

"Tell you what," Mr. Marawitz said. "You give me two bottles for my family *seder*, I'll give you a fixed pushcart."

"How long will it take?" Max said.

"How long does it take you for a bagel and coffee in Krasner's?"

"I'll eat slow," Max said.

Mr. Marawitz said, "And read the paper."

This was not easy. Most of the peddlers in Krasner's were talking about the death of Zalman Fruchter. Some peddlers had copies of the newspaper Mr. Marawitz had given Max. Small groups gathered around these newspaper owners. Five or six stood behind Max, sipping their coffee and munching their bagels as they read the paper across his shoulder. From what he heard, which was plenty, Max sorted out the two most widely held comments. Almost everybody wanted to know what Zalman Fruchter had been doing in a bathtub full of soapy water with all his clothes on, and nobody seemed to disagree with the general feeling that the accident couldn't have happened to a more appropriate victim.

"In Krasner's," Mr. Marawitz said when Max came back into the shop, "what's the talk about Zalman Fruchter?"

"I never knew so many people knew him," Max said.

"A man he's in the line of work a man like Zalman

Fruchter was in, lonely he'll never be," Mr. Marawitz said. He took the newspaper Max held out. "Dead once in a while, maybe," Mr. Marawitz said. "But lonely? Never. What did they have to say about him lying there in a bathtub full of soapy water with all his clothes on?"

"They think it's because he owned the building," Max said. "He could take the key without paying in the barbershop. The peddlers think he must have fallen in the bathtub and knocked his head or something while he was running the water, before he had a chance to take off his clothes."

Mr. Marawitz stared thoughtfully at the newspaper while his chest rumbled quietly like a threatening volcano.

"Who knows?" he said finally. "It could be. If the peddlers in Krasner's are wrong, only Zalman Fruchter could give them an argument, and from him from now on I think nobody is going to get any arguments."

Mr. Marawitz refolded the newspaper and shoved it into the back pocket of his overalls. He ran his hand along the side of the pushcart.

"How do you like?" he said.

"Good as new," Max said.

"Better," Mr. Marawitz said. "This hinge, here, it was loose. I took out the old screws, they were rusty, and I put in fresh.

Max opened the door and tested the new hinge.

"You're right," he said. "It's much better."

He reached into the pushcart and pulled out two bottles of Ida's wine.

"Your family should drink it in good health," Max said. "And thanks for putting me back in business."

"How is business?" Mr. Marawitz said.

"When nobody is stealing my pushcart," Max said, "I make a living."

"A young man like you," Mr. Marawitz said, "I think if you're not lazy you could make more than a living."

"I'm trying," Max said.

147

Mr. Marawitz slapped the pushcart.

"The bottles you got in here," he said. "They're all for customers they're already waiting for you to deliver?"

"Yes and no," Max said. "The streets I go, the people they know me, and they tell their friends, so I have no trouble getting rid of everything my wife makes."

"So these two bottles you gave me," Mr. Marawitz said, "I'm not upsetting your route?"

"Anybody I miss today," Max said, "I'll take care of them tomorrow."

"Where do you work?" Mr. Marawitz said.

"Columbia Heights mostly."

"A good neighborhood," Mr. Marawitz said. "If it's not too much trouble for you, I know somebody up there they could use a couple of bottles of wine for Passover."

"Just tell me who and where," Max said.

21

Who was a man named Boyle. Where was a beautiful two-story house on Southeast Eighth Street just off Rarig Avenue. The house was so beautiful that Max, coming around the corner into Southeast Eighth Street with his pushcart, stopped to admire it.

The large white clapboard structure with bright green shutters was the center of a nest of huge maple trees set on a slight rise. Not exactly a hill, but the land was just enough higher than the land on which the surrounding homes were built to make this house stand out from its neighbors as the special adornment of the neighborhood. Not that it needed the height to achieve this distinction. The amount of land in which the house sat was unusual even for Columbia Heights, which was, in the private definition of a tenement dweller like Max, "a very roomy section of the city." There were neatly trimmed lawns not only in front but on all four sides of this house. And all four lawns ended in the sort of substantial-looking metal-mesh fencing Max had previously seen only in public parks.

Shoving his pushcart around to the service entrance, Max noted that this fencing stuck up in the air at least ten and perhaps even twenty inches higher than the copper-colored hair that topped his own six-foot-two-inch frame. The service entrance was a locked door cut into the fencing at the back of the house. A small white enamel plaque set between the lock and a black push button bore the single word RING.

Max pressed the button. At the far end of the long cement walk that cut through the back lawn from the gate to the house Max was pretty sure he heard the clang of a bell. He waited. Nothing happened. Max pressed the button once more. Again he thought he heard the clang of a bell inside the house, but this second time Max was not sure. The puzzling lack of certainty may have had something to do with his sudden feeling of certainty about something else. He was being scrutinized.

Trying not to be obvious in his effort to determine from where this examination was coming, Max pressed the bell a third time. The back door of the house opened. A small, thin figure in pants emerged. Not slowly, but not on the double, either, the figure came down the cement walk toward Max. By the time it reached the door in the iron fence, the figure came clear to Max as a skinny little black man with a wrinkled face under a skullcap of tight white curls. He wore a loose-fitting white linen jacket that reminded Max of the coats the stewards on the *Friesland* had worn, and a look that could not be called friendly. Max, however, was not intimidated by the fact that the bright little eyes in the wrinkled black face were regarding him with so much suspicion. Max had grown accustomed to seeing that look whenever he rang the bell of any back door in this neighborhood for the first time. The residents of Columbia Heights had money. They were nervous about prowlers.

"Mr. Boyle?" Max said.

"Who you?" the black man said.

"Mr. Marawitz sent me," Max said.

The information did nothing to the look on the black man's face, but it set his hands in motion. He unlocked the wire-mesh door and pulled it open.

"Come on in," he said.

Max shoved the pushcart through the door and waited

until the black man locked it. When he started up the cement walk to the house, Max followed with the pushcart. He had been inside enough Columbia Heights houses to know, when the black man reached a screen door, that they were standing outside a kitchen. The black man said, "You bring something?"

Max opened the side doors of the pushcart and pulled out two bottles of Ida's wine.

"Fifty cents each," he said.

"Bring them in," the black man said.

That was what most housewives said. By the time Max had opened the pushcart, making sure he took his time doing it, the housewife had not wasted the opportunity thus provided to take in, along with his wares, the peddler's copper hair, and the look of suspicion had vanished. After the first visit, it was replaced by a smile, and the invitation that the peddler bring his wares into the kitchen was made before the housewife made her selection. The black man was obviously not a housewife. It was equally obvious that Max was expected. He carried the two bottles of wine past the black man, who held the screen door open for him. In the kitchen Max looked around for a place to set the bottles, but the black man had crossed the room to a swing door at the other side.

"Bring them in here," he said.

He punched his way through the swing door and held it until Max came through with the bottles. What Max came through into he found as surprising as his first sight of the house. His experience with large, lavishly decorated rooms was limited or nonexistent. Max had no yardstick to go by, so unconsciously he went by what the person who had built the room had intended: an intimidating impression of wealth.

It did not occur to Max until later that without this background he might not have been impressed at first glance by the occupant of the room: a short, fat, bald man in a blue bathrobe and yellow bedroom slippers. He had shapeless red blotches scattered across his scalp and his pale, pasty face, which glistened with sweat. The fat man sat in the center of an elaborate couch, arms spread wide along the back in a manner so strained that he might have been baring his breast to a firing squad. The look on the man's face gave Max the feeling that this impression was not totally outlandish. It was a look of pain or fear, perhaps both, crossed with a furious impatience to get it, whatever it was, over with.

"You from Marawitz?"

The rasping voice did nothing to impair the strange image. It was almost as though the man were taunting Max with his slowness in pulling the trigger.

"Yes," Max said.

"Okay, Ellis, beat it."

"Yes, Mr. Boyle," the black man said.

He stepped back into the kitchen. The swing door eased shut.

"Marawitz says you know how to drive a truck," Mr. Boyle said.

Wondering how Mr. Marawitz knew that, Max said, "Yes."

"You married?" Mr. Boyle said.

"Yes," Max said.

"If you stay away overnight," Mr. Boyle said, "your wife make any trouble?"

"No."

"You sure?" Mr. Boyle said.

"Yes," Max said, then realized he wasn't.

Mr. Boyle seemed to pick up the uncertainty that had followed the firm statement.

"Think it over," he said. "It's important. Unless you can stay away overnight without your wife making trouble, you're no good to me."

In this fancy neighborhood's most beautiful house, in this overwhelming room that so obviously had been brought into existence by limitless funds, as he faced this man who even more obviously owned both, a sudden feeling came thrusting up sharply through whatever uncertainty Max may have had about Ida's reaction to his staying away from home overnight. The feeling was a warning. It told Max to stop hesitating. It indicated clearly that being good to Mr. Boyle, whatever that meant, would bring Max closer to the consumption of lox-and-cream-cheese bagels without worrying about the cost than he had yet managed to come with his pushcart.

"In my house," Max said firmly, "my wife does not make trouble."

"How do you know?" Mr. Boyle said.

Max did not have to claw around in his mind for the right answer. It was ready and waiting. Max used it.

"She likes money," he said.

"How about you?" Mr. Boyle said.

"I like more than I'm making now."

Mr. Boyle's eyes, which were shot with smaller versions of the red splotches that decorated his face, narrowed abruptly. Max sensed that what he had said had carried the exploratory interrogation to a point at which Mr. Boyle felt it was now worth making an effort to bring his visitor into sharper focus for a serious examination.

"Be here at three o'clock this afternoon," he said "Tell your wife you'll be home by about eight or nine tomorrow morning."

"She'll ask me something," Max said.

"What's that?" Mr. Boyle said.

"She'll ask how much money I'll be bringing home with me."

"How much did you make with the pushcart last week?" Mr. Boyle said.

"Thirteen dollars," Max said.

This was a lie. Last week he had brought home to Minnehaha Avenue eleven dollars and thirty-two cents of "the soft." Mr. Boyle seemed to know the answer was a lie. He smiled, not unpleasantly.

"Okay, let's say you did," he said. "Tell your wife when you come home tomorrow morning you'll put twenty bucks on the kitchen table."

"When I come here at three o'clock should I bring anything special?" Mav said.

"Bring a sweater," Mr. Boyle said. "Where you're going it gets cold at night."

22

When he returned to Southeast Eighth Street at three o'clock, Max was carrying the sweater Ida had only the week before finished knitting for him.

This time, after he pressed the button under the word RING on the service-entrance door, there was no delay. The black man named Ellis was on his way down the cement walk from the kitchen almost before the clang of the bell died away. Unlocking the door in the metal fence, Ellis said, "Mr. Boyle is in the garage."

So were a long, sleek Buick touring car; a neat little Model T coupé; a battered Mack truck; and a tough-looking man of about forty who was introduced to Max by Mr. Boyle as Gabe Hanratty.

"Gabe is my foreman," Mr. Boyle said. "You take your orders from him."

These were delivered in a surprisingly squeaky, almost girlish voice which caused Max to examine the foreman more closely. He saw at once what at first glance had made Mr. Hanratty look so tough: a blue jaw that had not been shaved for at least several days, and a dirty gray turtleneck pullover that conceivably had never been washed since it was shipped from the factory where it had been made.

"You ride up here with me," Gabe Hanratty said.

He slapped the cab of the Mack truck and walked around the front to climb up behind the steering wheel. Max climbed up onto the front seat beside him and pulled the cab door shut. Hanratty started the motor and leaned out his window.

"See you tomorrow, boss."

Mr. Boyle may have replied, but Hanratty was easing the truck into first. Any words Mr. Boyle may have uttered were drowned out. Max thought as they pulled out of the garage that he caught a glimpse of Mr. Boyle's hand waving farewell, so Max waved back. Gabe Hanratty kept both hands on the steering wheel. Max, who had never driven a Mack truck, kept both eyes on what Hanratty was doing. It soon became clear that there was only one real difference between the lorries Max had known at Fürstenfeld and this truck in which he was being bounced out of Minneapolis into open country: weight.

"Mr. Boyle says he didn't tell you nothing," Gabe Hanratty said after a while.

"No," Max said.

"There's not much to tell," Hanratty said. "We're going north to make a pickup. It's a nine-hour drive, sometimes a little longer, sometimes shorter. Means we get there about midnight. When we do, we drop this truck. We shift to a couple of others that are waiting for us, already loaded, and we start right back. Going up it's not too bad, because we take turns driving. The rough part is coming back, because you're alone—me in one truck, you in the other. It's not all that bad, though, if you get some rest on the way up. You ever drive one of these babies?"

"No," Max said, "but it doesn't look too different from the trucks I've handled."

"It's not," Gabe Hanratty said. "Want to take a shot at it?"

"Sure," Max said.

Hanratty pulled over to the side of the road and stopped the truck. He and Max changed places. Starting the motor, Max could feel the older man watching him, but he sensed no suspicion or hostility in Hanratty's scrutiny. The foreman seemed genuinely interested in how Max would handle a piece of equipment that was new to him. In spite of a certain amount of nervousness he wasn't sure he managed to conceal, Max thought he handled it well. So, apparently, did Hanratty.

"Easy, isn't it?" he said.

There was no mistaking the friendly tone in the squeaky, girlish voice.

"Like you said," Max said, "it's not much different from the others. Heavier, but that's about all."

"This road we're on," Hanratty said, "it heads straight for the Canadian border like a rifle bullet, so you can't go wrong. Just stay on it, and when you get tired—say, in a couple of hours—give me a shove. I'm going to try for some shut-eye."

He curled up against the far side of the cab. Almost immediately he was snoring gently. The sound was not unpleasant. It gave Max the feeling that he was alone. He liked that. A great deal had happened since he had retrieved his pushcart that morning in the backyard at Minnehaha Avenue. He had not had the time to think it all through. After a few moments of trying, Max found to his surprise that the only thing he seemed to be able to think about was the twenty dollars Mr. Boyle had said Max would be carrying home to Ida in the morning. The next surprise was the poke in the ribs he got from Gabe Hanratty.

"Why didn't you wake me up?" the foreman said.

"I didn't feel tired," Max said.

Hanratty dug under the sweater and pulled out a large silver-colored watch. When the foreman struck a match and held the flame to the face of the watch, Max realized that aside from putting on the headlights some time ago, he had been unaware that day had given way to night.

"Holy hat," Hanratty said. "You know how long you been driving?"

With a grin Max said, "As long as you've been asleep."

Grinning back, Hanratty said, "You know how much that comes to in hours?"

"I don't own a watch," Max said.

"Nine," the foreman said. "We're almost there. Pull over and we'll change. This part gets a little tricky. When we cut off the main road, I mean."

Max pulled the truck to the side of the road. He and the foreman changed places. When he had the truck under way, Gabe Hanratty said, "Sitting there for nine hours, what were you thinking about?"

"Money," Max said.

The foreman's laugh was a surprise. Ida was not a giggler, but when Max tickled her in the right places she came through. It was odd to hear the same sound coming out of the blue-jawed foreman.

"When I was your age," Hanratty said, "and I had nine hours to think, it wasn't money I did my thinking about. Okay, now watch."

He swung the truck off the main road.

"You don't have to worry about remembering any of this," he said. "We'll be pulling out together, and you'll be right behind me all the way, so there's no chance you can get lost, but you might as well know how you got in, just in case. First we take this sharp right by that white farmhouse up there, see?"

Max saw, and he made it a point to remember. He made it another point to remember all the rest of it, too. Max didn't know where he was going, but he did know what it felt like to think for nine hours about the twenty dollars he was going to lay down on the kitchen table for Ida in the morning. He wanted to hold on to everything that was part of it.

When Gabe Hanratty pulled the truck out of a long tunnel of narrow dirt road covered with the overhang from close-packed maples, Max stared with a sense of excitement at the large cleared space into which they had emerged. He had not felt this way since Saul Sumeg had handed him his new papers at the foot of the hill outside South St. Stephen and Max had realized he was standing on American soil.

The moon was high but screened by the tall trees. Enough light came filtering through the thick foliage to show Max that the cleared space was well organized. From the opening in the overhang through which Gabe Hanratty had driven the Mack truck, the narrow dirt road cut straight across to what looked like a low, very wide shed at the far end. Smaller sheds to left and right, partially hidden by the trees, showed faintly lighted windows. On both sides of the road, neatly parked in rows, were what to Max's swiftly moving glance added up to about twenty or thirty trucks.

They all looked somewhat like the Mack in which he was riding beside Gabe Hanratty: big, untidy, powerful, and unmarked by any identification except the scars of much rough service. There was no time for second glances, because Hanratty was jolting the Mack across toward the big shed at a good clip, but Max did notice that the trucks were not all the same. Some were larger than others. A few were completely enclosed rectangles like freight-train boxcars. Most were platforms supporting heavy uprights covered with tightly laced weathered tarpaulins. Max was reminded of the far end of the Fürstenfeld barracks area where the lorries were parked, except for one thing. Aside from the dimly lighted shed windows, there were no signs of life in this area. Hanratty pulled up the truck in front of the big shed.

"I'm checking in here," he said. "You go over there to the left, the one with the two windows. There's a toilet, and someone on duty to see you get something to eat. I'll grab a bite and go to the can in here. Don't take too long, and then meet me out front here. By the time you've finished in there, we'll be ready to roll."

The one with the two windows, when Max entered, was a kitchen with several tables covered with blue-and-white-checked oilcloth. A fat old woman in work pants and a baggy black sweater was stirring something in a pot on the stove.

"Hello," she said with a smile. "The toilet is over there.

If you tell me before you go in what you want to eat, I'll have it on the table for you when you come out."

"You got anything *kosher?*" Max said.

"Eggs and cheese and bread and butter and like that," the old woman said. "But I don't have the extra dishes to make it in. The Jewish men sometimes they don't mind that, so long as what I give them it's *kosher* when it goes in the pot."

Max didn't mind either. He had stopped minding soon after he left his mother's farm in Vetzprem. If he hadn't, he would have starved at Fürstenfeld, and would have had nothing in his stomach to heave up during the crossing in the *Friesland* if it had turned out that he was, like Ida, a bad sailor. Whenever he was uncertain about the people he was dealing with, however, Max had found that asking for *kosher* food brought forth useful information that it would have been awkward, maybe even dangerous, to ask for directly. Now he knew, for example, that he was not the only Jew who had ever shown up at this aggressively un-Jewish-looking place on the Canadian border.

"Fried eggs will be fine, thanks, no matter what you fry them in," Max said.

The toilet was built to handle mass traffic. Soon after Max had locked himself in the stall in the far corner, he discovered that the old woman at the stove outside was not the only sign of life on the place. He heard the door open and shut, and from the talk they brought in with them, it was clear that two men had entered. They did not stop talking while they used the facilities. Max was finished before they were, but he remained seated, listening carefully. After they left, he moved as fast as he could, but when he came out into the kitchen area, the old woman at the stove was the only person in the place.

"Just in time," she said.

She came across to the nearest table with a platter of fried eggs and a plate piled high with bread and a fat slab of butter. "Coffee?" she said.

"You have milk?" Max said.

"Sure, if you want," the old woman said. "Most of the men like coffee on account of it keeps them awake when they're driving."

"I'd rather have milk, please," Max said.

He had two glasses to help wash down the eggs faster, but he wasn't fast enough. When he came out of the shed, two loaded trucks were standing in the place where Gabe Hanratty had parked the empty Mack. Max hurried across. Hanratty was at the wheel of the front truck. He leaned out of the cab.

"Step on it," he said. "Grab that other wheel and follow me."

"Listen," Max said.

"Not now," Hanratty said. "We gotta roll."

He gunned his motor and put the truck into gear. Max hesitated, but Hanratty's truck had started to move. Max ran down to the second truck. It was one of the big boxcar jobs. Max climbed in and hit the gas. As soon as the truck started to move, he felt the drag. He was driving more weight than he had ever carried at Fürstenfeld. So, quite clearly, was Gabe Hanratty. The foreman's truck was an open job, like the Mack in which they had come up from Minneapolis. The tarpaulins laced down tight over the uprights indicated clearly that like Max, Hanratty was carrying a full load of solid dead weight. Max wondered uneasily if the foreman should be carrying it so fast.

Trying to keep up with the man in front, Max did not realize until he sent his truck into the opening in the over-hang through which he and Hanratty had entered the clearing half an hour ago that he was moving too fast for the weight he was carrying. So, it seemed to Max, was Hanratty. The truck in front was swaying badly. Feeling the sway behind him, Max considered a fast decision and made it. He was not sure enough of his vehicle to keep it moving at this speed. He tapped the brake gently. The sway began to settle down.

By the time he was riding smoothly, the possibility Max

had weighed in making his decision became fact: up front, Gabe Hanratty's red taillight had vanished. Fortunately, Max remembered clearly what he had earlier made it a point to memorize: every turn Hanratty had followed from the point where he took the Mack truck off the main highway into the twisting route that had led them to the pickup depot in the clearing in the woods. Max was sure he could make it back to the main road without any trouble. He was equally sure that when he got there he would find Gabe Hanratty waiting for him.

Max was wrong on both counts. When he came out of the narrow dirt road onto the main highway, not only was the big broad paved road deserted, but more upsetting was the obvious fact that Max had not emerged at the place where he and Gabe Hanratty had entered. For a while Max sat quietly behind the wheel, not knowing what to do and not sure of what was going on in his mind. Then, slowly, two things came clear: his teeth were chattering with cold, and his heart was racing with fear.

"Okay," Max said aloud, trying to sound the way he would have sounded if he were in the kitchen on Minnehaha Avenue, toweling his hair after a day on the street with the pushcart while Ida cleared up the soup at the sink and explaining to her something that had happened during the day's work.

"Okay," Max said again, and listened for the sound of his own voice. Not quite. He tried a third time: "Okay."

Better. He could tell because the feeling of cold was now stronger than the feeling of fear. Knowing what to do about one of his problems broke the panic of immobility. Max pulled on the sweater Ida had finished knitting for him the week before. Like everything she did, she had done this well. The sweater was a dandy. Max could feel the chill begin to ease away at once. Not surprising him at all was the immediate feeling that the fear was easing away with it. What he was left with was a problem. There was only one thing to do with a problem. Handle it.

"Okay," Max said again, and now it was. He could not turn back. He could not wait here in the moonlight. Not after what he had heard in the toilet before he wolfed his fried eggs. Only one choice was available to him. He had to move forward. Forward meant Mr. Boyle in Minneapolis. The only remaining uncertainty, therefore, was which direction led to Minneapolis.

The skills acquired at Fürstenfeld slid the answer into place. Max put his forefinger into his mouth, then stuck it out the cab window into the cold wind. When he pulled his finger back into the truck, one side was still damp, the other chilled dry. Max put the truck into gear and turned it into the highway with the cold Canadian north wind at his back.

Nine hours later, at eighty-thirty in the morning, he rolled the truck into Mr. Boyle's garage on Southeast Eighth Street. By the time Max climbed down out of the cab, Ellis was waiting for him.

"Mr. Boyle wants to see you in the house," the black man said.

Max followed him across to the house, through the kitchen, and into the living room. As he came in, Max was aware of a slight faltering in the flow of movement that was carrying him forward. It was as though, on his way through the swing door, he had stumbled. Max looked around quickly, trying to figure out what was wrong. The room had lost none of its magnificence. Yet something was different. It was not Mr. Boyle. He looked exactly as he had looked the day before. Same blue bathrobe. Same yellow slippers. Same red face splotches. Same arms outflung to firing-squad position in the center of the couch. Same rasping, unpleasant voice.

"Where's Gabe Hanratty?"

That did it. The voice. Max knew what was wrong. The room had lost none of its magnificence. What it had lost was its unattainability. Max could suddenly see himself and Ida living in that room.

"I don't know," he said. "We got separated. He didn't tell

163

me what to do in case we did, so I figured the best thing I could do was get down here with my load as quick as I could."

He spoke without arrogance, but Max was aware of a sense of confidence. It had been a tense nine hours. Now that they were over, however, the tension was gone. Max knew he had done the right thing. There was something about that heavily loaded truck out there in the garage that gave Max the feeling of standing on a platform. He had been sent to bring that truck to this place. He had brought it. There was no arguing with that hard fact. Mr. Boyle didn't.

"Here," he said.

Mr. Boyle was holding something out. Max leaned down to look. A twenty-dollar bill. He had seen many of them. He had never held one in his hand. Max took it gingerly.

"Thanks," he said.

It did not occur to him that there was anything more to be said. Mr. Boyle seemed to feel the same way. So Max turned and pushed his way through the swing door into the kitchen and he walked across the kitchen to the screen door and through the screen door to the cement walk. He went down the cement walk to the service entrance, and out the service entrance and around Southeast Eighth Street, and across the city of Minneapolis to Minnehaha Avenue. On the fifth floor Ida was at the kitchen table, putting corks into the bottles of new wine.

Max walked across and put the twenty-dollar bill on the table in front of her. She looked down at the piece of paper, and then up at Max, and for the first time since they had faced each other at the barn door in Klein Berezna she did something that took him by surprise. Ida burst into tears.

In a small panic of astonishment he stared at her for several silent moments. Then, since he could think of nothing to say, Max came around the kitchen table, and he picked her up, and he carried her to the bed at the other side of the room.

23

Max came awake as though he had been hit. A couple of moments later he realized where he was. Then he heard the noise again. He fought to isolate it from the many noises darting through his sleep-fogged brain. He grasped and held on to a hard, fast banging on the door. Beside him Ida moved restlessly.

"Lie still," Max whispered.

He slipped out of bed and pulled the blanket up over her head. He crossed quickly to the door, then hesitated. The few swift physical movements had helped pull him out of the fog. The noise took on character. It was loud, but it was not being made by metal or wood. What was banging on the door was a fist. Max banged back. The noise stopped. He put his lips to the keyhole and hissed, "Who is it?"

A blast of wheezing cough preceded the single syllable: "Me."

The familiar sound dulled the edge of Max's panic. He slid back the bolt and twisted the knob. He pulled the door open until the chain caught. Through the narrow space he had no trouble making out Mr. Marawitz in the hall. The proprietor of the pushcart garage was standing directly under the gooseneck gas jet.

"What do you want?" Max said.

"Me, nothing," Mr. Marawitz said. "Mr. Boyle wants you."

Max had forgotten about Mr. Boyle. The man with the red-splotched face came back into Max's mind with a rush. He brought with him more than Max was at the moment capable of handling. He was still dazed with sleep.

"What does he want?" Max whispered.

"You," Mr. Marawitz said.

Max came awake completely. When he was asleep, with his arms around Ida, what had happened was in the past, neatly tucked away. Awake, Max was back in the middle of it: all the things he had been too exhausted to think about during the walk across from Southeast Eighth Street to Minnehaha Avenue. On that walk only one thing had mattered. Getting to the safety of Ida before he collapsed. Now that he'd had some rest, Max sensed rather than saw clearly a lot of other things that mattered.

"All right," he said.

Max pushed the door shut, unhooked the chain, and came out into the hall.

"Better put some clothes on," Mr. Marawitz said.

Max looked down at himself. He could feel his face grow hot. It was as though the proprietor of the pushcart garage had caught not Max naked, but Ida. He fought back an impulse to smash his fist into Mr. Marawitz' face.

"Wait for me," Max said.

He stepped back into the kitchen, clicked the door shut, rehooked the chain, and crossed to the bed.

"What's happening?" Ida whispered.

Max dropped to his knees beside the bed and pulled back the blanket. Seeing her face clearly, he realized he was seeing it by moonlight. He turned to look quickly at the alarm clock on the shelf over the sink. Ten-thirty. They had been asleep for almost twelve hours. Anyway, he had been.

"Mr. Boyle wants to see me," Max said.

"Now?" Ida said.

"Marawitz is waiting out in the hall."

She stirred in the bed. "I'll make you a cup of coffee."

166

He pushed her back. "No."

She put her hand on his. "Trouble?"

"I better go see," Max said.

He stood up. He went to the chair on which he had thrown his clothes and pulled them on fast. When his head came punching up out of the sweater, Ida was sitting up in bed.

"Wait till I come back," Max said quietly. "Lock the door. Don't open it for anybody until I get back."

"When will that be?" Ida said.

"As soon as I can," Max said.

When he and Mr. Marawitz came out into Minnehaha Avenue, Max saw that whatever the reason Mr. Boyle wanted to see him, he would not have to walk to Southeast Eighth Street to learn about it. Standing at the curb in front of the tenement was the neat little Ford Model T Max had seen yesterday in Mr. Boyle's garage.

Mr. Marawitz volunteered no information while he drove. Max was sure he would get none out of the pushcart-garage proprietor by asking. He kept his mouth shut and spent the time coming fully awake. It seemed the best way to face Mr. Boyle.

"You go on in," Mr. Marawitz said after he rang the bell and drove the Ford through the service entrance and into Mr. Boyle's garage.

Max got out and walked across to the kitchen door. Ellis was waiting.

"You go on in," the black man said.

On this, his third entrance into the magnificent room beyond the swing door, Max had his second surprise. Again the room seemed to have changed. This time, however, Max did not have to wonder what it was. He knew the reason immediately. This time Mr. Boyle was not lying back in the middle of the couch wearing the blue bathrobe and the yellow bedroom slippers. This time Mr. Boyle was standing in the middle of the room, directly under the enormous crystal chandelier, and this time Mr. Boyle was wearing a

167

dark business suit. The red splotches on his face were the same. So was the rasping, unpleasant voice.

"This morning you told me you got separated from Gabe Hanratty on the road down," he said. "You remember where it happened?"

"Not on the road down," Max said.

"What does that mean?" Mr. Boyle said.

"You know the layout up there?" Max said. "Where we picked up the two loaded trucks?"

Mr. Boyle's unpleasant face seemed to grow more unpleasant. His lips worked quickly. Max could feel himself wincing away from what was clearly going to be an explosion of sarcastic fury. Then Mr. Boyle seemed to change his mind.

"Yes, I know the layout." He said it so quietly that his voice sounded almost pleasant. "Why do you ask?"

"You know how you drive in off the main road?" Max said. "And it's a long way in? A lot of twists and turns through the woods till you come out in the open place where we picked up the trucks?"

"I know all that," Mr. Boyle said. "What about it."

"In there," Max said. "Going the other way, of course. Driving out to the main road, I mean. That's where all of a sudden first he was in front of me, then he wasn't. I mean I was watching Mr. Hanratty's taillight, because he told me to keep up with him, but all of a sudden he disappeared."

Mr. Boyle's eyes seemed to squeeze together. For several moments he stared at Max as though he had never seen him before. While he stared, Mr. Boyle's fingers, moving very slowly, undid the middle button of his dark jacket. Then he looked down at his hands. He seemed surprised by what they had done. Hastily Mr. Boyle rebuttoned his jacket.

"Gabe didn't disappear," he said. "His truck did."

"Where is he?" Max said.

"On a slab in the morgue," Mr. Boyle said. "They found him on the road with four bullets in his head outside Chisholm."

"What's Chisholm?"

"A town about halfway up to the Canadian border," Mr. Boyle said.

"Is it near a place called Hibbing?" Max said.

"Just down the road," Mr. Boyle said. "Why?"

"I tried to tell him," Max said.

"Gabe?"

"Mr. Hanratty, yes," Max said. "I heard it in the toilet."

"What toilet?" Mr. Boyle said. "Where? What did you hear?"

Max explained about going into the toilet while the old woman out in the kitchen area fried his eggs.

"I didn't see these two men when they came in," he said. "Because I was in the last stall at the end of the line with the door locked. But I heard them talking. I wasn't exactly sure what they were talking about, but I heard them say your name, and then Mr. Hanratty's name, and then something about two loaded trucks and how one of them would be driven back to Minneapolis by a new man. I figured by that they meant me. They said the place to do it was in the woods, up there where we were, but not the bodies; those their orders were they should get rid of them near Hibbing. It sounded like a place."

"It is," Mr. Boyle said.

"I didn't understand the whole thing, but what I understood was the names," Max said. "You and Mr. Hanratty and that about a new man, me. All these things, I thought I better tell Mr. Hanratty right away, but by the time I got out, he was already sitting in the first truck and he seemed very excited. He wouldn't listen and he wouldn't wait. He told me to hurry up and follow him. That's what I did, in the other truck, until like I said I lost him."

Mr. Boyle was staring at Max, and beginning to work on the button again, when a telephone bell rang out in the kitchen. The sound seemed to upset Mr. Boyle. His fingers abandoned the button as though it had suddenly become red hot. He started toward the swing door, moving very fast. Before he reached it, Ellis came through.

"That was the hospital," the black man said. "Mrs. Boyle has gone into labor. Dr. Cullinan says he doesn't think it will be very long and he feels you should come right over."

"Okay," Mr. Boyle said.

Ellis held the door for him. Mr. Boyle hurried out into the kitchen. The black man followed. Max stood quietly in the magnificent room, watching the swing door chunk back and forth in narrowing arcs, wondering what to do. Before he could make up his mind, the swing door was punched open again. Mr. Boyle came back into the room.

"These two men you heard while you were in the toilet," he said. "Were they talking English?"

"No, Hungarian," Max said.

"What?" Mr. Boyle said.

"They were talking Hungarian," Max said.

Mr. Boyle's eyes did that thing again, as though they were being sucked into his head by some force behind his forehead.

"You from Hungary?" he said.

"No, my wife," Max said. "She taught me to speak a little, but I understand better than I speak."

Ellis poked his head through the swing door.

"You be needing Mr. Marawitz anymore tonight?" the black man said.

"Yeah," Mr. Boyle said, slowly. Then, more rapidly: "Yes, tell him to wait."

Ellis faded back into the kitchen. Mr. Boyle turned to Max.

"My wife is in the hospital having a baby," he said. "I have to get over there, and I don't know how long I'll be, but when I get back I'd like to talk to your wife."

"My wife?" Max said.

Mr. Boyle gave him a quick look.

"Relax," he said. "Not alone. I want to talk to both of you. Marawitz will run you home and then drive both of you back here. Ellis will take care of you, food or whatever, anything you want, until I get back."

He started to shove the swing door, then stopped and turned back.

"I forgot your name," Mr. Boyle said.

"Lessing," Max said.

"No," Mr. Boyle said. "What does your wife call you?"

"Max."

Mr. Boyle touched Max's elbow with one hand and with the other started pushing his way through the swing door.

"This could be a very good thing for you, Max," he said. "For you and your wife."

Then Mr. Boyle did an astonishing thing. He smiled. It transformed his face. What made it astonishing was that Max suddenly realized that what had up to this moment been an undefined creature capable of enriching him, and therefore to be treated with respectful care, had emerged as a man it was possible to like.

"I'd appreciate it if when I come back from the hospital you'll both be here," he said. There was a slight pause, and Mr. Boyle added: "Please."

24

Max and Ida were waiting in the magnificent room on Southeast Eighth Street when Mr. Boyle returned to it from the hospital.

"It's a girl," he said with a happy smile as he came in through the swing door. "Is this Mrs. Lessing?"

"Yes," Max said, getting up quickly from the chair facing the couch, but he was not quick enough. Mr. Boyle had gone directly to the couch where Ida was sitting. He bent down and took her hand.

"I'm Harry Boyle," he said. "Your husband told me you speak Hungarian, but he didn't tell me you were beautiful."

Smiling up at the man who so far as Max was concerned was not the same disagreeable person from whom he had taken a twenty-dollar bill that morning, Ida said, "My husband is a modest man. Mrs. Boyle is all right, I hope?"

"Fine, yes," Mr. Boyle said. "Dr. Cullinan said she went through the whole thing like a trooper. She's asleep now, resting."

"The baby?" Ida said.

"Wonderful, absolutely marvelous," Mr. Boyle said. "Healthy as a prizefighter, six pounds eight ounces, not counting what looks like the beginning of a mop of gorgeous wavy blond hair."

"You've decided on her name?" Ida said.

"Claire, after my mother," Harry Boyle said. "Haven't you had a drink? What's the matter with Ellis?" He turned toward the swing door and yelled, "Ellis!"

The black man, who had come in with Mr. Boyle and was standing only a few inches behind him, winced away from the roar.

"They didn't want anything," he said. "Said they don't drink."

"On an occasion like this everybody drinks," Mr. Boyle said. "Stop wasting time."

"Yes, sir," Ellis said.

He went out to the kitchen. Max continued to watch Ida and Mr. Boyle. He didn't listen. Max just watched. He accepted the fact that when he had first met Mr. Boyle two days ago the man's conduct might have been peculiar because he was upset about something which Max now knew was the fact that Mr. Boyle's wife was in the hospital expecting a baby. What Max couldn't quite accept was the ease with which Ida was handling a conversation in her still awkward English that seemed completely appropriate in this rich man's room. Max found it upsetting to make the leap from the girl cleaning the fat off his soup at the sink on Minnehaha Avenue to the relaxed young lady discussing with Mr. Boyle under a crystal chandelier the choice of a name for his newborn daughter. It reminded Max of the uneasiness he had felt about what Ida had discussed two months ago when she had been alone with Rabbi Fruchter in the downstairs room of the house in Rivière du Cojot while Max had been upstairs examining the guest room with the rabbi's son.

"Is this your first child?" Ida said.

"The first one that's lived," Mr. Boyle said. "My wife had three miscarriages. The last one, she almost died, and Dr. Cullinan said that was it. We couldn't risk another try, he said. But we're getting on, my wife and I—not exactly old, but not kids anymore like you and your husband. Neither one of us, though, we just didn't have the right feeling about

173

adopting a baby, so we took a chance and, well, God was good to us. I don't suppose it's any secret that tonight Harry Boyle is one very happy man. Put it there, Ellis."

The black man set the silver tray on the low table in front of the couch.

"How do you take it, Mrs. Lessing?" Mr. Boyle said.

"Thank you," Ida said, "I do not drink."

Mr. Boyle's pink eyebrows went up into the middle of his red-splotched forehead. He said, "Is that true, Joe?"

"Max," Max said. "It's true, Mr. Boyle."

"The Irishman in my blood urges me to insist that this attitude is wrong," Mr. Boyle said. "The father of a brand-new daughter, however, tells me sternly I must not corrupt someone who can't be much older. Eighteen?"

"Seventeen," Ida said. "Next month."

Max was not finding the Ida–Boyle performance an undiluted pleasure, but he had to admit grudgingly to himself that the man on the couch beside Ida looked charming as he smiled and shook his head and said, "What an age to be. I know. I was there once myself. You sure you won't change your mind, Mrs. Lessing?"

"A little wine, perhaps," Ida said.

"Wine," Mr. Boyle said.

He uttered the word thoughtfully, scowling down at the silver tray, as though someone had asked him to identify his birthplace and all at once, in the midst of the grandeur by which he was presently surrounded, the lowly name had slipped his mind. The scowl vanished.

"Ellis!" Mr. Boyle roared.

Not quite nastily, but for Max the sound brought back onto the couch the man in the blue bathrobe and the yellow bedroom slippers, baring his breast to the firing squad. Ellis came through the swing door.

"We got any wine in the house?" Mr. Boyle said.

"We got that *kosher* stuff we bought two days ago from him."

The black man jerked his head toward Max.

"From now on 'him' is Mr. Lessing," Mr. Boyle said. "Bring the stuff in."

Ellis chunked his way out through the swing door as Mr. Boyle lifted the bottle high. He said, "You really should try some of this, Mrs. Lessing. Your husband brought it all the way down from Canada yesterday."

Max leaned forward for a better look at what he had brought down from Canada. It was a fifth of Scotch whiskey in a black bottle. The yellow label was jammed with tightly crowded print through which one word stood out boldly with unmistakable clarity: KIRKBEAN.

"It's very pretty," Ida said. "I would prefer the wine, however, if you don't mind."

Mr. Boyle said, "I do mind, but you are a guest in my house, and in Harry Boyle's house even an uncharming guest gets what he or she wants, and as I may already have indicated, Mrs. Lessing, I do not think you are uncharming. How about you, Joe?"

"Max," Max said. "Straight, please."

At his *bar mitzvah* in Vetzprem, when he completed his reading from the Torah, Max had been rewarded by the *gobbe* of the synagogue with a small square of *lekach* dipped in *brohmfin*. At Fürstenfeld, where *lekach* was unavailable, Max had learned to do without not only honey cake in his tipple, but anything at all that diluted whatever alcohol was being poured.

"Sorry," Mr. Boyle said. "Max. Max. Okay, three times and I've nailed down anything." He handed the glass across the low table. "Ask me what your name is."

Taking the glass, Max said, "What is my name?"

Mr. Boyle said, "Formerly Joe, now Max. Okay?"

Max laughed and said, "Okay."

The astonishing discovery made a few hours earlier was becoming less astonishing by the minute. Mr. Boyle was emerging more and more clearly as a man it was possible to like. Ellis came chunking in with one of the two bottles Max had delivered to Southeast Eighth Street by pushcart two days ago. Mr. Boyle pulled the cork and poured a glass for Ida.

"I'd like to propose a couple of toasts," he said. "This has been a very unusual day for me. Within the space of a few hours I have been handed the greatest blessing a man can know, and also dealt the worst blow a man can suffer. I would like you to join me in drinking first to the blow."

Mr. Boyle raised his glass.

"To the memory of one of the finest human beings I have ever been privileged to know," Mr. Boyle said. "A wonderful friend and a great business associate, Gabe Hanratty."

Downing a sip of Kirkbean, Max wondered about the phrase "business associate." It seemed to mean more than the word "foreman" by which Mr. Boyle had introduced Mr. Hanratty to Max.

"Max told me what happened," Ida said. "I am very sorry."

Mr. Boyle said, "It's because of what happened to Gabe that I asked your husband to bring you here."

Ida said, "I do not understand."

"Your husband tells me you are Hungarian," Mr. Boyle said. "I've been having trouble with a Hungarian for quite a while now. I haven't done anything about the problem because I didn't know how to tackle it. Today, from talking with Max here, I think I've got a handle on it."

"What is a handle?" Ida said.

"A grip on an idea," Mr. Boyle said. "You and Max are part of that idea."

"In what way?" Ida said.

"If I understood Hungarian," Mr. Boyle said, "I think Gabe Hanratty would be alive right now."

Ida said, "You want me to teach you Hungarian?"

"I'm too old to learn anything more complicated than how to bring a new daughter home from the hospital," Mr. Boyle said. "Hungarian is beyond my failing powers. Max seems to have learned enough of it from you to understand what a couple of men were saying when they thought nobody was listening. If Gabe had listened to Max, those men wouldn't

176

have found him where they expected to find him and put four bullets in his head. With Gabe dead, I need a new foreman. I have a feeling that if Max was my new foreman, and you kept working on his Hungarian, my business wouldn't suffer too much from Gabe's death, and I'd be on my way to solving my problem with this Hungarian who's been causing me trouble."

Ida said, "Is it rude to ask who is this Hungarian?"

"The brother of your landlord," Mr. Boyle said.

A puzzled look brushed Ida's face as she turned to Max and said, "Our landlord?"

Max had been following the conversation the way months ago in Klein Berezna he had followed Ida's conversation with the forger: letting her lead the way, waiting for his cue. She had just given it to him. Leaning forward into the conversation, Max said to Mr. Boyle, "You mean that Italian man, the barber downstairs in our building?"

"No," Mr. Boyle said. "I understand all he does is collect the rent. I mean this man Fruchter."

"Fruchter?" Max said.

He tapped the name smoothly along to Ida. With a neat assist, she flicked it into Mr. Boyle's court: "You mean our landlord is a man named Fruchter?"

"He was," Mr. Boyle said. "A couple of days ago he drowned in a bathtub on the top floor of your building."

"Oh, him," Max said. "Yes, that was the man Mr. Marawitz was talking about when I was in his shop."

"I thought you knew him," Mr. Boyle said. "Marawitz told me Fruchter brought you into his place a few months ago to buy a pushcart."

Ida fielded it deftly with "Now I remember, yes. When we first moved into the building and we paid the first rent to this Italian man downstairs, he asked what kind of work my husband did. I told him nothing yet, we just arrived in the city, he was looking for something, and this barber said I'll introduce him to Mr. Fruchter, he knows a lot about those things."

Max moved in nicely with "He sent for me to come down the next day. Mr. Fruchter was in the barbershop getting his hair cut. After he finished, he took me over to Mr. Marawitz, and I bought the pushcart."

"Well, this Fruchter down here in Minneapolis has a brother up in Winnipeg," Mr. Boyle said. "He's a Hungarian, and the men who work for him are Hungarian, and so far as my business is concerned the wrong member of the family got drowned in that bathtub on the top floor of your building. To take care of the one who is still walking around causing me trouble, I would like to hire your husband, Max, here as my new foreman, and you as my vice-president in charge of Hungarian problems. What do you say?"

Max grasped without difficulty that Mr. Boyle did not expect Max to be the one to say it. Ida had no trouble grasping the same point. She lifted her glass of wine and smiled at the man who had just made the Lessing family a business proposition.

"I say here is health and long life to Miss Claire Boyle, the new addition to your family," Ida said.

She said it in Hungarian.

25

The next day, for the first time since they had arrived on American soil, both the Lessings slept late. At eleven o'clock, when the peddlers on River Street were gathering in Krasner's Bakery for their late-morning bagels and coffee, Max shoved his pushcart into Mr. Marawitz's garage.

"I have something I think you can use," Max said, slapping the top of the pushcart. "A man who knows his business fixed this thing up for me a couple of days ago. It's in first-class shape. Are you interested?"

"How much do you want for it?" Mr. Marawitz said.

"Nothing," Max said. "My new boss said I should give it to you as a present."

"A finer boss you won't find in this whole city," Mr. Marawitz said. "I'm glad when I sent you to him I didn't make a mistake."

"So is my wife," Max said. "She said I should not only thank you, which I'm doing right now, but I should also ask you if there is something maybe I owe you for introducing me to Mr. Boyle."

"What you owe me is to satisfy Mr. Boyle he didn't make a mistake by hiring you," the proprietor of the pushcart garage said. "If you satisfy Mr. Boyle, then Hersh Marawitz has satisfied Mr. Boyle, and anybody who satisfies Mr. Boyle, such a person will always eat bagels with lox and cream cheese at eleven o'clock in the morning. Let's go over to Krasner's right now, and I'll buy you one for a celebration."

"Thanks, but not today," Max said. "Today I have to meet Mr. Boyle in his warehouse at twelve o'clock. Is that clock up there right?"

Mr. Marawitz opened his mouth to reply but was caught by a coughing fit. When he came out of it, the proprietor of the pushcart garage said, "Would I keep a clock on my wall that isn't right? Don't be late. It's the one thing Mr. Boyle hates. And while the clock is right, a clock you can't carry in your pocket. Don't you own a watch?"

"Not yet," Max said.

Mr. Marawitz stepped behind a counter piled with bicycle tires and tools. He opened a drawer, shoved his hand around among the contents, and came up with a large silver-colored watch. It looked like the timepiece Gabe Hanratty had pulled from under his sweater three days ago while he and Max had been driving the Mack truck up to the Canadian border. Mr. Marawitz wound the watch, set it by the clock on the wall, and handed it to Max.

"A first-class item," the proprietor of the pushcart garage said. "In this country a finer piece of merchandise nobody makes. It said in the papers last year President Wilson along with the Fourteen Points he was also taking an Ingersoll in his pocket to the Peace Conference there in Paris."

"How much?" Max said.

"One dollar," Mr. Marawitz said.

"Could you wait for the money until my first payday?" Max said.

"For that dollar nobody has to wait," Mr. Marawitz said. "This is a present. Tell your wife it's from one friend of Mr. Boyle to another. Now you better shake a leg. It's a fifteen-minute walk from here to Wayzata Boulevard."

According to his new watch, Max made it in twelve. He would not have known he had made it at all if Mr. Boyle had not warned Max to look sharp when he turned into

Wayzata Boulevard for the numbers 817 on a dark brown door in the middle of the block. He pressed a black button under the brass doorknob. There was a buzz inside the lock and the door jumped free. Max pulled it wide, stepped in, and found himself facing a short, amply proportioned woman with complicated white hair. She could have been his own mother back in Vetzprem, except that his mother did not own a black bombazine dress with white pearl buttons, and his mother did not wear narrow half-moon eyeglasses that sat low on her nose. Nor, when she smiled, did Max's mother reveal the number of gold teeth this woman was now flashing at him.

"I'm Mrs. Gutera," she said. "Mr. Boyle called this morning and told me you were coming."

She stepped around Max to reach the door, which she attacked with both hands, shoving hard until the lock clicked. Watching this performance, Max saw that the inside of the door was more informative than the side that faced the passerby out in the street. High up, in large letters, appeared the words INNISFAIL TRADING CO., INC. Underneath, in larger letters, a block of type read:

IMPORTANT!
AFTER ENTERING ALWAYS CLOSE THIS
DOOR BY PUSHING HARD UNTIL YOU
HEAR THE LOCK CLICK

"Anybody comes here the first time," Mrs. Gutera said, "I always come up front here from the office and let them in personally, to sort of remind them this is how Mr. Boyle wants it." With a pleasant laugh she added, "Nobody has to be reminded twice. This way, please."

Max followed her out across a large garage space with a cement floor. Among the parked trucks Max noticed at once the big one he had driven down from the Canadian border two days ago. Beyond the trucks Mrs. Gutera led the way through a wooden arch into a partitioned-off area that was her office.

A heavyset man with a cigarette pasted to his lower lip was standing behind a golden oak rolltop desk, resting his weight on one elbow as he flipped the pages of a tabloid newspaper. He couldn't seem to find anything interesting enough to hold his attention. He wore a blue work shirt and a pair of grease-stained overalls. The overalls sagged with the weight of several tools that hung through loops on both his hips. The man looked up across the newspaper when Max and Mrs. Gutera came in. He did it without removing the cigarette from his lip, so that he had to squint through smoke at the newcomers. The way he did it made Max feel the man could have been sighting a rifle pointed at the newcomer.

"Bert, this is Max Lessing, the man Mr. Boyle told me about on the phone," Mrs. Gutera said. "Mr. Lessing, this is Bert Bartholdi, our chief mechanic."

Mr. Bartholdi came out from behind the desk, removing the cigarette from his lip as he moved. The disappearance of the smoke that had been irritating his eye caused the squint to vanish as well. With it went the sinister look of a man trying to get a target into his gunsights. Mr. Bartholdi emerged from the smoke screen as a reasonably pleasant-looking middle-aged man of the kind who occasionally showed up for coffee in Krasner's.

"You call me Bert," he said, pushing out his hand. "I'll call you Max. Okay?"

"Okay," Max said, taking Bartholdi's hand. It was like taking several pounds of cement into which before it hardened small bits of broken glass had been set. The next thing Max said was "Ouch!"

Bartholdi laughed, revealing a few tobacco-stained teeth separated in a clearly unplanned way by spaces of varying width. As a result his mouth, when open, resembled a wedge of Roquefort cheese.

"Mrs. Gutera says you speak languages like a college professor," he said. "Pick a good one and say a few words."

"If you do that to my hand again," Max said in Yiddish

through a friendly grin, "I will tear your head off your neck and shove it up your ass."

"What does that mean?" Bert Bartholdi said.

" 'Glad to meet you' in Yiddish," Max said.

"Same here in English," the mechanic said. "It's the only language I know."

"You know it better than I do," Max said in English. "But I'm learning. Now what I want to learn is what Mr. Boyle told me you're the only one who can teach me, which is how to be the foreman of this place."

He said it without changing the grin, only the tone of his voice. Mr. Bartholdi's face indicated that he had recorded the change. He disposed of what was left of his laughter by pasting the cigarette back on his lower lip and squinting through the new smoke screen.

"Let's go," he said, starting for the door.

"Bring him back when you're finished," Mrs. Gutera said. "Mr. Boyle said I should show him how we keep the books."

Out in the garage area Mr. Bartholdi said, "Tough luck what happened to Gabe Hanratty."

"The police arrest anybody yet?" Max said.

"In this state nobody ever heard that word," the mechanic said. "Especially cops. Down here, this part, we load and unload. Upstairs, the other floors, it's all storage. The trucks come in over here, these doors."

He kicked a metal bar out of a hasp sunk in the cement floor, dipped down to grasp an iron ring, and pulled hard. What seemed to Max an entire wall of the building started to go up in the air on oiled pulleys. Mr. Bartholdi stopped the moving door at shoulder height and pointed out across a paved turnaround back of the building.

"The trucks come in through Twelfth Street, over there," he said. "All hours of the day and night they come in, so around the clock we're never shut down, because the stuff has to be unloaded with no time wasted, and the trucks moved out for new pickups. We don't make our money by piling the stuff up here and looking at how pretty it is. We make our money by moving the stuff out to customers. That means at least two shifts a day, sometimes three, depends on the traffic. The traffic depends on Mr. Boyle, and Mr. Boyle depends on his foreman, which used to be Gabe Hanratty and is now you."

Mr. Bartholdi hauled down hard on the ring. The wall came back into place smoothly on the oiled pulleys. Mr. Bartholdi bent over, slid the metal bar back into the hasp, and with a hard backward kick of his heavy shoe locked it into place. Straightening up, he said, "Anything else you want to know?"

"Yes," Max said. "What's eating you?"

Mr. Bartholdi spat the end of his cigarette free from its damp anchorage on his lower lip and with his heavy shoe pounded it into a stain on the cement floor as though he were driving a spike.

"Gabe Hanratty was a friend of mine," he said.

"I didn't know him long enough to get that far," Max said. "Twelve hours after we met he had four bullet holes in his head."

"I notice you haven't," Mr. Bartholdi said.

"Men with holes in their head are in no position to accept Mr. Boyle's offer to become his new foreman," Max said. "He told me the job is mine as long as I know how to hold on to it, so here's something you better know. If holding on to this job means getting myself a new chief mechanic, I know how to do that too."

Max turned on his heel to put a dramatic terminal point on his performance. It had taken everything he had, including his not exactly total grasp of the language he was using, to get this far. He couldn't risk having to go any further. Not until he had a chance to catch his breath and Mr. Bartholdi had a chance to think things over. Max was astonished to find he had turned on his heel into the full glare of Mrs. Gutera's gold-toothed smile.

"Excuse me for interrupting," she said. "Mr. Boyle wants you on the telephone and he says it's important."

Max didn't doubt it was important as soon as he heard Mr. Boyle's voice. The man at the other end of the phone was not the charmer of the night before. The man at the other end of the phone was the man in the blue bathrobe and the yellow bedroom slippers who had introduced Max to Gabe Hanratty.

"I want to see you right away," the unpleasant voice rasped. "Get up to the house as fast as you can."

The line went dead before Max had a chance to put together any kind of comment. This was just as well. Mrs. Gutera was watching him nervously, and as Max hung up the receiver Bert Bartholdi was coming into the office from the garage area. Mrs. Gutera's gold teeth were under cover, and the mechanic was squinting through the smoke from a freshly lighted cigarette.

"I have to get to a meeting in Mr. Boyle's house," Max said. "Until I get back, carry on."

Not until he was out on the street did he realize the source of his parting shot. It had been one of Oberfeldwebel Sauerlich's favorite exit lines. At the service entrance to Southeast Eighth Street, Max was greeted by what seemed to be one of Ellis' favorite entrance lines: "Go right in."

Max did, and found himself alone under the crystal chandelier. He returned to the swing door and poked his way back into the kitchen.

"Where's Mr. Boyle?" he said.

"On his way home from the hospital," the black man said. "Want something while you're waiting?"

"Is that coffee?" Max said.

"Just made it fresh," Ellis said. "Cream and sugar?"

"Thanks," Max said. He started to move back through the swing door, then stopped. "There's trouble?" he said.

The black man with the woolly white skullcap looked up from the cup and saucer. He gave Max a short glance, then turned back to pouring the coffee.

"He call you at the warehouse?"

"Yes," Max said.

"How'd he sound?" the black man said.

"Not like last night."

"Then there's trouble," Ellis said.

He came toward Max with a cup of coffee. Taking it, Max said, "What kind of trouble?"

"I never know," the black man said. "I just watch for it. When it comes, I handle it. You want to be around here any length of time, Mr. Lessing, you learn how to do the same. Now you go on in there and enjoy your coffee."

Max went on in there, but he did not enjoy his coffee. His mind was still back on Wayzata Boulevard, working on the Bert Bartholdi problem, double-checking on how he had handled it, trying to figure out how to take it from there and wrap it up without any loose ends. A car door slammed out in the garage. Max was on his feet when Mr. Boyle came through the swing door.

"Hello, Max," he said. "Nice of you to get over here so fast."

Max tried not to show his surprise. Gone was the voice that had rasped at him on the telephone. The voice he had just heard, however, did not belong to the night before either. The dark business suit did. The dark business suit and the red splotches on the pale face and the bald head. Everything else was new. To Max, anyway.

"Sit down," Mr. Boyle said.

He sounded as though he were instructing himself as he settled into the middle of the couch. The way he did it was also new. It reminded Max of a piece of heavy machinery being lowered slowly into a place that had been carefully prepared by technicians to receive it. Max sat down next to his cup of coffee, in the chair facing the couch. Ellis came in with the silver tray and set it on the low table. He uncorked the Kirkbean, poured one of the two glasses full to the brim, and turned to Max.

"You, Mr. Lessing?"

"No, thanks," Max said. "I'll finish my coffee."

The black man nodded and went out through the swing

door. Mr. Boyle continued to sit without movement. It was as though the entrance of Ellis and the exchange between Max and the black man had not taken place. Then Max noticed that Mr. Boyle, who seemed to be looking at him, was not doing that at all. He was looking toward Max, but he was doing it as though his glance were on a leash and, having started to send it toward Max before he realized the leash was too short, he now lacked the desire or the energy to pull it back.

Then Max noticed that Mr. Boyle's lips were moving. They were not moving at what Max would have identified as the speed of normal speech, and they were not moving with conviction. It was as though Mr. Boyle were trying to do an arithmetic problem, or pass on to someone beyond Max's sight lines a street address or a telephone number, but the same lack of will or failure of energy that prevented him from drawing back the glance that hung suspended in the air between him and Max now prevented him from either remembering the words or speaking the numbers.

With a sense of shock it occurred to Max that he could have been sitting in the room with a dead man who refused to acknowledge or had not yet learned his life was over. Max drew in his breath sharply.

The small sound seemed to jolt Mr. Boyle from his trance. His body jerked upward. A single movement, but it was apparently enough to bring him back from wherever he had been.

Mr. Boyle reached out, picked up the glass of whiskey, and took down half the contents in a long, slow pull. When he set the glass back on the table, the small click of glass on wood seemed to do for Max what his sharp intake of breath had done for Mr. Boyle. It was as though the teacher in his old classroom in Vetzprem had come up behind Max at his desk and with a sharp poke of her wooden pointer had told him to stop daydreaming and get back to work.

"Mrs. Boyle," he said. "How is she?"

"Dead," Mr. Boyle said.

What Max said next was not clear even to Max. Later, when he was putting the pieces together for Ida, it occurred to him that he might very well have said nothing. Actually all Max remembered was the struggle to assemble and release, in reply to Mr. Boyle's one-syllable statement, any kind of sensible sounds. Whether Max succeeded in releasing them did not, in retrospect, matter. What did matter was that when he did begin to hear clear, sensible words, they were being uttered by Mr. Boyle.

"They called me from the hospital a little after six this morning," he said. "She was hemorrhaging badly. Cullinan had been called already, and he was on his way. I was outside her room in twenty minutes, a half hour at most, but it was too late. Cullinan got there a few minutes after I did, and the poor bastard, you can imagine how he felt, but it wouldn't have mattered when he got there. Once it started, he said, nothing could have saved her. Any other guy would have said 'nobody,' not 'nothing,' but not Steve Cullinan. Not to me, anyway. We've known each other since we were kids. That's how he cried. Just like a kid. Blaming himself because we hadn't listened to him, because he'd let us take a chance—as though anybody could have stopped Molly once she decided she wanted to do something."

Mr. Boyle's voice stopped the way Max had seen spinning tops stop. His voice seemed to wind down, then begin to totter, and finally it keeled over slowly and lay still. Max had a desperate feeling that it was important to get it going again.

"What about the baby?" he said.

"Baby?" Mr. Boyle said.

He looked like a man who, while reading something with total absorption, had had his attention jolted from the printed page by a hard shove.

"Is she all right?" Max said. "Claire?"

"Who?" Mr. Boyle said.

"The baby," Max said. "Little Claire."

"The baby," Mr. Boyle said. Then, more quickly: "Yes,

the baby is fine. Yes, just fine. Matter of fact, come to think of it, that's why I called you. I thought—"

Again Mr. Boyle's voice wound down, tottered, and keeled over like a spent top. He picked up his glass and, with another long, slow pull, drained it. Setting the glass back slowly, Mr. Boyle missed the edge of the table by an inch or two. His body came forward with a jerk, as though he had been walking across the room and had stumbled, but he recovered and set the empty glass down properly. In the silence that followed, Max saw that Mr. Boyle's glance had gone out again on its invisible leash. It was hanging somewhere in the air between him and his visitor, and Mr. Boyle's lips were moving in that same slow, indecisive way.

"The terrible thing is," his suddenly audible voice said, "I kept saying to myself all the way to the hospital, I kept saying, Even if I only get there in time to say goodbye, then it will be all right, but I didn't get there in time, so I never had a chance to say goodbye."

The voice sank back into inaudibility, but the lips continued to move, and Max had another moment of shock. All at once he knew where Mr. Boyle's glance had come to rest in the air between them. All at once Max knew what Mr. Boyle's inaudible words were doing. They were saying the goodbye he had arrived too late to say at the hospital.

"That's why I called and asked you to come over and meet me here," Mr. Boyle said.

He said it so crisply, the voice completely matter-of-fact, that a few moments went by before Max grasped what had happened. Mr. Boyle had finished saying goodbye. He was back to the business at hand.

"If there's anything I can do?" Max said.

"I think maybe you can," Mr. Boyle said. "I'll be bringing little Claire home in a few days. I don't suppose it will matter to a tiny baby like that if what she comes home to is a hired nurse, but it will matter to me. All my family is gone, and my wife's family is mostly in Ireland. The parts that aren't, they don't like me and I don't like them. I don't want them in the same house with my daughter. In my business I have to go out of town a lot, sometimes overnight, sometimes longer. I was never very happy about leaving Molly alone here in the house, even though with Ellis around there was nothing to worry about; but a little baby, I don't know. With a little baby I feel different, if you understand what I mean."

Max didn't, but he thought he ought tŏ feel he understood so he said, "Sure."

"Which is what made me think of your wife," Mr. Boyle said.

"My wife?" Max said.

The look Mr. Boyle gave him needed no marginal reminder notes to be recognized at once as a footnote to the look Max had received the night before.

"Both of you," Mr. Boyle said. "You and Mrs. Lessing. Now that you're my foreman, we're going to be working very closely together. I think it would be better for both of us, not to mention for your wife, if you were nearer to the warehouse and to this house than you are now on Minnehaha Avenue. Besides, I know Minnehaha Avenue, so I know the kind of place you're living in, and what they're probably soaking you for it in rent. I happen to have a very nice three-room apartment out there over the garage, complete with a modern bathroom and all conveniences, which nobody's using. You and your wife could have it rent free if you and Mrs. Lessing said yes and took on the job."

"I've just been over to Wayzata Boulevard, so I know what my job is," Max said. "I don't understand, though, what my wife's job would be."

"Whatever she wants to make of it," Mr. Boyle said. "Not exactly a nurse, because I'll get a professional to do the work for her, or even two if she wants them. What I'm saying is that I don't want the baby to grow up with nothing but strangers around. If you and Mrs. Lessing were around, in the house all the time, she might have the same feeling I'd have when I go out of town, the feeling that I'm leaving my daughter with family. What do you say, Max?"

"I can't say it," Max said.

"Why not?" Mr. Boyle said.

"A thing like this," Max said, "my wife will have to do the saying."

26

What Ida said was "Rabbi Jobsky wouldn't like it."

"Why not?" Max said.

Ida laughed. "I might learn a few things he doesn't know."

The first thing Ida learned, as soon as she finished distributing their few belongings in the apartment over the garage on Southeast Eighth Street, was not unlike the discovery Archimedes made in his bathtub. Freedom from the necessity to climb down four flights of stairs to a toilet in a backyard, freedom to walk into a room in your own home and close the door against the world to perform a bodily function in privacy was a change that enlarged the human spirit as surely as it was enlarged for a short man who woke up one morning to find himself tall, or an ugly girl who by the wave of a good fairy's wand was made beautiful.

"The second thing," Ida said to Max when he came home from Wayzata Boulevard for his first meal in their new home, "is look."

Max looked at the plate from which rose an intoxicating odor that filled the sunny kitchen.

"What is it?" he said.

"I don't know," Ida said. "All I know is you don't have to boil it for three days and clean off the fat every night to be able to chew it. In fact, you don't even have to pay for it."

"Why not?" Max said around a succulent mouthful.

"Mr. Boyle pays for everything," Ida said. "Ellis told me this morning he goes out every day to do the shopping, and Mr. Boyle told him from now on to make sure before he went out to ask me what we wanted. I didn't know what to say, because I never know what we want till I go to the butcher and see what's cheap. I think Ellis must have guessed what was going through my mind, because he said Mr. Boyle also told him to tell me all our groceries were like our rent: free."

Max cut another generous piece of meat and said, "So how did he know to get this?"

"I don't know," Ida said. "I told Ellis anything he got for Mr. Boyle to eat would be all right for you and me, and this is what he brought from the butcher."

"Next time you see Ellis, ask him the name of this meat," Max said.

"Why?" Ida said.

"When you learn how to write a letter to your mother you should spell it right," Max said. "So when Rabbi Jobsky reads it for her, he'll learn it right."

Ida did not have time to think about a letter to her mother for quite a while. She spent almost a week helping Mr. Boyle hire a nurse for the baby, and after they settled on Miss Liddy, the nurse proved to have firm ideas about how a nursery should be furnished.

"She could be right," Ida said to Max the night before Mr. Boyle planned to bring his baby daughter home from the hospital. "It's just that I don't know about these things here in America, and I don't want Miss Liddy to know I don't know, so I have to say no to everything at least twice before I say yes once. The meat you're eating, Ellis told me, is called porterhouse steak. He wrote it down for me, but how I will ever write it in Hungarian in a letter to my mother I don't know."

"Put your mind to it," Max said, chewing contentedly. "You can do anything."

It was a feeling Ida shared, but she kept the sentiment to herself. She had not been married long enough to feel she could safely put all her cards on the table. It seemed wise to hold something back for a time when she might need a surprise to carry her through a sticky situation. The time arrived sooner than she had thought possible.

"Mr. Boyle was here for lunch today," she said to Max when he came home from work a few days after little Claire had been settled in the nursery in the main house.

"I know," Max said.

"How?" Ida said. She was clearly surprised.

"He told me," Max said.

Ida brought the porterhouse from the stove. She set it on the table between them and sat down facing him.

"What did he say?" Ida said, cutting the steak in half.

"What he planned to tell you," Max said.

He took the plate Ida handed him and picked up his knife and fork.

"What do you think?" Ida said.

"Of what?" Max said.

"What he told me."

"I don't know what he told you," Max said. "I wasn't here. This porterhouse is tougher than the last one."

Ida cut a piece from her half, put it into her mouth, and chewed thoughtfully.

"You're right," she said. "I'll tell Ellis. You think Mr. Boyle told me something different from what he said to you he was going to tell me?"

"No," Max said. "That would be stupid, and Mr. Boyle is not stupid."

"Then what do you think?" Ida said.

Max said, "I think he may have told you more here on Southeast Eighth Street than he told me he was going to tell you on Wayzata Boulevard."

Ida cut herself another piece of steak, a very small piece, chewed for a while, then put down her knife and fork.

"You better tell me what you think about Mr. Boyle,"
she said.

"I think he's a man about forty years old," Max said.
"For a long time he was living with a woman something
younger; according to the pictures around the house, a
good-looking lady; according to the way he acted the day
she died, a woman he was crazy about. Now, this last month
since his wife died, Mr. Boyle is living in a house with
what? A black man with white hair he calls a butler. A
tough nurse with a shape like an ash can, and buck teeth,
and a face it could be made from the leather bottom of
your yellow wicker suitcase. And a *zaftig* little blonde with
only seventeen birthdays to her credit plus all the right
things in the right places that go with girls who have only
seventeen birthdays to their credit. I don't know what it feels
like to be forty years old, but if I was in Mr. Boyle's shoes,
living with those three choices, I don't think I'd feel
much different from the way Max Lessing feels now at
eighteen."

Ida laughed and cut herself another wedge of porterhouse,
a much larger piece.

"You mean that's all there's to it?" she said.

"What do you mean by I mean that's all there's to it?"
Max said.

"You're jealous," Ida said.

It was Max's turn to laugh.

"Not yet," he said. "But I don't want to get there."

"Neither do I," Ida said. "So here's what happened. I was
in the nursery with Miss Liddy, helping her bathe Claire,
when Mr. Boyle came in. He played with the baby awhile,
then asked me to come out in the living room, he wanted
to talk to me. In the living room he got himself fixed into
the middle of the big couch, the way he always does, and I
sat down facing him, and he yelled for Ellis. Would I like
some lunch while we're talking? I said no, you and I were
having a steak for supper and I didn't want to spoil my

appetite, but he said he was hungry, so he told Ellis to bring us some sandwiches and coffee."

Max said, "Do I have to listen to what kind of sandwiches and whether you had cream and sugar with the coffee?"

"A man who is not yet jealous but he doesn't want to get there," Ida said, "I think you should hear everything."

"You mind if I go on eating?" Max said.

"All I mind is don't be a smart aleck," Ida said. "This is important."

"I'm listening," Max said.

"Mr. Boyle said since he'd never been a father before, he wasn't surprised to find that these last few weeks he's been thinking a lot about the subject. What did surprise him, Mr. Boyle said, was the kind of thoughts he was having."

"See?" Max said.

"No, I don't, and neither do you," Ida said. "Go on eating. The kind of thoughts he was having, Mr. Boyle said, were about this man who drove up with you to Canada and you came back but he didn't."

"Gabe Hanratty," Max said. "Former friend of Bert Bartholdi."

"That's the man," Ida said. "And just because you don't like this Bert Bartholdi, I don't think you should say bad things about the other one, Hanratty. If he hadn't got himself killed, Mr. Boyle wouldn't have hired you as his foreman, and I wouldn't be telling Ellis to bring us porterhouse steak every night and we wouldn't be eating it in this beautiful apartment which doesn't cost us any more than the steak does."

"Don't put words in my mouth," Max said. "I never said a bad thing about Gabe Hanratty."

"If you'll just keep putting steak in your mouth," Ida said, "I'll be able to tell you what Mr. Boyle told me, which was that he didn't want to happen to his little daughter, Claire, what happened to this Gabe Hanratty's daughter. One day she had a father, the next day she didn't."

"It happens to everybody," Max said.

"Mr. Boyle knows that," Ida said. "He also knows his wife's relatives—not the ones in Ireland, the ones in this country that he doesn't like and that don't like him; Mr. Boyle says the minute something happens to him they'd close in on the baby because of his money, and he wants to prevent that. What he wants to do, he told me, he wants to fix it so if what happened to Gabe Hanratty and what happened to your father, if it ever happens to him, his little daughter, Claire, will be protected from his wife's relatives as well as anything else and anybody else who might want to move in on her because she'll have somebody else right there, doing the same things for her that Mr. Boyle was doing, so the little girl won't notice there's been this big change."

"By this somebody he means me?" Max said.

"No," Ida said.

"You?"

"No," Ida said.

"Who?"

"Us," Ida said.

"That's funny," Max said.

"Why?"

"That's exactly what he told me on Wayzata Boulevard this morning before he came over here to Southeast Eighth Street to tell it to you," Max said.

"Does that make you feel better?" Ida said.

"If that's all he told you," Max said.

"It is."

"Something's missing," Max said.

Ida laughed. "There is," she said.

"What?"

"What I said to Mr. Boyle."

"What was that?" Max said.

"I said he'd have to ask you," Ida said.

Downstairs there was a sharp rapping on the garage door. Ida pushed back her chair and crossed to the kitchen door.

"Hello?" she called.

"Mrs. Lessing?" Ellis called back.

"Yes."

"Mr. Boyle said when you and Mr. Lessing finish supper, if it's not too much trouble could he see Mr. Lessing over at the house for a few minutes?"

Max came across the room and called down the stairs, "I'm on my way."

Mr. Boyle was waiting in the middle of the couch under the crystal chandelier.

"Mrs. Lessing told you?" he said.

"She also told me she said you'd have to ask me," Max said.

"I've known you both long enough so that didn't come as a surprise," Mr. Boyle said. "Sit down and make yourself comfortable and consider yourself asked."

Max sat down and said, "If you want it, Mr. Boyle, and you think it's right, Ida and I will be glad to do it, whatever the way is that these things are done."

"I do want it," Mr. Boyle said. "And I know it's right, not only for little Claire and for me, but also for you and Mrs. Lessing. When we get down to the financial arrangements I'm sure you'll agree. Right now, do you have any questions?"

"Only one," Max said.

"What's that?"

"I want you to fire Bert Bartholdi," Max said.

Mr. Boyle pursed his lips, then reached across to the silver tray and picked up his glass. He took down a couple of ounces of Kirkbean, staring at Max without blinking across the rim of his glass. When he put the glass back on the tray he said it it, "Is that a question or a condition?"

"What's a condition?" Max said.

Mr. Boyle said, "If I say no to firing Bert Bartholdi, and you say In that case I won't say yes to what you want me to do about your daughter, Claire, that's a condition."

Max pursed his lips, the way Mr. Boyle had pursed his, and he tried to underscore the imitation of Mr. Boyle's manner by staring for a few moments at his boss without blinking, before Max saying, "When you hired me as your foreman, Mr. Boyle, you said the job was mine as long as I know how to hold on to it. The first morning on Wayzata Boulevard, my first meeting with Bert Bartholdi, the way the meeting went I had to tell him what you told me, and then I told him something nobody told me."

"What was that?" Mr. Boyle said.

Max said, "I told him if holding on to the job meant getting myself a new chief mechanic, I knew how to do that too."

The red splotches on Mr. Boyle's face rearranged themselves. They always did when he smiled.

"You told him the truth," Mr. Boyle said.

Max said, "Will you fire him, or should I do it?"

"I'm not the foreman," Mr. Boyle said.

Max took a chance. He smiled back. "Then what I said, it was not a condition," he said. "It was just a question."

"Which I have answered, "Mr. Boyle said. "Now you answer mine."

"What you want me and Mrs. Lessing to do about your daughter," Max said, "we'll be glad to do it."

"I appreciate that," Mr. Boyle said. "I'll call Coley Scudder and have him fix up the papers."

"Who is Coley Scudder?" Max said.

"My lawyer," Mr. Boyle said. "You'll like him."

27

Fortunately, Ida liked him too.

Max was not aware of this for almost a month after he and Ida were taken by Mr. Boyle to Scudder's office on Chanhassen Circle where the papers were signed that established their legal relationship to Mr. Boyle's infant daughter, Claire.

Almost three weeks later, Max had his first experience with the more unsettling aspects of his new job. He got the news from Mrs. Gutera as soon as he arrived at Wayzata Boulevard in the morning. By the time he came home to Southeast Eighth Street at the end of the day, the unsettling aspects had settled down, at least so far as Max was concerned, and he decided not to say anything about it to Ida. Her relationship with Miss Liddy had just started to work smoothly enough so that Ida was beginning to enjoy taking care of the baby. This kept Mr. Boyle in a pleasant frame of mind for longer periods of time. Which in turn made life easier for Max on Wayzata Boulevard. For this reason, when he came into the kitchen over the garage that evening, Ida's first words were a shock.

"Did they find the killers?" she said.

The temptation to say "What killers?" was almost irresistible to a man who had decided to put an unpleasant experience behind him by pretending it had not happened. Max resisted the temptation. He knew Ida. Or rather, he was getting to know Ida.

Instead, he said, "How did you know about it?"

"Mr. Boyle told me," Ida said.

"When?"

After getting the bad news from Mrs. Gutera, discussing it with Max, and making a few phone calls from his private office, Mr. Boyle had left the warehouse on Wayzata Boulevard late in the morning.

"Around twelve," Ida said. "He came here to watch Miss Liddy bathe the baby and have a sandwich."

"And talk to you," Max said.

"That's why he pays for our porterhouse steaks."

"What did you have to tell him today to earn our supper for tonight?" Max said.

"He wanted to know what *dudky brott* means."

"That's what he asked me this morning," Max said. "I told him I didn't know enough Hungarian to be sure I was translating it correctly, but I thought it was something people said when they lifted a glass of wine in the air and made a toast."

"It could be used that way," Ida said. "It depends on the person who says it. I mean what he's making the toast about."

Max said, "That's what you told Mr. Boyle?"

"How else could I get him to tell me why he came home to ask me?"

"Don't make me answer that," Max said. "Just tell me what Mr. Boyle told you."

"He said three of his trucks were hijacked last night near a place called *matzo* something," Ida said.

"Mahtowa," Max said. "It's an Indian name. About halfway down from the Canadian border."

"Mr. Boyle said all three of your drivers were shot," Ida said. "By the time the police found them only one man was still alive, and he didn't stay alive long. The police

asked him what happened, did he recognize any of the
people who shot them, things like that. All the man had
strength enough left to say, he said those two words, *dudky
brott.*

"This morning, when Mr. Boyle learned what happened,
he figured because he'd been having all this what he called
Hungarian trouble, and those men you heard talking in
the toilet up there that first time, when you went up in the
truck with Mr. Hanratty, they were talking Hungarian, from
these things Mr. Boyle figured the two words, *dudky brott,*
they were Hungarian."

"That's the way I figured too," Max said. "But that's
as far as I got."

"Here on Southeast Eighth Street Mr. Boyle got further,"
Ida said. "Because as soon as he told me what happened,
the three trucks hijacked, the three men killed, I could see
somebody using those words *dudky brott.*"

"Who?" Max said.

"A man who is Mr. Boyle's enemy," Ida said.

"The man he called his Hungarian trouble?"

"Don't you think that sounds right?" Ida said.

"What did Mr. Boyle think?" Max said.

"I don't know," Ida said. "I'm not always sure I know
what goes on inside his head. Leaving out his thinking, but
just what he said, Mr. Boyle said You mean if somebody
wanted to destroy an enemy, and by hijacking three of his
loaded trucks and killing three of his enemy's drivers this
man felt he had destroyed his enemy, even without a glass
of wine in his hand he might say those words to show he'd
won a victory?"

"What did you say?" Max said.

"What you would have said," Ida said. "Absolutely. Not
only that, I said to Mr. Boyle, I said I could see how the
man who was shot, the man who was dying, when he was
talking to the cop, trying to tell him what happened, he
could have repeated those words because that's all the
strength he had left, to say those words."

"That makes sense," Max said.

"To a Hungarian," Ida said.

"How did it sound to an Irishman?" Max said.

Before Ida could answer, the voice of Ellis rose from the garage downstairs.

"Mrs. Lessing?"

"Yes?" Ida called.

"You put the supper on the table yet?" the black man said.

"Not yet," Ida said. "Why?"

"You mind holding off just a little while?" Ellis called. "Mr. Boyle would like to see Mr. Lessing for a minute over at the house."

Mr. Boyle saw Max in a part of the house that had grown familiar to Max but tonight looked strange. After a moment he understood why. He had never seen Mr. Boyle in his own kitchen. Max had seen him many times, however, doing what he was doing now. Mr. Boyle was standing at the counter near the stove, pouring Kirkbean into a glass on the silver tray.

"I hate to tear you away from your supper," he said, "but we've got to move fast. Tell Mrs. Lessing we'll be back sometime tomorrow, and she has my assurance you won't starve. Ellis has packed sandwiches and fruit and a thermos of coffee."

Mr. Boyle drank down half the contents of his glass, paused to wipe his lips with the back of his free hand, and said, "I've got the Buick out front."

He raised the glass for the second half of his stirrup cup, then paused with his hand in the air.

"Tell her not to worry," Mr. Boyle said. "You'll be perfectly safe." He set the glass back in motion toward his lips, then stopped it again. "And don't forget to bring your sweater," he said.

What Mr. Boyle brought was a heavy red-and-black-checked mackinaw with a loose collar that flipped over his head to form a hood. At first, when he stood on the Southeast Eighth Street sidewalk beside the car, struggling to get his arms into the stiff sleeves, it seemed to Max an odd outergarment for Mr. Boyle, because he was wearing the dark business suit he always wore in the warehouse on Wayzata Boulevard.

Once he was settled behind the wheel of the Buick, however, and Max had worked himself into a comfortable position on the seat beside him, it seemed to Max that after all these months he was finally seeing Mr. Boyle dressed in a manner that seemed appropriate to his red-splotched face, his bald head, and his occasionally pleasant but usually raspingly unpleasant voice.

Mr. Boyle did not use it for a long time as he guided the Buick out of Minneapolis in the gathering dusk, onto the road that Gabe Hanratty had said went straight for the Canadian border like a rifle bullet. It was almost two hours by Max's Ingersoll before Mr. Boyle broke the silence.

"I talked it over with Coley Scudder," he said without so much as a preparatory throat-clearing rasp. "Counting the three truckloads they got away with, and what it's going to cost to do something for the families of the dead drivers, I can't go on like this."

That was all Mr. Boyle seemed to have to say on the subject.

For the time being, anyway. About an hour later, while Max was munching one of Ellis' salami sandwiches, Mr. Boyle's voice rasped back into action.

"Want to drive for a while?" he said.

"Sure," Max said.

The shift seemed to jolt Mr. Boyle into a renewed desire to talk.

"Coley Scudder said the way to handle these things is to face up to them," he said. "Have a head-to-head meet with this guy, Coley said. Get it all out on the table. Maybe he'll listen to reason. There's enough to cut up without putting bullets in people's heads. He won't listen to reason? He won't cut? He wants it all? Okay. At least you'll know when you make your move there was no other move you could make. I buy that. Coley has good sense."

Mr. Boyle, who eventually was back at the wheel, obviously knew the way in from the main road as well as Max by now had learned it. Mr. Boyle made the sharp right at the white farmhouse without hesitation. He guided the Buick easily around every turn in the twisting dirt road through the woods. When the car came out through the opening in the overhang into the cleared space, Max realized for the first time since they had left Minneapolis that the moon was no longer hanging in the sky where it had hung during his first visit to the place with Gabe Hanratty. The sky, however, was clear and jammed with stars. Enough light came filtering through the thick foliage to show Max that the cleared space, which had impressed him on his first visit by the neatness with which its traffic was organized, on this visit seemed almost deserted.

From the opening in the overhang through which Mr. Boyle had driven the Buick, he sent it straight across toward the long, wide shed at the far end of the dirt road. The sheds to left and right, partially hidden by the trees, showed no lights. The neatly parked rows of trucks on both sides of the road were gone. There was only one vehicle in the area: a shabby Ford touring car that reminded Max of the vehicle in which Saul Sumeg had driven him and Ida from the dock on the Maine beach to the foot of the hill that led up into South St. Stephen. This car was parked in front of the long wide shed at the far end of the dirt road in front of which, months ago, Gabe Hanratty had parked the Mack truck in which he and Max had driven up from Minneapolis. Mr. Boyle pulled his Buick up beside the Ford and cut the ignition.

"You know where the toilet is," he said.

"Sure," Max said.

"I don't know how long I'll be," Mr. Boyle said. "Get back as quick as you can and wait for me here in the car."

He got out of the Buick, walked up to the door of the long, wide shed, and disappeared inside. Max got out on his side. Slamming the car door, he noticed the license plate hanging down between the front wheels of the Ford. Black numbers on red tin. Canada.

Max walked down to the only shed that showed any lights. When he came in, the fat woman in work pants and a baggy black sweater was at her post, stirring something that smelled good in a pot on the stove.

"Fried eggs?" she said.

"Not tonight, thanks," Max said. He came across with the thermos Ellis had put into the Buick. "Could you fill this with coffee?"

"Glad to," the woman said. "Sugar and cream?"

"Black, please," Max said.

When he came back out of the toilet, the thermos was waiting for him on the blue-and-white-checked oilcloth that covered the table nearest the door.

"Thanks," Max said, picking it up.

"Nothing," the woman said. "Have a good trip."

Walking back toward the wide, low shed, Max noticed a man walking slowly around the Buick. There was something familiar about the way he kept his head tipped to one side. A few moments later Max saw why. The man had a cigarette pasted to his lower lip. He was squinting through the smoke as though he were sighting a rifle at the Buick.

"Hello, Bert," Max said.

"I thought I recognized the car," Bert Bartholdi said. "What are you doing up here?"

"I like the toilet," Max said. "I always drive up from Minneapolis when I have to go. How about you?"

"I got me an honest job," Bert Bartholdi said. "I'm too old to earn a living for my family ducking bootleggers' bullets."

He walked off to the shed where the old woman had re-filled Max's thermos. Max got into the Buick and poured himself a cup of coffee. Soon after he finished it, and screwed the cap back onto the thermos, Mr. Boyle came out of the

206

long, wide shed. He flipped the hood of the mackinaw up over his head and climbed in behind the wheel.

"Anything happen?" he said.

The two words, emerging through Mr. Boyle's tight lips, made a sound that reminded Max of a carving knife running along the edge of a whirling carborundum wheel. His gut tightened. Inside the shed, things had not gone well.

"I ran into our former mechanic," Max said.

"Bert Bartholdi?"

The surprise in Mr. Boyle's voice was more disturbing than the nastiness.

"He's up there in the toilet shack," Max said.

"What's he doing in this place?"

"He's got a new job," Max said. "With an honest man, he said, where he doesn't have to duck hijackers' bullets."

"Anybody we know?" Mr. Boyle said.

"He didn't say."

"If he's up in this wilderness going to the toilet this time of night," Mr. Boyle said, "there's not much future in his new job, I don't think."

Mr. Boyle clearly had other thoughts, but he kept them to himself. He scowled in silence through the windshield as he guided the Buick out of the woods on the twisting narrow dirt road.

"Want me to drive?" Max said when they emerged onto the main road.

"In a while," Mr. Boyle said.

A while proved to be almost two hours later. Mr. Boyle pulled the car over to the side of the road. He and Max changed places. Putting the Buick into gear, Max noticed a metal road sign: KEEWATIN 2MI. It was the last thing Max remembered noticing. As he swung the car back onto the road, the steering wheel seemed to come free in his hands. The car kept going, however, gathering speed as it moved at right angles to the road.

"What the hell—?"

It was Mr. Boyle's voice, rasping upward in the beginnings of an enraged outburst, but Max never heard the words. He remembered clutching the steering wheel as thought it were a soup plate he had snatched in midair from an unexpectedly kicked-over table. He remembered the total disregard the automobile under him suddenly seemed to have for his attempts to change its direction. He remembered, as the car went shooting off the side of the road like a child going down a slide in a park playground, his surprise on discovering that the Buick seemed to be heading out into space. Then the nose of the car dipped down sharply, as though it had been yanked like a bell rope, and Max remembered thinking there was absolutely nothing below the Buick but what looked like an enormous bottomless hole.

When the car hit, he remembered being hurled straight up in the air, off the seat, and that was the last thing Max remembered.

28

When he started coming awake, it seemed to Max he was doing it in a place where it was perfectly reasonable for him to be: his own bed in the apartment over the garage on Southeast Eighth Street. When he was fully awake and he tried to move, Max was astonished to hear himself scream. He had no choice. The sound was ripped out of him.

"You awake, Mr. Lessing?"

Max did no more moving. Not with the lower part of his body. All he risked was a slow, very slow turn of his head in the direction from which the voice had come. It had come out of Ellis. The skullcap of tight white curls came into Max's line of vision before he realized that the black man was sitting beside the bed.

"What are you doing here?" Max said.

Ellis said, "Waiting for you to wake up and start asking questions."

"Where's Mrs. Lessing?" Max said.

"Over at the house with the baby," Ellis said. "You really bad?"

"Only when I move," Max said.

Then he started to remember, and it came back fast. All of it. Even the road sign: KEEWATIN 2 MI.

"Mr. Boyle?" Max said.

"Dead," Ellis said.

Considering what Max remembered, that piece of information was not surprising. Merely shocking. With the shock so many other things came crowding at him that Max felt he'd better not try to handle more than one piece at a time.

"How come I'm not?" he said.

Ellis said, "The police and the ambulance doctor they think it's mostly just luck, but mainly you didn't go through the windshield the way Mr. Boyle did. It cut off his head."

Max held on tight, waiting for the sick feeling in his stomach to level off.

"You want some water?" Ellis said.

"I think yes, thanks," Max said.

The black man took a glass from the table next to the bed.

"Mrs. Lessing fixed this thing so you won't have to lift your head," Ellis said. "I'll hold it. You suck in."

He steadied the glass against Max's cheek and bent the straw until he was able to slip the end between Max's lips. Going down, the water stopped the sick feeling from coming up.

Ellis said, "Not too much, Mrs. Lessing said."

He put the glass back on the table. Max took several long, deep breaths with his mouth open.

"Please ask Mrs. Lessing to come over," he said.

Ellis pulled an Ingersoll from the watch pocket under his pants belt.

"She'll be here in a few minutes," he said. "The important thing right now, she don't want the baby upset. Not much chance of that, Miss Liddy says, a little thing in a cradle as small and tiny as that, but Mrs. Lessing says you and she promised Mr. Boyle if anything like this happened you'd do everything you could to keep the baby easy in her mind, no matter how small or tiny she is, and since you can't do anything about it yourself right now, Mrs. Lessing is doing it for both of you. She said if you wake up, and she wasn't back yet, I should explain that, so you won't think she's neglecting you. That sound all right?"

It didn't. He wanted Ida. But he couldn't say that to Ellis.

"Sure," Max said.

"Mrs. Lessing also said if you wake up before she comes over," the black man said, "I should fill you in. You want to rest some more? Or you want to hear?"

"I want to hear," Max said.

"The Buick went down into the gulley with such a crash," Ellis said, "it brought a farmer from up the road to see what happened. When he saw, he went back to his house and called the police."

"Keewatin," Max said.

"How come you remember that?"

"There was a road sign," Max said.

"The police came out with the ambulance," Ellis said. "They took Mr. Boyle to the morgue, and they took you to the hospital."

"Is there anything—"

"No," the black man said. "Put your mind easy on that. You've got two busted legs, one broken wrist, a few cuts, a lot of scratches, and some cracked ribs, but nothing of a permanent nature, as they say."

"That's the truth?" Max said.

"You check it out with Mrs. Lessing."

"I didn't mean—"

"I know you didn't," the black man said. "When you ask anything I wouldn't have asked if I was in that bed and you was sitting here in this chair, I'll let you know. Before the doctors had you patched up, the police knew what happened. Somebody was trying to kill you. They fooled around with the steering wheel on that Buick. The shear pin was sawed halfway through. Once you got that automobile rolling, it was just a matter of time. Every time you moved the steering wheel it dug that cut in the shear pin a little deeper. Any thoughts you got on that, don't tell me about it."

"Why not?" Max said.

"Mrs. Lessing's been talking to Mr. Scudder," Ellis said. "He wants to ask you a few things when you're up to it.

211

Mrs. Lessing says you're not up to it when you're talking to me alone. Okay?"

"Okay," Max said. "How did I get back here?"

"Mrs. Lessing," the black man said. "That lady has a head on her shoulders. When the police called from up in that place with the name—"

"Keewatin," Max said.

"—they told Mrs. Lessing she better come up because nobody was going to be able to move you out of there for quite a while. Mrs. Lessing didn't agree. She called Mr. Scudder, and he arranged for a private ambulance, and Mrs. Lessing and I we rode up there together to this place—"

"Keewatin," Max said.

"Why you keep repeating that?"

"I don't know," Max said.

He didn't, but it seemed important.

"Well, hold off till I finish," the black man said. "The doctors up there made a fuss. Anyway, they tried to, but I notice nobody gets very far fussing at Mrs. Lessing. She told them doctors she couldn't waste no time. She had a baby down in Minneapolis, and if they didn't want to help get you in that there ambulance, we'd get by without them. So they helped, and we got you back here, and that was just about seven o'clock last night."

Ellis examined the face of his Ingersoll.

"It's now six minutes after twelve the next day," he said. "And those steps I hear downstairs is Mrs. Lessing."

Ida came in. Ellis stood up and nodded toward the bed.

"Doesn't look too bad, does he?" the black man said.

"Except for the bandages," Ida said. "Thanks, Ellis. The baby's asleep. You go on over and have your lunch."

"Want me to cook up something for you and Mr. Lessing?" Ellis said.

"Thanks, no," Ida said. "I'll make some soup or something. The minute the baby wakes up, you come and get me."

"I will do that, Mrs. Lessing," the black man said.

He went out. Ida sat down beside the bed. She and Max stared at each other. When Ellis' shoes stopped tapping wood on the stairs and slapping cement in the garage and started sending up the sound of kicked gravel as he made his way back to the house, Ida nodded. Max understood. It was safe to talk.

"It's all right," she said.

"How do you know?" Max said.

"Mr. Scudder," Ida said. "I think we can trust him."

"Why?"

"You know the Innisfail Trading Company?" Ida said.

"Of course I know it," Max said. "I work for it."

Ida said, "You also work for Mr. Scudder."

"Since when?"

"Since he's been what he calls a stockholder in the Innisfail Trading Company," Ida said. "He explained it to me. It's a corporation. Mr. Boyle owned most of the stock. Mr. Scudder owns the rest. I'm not sure why. Maybe because he's Mr. Boyle's lawyer. Maybe for some other reason. I haven't found that out yet, but I'll keep my eyes and ears open and I'm pretty sure sooner or later I will. Right now that's not important."

"Right now what is important?" Max said.

"Mr. Scudder likes us," Ida said.

"He does?"

"I'm sure of it," Ida said. "I felt it that day Mr. Boyle took us over to Mr. Scudder's office on Chanhassen Circle to sign the papers about the baby."

"How does that make things all right today?" Max said. "With Mr. Boyle all of a sudden dead?"

"You're thinking only of losing your job," Ida said. "And our losing this apartment."

"Don't forget the porterhouse steaks."

"This is no time for jokes," Ida said.

"Every bone in my body that isn't already broken feels like in a few minutes it will be," Max said. "My boss has just been murdered by some gangsters who were trying to murder me along with him. What makes you think I think this is a time for jokes?"

"Because you haven't had time to find out what I've found out," Ida said.

"Which is what?"

"It's more important to Mr. Scudder that the Innisfail Trading Company should stay in business than it is for us," Ida said.

"Who cares what's important to a rich *goy* lawyer?" Max said. "I care about what's important to us."

"So does Mr. Scudder," Ida said.

"Are you crazy?"

"Not yet," Ida said. "But I will be if I have to keep on talking and you won't listen."

"I'm listening," Max said.

"Mr. Boyle is dead," Ida said. "Everything he owned now belongs to his daughter. His daughter is two months, one week, and three days old. Among the things little Claire owns is her father's stock in the Innisfail Trading Company. That makes her Mr. Scudder's partner. You and I are little Claire's foster parents. Mr. Scudder knows that. He made out the papers for us to sign. He also knows we're a couple of dumb greenhorns from Europe who don't know anything about this country, especially how things like the Innisfail Trading Company work over here. So how could it be better for a man like Mr. Scudder who wants his business to keep on going than to have as a partner a two-month-old baby with two greenhorns as foster parents?"

Max could feel the pieces begin to fall into place. The clunks were almost painful.

"That's why he sent the private ambulance up to Keewatin to get me," he said.

"That, plus what I told you," Ida said. "He likes us."

"Us or you?" Max said.

"What's the difference?" Ida said. "Mr. Boyle liked us the same way."

"Look what happened to Mr. Boyle," Max said.

"He was a big stockholder," Ida said. "Someday the same thing could happen to a small stockholder."

Max embarked on a laugh. It emerged as a scream.

"The doctor told me every move will hurt for a while," Ida said. "But he also told me everything will get better. So all you have to do is wait for it to get better and then go back to Wayzata Boulevard, where you will go on being the foreman of the Innisfail Trading Company as though nothing happened, but you and I know better."

"That's all?" Max said.

"Except for one thing."

"What's that?" Max said.

"I want you to tell Mr. Scudder you understand everything I told you," Ida said.

"When do you want me to do that?" Max said.

"Right now," Ida said. "That's his machine I just heard pulling into the driveway."

A few moments later Mr. Scudder's shoes were kicking gravel toward the garage. Ida went to the bedroom door and called down the stairs, "Please come up, Mr. Scudder."

He came into the room with a fat briefcase under his arm and on his gaunt, ageless *goy* face a troubled smile.

"Am I disturbing him?" he whispered.

"Just for a few minutes it won't matter," Ida said. "Max, tell Mr. Scudder what you just told me."

Max said, "I understand everything."

Mr. Scudder's smile changed from troubled to sweet. He came to the bed, started to put out his hand, then stopped and sent a nervous glance at Ida.

"Is it all right?" he said.

"If you don't shake it too hard," Ida said, "I'm pretty sure it won't fall off."

Mr. Scudder picked up one of Max's hands as though with with a pair of tongs he were lifting a chocolate cream from a box of bonbons.

"I'm very pleased," he said. "Take your time getting well,

Max, and then come back to Wayzata Boulevard, where we need you."

"Thank you," Max said.

"Until then," Mr. Scudder said, "if there's anything you want, please don't hesitate to ask me."

"There's one thing," Max said.

"What is it?" Mr. Scudder said.

"I don't want my wife running back and forth between the baby in the house and her crippled husband over here in the garage," Max said. "For a young girl, it's too much work."

"I hadn't thought of that," Mr. Scudder said. "Is there anything you can suggest?"

"Yes," Max said. "I think it will make things easier for everybody if my wife and I move out of the garage and over into the big house."

29

The first move was into Mr. Boyle's billiard room. It was on the ground floor. This eliminated the problem of a man encased in sixty pounds of plaster casts getting himself up and down stairs. Mr. Boyle's billiard table was pushed into a corner of the large room and the double bed from the garage was moved in.

The second move was from the billiard room to the even larger drawing room. This did not involve the invalid's sleeping hours. During his third week of convalescence, Max was able with the help of crutches to start moving about in an upright position under his own power. Every morning he moved to the center of the large couch under the crystal chandelier.

Sprawled in the place where Mr. Boyle used to alternate, while consuming Kirkbean, between irascibility and affability, Max received his daily visit from Mrs. Gutera. Through her he routed the trucks into and out of the Wayzata Boulevard warehouse by remote control. Occasionally Mr. Scudder came in to discuss business manners and bring papers for Max to sign. They never discussed Mr. Boyle. Three months after the accident outside Keewatin, Max was able with the help of a single cane to walk adequately on the flat.

One morning, while Ida was in the nursery with Miss

Liddy helping Dr. Schieffelin give the baby her smallpox vaccination, the front-door bell rang. Max was on the couch, checking the week's shipping figures Mrs. Gutera had left with him earlier in the morning. He was unaware that nobody had answered the bell until it rang again.

Max looked up from his papers, then remembered that Ellis had gone downtown with the daily shopping list. Max got the cane into position, hoisted himself up onto his feet, and went out to the front door. He opened it and found himself facing Jekuthiel Fruchter.

"Say something friendly," the big man said.

"What do you want?" Max said.

"You call that friendly?" Jekuthiel Fruchter said.

"It's as friendly as I feel to anybody named Fruchter," Max said. "What do you want?"

"On my feet I've always found it impossible to do two things," Jekuthiel Fruchter said. "Give a girl a *shtip*, and talk business."

"In my house you're not going to do either," Max said.

He started to close the door. One of the knee-high hunting boots laced with yellow leather thongs came forward in a slow kick. The door stopped moving.

"I hear all your bones are pasted together again," Jekuthiel Fruchter said. "You want to keep them that way, all you have to do is invite me in for a sitting-down talk."

"Max."

He turned. Ida had appeared in the hall behind him.

"Let him in," she said.

"I always figured the women have the brains in this family," Jekuthiel Fruchter said. "How are you, Mrs. Lessing?"

"I'll be better when you finish your business with my husband and get out," Ida said.

She didn't help Max back into the living room, but she kept close to him until he was back in the middle of the couch.

"If you want me," she said to Max, "I'll be in the nursery."

She walked out. Jekuthiel Fruchter removed his red-and-black-checked hunting cap with the black duckbill visor. He undid the two top buttons of his sailor's pea jacket. He dropped his two hundred and fifty pounds into the chair facing Max.

"A nursery," Jekuthiel Fruchter said. "Wait till I call my brother on the long-distance in Rivière du Cojot. He'll be very happy. Not only because he likes you and Mrs. Lessing so much, but also because he's crazy about babies."

"Just tell me what you're crazy about," Max said.

"Collecting my family's debts," Fruchter said. "What I want to know is When can I tell my brother we're going to collect the twenty thousand dollars you owe us?"

"Since when did it become twenty thousand?" Max said.

"Since our brother Zalman got drowned in a bathtub," Jekuthiel Fruchter said.

"If I were you," Max said, "I'd start taking swimming lessons."

"Until we collect our twenty thousand dollars from you," Fruchter said, "I won't be able to afford it."

"In that case," Max said, "I think you better spend the rest of your life staying away from water."

Jekuthiel Fruchter said, "You won't have much of a life to spend if I don't get my family's twenty thousand before Yom Kippur."

"There's some debts I never pay before the High Holy Days," Max said. "The rest I never pay after the High Holy Days."

"You'll pay this one," Jekuthiel Fruchter said.

"Tell your brother up in Rivière du Cojot not to hold his breath," Max said.

"Funny you should give me a message for him," Jekuthiel Fruchter said. "On the long-distance this morning my brother said I should give you a message."

"Leave it on the table by the door on your way out," Max said.

"My brother said Give the little Austrian *putz* the name of Harry Boyle's Hungarian problem," Jekuthiel Fruchter said.

Max's gut did that thing he had come to recognize but no longer feared.

"When it comes to murderers," Max said, "I like to hear the names clearly so I can repeat them to the district attorney. Say this one nice and slow."

"The last name is Fruchter," Jekuthiel Fruchter said. "The first name, you got a choice from a list."

"Now that Zalman got himself drowned," Max said, "I guess the list is shorter."

"It's long enough to collect the family debts," Jekuthiel Fruchter said. "You just deliver that twenty thousand where it belongs."

He stood up.

"You deliver my message where it belongs," Max said. He got the cane into position and pushed himself up onto his feet. "If you don't want that list to get shorter," Max said, "you just keep everybody named Fruchter out of Minneapolis."

"Since when did you get to own the place?" Jekuthiel Fruchter said.

"Since Harry Boyle was murdered," Max said.

PART III
1974

30

Half a century later, it was the name that attracted Paavo Ohmstetter.

"Lessing," he said on the morning in 1974 when news about The Frontenac first crossed his path. "Lessing."

Liv was at the sink, rinsing the grapefruit seeds. She looked down the kitchen toward the dining alcove. Her husband was hunched over *The Miami Herald* with his second cup of Postum.

"You say anything to me?" Liv said.

"Lessing," Paavo said again, obviously not to her. This did not surprise Liv Ohmstetter. Her husband did quite a lot of talking to himself.

She turned back to the sink and counted the seeds. Eleven. Not bad, considering it was June. The season was almost over. In 1969, when they had first arrived in Florida, getting fifteen or twenty seeds out of a single grapefruit had been commonplace. Liv had not realized then the significance of the fact that it was November when she and Paavo had settled into their house in Ce Esta Village. Later she learned that they had arrived in Florida at the height of the grapefruit season.

In November a sack of ten beautiful Indian Rivers went for forty-nine cents at Winn-Dixie. They made lovely eating—nothing like the pulpy lumps of cotton wool that passed for grapefruit up in Minneapolis. These were so delicious that Liv and Paavo didn't mind the seeds. At that time they considered the seeds a nuisance. Then they discovered that almost every one of their neighbors in Ce Esta Village had a grapefruit corner in the gardening plot that came with each house. Almost immediately what had been a pleasant addition to the Ohmstetter breakfast menu became also an important event of the day.

They grew accustomed to the fact that as the grapefruit season waned, the morning seed take diminished. Not, however, the eagerness with which Liv picked the seeds out of the fruit. Certainly not the diligence with which, after he finished his morning stint at the easel in his garage studio, Paavo later planted them out back. In June anything over six seeds was considered a decent haul. Eleven added up to a bonanza.

"Guess how many this morning," Liv said.

"Lessing," Paavo said.

He tapped his forefinger on the newspaper.

"It's the real estate section," she said.

"Congratulations," Paavo said. "Five years in Florida with all those grapefruit seeds, I was afraid maybe you forgot how to read."

"I never learned how to read the real estate section in Minneapolis when I was young and had my eyesight," Liv said. "Why should I start now when I can't see without glasses and I'm on Social Security?"

"I'm the one who's on Social Security," Paavo said. "You're on one half what I get because you're my spouse, and if you learned to read the real estate section you might learn something that could maybe get me off Social Security and you off my back. Here, genius."

He thrust the paper at her.

"I left my glasses in the bedroom," Liv said. "You'll have to read it to me."

"It's an article by the *Herald*'s top man on real estate,"

Paavo said. "Larry Conyers his name is. In fact, he's the paper's real estate editor."

"By that I should be impressed?" she said.

"Close your mouth and open your ears and we'll see," Paavo said. "*The Frontenac enjoys two distinctions on the Florida Gold Coast*, this Larry Conyers writes here on the front page of the real estate section. *It is probably the most eye-catching structure built south of the Mason-Dixon line, and it is the only high-rise between Key West and Palm Beach on which Lloyd's of London is willing to write hurricane insurance. It is also a pet project of Max Lessing, founder of the worldwide conglomerate empire that bears his name.*"

"Say!" Liv said.

Paavo looked up from the paper. His right eye, naturally, looked up somewhat higher than his left.

"Yes?" he said.

"Is that the Max Lessing who—?"

"It's got to be," Paavo said.

"Why?" Liv said.

"In your imagination can you conceive of a world containing two of them?" Paavo said.

"No way," Liv said.

"Which means—" Paavo said.

"Where you going?" Liv said.

Across his shoulder he shot her a look of loathing. In his endless struggle against the bastards who were out to destroy him, Paavo Ohmstetter had never found a more able or willing lieutenant than Liv. After forty-one years, however, the dumb bitch still had not caught on that stopping stupid remarks in mid-flight was his province, not hers.

"To make a long-distance phone call," Paavo said.

"Who to?"

"You remember Joe Catalini?" Paavo said.

"Joe Cat—?" Liv said.

"The same."

"You know how to reach him?" Liv said.

Paavo said, "Would I be breaking my neck to get to

225

the telephone to make a long-distance call to a man I don't know how to reach?"

"But how—?" Liv began.

"I've kept in touch," Paavo said.

"All these years?"

"A man at the apex of his powers who is shoved out of the stream of life just because he has reached the number sixty-five on a chart and gets dumped on the trash heap called Social Security," Paavo said, "what else have I got to do?"

Quite a lot, as it turned out. Once he landed the job as manager of The Frontenac.

Paavo Ohmstetter never doubted he would land it. As soon as he got Joe Catalini on the phone, anyway. This was not easy, but it was not so very difficult, either. Through what sounded like a screening staff of switchboard operators and secretaries, Paavo set in motion a few appropriate references to Minneapolis in 1920. From that moment on, Paavo knew it was all wrapped up.

"Hold on, please," the fourth secretary said.

She could have been the fifth. Paavo had stopped counting.

"My arm hurts," he said to her. "I've run out of holding-on juice. You tell Mr. Catalini to call me back. I'm going out in half an hour to plant my grapefruit seeds, so he'd better call before then. Every day after I plant my grapefruit seeds, I go to my studio. When I'm painting I do not take phone calls. So listen carefully to this phone number, dear. I'm not going to repeat it."

He spelled it out clearly and hung up without waiting for any more talk from the New York end. Liv was standing over him. Her lips were pursed.

"You think—?" she said.

"What else?" Paavo said. "This Postum is cold. Could you pull yourself together long enough to make me a cup of hot?"

By the time she brought the fresh cup into the living room, the phone was ringing. Paavo picked it up.

"Hello?"

"Paavo?"

Good. Very good indeed.

"The same," Paavo said.

"Where you calling from?" Joe Catalini said.

"Florida."

"Any special part?" Joe said.

"The part I own," Paavo said. "Me and the First Atlantic Savings and Loan."

"Keeping you busy?"

"I got a little studio in the garage where I add a couple of square inches to an abstract every day," Paavo Ohmstetter said. "I got a little garden out back where every day I plant the grapefruit seeds Liv and I pick out of our breakfast. And I own a little souvenir paper knife I got with Publix green stamps that every third day of the month I use to open the brown envelope in which the Department of Health, Education and Welfare sends me my green Social Security check."

"Sounds like a full life," Joe Catalini said.

"Leonardo da Vinci it wouldn't make jealous."

"Funny you should call just now," Joe Catalini said.

"Funny like in Milton Berle?" Paavo said. "Or funny like in Dear me what a surprise?"

"Looks like we're going to be neighbors," Joe said.

Paavo nodded. He not only did quite a bit of talking to himself. Paavo also did quite a lot of nodding to himself. His mind was like a jigsaw puzzle. He liked to fill in the empty spaces. The one that Joe Catalini's remark had just filled in was the seven minutes that had elapsed between the time Paavo hung up on the fourth or fifth secretary and the time Joe Catalini returned the call. For years Paavo had been hearing that the Lessing family intelligence network kept the CIA colored bright green with envy, but Paavo had not realized it was as fast as this.

"You moving down here?" Paavo said.

"Me personally, no," Joe said.

"Too bad," Paavo Ohmstetter said. "For a moment there, I thought I was about to pick up a chum so every third day of the month we could go to the mailbox hand in hand and wait for our Social Security checks side by side."

"Not yet, Paavo, but I may join you in a couple of years," Joe Catalini said. "Meantime, though, we're building a big apartment house on the beach down your way."

"I didn't tell you yet what my way is," Paavo Ohmstetter said.

"The way I remember you, Paavo, what you had between your ears in Minneapolis wasn't exactly cold farina," Joe Catalini said. "The way I figure, anybody with brains who retires to Florida, he'd do it by buying himself a nice little three-room cottage in this place called Ce Esta Village, 1130 Southeast Second Street, Pompano Beach, Florida 33060."

"Pretty good, Joe," Paavo Ohmstetter said. "For seven minutes."

"Hold it, Paavo, that may not be all. My secretary seems to have something for me." Pause. Joe Catalini came back on the wire with "Purchase price nineteen thousand five, mortgage ten. Not a bad deal, Paavo. Not bad at all."

"Not great, either," Paavo Ohmstetter said.

"Maybe you could do better," Joe Catalini said. "If you read this Larry Conyers, he's the real estate editor of *The Miami Herald*, I'm sure you'll agree, Paavo."

"Funny you should mention Conyers," Paavo Ohmstetter said. "I was just reading him aloud to my wife, Liv, with my Postum."

"Funny like in Milton Berle?" Joe Catalini said. "Or funny like in Dear me what a surprise?"

"I don't know yet," Paavo said. "I thought we could maybe have a talk."

"Be at Miami International Airport at two o'clock sharp," Joe Catalini said. "I'm sending Abe Shantz down with one of the jets to pick you up."

"As long as you're sending one of the jets down," Paavo Ohmstetter said, "why don't you climb aboard? We could talk here in my comfortable little living room and I wouldn't have to get out of my swimming trunks and climb into city clothes."

Joe Catalini's voice did not change. Only the tempo of his delivery.

He said, "Don't push, Paavo. We could you use you, but we don't need you. Be at the airport at two o'clock sharp."

Paavo was there. At five o'clock he was in Joe Catalini's office on the top floor of the Lessing Tower on Park Avenue. At eleven-thirty he was back at Miami International Airport. Liv met him. He did not speak until they were on the Thruway, heading home to Ce Esta Village.

"You are driving the new manager of The Frontenac," Paavo said. "An oceanfront luxury apartment house halfway between Miami and Palm Beach which is not yet completed but which is taking shape so rapidly that it has attracted the attention of the *Miami Herald* real estate editor, Mr. Larry Conyers."

"Is that good?" Liv said.

"It's better than Social Security," Paavo said.

"How much better?"

"Salary fifteen thousand," Paavo said.

"That's three hundred a week," Liv said.

"Minus we have to give up our Social Security," Paavo said.

"With three hundred a week gross coming in," Liv said, "who needs Social Security?"

"Are you asking questions?" Paavo said. "Or am I answering them?"

"Pardon me for breathing," Liv said.

"Part of the deal," Paavo said, "we get an apartment in The Frontenac rent free."

"How big?"

"The building isn't finished yet," Paavo said. "We can run over and look at the model. From what Joe Catalini told me, the manager's apartment is somewhat smaller than the owners' apartments."

"Naturally," Liv said.

"If you were building an apartment house," Paavo said, "would you make the manager's apartment as big as the others?"

"Are you asking questions?" Liv said. "Or am I answering them?"

"Even though it is smaller than the owners' apartments," Paavo said, "I was told by Mr. Joe Catalini the space we will have will be four hundred and eighty square feet larger than the space we now have at 1130 Southeast Second Street, Pompano Beach 33060."

"How does he know?" Liv said.

"Try not to be stupid," Paavo said. "I've had a long day."

"What else?"

"Free utilities," Paavo said.

"Including telephone?"

"Especially including telephone," Paavo said.

Liv said, "What's with the especially?"

"No matter where he may be," Paavo said, "from wherever it is, Joe Catalini wants to be able to keep in touch with the manager of The Frontenac."

He did it by installing in Paavo Ohmstetter's apartment a telephone with a panel that had more buttons on it than an accordion.

31

The installation of the tinted glass was Paavo Ohmstetter's own idea. He knew what the morning sun did to the Ohmstetter living room at Ce Esta Village. It was not difficult to project a guess about what that same sun would do to a living room with a forty-foot picture window facing the Atlantic Ocean.

After inspecting the manager's apartment a month before he and Liv were scheduled to move in, Paavo ordered the window replaced with a seamless sheet of tinted glass. This effectively cut from the apartment all the heat as well as all the glare of the morning sun.

Two years later, on the night when Hurricane Carla was threatening the southeast coast of Florida, Paavo Ohmstetter realized the tinted glass also cut from his apartment in The Frontenac the more terrifying aspects of flashing lightning. Coming in from the bedroom, he said, "You buzzed?"

"Yes," Joe Catalini said.

He was sitting where Paavo had left him. On the couch, next to his folded raincoat. Staring out at the Atlantic across the coffee table. On it sat the telephone with the push-button console that resembled the control panel of an old C-51. Catalini was thinking of the telephone talk he'd had with Lou Mangan up in Boston. Joe had used the ex-policeman on a number of occasions when he wanted something done in the Boston area. It seemed to him Mangan would probably handle the assignment Joe had given him as well as it could be handled. Mangan was a reliable man. It seemed to Paavo Ohmstetter that Joe Catalini looked tired.

Paavo said, "Anything more I can do?"

Joe said, "That's lightning isn't it?"

Surprised, Paavo looked over his visitor's head. Beyond the tinted glass the smudged darkness seemed restless. A sort of rubbery curtain of not very clearly identifiable color. Like the layer of fat on top of a slowly bubbling pot of greasy soup stock viewed in a dimly lighted kitchen. With one odd difference. Across the restless mass of squirming darkness, slashes of dull silver sped back and forth, sometimes up and down, in a darting but curiously lazy way.

"Yes, it is," Paavo said. "It doesn't look like lightning because the window is tinted glass. Like a windshield."

"That taxi driver waiting for me outside better have one of those windshields," Joe said.

He heaved himself up onto his feet. To make it, Paavo noted, Catalini had to use both hands, shoving down hard on the couch.

"He has," Paavo Ohmstetter said. "While you were upstairs in the penthouse I had him down in the basement drying off. I checked out his rig, just to make sure. Nothing wrong with it. Palm Beach Taxi is a good outfit. They use only late-model Caddys."

It was done so smoothly that it might have gone unnoticed. Not, however, by Joe Catalini. His life consisted of not unnoticing anything. Paavo Ohmstetter had wanted Joe Catalini to know Paavo was aware Joe had come to The Frontenac in this storm by way of Palm Beach, which was north, and not as Joe Catalini always came, by way of Miami International, which was south. Joe Catalini had not only noticed it. He had recorded the more important point: Paavo Ohmstetter had wanted him to notice it.

"What do the weather boys say?" Joe said.

Paavo crossed back to the bedroom. He opened the door
and poked his head in.

"Liv," he said. "Turn it up."

The TV sound track came blasting into the living room."

"—no significant change."

The gargling voice of the newscaster oozed into the living
room like olive oil sliding down a drainboard.

"Our latest report from the National Hurricane Tracking
Center, monitored in Miami eight minutes ago, indicates
that as of this moment, which is two-ten A.M., the threat to
the Florida southeast coast seems to be mounting, but it
cannot yet be identified as certain. From the Keys up to
Palm Beach there has been an increase in wind velocity, but
not of a significant nature, and the rain can still be described
as unpleasantly incessant, but there is not yet, repeat not yet,
any cause for evacuation. Dr. Jonas O'Malley, Director of the
National Hurricane Tracking Center, just told us in a telephone interview that the chances are excellent we will make
it through to daylight with nothing more serious than the
present unpleasantness of gusting wind and pelting rain.
However, that does not mean it is wise or safe to relax the
precautions we have been urging since—"

Paavo Ohmstetter pulled the door shut. The gargling
voice vanished.

"I guess that's enough," Paavo said.

"Plenty," Joe said. "I'm sure the driver will be able to
get me through."

He bent over to pick up his raincoat.

"If you're going north," Paavo Ohmstetter said.

This settled what Joe Catalini had begun to feel from the
moment he had come down from the Lessing penthouse ten
minutes ago and found Paavo waiting for him as usual in
the lobby. Except that this time it was not as usual. This time
Paavo clearly had something on his mind. Joe Catalini would
have to give the manager a chance to unload it. They had
met once in Minneapolis in 1920, when Joe Catalini was a
boy of eleven and Paavo Ohmstetter had been sixteen. Joe

had no recollection of the meeting. He remembered clearly, however, the circumstances that had brought the meeting about.

Half a century later, Joe Catalini and Paavo Ohmstetter had met again. At Paavo's request, in Joe's office at the top of the Lessing Tower on Park Avenue in New York. The meeting had resulted in Paavo Ohmstetter's coming to live with his wife, Liv, in the manager's apartment at The Frontenac.

During the next two years he and Joe had met frequently, whenever Joe flew down for a meeting with Ida Lessing in the penthouse.

These meetings were always the same—except, of course, that this one, tonight, was embedded like the whole state of Florida in Hurricane Carla. The meetings always took place in Paavo Ohmstetter's apartment after Joe Catalini came down from his meeting in the penthouse. They always consisted of a session by Joe with the Ohmstetter telephone in the manager's living room. While Joe caught up with his work, Paavo and Liv remained secluded in the bedroom. The meetings always ended with an exchange of innocuous information about things like the weather.

Aside from the enveloping presence of Hurricane Carla, this meeting tonight was different in one other respect. Instead of discussing the weather Paavo had said, "If you're going north."

Joe Catalini was surprised by his surprise. Nobody had used that tone of voice to him in a head-to-head conversation for a long time. Not for half a century.

"When you called me two years ago and said you wanted to talk to me," Joe Catalini said, "I told you I'd send Abe Shantz down in the jet to pick you up. You said it would be easier for you if I flew down with Abe and we had our talk down in Florida. You remember my answer?"

Paavo Ohmstetter said, "You said, 'Don't push Paavo.'"

"Do I have to say it again?" Joe Catalini said.

Paavo said, "I don't think you'll want to."

Joe looked down at the raincoat hung across his forearm. He tossed it back on the couch.

"If this will take long," Joe said, "I'll get off my feet. Should I sit down?"

"I don't care whether you sit or stand," Paavo Ohmstetter said. "All you have to do is listen."

"I'm doing that," Joe Catalini said.

"Fifty years ago the son of a bitch you work for destroyed my wife's father," Paavo said. "You helped him. It's taken me half a century to work my way into a position where Liv and I can pay you both back. Plus that bitch upstairs who washes the bloodstains out of your assassination uniforms."

"Don't take on too much, Paavo," Joe Catalini said.

"I told you to listen," Paavo Ohmstetter said. "You better do that, and you better get it right the first time around. The way this thing is set, I don't have to give any second chances. You ready?"

Joe Catalini said, "I will be, after you tell me who was your wife's father."

"Zalman Fruchter," Paavo Ohmstetter said.

In a tired voice Joe said, "I'm ready."

"I know who's got Stevie," Paavo Ohmstetter said. "They told me what it's going to cost you to get him back alive. They instructed me to pass the terms on to you."

"Do it carefully," Joe Catalini said. "I'm going to sit down."

32

Joe Catalini had not been sitting down on the rainy Sunday in 1922 when Mr. Shale led Troop 24 out of the basement of the public library on Edina Street for the weekly hike to Falcon Island. The rain was unpleasant, but it took more than rain to stop Mr. Shale.

To him the Sunday hike was the most important activity of the troop week. During the bad winter months he was forced to restrict this activity. Floating ice in the Mississippi put the Falcon Island ferry out of action from December to February. During those months, therefore, the actual hikes did not take place. Under Mr. Shale's direction, however, the preparations for these hikes went on relentlessly. According to the janitor of the Edina Street Public Library, planning activities in the basement on winter Sundays were more punishing to his building than anything that happened after the actual hikes started in the spring.

These activities were particularly strenuous during the 1921–1922 winter months. That year the All-Minneapolis Boy Scout Council announced a city-wide Summer Rally for mid-July. Mr. Shale's pride in his troop was not small. His competitive instinct was enormous. Mr. Shale made no secret of his determination that Troop 24 turn in a creditable performance. When he was not leading Troop 24, Mr. Shale was teaching high school English. He was precise about the use of words.

"By creditable," he told the boys in his troop at the Friday-night meeting that preceded the first Sunday hike of the 1922 season, "I mean you see that wall?"

Mr. Shale pointed behind him and over his head.

"We're coming back from that rally in July with at least one first-place pennant to hang up there," he said. "Sunday morning, when we get over to Falcon Island, the first thing we'll do around our campfire is lay out our strategy."

Because of the rain it didn't quite work out that way. Getting down to the river was not difficult. In good weather, under Mr. Shale's sharp disciplinary eye, it was a twenty-minute walk from the library. In the rain it took half an hour. Also, even under Mr. Shale's sharp disciplinary eye, thirty-seven soaked-to-the-skin boys ranging in age from eleven to fifteen were not a very impressive spectacle of coordinated physical movement. Fortunately, nobody showed up at the Falcon Island ferry slip to watch the scouts of Troop 24 and their scoutmaster embark.

"Pick it up, men," Mr. Shale said tartly.

What he had himself picked up as an artillery-battalion second lieutenant at Château-Thierry was a memory that in 1922 had not yet dimmed. Mr. Shale knew from personal experience how human beings gathered under stress for group action could perform. He was not yet old enough, nor had he yet lived far enough away from his war experience, to begin to grasp that having once seen men at their best, he was doomed from then on to one long descent into dis-illusion.

On that rainy Sunday in 1922, young Mr. Shale was aware only that the men with whom he had forged a shining memory at Château-Thierry had been cut from a different bolt of cloth than these thirty-seven rain-soaked boys on the banks of the Mississippi.

"Pick it up," he continued to say with waning conviction and mounting irritation. "Pick it up."

They did, at least to the extent of managing to stumble onto the ferry without physical injury or numerical loss. It was a short ride. So that when they stumbled ashore on Falcon Island, the thirty-seven dripping boys were still a reasonably cohesive unit. Mr. Shale's sharp eye told him that without help this could not continue for very long.

"Senior Patrol Leader Catalini!" he rapped out.

"Yes, sir!" Joe rapped back.

He was still two months short of his fourteenth birthday. Joe's experience in the barbershop on Minnehaha Avenue, however, and selling newspapers on Anoka Avenue, had cemented into his makeup bits and pieces of knowledge that the advancing years might sharpen but would never basically change. One of these was an acute awareness of the importance of responding with confidence to the call of a superior who was clearly losing it.

Mr. Shale said, "You know the island better than a lot of the younger boys."

It was intended as a statement of fact. Only the boy to whom it was addressed sensed in the firm voice the faint tremor of the not quite totally concealed orison.

"Yes, sir," Joe Catalini said.

"You know Whampoa's Open," Mr. Shale said.

"Yes, sir," the boy said.

"That's where we're heading," Mr. Shale said. "As long as it's still raining, I'm going to keep the troop here with me in the ferry shed for the briefing. That should take about an hour. By that time the worst of this rain will be over. The ferry captain just had a radio report, so here's the plan. While I stay here and conduct the briefing session in the ferry shed, I want you to head across to Whampoa's Open and do a thorough recce. You know what I mean, Senior Patrol Leader Catalini."

"Yes, sir," Joe Catalini said.

He didn't, but Joe suspected Mr. Shale didn't either. Out of the boy's suspicion, however, came the certainty that anything Joe did at Whampoa's Open would meet with Mr. Shale's approval if, when the scoutmaster arrived with the thirty-six other members of the troop, the facility was ready to receive them.

Not, of course, with open arms. Whampoa's Open had not been designed to do that even under the best conditions. On this dreary day anything into which the boys of Troop 24 marched would be a triumph if it was even slightly better than the conditions under which they had been traveling since they had left the Edina Street public library on the mainland.

"On the double, then, Senior Patrol Leader Catalini," Mr. Shale said. "We'll see you in about an hour."

In spite of the pouring rain, this estimate seemed reasonable to Joe Catalini. Whampoa's Open was a forty-acre tract of undeveloped land two miles from the ferry. The dirt road, like all the roads on Falcon Island, was not very good. Nothing on Falcon Island was very good, which was the reason the All-Minneapolis Boy Scout Council had inherited Whampoa's Open from a bankrupt real estate developer.

On this Sunday, plowing his way through the mud and the rain into the campsite, Joe skirted the huge central area. This consisted of a sprawled mass of large square wooden platforms separated by winding lanes. On these platforms visiting Boy Scouts pitched the pup tents they brought to Whampoa's Open in pack rolls on their backs, or set up the larger group tents that were supplied by the caretaker from the store at the north end of the tract. The words "supplied" and "caretaker" were a little confusing.

At one time, when the project had been started, it seemed reasonable to guess that provision had been made for some sort of hired help to look after the place. If so, the provision had been abandoned before Joe Catalini started coming to Whampoa's Open. He had never seen anybody on the place except, once in a while, another group of Boy Scouts from some other part of Minneapolis. These meetings were rare.

Most of the time when Joe and the members of Troop 24 came to Whampoa's Open they were the only human beings visible on the not very attractive place.

It was not surprising, therefore, that the place always looked run-down. To a camping party, especially a camping party led by so resourceful a man as Mr. Shale, this was no drawback. In Mr. Shale's view, campsites were supposed to be rough affairs. They were challenges. Experienced campers, applying their Scouting skills, were supposed to turn these rough surroundings into civilized habitations.

The fact that they always succeeded was a tribute to Mr. Shale and a surprise to Joe Catalini. The surprise was based on the fact that in spite of no caretakers and the run-down look, there were no evidences of vandalism. Nobody seemed to do very much for Whampoa's Open, but nobody seemed to do very much to it, either.

Joe Catalini knew that a vacant tenement on Minnehaha Avenue, for example, would not have been left with a single unsmashed window the day after the kids on the block learned nobody was living in the building.

The only windows at Whampoa's Open were in the sprawling log cabin that served as the area headquarters and storehouse. These were always, whenever Joe Catalini visited the place, filthy. They were also, however, always unbroken.

Joe was glad to see, as he came in out of the mud and the rain, that the windows were still intact. He crossed to the huge fireplace. It looked all right except for the woodpile, which was low. It didn't take Joe long to figure out the best thing he could do to get the place ready for his soaked-to-the-skin fellow members of Troop 24. It was what Mr. Shale would want him to do. Joe Catalini went out the back door and crossed to the woodshed.

The shed didn't look much different from the way it had looked when Joe had last been here at Whampoa's Open, back in October, but it felt different. It was a funny feeling to have about a shapeless, not very well constructed, clearly deteriorating woodshed.

Wondering why, as he stood in the doorway, Joe became aware that the funny feeling seemed to have something to do with the stacks of wood on the right. He moved across toward them, then stopped. Another funny feeling had entered the puzzling picture.

This new feeling nudged the boy to an uncomfortable awareness that he was doing something familiar, something he had done once before, in some other place. Then he saw the man lying at the base of the last stack on the right, and Joe Catalini knew what was giving him that sense of familiarity.

Not that the men looked alike. Not even remotely. This man was enormous. Six feet four, easy. Even more easily, two hundred and fifty pounds, maybe more. The huge body was encased in a sailor's navy blue pea jacket. The legs were tucked into knee-high hunting boots laced up tight with yellow leather thongs. The red-and-black hunting cap with a duckbill visor sat crookedly on the dead man's head because the head lay at an angle against the bottom log in the pile. And of course this man was not lying in a bathtub full of soapy water.

Just the same, Joe Catalini knew at once that the two men were brothers.

33

"How did you know that?" Max Lessing said.

"Well, you remember two years ago?" Joe Catalini said. "That Mr. Zalman Fruchter? A few days after he drowned in the bathtub up on the top floor?"

"Sort of," Max said carefully. "I never knew Mr. Fruchter personally. In those days, when my wife and I lived on Minnehaha Avenue, I used to pay the rent to your father downstairs in the barbershop. You want another cup of cocoa?"

"Yes," the boy said.

"Ellis!" Max Lessing shouted.

The swing door opened. Ida poked her head in.

"Ellis took the Buick down to Hueffer's for gas," she said. "Can I help?"

Max nodded toward the boy on the couch. "He wants more cocoa."

Ida said, "Bring in the cup."

She stepped back into the kitchen. Max pushed himself up out of the couch and came across to Joe Catalini's chair. He took the boy's cup and carried it across the living room to the swing door. Max pushed his way in to the kitchen.

"Besides cocoa," Ida said, "what else does he want?"

Max was not surprised by her asking the question that

was going through his own mind. Ida did that all the time. What surprised him was that she seemed troubled. She had been surprising him that way several times daily. Dr. Schieffelin assured him it was nothing to worry about.

"She's acting the way any other pregnant girl acts," Dr. Schieffelin said. "You're mixing up the way she took over little Claire two years ago with what's happening to her now. Taking over the Boyle baby was no problem. All girls like babies. It's like being given a new doll. But her own baby, that's something different. It's not like going to a toy store and buying a doll. Or finding one under the Christmas tree. It's a serious business. It takes a long time. All that time she's carrying a living thing around inside her, and all that time, no matter what I tell her, she's never quite sure what's going to happen. What the doll will look like. If she's going to have the baby successfully. Will it be painful. Things like that. For nine long months she has to live with a physical and mental discomfort that men don't understand. You're lucky that all you see is that now and then she seems worried. My advice to you is Don't you make things more difficult by also worrying. Everything will clear up once the baby is born."

Max could not help thinking how it had cleared up for Mr. Boyle, but he did not think about that long. He concentrated on what Ida had just said and answered with "What makes you think this kid wants something?"

"I'm not sure," Ida said. "But I remember him from Minnehaha Avenue, and he always made me a little uncomfortable."

"In what way?" Max said.

"I'm not sure about that either," Ida said. "You be careful, Max."

"With a fourteen-year-old boy?"

"That's what makes me uncomfortable," Ida said

"What makes you uncomfortable?" Max said.

"That he's only fourteen years old," Ida said.

Max took the fresh cup of cocoa and went back into the

living room. He was aware that his movements were slow and deliberate, as though he were walking along a stretch of sidewalk and trying to avoid stepping on the cracks. In a way, he was. He paused at Joe's chair.

"You warm enough?" he said.

"Yes, sir," Joe Catalini said.

Max pulled the blanket up around the boy's neck.

"Stay covered," he said. "Your Scout uniform is drying out by the kitchen stove."

Max dropped back onto the couch. The movement un-expectedly supplied a surprising clue to his discomfort. It reminded Max of that day on the *Friesland* when he had dropped into the shallow scooped iron of the pawl ring be-side the total stranger named Saul Sumeg. Max had that same feeling of expectancy. A move was being made in his direc-tion. All he had to do was sit and wait. What made it un-comfortable now, what made it even a little scary, was that the move Max was sitting and waiting for would be coming from a naked fourteen-year-old kid wrapped in a blanket.

"This man today," Max said in a manner it annoyed him to realize was fake casual. "You say you knew he was this Zalman Fruchter's brother?"

"Yes, sir," Joe Catalini said.

"How did you know that? Max said.

"After the first Mr. Fruchter drowned," Joe said, "this second man came to see my father in the barbershop. When he was in the barber shop he was wearing the same clothes he wore when I saw him this morning in the woodshed out at Whampoa's Open. He wasn't dead then, of course. I mean, he was alive two years ago when he came into the barbershop to talk to my father. But the thing was, you see, I never saw anybody dressed like that in Minneapolis, like a lumberjack, so I asked my father who this lumberjack was. He's Mr. Zalman Fruchter's brother, my father said, from Winnipeg. That's how I knew."

It was all said very carefully and clearly, the way a child would recite for a teacher who had called on him to answer a question in a classroom. The trouble was, Max did not feel like a teacher. He felt like a fool.

"This morning," Max said. "When you saw him out there in that woodshed on Falcon Island, you're sure it was the same man?"

"Not exactly the same," Joe Catalini said. "This morning he was dead."

Max squirmed a little in his chair. It was the sort of remark Oberfeldwebel Sauerlich used to make in the orderly room at Fürstenfeld.

"You find that makes a difference?" Max said, trying not to sound too obviously acidulous.

The boy said, "Well, you know, Mr. Lessing, lying down there by the pile of wood this morning he didn't look as big as he looked two years ago standing up in my father's barbershop."

"How did he look to the police?" Max said.

Joe said, "The police haven't seen him yet."

Max gave the boy another look. This was not an Oberfeldwebel Sauerlich remark. This was a Harry Boyle remark. And this was a fourteen-year-old boy.

"What about the other people who have seen him?" Max Lessing said. "Like your scoutmaster, for instance."

"You mean Mr. Shale," the boy said.

"Whatever his name is," Max said.

"John Quincy Adams Shale," Joe Catalini said.

"What did John Quincy Adams Shale say when he saw this dead man in the woodshed?"

"Nothing," the boy said.

Max Lessing said, "Your scoutmaster saw a dead man in the woodshed and he said nothing?"

"Mr. Shale didn't see him," the boy said.

Max Lessing's uneasiness raised a cautioning finger. Nothing would be accomplished if he smacked this kid.

"How could that happen?" Max said.

"On account of the rain," the boy said. "It didn't stop. This morning, when we got off the ferry at Falcon Island,

Mr. Shale said as long as it was raining so hard he'd keep the troop in the ferry shed for a briefing session, and he sent me ahead up to Whampoa's Open to get things ready for when the rain stopped."

"You told me all that," Max said. "That's why you made the big fire in the fireplace."

"Yes, sir," Joe Catalini said.

Max Lessing said, "Now tell me what happened after you had the fire going."

"The ferry captain who gave Mr. Shale the radio report, he was wrong," the boy said. "The rain didn't stop. When Mr. Shale and the troop arrived they were all pretty wet. So everybody stayed inside, around the fire, drying out their uniforms."

"How long?" Max said.

"All day," Joe Catalini said. "It takes a long time to dry a Scout uniform in front of a fire. Most of them were still a little wet when it came time to hike back to the four-o'clock ferry."

"You kept the fire going all day?" Max said.

"I had to," the boy said. "Everybody was soaked."

"Keeping the fire going all day," Max said, "you must have needed a lot of wood."

Joe said, "There's always plenty stacked out there in that woodshed."

"That's what I'm getting at," Max said. "Going out for more wood, somebody must have seen this dead man in the shed."

"No," the boy said.

Max Lessing said, "What do you mean, no?"

The boy said, "I thought right away If anybody goes out to that shed for wood they'll find what I found when I went out to that shed for wood. But it didn't happen."

"How come?" Max said.

"Because I was the only one who went out to that shed for wood."

"I see," Max said.

246

He didn't. He wished Ida were in the room.

"You arranged that?" Max said.

"It wasn't hard," the boy said. "When it comes to carrying wood for a fire, nobody will fight you for the chance to do it. Especially when it's raining."

"Not even this John Quincy Adams Shale?"

"He's our scoutmaster," Joe Catalini said. "Scoutmasters don't carry wood."

"I didn't know that," Max said.

"Never," the boy said. "Most of the time not even senior patrol leaders."

"What's a senior patrol leader?" Max said.

"Me," Joe Catalini said.

"But today a senior patrol leader did carry wood?"

The boy said, "On account of I didn't want anybody but me to see that dead man."

Max Lessing looked up at the glass clock on the marble mantelpiece.

"It's almost six o'clock," he said. "You found him in the woodshed when?"

"The ferry left for Falcon Island at nine sharp," Joe Catalini said. "That's the schedule. Eight minutes to get across; then Mr. Shale sends me up to Whampoa's Open, it's two miles; the rain and the mud and all, say it took me an hour. It didn't, but say an hour. Okay?"

"Sure, yes," Max Lessing said.

He could see the importance of trying to think ahead of this kid. Unfortunately, he didn't see what direction his thinking should take.

"So I get to the log house say around ten-fifteen," the boy said. "And a few minutes later I found the man in the woodshed."

"Say ten-thirty?" Max Lessing said.

"About, yes," Joe Catalini said.

"And now it's almost six o'clock," Max said. "So what you're saying, you think for seven and a half hours nobody except you has seen that dead man?"

The boy said, "That's right. Except of course I don't know about since we all left Whampoa's Open. We came back on the four-o'clock ferry."

"The police, then, they could have found the body since you and Mr. Shale and all those Scouts left the place?"

"They could have," the boy said. "But I don't think they did."

A suspicion crossed Max's mind. Could it be this little bastard was playing with him?

Max said, "What makes you so sure the police haven't found the body since the whole bunch of you left the place?"

"Well, you see how it is," Joe Catalini said. "In this kind of weather, this rain today, nobody is going out to Whampoa's Open on a hike."

"Nobody except you and this John Quincy Adams Shale and thirty-six other kids," Max Lessing said.

The sarcasm clearly went over the boy's head.

"Nobody after us today is what I mean," he said. "This time of day it's too late for a hike, and the police, they don't go out there except maybe when the weather's good, for a checkup or something. Days like this, though, the rain and all, the police don't go out on checkups. Even suppose they did, say they went out after we all left on the four-o'clock ferry, it still wouldn't matter."

"Why not?" Max said.

"Because the last trip I made out to the woodshed for a log to put on the fire, I shoveled up over the body a lot of kindling. I mean I covered it up is what I mean."

"I see," Max said once more.

Max was aware, of course, that he did not see a damn thing. It occurred to him that he was only six years older than this kid. At twenty, he shouldn't be having all this trouble with a fourteen-year-old. Max wondered if it was because he had never before dealt with a boy on this level, or because he had never before dealt with this kind of boy. He was not handing out a Hershey bar to a kid. It was he, Max Lessing, who was being handed something, and what he was

248

being handed was a tough ticket by a smooth operator. It was like starting out across the street and finding in the middle of the gutter you had put on the wrong shoes for this kind of unexpectedly dangerous slippery paving.

"Where is Mr. Shale now?" Max Lessing said.

"Home," Joe Catalini said.

"And the other thirty-six boys from your troop?"

"From the ferry they all went home," the boy said.

"But you didn't," Max said.

"No sir."

"You came up here to Columbia Heights," Max said.

"Yes, sir," Joe Catalini said.

"Why?"

The boy said, "This thing from the dead man."

"The dead man in the woodshed on Falcon Island," Max Lessing said, nailing it down the way Coley Scudder nailed things down in a meeting.

"In Whampoa's Open on Falcon Island," Joe Catalini said. "Yes, sir."

"Okay," Max Lessing said. "Now what thing are you talking about?"

The boy set down the cup of cocoa on the end table next to the silver-framed picture of Ida holding Claire all wrapped up in a blanket the day she had helped Mr. Boyle bring the baby home two years ago from the hospital. Then Joe Catalini's hand came up out of the blanket. He was holding a white envelope.

"This thing," the boy said.

Max reached across from the couch and took the envelope.

"There's nothing in it," he said.

"No, sir."

"Why did you bring it to me?" Max said.

"Up in the corner," the boy said. "The return address. It's printed."

"I see that," Max said. "It's my address. This house here on Southeast Eighth Street. This is one of my envelopes."

"That's how I knew to come here," Joe Catalini said.

This time Max did see. What he saw was an eye-opener. This little fourteen-year-old punk was blackmailing him.

Almost with relief, Max Lessing said, "Mr. Shale and the other boys when you all got off the ferry from Falcon Island, they all went home, but you didn't. You came up here to see me just because my name and return address are printed in the upper left-hand corner of this envelope."

"Not just because of that," the boy said.

"What else?"

"The dead man in that woodshed," the boy said. "He was holding the envelope in his hand."

"I see," Max Lessing said again. This time he said it with something not unlike admiration. He added, "How old are you?"

"Not exactly fourteen," Joe Catalini said. "In two months I'll be."

"When you grow up," Max said, "what do your mother and father want you to be?"

"I have no mother," the boy said. "She died."

"Your father?" Max said. "What does he want you to be?"

The boy said, "Anything but a barber."

Pause. It took Max by surprise. Not because at this moment he did not welcome a pause. On the contrary. In his mind Max had planned a pause as the next beat in this conversation. The boy, however, quite clearly had his own plans.

From the way Joe Catalini picked up his cup of cocoa and took a sip, Max had the feeling the boy had arranged the pause. More important, however, was another feeling. Max Lessing's feeling that he had found the place where he could move in and take hold of this situation.

He said, "Maybe I better have a talk with your father."

34

The results of the conversation were several. Some immediate. Others long-range. All the results, however, were, in Max Lessing's new English phrase, on the plus side.

"What's the plus side?" Ida said.

Picking up new English phrases had started as a game. It had become a small rivalry.

Max laughed and said, "The Lessing side, of course."

"Yours and mine," Ida said.

"Ours."

"Never forget that," Ida said.

Max wondered what she meant. Since the baby's birth she had put on a little weight. Max liked that. Ida didn't. She wasn't going to become one of those fat Hungarian farm girls with whom she had grown up. This was America. Ida was modeling her figure on Norma Talmadge. That was all right with Max too. These days everything was all right with Max except Ida's occasional remarks like this one.

He wondered uneasily if she had ever wondered about all those women at the back doors of the houses in Sunningdale to whom he used to sell things from the pushcart. Those days were over, of course, but there were other women. Maybe that was why he thought he heard things in Ida's remarks that were not there. Or perhaps it was because of the book Ida gave him the next day. It was called *One of Ours*.

"You want me to read this?" he said.

"If your English is good enough," Ida said.

Max said, "It's good enough to get us this house on Columbia Heights."

He was sensitive about his English.

"We've had this house on Columbia Heights for two years," Ida said. "There are other things in this country besides Columbia Heights."

Max Lessing was well aware of this. The knowledge kept him awake at night.

"I'm willing to learn anything," he said. "Even English."

Ida said, "From this book Susie Shale says you'll learn faster."

Susie Shale was the wife of the Troop 24 scoutmaster. The Shales had come into the lives of Ida and Max Lessing soon after Max had his on-the-plus-side talk with Angelo Catalini. The talk had taken place the day after young Joe Catalini showed up in his dripping Scout uniform on the Lessing doorstep.

"My son, Joe, says you want to have a talk with me," the barber said to Max Lessing when Ellis showed him into the living room. "Joe said I should come here tonight."

"What I wanted to talk to you about," Max said, "I didn't think a barbershop is the right place."

Angelo Catalini said, "Not my barbershop."

The words were not much. The manner of their delivery was a biography. Max saw at once where young Joe Catalini had come by his unique quality. This comic-opera wop was clearly no *shmuck*.

"You'll have something to drink?" Max said.

"So long as it's not sacramental wine."

"I don't handle that stuff anymore," Max Lessing said.

The barber said, "I've tried some of the stuff you handle now."

"You like it?"

"Except for what it costs," Angelo Catalini said. "I have to cut a bushel of hair to pay for a belt."

"In this house my friends don't pay for anything," Max Lessing said.

He went to the golden oak sideboard. After the crystal chandelier it was the thing Max liked best in Harry Boyle's former living room. It reminded him of the sideboard in which his mother in Vetzprem kept the plates she used on Friday night for the sabbath dinner. Max opened the carved door. He took out a bottle of Kirkbean and a couple of glasses. He poured generously and brought the glasses back across the room.

"Here's to Joey," Max said.

"Not Joey," Angelo Catalini said. "Joe."

"Here's to Joe," Max Lessing said.

They drank. Catalini made a complimentary noise with his lips.

"Better than that sacramental wine I used to steal out of your pushcart in the backyard," he said.

"When did you do that?" Max said.

"Barbers get up a lot earlier than you think," Angelo Catalini said.

"Sit over there," Max said. "It's a very comfortable chair."

"I know," the barber said, sitting down. "This is where Joe sat yesterday while you had his uniform drying by the stove out in the kitchen."

"How do you know that?" Max said.

"Joe told me."

"He tells you everything?" Max said.

"Not much the kid leaves out," Angelo Catalini said.

"Another belt?" Max Lessing said.

"If we earn it," the barber said.

"How do you mean?"

Angelo Catalini lifted his glass.

"One to get started," he said. "The second to finish. If there's anything that gets finished."

Max Lessing started to say "I see." He caught himself in

time. Yesterday, when the barber's son was sitting in that chair, Max had grown a little tired of saying "I see" to a fourteen-year-old boy wrapped in a blanket. No point in risking the same thing happening while talking to the kid's father.

"I'll tell you why I asked Joe if you and I could have a talk," Max said.

Angelo Catalini said, "I'm listening."

"I never got to know you very well when we lived down on Minnehaha Avenue," Max Lessing said.

The barber said, "Our hours were different."

Max laughed and said, "If they weren't, you wouldn't have had a chance to swipe those samples of my Passover wine."

"I got to know your wife a little," Angelo Catalini said. "She was never late with the rent every month, and Mrs. Schiff on the third floor, she always said nice things about you. I hear the missus is expecting a baby."

"Our first," Max Lessing said. "We have a little foster daughter two years old, but this will be the first of our own. That's the reason I wanted to have this talk with you."

"I'm a barber," Angelo Catalini said. "What can I do for a baby?"

"You could do something for his father," Max said.

"Any barber?" Angelo Catalini said. "Or just me?"

"Just you," Max Lessing said.

The barber said, "I must have something you want."

"That's right," Max said.

"What?"

"Joe," Max Lessing said.

"The boy makes an impression," the barber said.

"He made an impression on me," Max said. "Two years ago? That man who owned the tenement? What was his name?"

"Fruchter," the barber said. "Zalman Fruchter."

"That's it," Max Lessing said. "You remember when they found him drowned in the bathtub on the top floor?"

254

"They?" Angelo Catalini said. "You mean Joe. Didn't you read the papers?"

Max Lessing said, "You bet I did. That's when Joe made such an impression on me. The way he handled himself. The way he talked to the police."

"That's one of the things he learned in the barbershop," Angelo Catalini said.

"What?" Max said.

"How to talk to the police."

"I never saw any police in your barbershop," Max said.

"Different hours," Angelo Catalini said.

"I forgot that," Max Lessing said.

"Most people do," Catalini said. "They think, What's a barbershop? A place to get your hair cut. It's that, naturally. But because it's that, it's also a hell of a lot more, if you know what I mean."

Max Lessing said, "I think I do."

"I'll bet you do," Angelo Catalini said. "A man doesn't move from sacramental wine on a pushcart to Kirkbean Scotch whiskey on Columbia Heights in two years unless he knows things like that."

Max was pleased by the older man's compliment, but it seemed sensible not to dwell on it. What he wanted was going to cost money, and he had money, but not as much as Mr. Catalini seemed to think. Not yet, anyway.

"I asked you to come for a talk," Max said. "But all of a sudden I have this feeling."

"What feeling?" the barber said.

"If I hadn't asked you to come here," Max Lessing said, "I'd have got an invitation to your place."

"Close," Angelo Catalini said. "But no cigar."

"How close?"

"A boy like Joe," the barber said. "He's got a father like me. He finds things on rainy days in places like Whampoa's Open. You think a boy like that gets off the ferry from Falcon Island and he comes running up here to show them to strangers?"

"I might have thought that yesterday," Max Lessing said.

"What do you think today?" Catalini said.

"I think today from the ferry Joe went home," Max Lessing said. "He told you what he found at Whampoa's Open, and you told him to come right up here, wet uniform and all."

"You got the cigar," the barber said.

"I think I've got something else, too," Max Lessing said.

Angelo Catalini said, "Tell me."

"You and me," Max said. "I think we want something from each other."

"Not 'you and me,' " the barber said. " 'You and I.' "

"What's the difference?" Max Lessing said.

"You need help with your English," Catalini said. "You're not going to stay here on Columbia Heights any more than you stayed on Minnehaha Avenue. You'll be moving on. Men like you always do. Where you're going, you'll go faster and you'll stay longer if you talk the language right. I'll tell Mrs. Shale to come see you. She's a nice girl, Susie Shale. A very fine American type. College graduate and everything. She's the wife of Joe's scoutmaster. I cut his hair. She gives English lessons. She's helped me a lot, and I've got her helping Joe. After a while you'll know not to say to a barber 'You and me want something from each other.' You'll say 'You and I want something from each other.' "

"Let's say I said it," Max Lessing said. "Now I'll tell you what I want from you."

The barber said, "You don't have to say it again. You already told me you want Joe. All we have to figure out now is the terms."

"That's what I call laying it on the line," Max said. "I like that, Mr. Catalini."

The barber said, "I don't have time to lay things any other place."

"Why not?" Max Lessing said.

"I'm dying," Catalini said.

Max didn't know what to say to that, so he fell back on Oberfeldwebel Sauerlich's rule: Say nothing. For a while, neither did the barber. Catalini finally broke the silence with "I had you figured for the sort of man who wouldn't come riding in with that shit you're sorry. I had you figured right. For Joe's sake I'm glad."

Irrelevantly, Max found himself wishing he could do something to keep this wop from dying. Max Lessing had not found many people in America about whom he felt this way.

"The way I'm beginning to do business," Max said, "I find I have to go away a lot. It makes me uncomfortable to leave my wife alone in the house while I'm away. Not only with a two-year-old little girl, but now also with a new baby boy. By alone I don't mean servants or bodyguards or those things. We've got Ellis, the butler, and Miss Liddy, she's the nurse, and if I need muscle there's the staff in my warehouse on Wayzata Boulevard. But that's not what my wife and I want. What we want, we want somebody that's part of the family. An older man or an older woman wouldn't be right. A boy of fourteen, a boy that you could say was growing up with the same family, like an older brother, that sort of boy is exactly right."

Angelo Catalini said, "There are other boys of fourteen."

"They're not Joe," Max Lessing said.

"The time you lived on Minnehaha Avenue," the barber said, "I'm beginning to think maybe our hours weren't all that different."

Max said, "He's not the kind of boy you'd have to wait until you had the same hours before you notice him."

"You got plans for him?" Catalini said.

"Right now only one," Max Lessing said. "To grow up here with us as a member of the family."

The barber said, "Joe is pretty grown up already."

"You must have had some plans in mind for him yourself," Max Lessing said.

257

"I shave a lot of politicians," Angelo Catalini said. "I've never known one of them was in the same league with what Joe could be."

"He could be even better," Max Lessing said, "if he was trained as a lawyer."

The barber held out his glass.

"Looks like we've both earned that second belt," he said.

Max took the glass and carried it with his own to the sideboard. Pouring the Kirkbean, he said, "You don't have to answer this one."

"If I can't," the barber said, "I won't."

"How long do the doctors say?" Max Lessing said.

"Fuck the doctors," Catalini said.

"That gives us something to drink to," Max said.

He came across the room with the glasses and handed one to the barber. "Fuck the doctors," Max Lessing said.

"I'll drink to that," Angelo Catalini said.

"When Joe walks up there to that platform to pick up his law-school diploma," Max Lessing said, "you and I we'll be sitting side by side down in front."

PART IV
1932

35

Angelo Catalini did not make it. He died in 1922, six months after Joe, just turned fourteen, came to live with the Lessings in the big house on Southeast Eighth Street.

Max Lessing, on the other hand, was seated ten years later in the Sanders Theatre audience, down in front as promised ten years earlier, on the day Joe graduated from Harvard Law School. Max could not see Joe. The boy was just another mortarboard in the phalanx of 379 young men who made up the 1932 Cambridge graduating class.

"They call out the names one by one," Ida explained in her seat beside Max. "As each boy's name is called he gets up from over there on our left, all those square black hats, and he walks up there to the platform, and his diploma is handed to him. It's done alphabetically, one by one, so stop being nervous. After all these years you know what Joe looks like, and you certainly know what his name sounds like when it's called out loud, so sit back and relax. You won't miss him."

Max sat back, but he could not relax. There were too many preliminary speeches. Finally, the man on the platform cleared his throat and said into the microphone: "George McCallister Aaronson." The first mortarboard broke from the phalanx on Max's left. A boy rose under the mortarboard and started down the aisle to the platform. Somebody tapped Max's shoulder. He turned. It was Hymie Shantz, halitosis and all, standing in the aisle. He was bent over obsequiously, as though angling for the proper point of attack from which to bite Max's ear.

"Mr. Max," he whispered.

"For God's sake," Max said, "not now."

Several heads turned.

"Max, please," Ida murmured.

"Later," Max forcefully whispered.

The bodyguard flinched but stood his ground.

"Long distance," Hymie Shantz whispered.

Max said, "I just told you—"

"You're telling it to everybody in the Sanders Theatre," Ida said.

Her voice was lower than a murmur, but sharper than a slap.

Max said, "You were the one who insisted we should bring him along from Minneapolis."

"As a bodyguard," Ida said. "Not as an interrupter of Joe's graduation."

Hymie Shantz did not move. His sad, sagging face brought his penetrating voice closer to Max Lessing's ear.

"Chicago," he said.

Max shot a glance at Ida. She was watching George McCallister Aaronson, now bareheaded and with his flat hat under his left arm, take his diploma with one hand from the man at the microphone; transfer it to the other; receive a handshake; then, after passing the lectern, restore the mortarboard to his head. Its tassel, which before had hung from its right edge, now fell to the left. Ida was telling herself she was sure when Joe's turn came he would manage the little ceremony with much more grace, when she became aware of an eruption on her left. She turned. Max was on his feet.

"Be right back," he muttered.

He placed his commencement program on the seat and grunted something unintelligible. He edged out into the aisle and followed Hymie Shantz up to the back of the auditorium.

"Gregory Caulfield Atwater," the man on the platform said into the microphone.

Ida turned back to the platform. She had left her home and little Claire and Norman to come all the way across the country to sit here in Cambridge and watch Joe receive his diploma. She was going to do just that. If Max couldn't arrange things better than to receive long-distance calls from Chicago in the middle of a ceremony to which he had been looking forward eagerly for ten years, that was Max's problem.

Then one of the words Ida had just spoken to herself seemed to pop up in her mind, the way the numbers popped up on the call box in the kitchen at home when somewhere in the house somebody wanted to summon Ellis. Ida felt her forehead crease as she examined the word.

"Chicago," she said to herself.

Out in the hall, following Hymie Shantz to a booth in which Hymie's assistant was immobilizing the phone for his boss by holding the receiver free of the hook, Max said the same thing.

"Chicago?"

"Yes, sir," Hymie Shantz said. "I wouldn't have bothered you, because I know what you said how important this is, Mr. Joe's graduation, but she said it was very important and if I interrupted you she said you would understand why."

"All right, all right," Max said.

He took the phone from Hymie's assistant and stepped with it into the booth.

"Hello?"

"Max?"

"Yes."

"Alma."

"What do you want?"

"We'll begin," Alma Pine said, "with I don't want to be talked to in that tone of voice."

263

"For God's sake," Max Lessing said. "It's the middle of the graduation. They've started to call the kids up for their diplomas. I told you how important this is."

"Before you left Minneapolis yesterday," Alma said, "you called me here in Chicago and told me how important Chicago is."

Max's mind came out of the Sanders Theatre auditorium and took up a listening position in the phone booth.

"Sorry, honey," he said.

"Don't be sorry," Alma Pine said. "Just be a little polite for a change."

Max Lessing said, "I said I'm sorry."

"It would be nice," she said, "if once in a while you'd stop treating me so you always have to end up saying you're sorry."

"Oh, God," Max Lessing muttered.

"I heard that," Alma said.

"How is Chicago, honey?"

"If you have to work for Billy Minsky," Alma Pine said, "don't do it in Chicago."

Listening to her babble was not for Max Lessing a new experience. Listening to her doing it at the other end of a long-distance call transformed an old experience into a new excitement. Max had been seeing her for years while she talked on the phone in the bedroom of her suite in the Nokomis Hotel on Anoka Avenue in Minneapolis, sprawled on her stomach while with her free hand she lazily scratched herself. Now, standing in the phone booth out in the corridor of the Sanders Theatre, he could see her out there in Chicago, scratching away, and all of a sudden with a sinking heart Max Lessing knew again, as he had known over and over during the past nine years, why it had lasted nine years, and why it would probably last another nine or another ninety or another nine hundred, God help him.

"Alma," he said.

"Yes, Max," she said.

"I apologize," he said. "It's just you know how I feel, how

264

much this kid's graduation means to me. It's made me jumpy. I apologize, like I said. Now tell me why you called, honey."

"You listening?" Alma said.

"Didn't I just say so?"

"Really listening?" she said.

"Really listening, honey," Max Lessing said.

"McAdoo just switched from Smith," Alma Pine said.

"What?"

"McAdoo just threw his votes to this Roosevelt," Alma Pine said.

Max Lessing said, "Oh, Jesus."

She said, "It just came over the radio here in my dressing room."

"It say how many votes?" Max said.

"No, but it said all the votes McAdoo had," Alma said. "And it said they're enough to swing the convention to this Roosevelt."

"Listen—" Max said.

"I can't," Alma Pine said. "I've got to run now, so here it is again. McAdoo just swung all his committed delegates to this Roosevelt. Al Smith is shitting bricks. The McAdoo votes put this Roosevelt over the top. You know what that means?"

Max Lessing said, "Yes, honey, I do."

"It means this Roosevelt, whoever he is," Alma said, "it means he's got the nomination."

Max Lessing said, "It means more than that."

"What?" Alma Pine said.

He could see her scratching herself again.

"Tell you what," Max said. "On the way home I'll stop off in Chicago for the night and tell you in person what it means."

"How about the ball and chain?"

"It beats me the way you keep worrying about that," Max Lessing said. "I've been handling it for nine years without any skin off anybody's nose, haven't I?"

She was saying some more, but he didn't wait to listen. He hung up and came out of the booth.

"While I'm in the auditorium," he said to Hymie Shantz, "do something about the train tickets. Mrs. Lessing is going back to Minneapolis alone. I'm stopping over in Chicago."

"Yes, sir," Hymie Shantz said.

"Did I miss anything?" Max said as he slipped into the seat beside Ida.

She said, "Listen."

"James Russell Jennings," the man on the platform said into the microphone.

A mortarboard rose from the phalanx on Max's left. The boy started down the aisle to the platform.

"Jennings is a J," Ida said. "The tenth letter in the alphabet. Catalini is a C, the third letter in the alphabet."

"I missed it, huh?" Max Lessing said.

"Maybe it was worth it," Ida said.

"What?"

"Who was calling?" Ida said.

"One of the usual birdbrains from Winnipeg," Max said.

"I thought Hymie Shantz said Chicago."

"What?" Max said.

"Never mind," Ida said. "Joe won't know you missed seeing him get his diploma. I won't tell him."

"Thanks," Max said. "I wouldn't want to hurt the kid's feelings."

"Don't worry about it," Ida said. "At least you won't miss him at Ganyi's Gardens."

266

36

The last person who had been missed at Ganyi's Gardens was William Jennings Bryan. That was in 1896.

The train carrying the Boy Orator of the Platte by accident failed to make its scheduled stop in Minneapolis on the tour that took Bryan through his record-breaking six hundred deliveries of the Cross of Gold speech in every corner of the country. Sandor Ganyi, founder of the pleasure dome that bore his name, was furious.

The Grand Ballroom of his Gardens had been reserved by the Democratic National Committee for Bryan's only appearance in Minnesota. Ganyi had spent a good deal of money advertising the event. Every ticket had been sold. When Bryan did not show up, Ganyi had to return every penny. The deposit forfeited by the Democratic National Committee was a small fraction of the sum he had paid out on promotion.

Worse than this financial loss, however, was Ganyi's loss of face with the citizens of Minneapolis. The fact that he had been scrupulous about returning their money did not change the fact that the ticket holders had been denied an event to which they had looked forward. Ganyi sank for a while into a dark mood of contemplation. He came out of it with an idea.

Sandor Ganyi got in touch with the Republican National Committee. He offered them the free use of Ganyi's Gardens if they would arrange an appearance in it for their candidate. The Republican National Committee saw a chance to plug a hole. Minneapolis was not a Republican stronghold. Ganyi's offer was accepted.

The Republican candidate showed up on schedule. As an orator he was not in the same league with Bryan. But he did step up to the plate in Minneapolis. The day after the votes were counted, Sandor Ganyi pointed this out in a full-page ad in the *Minneapolis Star*.

WE PUT MC KINLEY IN THE WHITE HOUSE, his advertisement said. COME TO GANYI'S GARDENS AND PUT SOME JOY IN YOUR LIFE.

The citizens of Minneapolis adopted the suggestion with enthusiasm. In the course of their adoption they also put into their stomachs vast quantities of the best Pilsner brewed in the Midwest. The Eighteenth Amendment changed the place where it was brewed, but not where it was consumed. Max Lessing's business was responsible for maintaining the steady flow between brewer and consumer. The popularity of Ganyi's Gardens was at its peak when Max rented the Main Ballroom for a party to celebrate Joe Catalini's graduation from law school.

"Here's what I want," Max Lessing had said to the bowling-ball-shaped Hungarian the day he and Ida took the train to Cambridge.

"Mr. Max," Sandor Ganyi said, "let me tell you what you want. For this boy you want the biggest and the best and the most wonderful thing in this city we've had since I put Mr. McKinley in the White House."

Max Lessing's forefinger went up.

"Plus?" he said.

"Plus the Pilsner should be Sauerlich," Sandor Ganyi said. "And the Scotch only Kirkbean."

"And if everybody in this town doesn't show up, from Mayor Nagel down—"

"From Governor Berg down," Sandor Ganyi corrected.

"—wearing their best bib and tucker—"

"—Sandor Ganyi better take the next ship back to the country where Mrs. Lessing and I we were both born," Sandor Ganyi said.

"Don't do that," Max Lessing said. "Mrs. Lessing is very fond of you."

"Likewise," Sandor Ganyi said. "This party, Mr. Max, believe me, they won't forget."

They didn't, in their different ways. It was his own way, of course, that Max Lessing remembered best. Mainly because he was late getting out of Chicago. The morning after he left Cambridge, Coley Scudder's phone call woke Max up in Alma Pine's suite at The Drake.

"Hate to do this to you," Max's lawyer said.

"You're not doing it to me," Max said. "You're doing it to Alma."

"Apologize to the lady for me," Coley Scudder said. "This is important. When did you plan to be back here in Minneapolis?"

Max said, "You're coming to Joe's party tonight?"

"The whole state of Minnesota is coming to Joe's party tonight."

"I'm giving the party," Max said. "Remember?"

The lawyer said, "What train you taking?"

"Two something," Max said. "Why?"

"There's a four-eleven," Scudder said. "Could you take that instead?"

Max said, "If you give me a good reason."

"This Roosevelt," Coley Scudder said, "is flying from Albany to Chicago to give his acceptance speech to the convention in person. There are people we do business with who are flying to Chicago from another place to hear the speech. If you could stay in Chicago long enough to have a talk with one of these men early this afternoon, it would be very helpful, Max. Very helpful indeed."

"Coley, I can't screw up the kid's party tonight," Max said.

269

Coley Scudder said, "The four-eleven will get you back here to Minneapolis in plenty of time."

"It's important?" Max said.

"Very."

In the twelve years since Harry Boyle had died and Max, as the foster father of little Claire, who was the major stockholder in the Innisfail Trading Company, had become Coley Scudder's most important client, Max could recall only one or two times when Coley had used the word "very" in just that way.

"Okay," Max said. "What do I have to do?"

"Stay where you are," Scudder said. "He'll come to Alma's suite at two sharp."

Max said, "What's his name?"

"Sir Digby Locksmoor," Coley Scudder said.

Sir Digby and Max had no trouble understanding each other. Susie Shale's lessons had done quite a lot for Max's accent. The subject of their discussion did all that was necessary for Sir Digby's accent. Max caught the four-eleven. When he came into the house Ellis had his bath ready and his dinner jacket laid out.

"Mrs. Lessing took Miss Claire and Mr. Norman and they went on ahead with Mr. Joe," Ellis said. "She thought it would be nice if in addition to the children one adult member of the family was at Ganyi's when the Governor arrives."

The twelve years had not changed Ellis' skullcap of woolly white corkscrew curls. Under Susie Shale's direction, however, Ida had been moving into areas of elegance that it seemed to Max, from what he saw in the movies, were British in tone. Ellis was beginning to sound not unlike Clive Brook.

"Mrs. Lessing is up there with the children at the top of the stairs waiting," said Sandor Ganyi when Max came into Ganyi's Gardens a half hour later.

Also waiting at the top of the stairs with his entourage was the Governor. He was chatting with Ida. She waved. So did Claire and Norman. Max waved back.

"How's it going?" Max said.

Sandor Ganyi said, "Listen."

He tipped his head so sharply that both wings of his sweeping mustache swayed. Max did the same. He had no mustache, but he had a good ear.

"Meyer Davis?" Max said.

"You ordered I should make the party the best," Sandor Ganyi said.

Max patted the shoulder of the bowling-ball-shaped proprietor of Ganyi's Gardens. "Thanks, Sandor."

It was the sort of exchange, Max realized with a sardonic inward grin, that belonged, like the restructured Ellis, in a Clive Brook movie. Max tried to remember what he and Ida had looked like on that day in Klein Berezna thirteen years ago when he had stopped to beg a cup of milk, but the attempt was shattered by Sandor Ganyi, who said, "For you, Mr. Max, anything. You better shake a leg. The Missus is looking impatient."

Moving up the sweeping white marble stairs with Hymie Shantz behind him, Max wondered about these Hungarians. They didn't use English words the way Angelo Catalini had used them, and the way Susie Shale was teaching Max to use them. The last word in the world you could apply with accuracy to Ida was impatient. She was a slow but steady girl. She waited things out.

"I almost got tired of waiting," Ida said when Max got to the top of the stairs.

As he always did when he came home from a trip, he stared at the children in surprise. Claire, at twelve, was turning into a blond beauty. Norman, at ten, was clearly going to be a football player. Already he came almost to Max's shoulder. Ida took his hand and Max kissed her as the children moved in, and he put his arms around them for a hug.

Ida said, "I told the Governor not even a presidential convention in Chicago could keep you away from this party for Joe."

"It didn't, but it tried," Max said. "Sorry to be late, kids."

"Better late than never," said Gerhardt Berg. "It's the first lesson you learn in that hot seat they call the gubernatorial chair. Max, I'd like a minute with you."

Claire and Norman trotted off into the ballroom.

"At your service, Gerry," Max said, peering across Ida's head in the direction taken by the children. "Where's Joe?"

"By the bandstand," Ida said. "With the Mayor's daughter. Come, I'll take you."

"Ida, darling," Governor Berg said. "You promised."

"That's true, Max, I did," Ida said. "I told the Governor if he stood by my side here at the top of the stairs, he'd see you before anybody else saw you when you came in, and I promised him he could have a few minutes alone before you went into the ballroom. I promised, Max. You keep my promise."

She pushed him toward Gerhardt Berg. The Governor took Max's left biceps in both his hands and tugged him out of the stream of merrymakers moving up the marble stairs to the ballroom. The walls sheltering the staircase were broken by alcoves from which statues of men and women famous in Hungarian history stared out at Sandor Ganyi's guests.

Governor Berg pulled Max Lessing into the shadow of the mounted legendary hero Arpad. Sword drawn, he glared out fearlessly across a mustache on which Sandor Ganyi had clearly modeled his own. It was not clear at what Arpad was glaring, but the legend on the bronze plaque at the feet of the marble hero indicated that he might be regarding balefully an invading horde led by Attila the Hun. The legend on the plaque was printed in Hungarian. Governor Berg's excited words were spoken in English.

"Max," he said, "I think we can beat him."

"Who?" Max said.

"This Roosevelt," Gerhardt Berg said.

"What makes you think that?"

"Just before I came over here, Pat Hurley called me from

the White House," Governor Berg said. "Pat had just been in with the President, and he said the President was relieved it's going to be this Roosevelt he'll be running against, but he wants all the help he can get."

Max said, "You going to give him any?"

"If I can get you to run for Mayor."

"What about Matt Nagel?" Max said. "How many mayors does this town need?"

"One, if he's a Republican," Governor Berg said. "Matt Nagel is a Democrat."

Coley Scudder came in under Arpad's drawn sword.

"Governor, I'm going to have to tear my client away for a minute," the lawyer said. "Once he gets upstairs into that ballroom I'll never get a chance to say the few words I've got to say before the festivities close in around him."

"Sure thing, Coley," the Governor said. "I've got my few words in. All I need is one from Max. How about it, Max? Yes or no?"

"Let me think about it," Max said. "I'll call you tomorrow."

"The President will be grateful," Governor Berg said.

He tapped Max's elbow and moved off to join Ida at the top of the stairs. Coley Scudder pulled Max into the shadow of King Louis II being speared by an Ottoman Turk at the Battle of Mohács in 1526.

"I don't know what kind of hot air Gerry Berg was feeding you," Scudder said. "But I don't think the gratitude of President Hoover is going to be worth much in the open market once this Roosevelt hits his stride."

"Neither do I," Max said. "Not after what I heard this afternoon in Chicago from your Englishman friend."

"Sir Digby called me a few minutes after your meeting at The Drake," Coley Scudder said. "Locksmoor said he liked you."

"He'd better," Max Lessing said. "Ida and I are going to be his houseguests in London next month."

37

They overstayed their visit. Max did not realize this was going to happen until the morning after he and Sir Digby signed the memorandum of agreement.

On that morning in 1932, when Max came out of the bathroom in the guest suite of the Locksmoor house on Park Lane, Ida was sitting up in bed, holding aloft a folded copy of *The Times* of London. She might have been acting out a charade that involved the arm and torch of the Statue of Liberty.

"Watch out," Max said to the maid who was setting the breakfast tray across Ida's lap. "My wife is about to play a chukker of her favorite sport."

In a deft crouch, Trimmer whipped her starched white cap away from the bed. The folded copy of *The Times* thwacked down on the delicately lace-trimmed pink crepe de chine blanket cover.

"Missed," Ida said.

"Pity," Trimmer said. "Better luck next time, Mrs. Lessing."

"The trouble with this country is there's always a next time," Ida said. "Where do you get all the flies?"

The maid said, "Do we have so many more than you have in America?"

"In America only poor people have flies," Ida said. "A rich man's house like this one, in America a fly would never get past the front door."

"Odd," Trimmer said. "How do the flies know they're forbidden to enter?"

"Screens," Ida said.

"Screens?" the maid said.

"I'll explain later," Ida said. "Right now you explain what you have to explain to Mr. Lessing."

Trimmer said, "Why, Mrs. Lessing, how ever did you know?"

"We've been living in this house a week," Ida said. "I noticed, Trimmer, whenever you bring in my breakfast and you have a message for Mr. Lessing, that piece of black lace up there on your cap, you have it pulled across so it hangs down in front as a reminder."

"Scotland Yard could do with you, Mrs. Lessing," the maid said. "Indeed they could."

"What's Scotland Yard?"

Max said, "First give me the message."

"There's a trunk call for you, sir," Trimmer said. "In the business room."

Reaching into the armoire for his jacket, Max said, "Who is it?"

The maid said, "Mr. Scudder, sir."

"You come all the way up here to tell me there's a trans-atlantic call waiting for me," Max said. "But first you have to finish a conversation with my wife about why in America we have flies in poor people's houses but not in rich people's houses?"

Trimmer said, "We didn't finish, sir."

"And we won't as long as Mr. Lessing is in the room," Ida said. "He's a born interrupter. Max."

"Not now," Max said. "Coley's waiting."

"He'll wait," Ida said. "He works for you. Come here."

Max crossed to the bed and dipped down. Ida reached across the breakfast tray and fussed expertly with his tie.

"All right," she said, tapping the knot. "Now on the long-distance phone you won't look like a bum."

Trimmer whinnied.

"Watch it, Ida," Max said as he moved to the door. "Susie Shale set me straight on that one. My last lesson she warned me the word means something entirely different over here in England."

Ida said, "What word?"

Max said, "Tell her, Trimmer."

He stepped out into the complicated viscera of the Locksmoor house. It was high and narrow, with a magnificent view of Hyde Park. The view was available only from the front rooms. The windows at the rear looked out on what seemed a haphazard mass of chimney pots and dirty gray stone arranged apparently without plan to form backyards of different sizes and shapes. For Max they were surprisingly similar to the backyards of Sunningdale and Columbia Heights through which he had shoved his pushcart when he was a kid of eighteen during his first few months in America.

Now that he was a young man of thirty, Max noted that these surprisingly similar backyards were also totally different. In Sunningdale and Columbia Heights Max did not remember seeing lace-capped maids hanging out laundry; liveried footmen polishing silver; parked Bentleys serving as footrests for cigarette-smoking uniformed chauffeurs; and men in knee-length white smocks delivering groceries from vans marked FORTNUM & MASON.

Another thing Max did not remember was anybody in Minneapolis who had any kind of money, living the way Max and Ida were now living on Columbia Heights, who did not have a telephone in the guest bedroom.

"Good morning, sir," the butler said at the door of what everybody in the house called the business room.

"Good morning," Max said. "If you want to know will I have coffee while I'm taking the call, the answer is yes, Bryce, thanks, I will."

"Very good, sir," the butler said.

276

Max went into the business room. Bryce pulled the door shut. Max circled the pieces of furniture about which all week Ida had been secretly making notes. He sat down at Sir Digby's desk, which Ida said was signed, meaning there was no chance of getting one like it, but it was so beautiful she was certainly going to try. Into the phone Max said, "Coley."

Coley Scudder's secretary said, "One moment, Mr. Lessing. I'll put him right on."

Running his hand along the satiny edge of the desk top, Max wondered why, if Ida was crazy about it, she shouldn't have the damn thing.

"Max?"

"Hi, Coley," Max said. "What are you and your secretary doing in the office at this hour? It's two in the morning back home, isn't it?"

"Yes, but I couldn't wait to hear," Coley said. "Are we in?"

"Like Flynn," Max said.

"You mind if I ask questions?"

"Everything went on schedule," Max said. "There's nothing to ask questions about."

"There's a question of time," Scudder said. "It will be a week at least before you and Ida get back here to Minneapolis. There's no point in wasting that many good working days. While you're on the high seas I can get with Locksmoor's people on this side. They're eager, Max. Waiting to go to contract. If you don't mind, I'd like to double-check and make sure when I go into a meeting with those boys I've got it direct from you, every word, every point, exactly the way you and Sir Digby hammered it out last night. We're not dealing with kindergarten kids, Max."

"After last night," Max said, "they know they're not dealing with Boy Scouts, either."

Coley Scudder said, "Rough?"

Max said, "Nothing like crossing in steerage on the *Friesland* thirteen years ago."

"I'll put Myra on the extension," Scudder said.

Max hesitated. He always did when he was in contact with Coley Scudder and something happened to remind Max he was dealing with a human being.

When Harry Boyle had introduced Max and Ida to the lawyer in his office on Chanhassen Circle twelve years ago, Max had thought of Scudder the way he thought of the lawyer's office. A place to which in America you had to go as a necessary precaution if you wanted certain things arranged in such a way that the authorities would not in the future be attracted to question the way you were doing those things. The papers Max and Ida had signed with Mr. Boyle in order to make his infant daughter Claire their legal responsibility had been part of that place. So had the man who had drawn up the papers.

Max did not think of that man as a human being any more than he thought the office in which he functioned or the papers he created in that office were human. They were all part of the machine. Nothing about this feeling for Coley Scudder had changed after Mr. Boyle's death. Scudder continued to do the things for Max that he had done for Mr. Boyle, and he did them in the same way.

Every now and then, however, something happened that jolted Max into a different awareness about the tall, gray-haired, good-looking, not young and not old, impeccably tailored man who never smiled, always smelled of Sen-Sen, and, in spite of the fact that he was almost bamboo-pole thin, bore a remarkable resemblance to Herbert Hoover.

"It's the collar," Ida had said when Max once mentioned to her his occasional odd reaction to Coley Scudder. "Next time there's a picture of President Hoover in the paper, you take a good look at it, then you take a look at Coley, and you'll see what I mean."

Max did see, but he didn't understand.

"Every once in a while something happens," he had said to Ida. "I never really know what it is until I force myself to think back. He uses a word I never heard him use, or he feels maybe he ought to smile and he tries, and all of a sudden it's like when you buy a suit and you see yourself in one of those clothing-store triple mirrors. You never knew you looked like that, and you never knew Coley looked like that."

Ida had surprised him by saying, "You know the bicycles you bought last week for the children?"

"What about them?" Max said.

"Have you watched them in the driveway while Ellis is giving them a riding lesson?"

Max had tried to remember. He was up in Canada so much of the time these days, it occurred to him that he didn't see as much of the kids as he used to.

"I've seen them," Max said. "I can't say I've stood around watching them. It seems to me Norman is catching on fast, but Claire, she's going to break her pretty neck if she doesn't watch out."

"That's the difference," Ida said. "Norman takes to it as easily as he took to walking, without any sweat. Poor Claire, though, she's so afraid she'll fall over, she gets tense and so she does fall over. Ellis keeps telling her she'll never ride easy until she stops hunching over the handlebars, but she keeps hunching over the handlebars. The same with Coley Scudder."

"I don't see anything the same between that ice-cold *goy* and that beautiful little girl," Max said.

"Not normally," Ida said. "Because he's always hunching over the handlebars, so it doesn't look unusual. It's just the way Coley Scudder is. Once in a while, though, the way you just said, he uses a word he never tried on you before, or he feels he ought to smile, and it comes out so wrong, you suddenly realize he's not a machine, he's a human being who has made himself into a machine, and for a moment he forgot, so you look at him in surprise, even a little nervous, because you're afraid all of a sudden he's going to fall off the bicycle."

It was an odd feeling for Max to find himself caught up in one of those moments while sitting at Sir Digby Locksmoor's signed desk in the business room of the house on Park Lane talking on the transatlantic telephone to Coley Scudder in Minneapolis. All the confidence and pleasure with which Max had come down from the guest suite to take the call were suddenly gone. All at once Max in London could see Coley Scudder on Chanhassen Circle trying to smile. Max decided he'd better get Coley back to hunching over the handlebars.

"Okay," Max said. "If you really think it's important to put Myra on the extension, put her on."

"I really do think it's important," Scudder said.

Max pulled the memorandum from his breast pocket.

"Myra, take this down, will you?" Coley Scudder said.

"Yes, sir," his secretary said.

"One," Max said, reading from the memorandum. "We get the exclusive right for ninety-nine years to import all Kirkbean products into the United States and the entire Western Hemisphere."

Scudder said, "Got that, Myra?"

"Yes, Mr. Scudder," his secretary said.

"Two," Max said. "The schedule of payments is in American dollars fixed at the rate you and Sir Digby's people worked out in Chicago before Ida and I sailed for England."

Scudder said, "Got that, Myra?"

"Yes, Mr. Scudder," his secretary said.

She got the remaining sixteen points as well.

"Max, that's great," Coley Scudder said when Max finished. "And it's all down on paper in a handwritten memorandum as agreed?"

Max said, "On Sir Digby's personal stationery, which I took with his permission right here out of the top drawer of his desk. Handwritten by me last night on the same desk from which I'm talking to you now. I made two copies, then Sir Digby and I signed both copies, and Bryce, the butler, and Trimmer, the upstairs maid, signed as witnesses. Sir Digby took his copy. I took mine. It's right here in my hot little hand."

Coley Scudder said, "Max, I must congratulate you, I really must. I don't know any businessman, certainly nobody I've ever met in all my years as a lawyer—nobody, absolutely nobody—who could take something of this magnitude, of this magnitude and complexity, Max, and follow it through in a tough negotiation as perfectly to the letter as you've followed it."

Max said, "I didn't quite follow it so perfectly to the letter as you laid it out."

"How do you mean?" Scudder said.

"I added a few letters of my own."

"You better tell me," Coley Scudder said.

"Myra?" Max said.

"Yes, Mr. Lessing?"

"Take this down," Max said.

"Yes, sir," the secretary said.

"I added one point," Max said.

"What point?" Scudder said.

"If come November this Roosevelt character is not elected," Max said, "the whole deal is off."

Pause. Max ran his hand again along the edge of the desk. It felt nice. Like Alma when she was—

"Max?"

"Yes, Coley?"

"Why did you want to do that?" Coley Scudder said.

"I've been living here in London with this funny accent for a week," Max said. "It's been a lot different from an hour at The Drake in Chicago. It's like you read a letter from somebody you never met. You get an impression. Then all of a sudden the guy who wrote the letter comes into the room and he reads it aloud to you. You catch things you missed before."

Scudder said, "What did you miss in Chicago?"

"The direction of their thinking," Max said. "From Sir Digby in Chicago and from the briefings you gave me, I could see they saw what we saw. With Prohibition on the books, getting stuff like Kirkbean into the country was where the money's been at. If this Roosevelt gets in, the first thing he's going to do is give the gate to your good friend and mine, the Eighteenth Amendment, and you know what that means."

Coley Scudder said, "Yes."

"For the boys over here who own things like Kirkbean Distilleries it's going to be a jolt. From years of running a seller's market, all of a sudden they're going to be on the short end of a buyer's market. For a dozen years we've been willing to pay Sir Digby and his boys anything they've asked for their stuff because we've been able to get it back from the suckers at home for anything we've wanted to ask them to pay us. With Prohibition dead we won't be able to write our own price tags anymore with the folks back home, because the folks back home will be able to shop around. That's not good."

"No," Scudder said.

"Up to now," Max said, "we've had no competition. Nothing we couldn't handle, is what I mean. With this Roosevelt in and Prohibition out, it's going to be an entirely different ball game. If you'll pardon me for using a dirty word, Coley, everybody is going to have to go *kosher*. The boys who will come out ahead will not be the boys who under Prohibition had the muscle. No more, Coley. Not with this Roosevelt in and Prohibition out. When that happens, the boys who will come out ahead are the boys who had the brains to see the *kosher* scene coming and prepared for its arrival by signing the boys like Kirkbean to watertight exclusive-distributor contracts."

Coley Scudder said, "Boys like us."

"Coley, we live in an uncertain world. Things that look surefire have a way of taking you by surprise. If come November this Roosevelt falls on his ass, I want us to be able to do business exactly as we've been doing it up to now, because up to now nobody in the business has done business better than we've done it, have they, Coley?"

"No," Coley Scudder said.

"So you could say," Max said, "this point I added last

night to your memorandum, it's a nice big fat insurance policy."

Pause. Max's hand slid once more across the satiny desk edge. There was a stirring in his loins.

"Max?"

"Yes, Coley?"

"Sir Digby," Coley said. "How did he take all this?"

"He signed," Max said.

Coley Scudder said, "I see."

At that moment, Max saw something too. Not just the movement of the opening door through which Sir Digby Locksmoor now came into the business room. Max saw something he should have seen all the way back in Chicago. What it was about Sir Digby Locksmoor that had made him seem familiar to Max from the moment he first saw the Englishman walk into Alma Pine's suite at The Drake.

"Am I interrupting?" Sir Digby said.

It was Mr. Marawitz he reminded Max of. Wheezing old Mr. Marawitz, owner of the pushcart garage on River Street in Minneapolis.

Max said to the newcomer, "I'm talking with Coley in Minneapolis."

Sir Digby said, "Oh, I say, may I cut in? Just for a moment?"

Max said, "Be my guest." Into the phone: "Sir Digby just came into the room, Coley. He wants to say a few words."

Sir Digby Locksmoor took the phone from Max.

"Coley?" Sir Digby said into the phone. "Digby here. I'm on my way out with Max's and Ida's passports. . . . Yes, I thought I'd take them to the office personally. My staff will have them validated at the Embassy for tomorrow's sailing. . . . Nonsense. No trouble at all. On my way out of the house, however, I could not resist pausing to seize this opportunity to tell you something that came to me last night in this very room. Are you listening, old boy?"

Scudder said, "I am."

"For a week," Sir Digby said, "I have been under the

impression that I have been conducting a complex business negotiation with a sensible, shrewd, and attractive businessman."

Coley Scudder said, "Weren't you?"

Sir Digby said, "Not a bit."

He reached out his free hand and placed it on Max's shoulder.

"What I learned in this room last night, Coley," Sir Digby said into the phone, "I learned that when Max Lessing sails for home on the *Leviathan* tomorrow, I will be saying farewell to a brilliant young businessman, of course, and I will also be saying *au revoir* to a highly treasured new friend, yes."

Sir Digby Locksmoor smiled gently into the telephone mouthpiece. His upper plate here on Park Lane, Max noticed, like the upper plate of Mr. Marawitz on River Street, could have done with a little attention from a good dentist.

"More importantly," Sir Digby Locksmoor wheezed through his marred dentures, "when Max Lessing leaves London tomorrow, when I say goodbye to this young man of thirty, I will be saying goodbye to a kind of human being who is very rare in our society today."

Coley Scudder said, "What's that?"

Sir Digby Locksmoor said, "I will be saying goodbye to a merchant statesman."

38

The thirty-year-old merchant statesman spent a busy morning moving around London with Hymie Shantz. Shortly
before noon, when Max got back to Park Lane, Ida said,
"Where have you been?"

"Buying you a souvenir of London," Max said. "I've fixed
to have it shipped on the *Leviathan* when she sails tomorrow.
That way all three of us, you and me and the souvenir, will
arrive in Minneapolis together."

Ida said, "Is it something I like?"

"You've been writing valentines to it," Max said, "the
whole week we've been living in this house."

"Sir Digby's desk?"

"Now known as Ida Lessing's desk," Max said.

Ida said, "I guess I'll never teach you to keep your nose
out of things you don't understand."

"Anything I don't understand," Max said, "I pay for an
explanation from somebody who does."

"Without getting paid for it," Ida said, "I told you what
Susie Shale explained to me a signed piece of furniture
means. The desk downstairs in the business room is a
Hepplewhite. It's the only one in the whole world. That
desk, Max, is like a painting. The man who made it signed it."

Max said, "I found a forger."

"Who?"

"The same clown who signed the desk downstairs."

Ida gave him a look, then a laugh. "Does Sir Digby know?" she said.

"Not if you and I don't tell him," Max said.

There was a tap on the door.

"Yes?" Ida said.

Trimmer came in.

"Mr. Lessing," the maid said.

"I know," Max said. "There's a trunk call for me in the business room."

"No, sir," Trimmer said.

Max said, "You've got that piece of black ribbon hanging down in front."

"Well, yes, but not a trunk call, sir," Trimmer said. "Sir Digby is calling from his office in Berkeley Square."

"Close," Max said. "But no cigar."

"I beg your pardon, sir?"

"Tell her," Max said to Ida. "I'll go see what the other owner of a Hepplewhite signature wants."

What Sir Digby Locksmoor wanted was not very clear the first time around. The marred upper plate plus the asthmatic wheeze sometimes made his telephone conversation difficult. This seemed to be one of those times.

Max said, "Let's see if I've got this straight." He turned with the phone and looked out at Hyde Park as he talked. "Your secretary took our passports over to the Embassy," Max said. "She went directly to this man you know on the Ambassador's staff."

"An old friend," Sir Digby said at the other end of the phone. "Known him for years, Max."

"He does this sort of thing for you all the time," Max said. "Sandpapers rough spots. Cuts corners. Slices through red tape. Eases the pinch. Helps people over hurdles. Gets things wholesale. Expedites passports so you don't have to stand in line on docks or in customs sheds like the rest of the peasants."

"He's quite high up in the pecking order," Sir Digby said. "We've been doing favors for each other for years."

"But today he's not playing," Max said.

"Not at all," Sir Digby said. "What he said was could you and I lunch with him today at his club."

"Why not?" Max said. "We've all got to eat."

"One-thirty at the Bath, then?"

"That's the one you turn right from Piccadilly at The Ritz?" Max said. "You're walking down St. James's Street? And it's about halfway along the block on the right?"

"Quite," Sir Digby said. "Just beyond Prunier's."

Max said, "What's this boy's name?"

"Klemperer," Sir Digby said. "Orville Klemperer. Terribly decent chap, Max. You'll like him."

Max said, "For you the young merchant statesman will try."

He hung up and looked at his watch. Ten minutes to twelve. Max walked out of Sir Digby's business room. Bryce was waiting in the hall.

The butler said, "Will you and Mrs. Lessing be lunching in, sir?"

Max said, "My wife hasn't told you yet?"

"Mrs. Lessing says she never makes plans for her next meal, sir, because invariably at the last moment you change them."

"Today I'm not going to disappoint her," Max said. "Tell Mrs. Lessing I was called away."

"Of course, sir," the butler said.

He helped Max on with his coat and handed him his hat. Opening the front door, Bryce said, "Could you say when you'll be back, sir?"

Max wondered if Ellis, back on Columbia Heights, would have asked that question.

"I could," Max said, "but I'll probably change my mind about that too."

"I merely thought Mrs. Lessing might ask," the butler said. "I didn't want her to worry."

"She'll ask," Max said, "but she won't worry."

Sir Digby's maroon Bentley was waiting at the curb. Hymie Shantz and the chauffeur were having a cigarette on the sidewalk.

Max said to the bodyguard, "You smoke too much."

"Don't I know it," Hymie Shantz said. "We rolling?"

"Yes," Max said. "Slote, you know the American Embassy? On Grosvenor Square?"

The chauffeur said, "Of course, sir."

He dropped his cigarette, ground it out with his shoe, and opened the rear door of the car.

Max said, "Take me over, please."

He got in. Hymie Shantz followed. Slote slammed the door and went around to the driver's seat. Max had considered walking. What Hymie knew didn't matter. About this Slote, however, Max was not so sure. He would have preferred to keep the chauffeur out of the next hour or so. Walking, however, would probably make more of an impression on a chauffeur's memory than a short run in the car.

When they got to the Embassy, Slote came around to open the door. "Will you be long, sir?" he said.

It occurred to Max that Sir Digby's staff in London had one thing on Ellis in Columbia Heights. They would have made better pollsters. Sir Digby's team never missed a chance to ask a question.

"Not very," Max said. As Hymie heaved himself out to the sidewalk, Max said to the bodyguard, "About two cigarettes' worth."

There was a surprising amount of traffic in the lobby, but the girl at the reception desk was free.

"Mr. Klemperer," Max said. "Orville Klemperer."

"You have an appointment, sir?"

"Yes," Max said.

"What name, please?"

"Berg," Max said. "Gerhardt Berg."

The girl picked up her telephone. It had a bulky black masking device over the mouthpiece. When she spoke into it the lower half of her face disappeared. Max could not hear what she said or what was said to her. Whatever it was, though, the reply caused the girl's eyes to roll toward him in a look of surprise. With the lower half of her face concealed by the instrument, her eyes attracted more attention than Max guessed they ordinarily would. The girl's eyes were gray, with small golden flecks surrounding the very black pupils. Like Alma's.

"Sorry to keep you, Mr. Berg," the girl said. She put down the telephone. "If you'll take that elevator on your left, sir? Mr. Klemperer is on the second floor. His secretary will be waiting for you at the elevator door, sir."

"Thanks," Max said.

He thought the elevator would have been an insult to Montenegro. Max found himself wondering about the State Department. The boys who ran it seemed to have less pride in how America looked to people in the great capitals of the world than Ida had in how her home looked on Columbia Heights. They were on the ball about secretaries, though. On the second floor Orville Klemperer's girl was waiting at the elevator door, as advertised.

She said, "This way, Mr. Berg."

The room Max entered went with the elevator. Sandor Ganyi ran his Gardens out of a hole-in-the-wall on Hennepin Avenue that was more spacious and better-looking than this. Still, it was an outer office, a place in which a secretary stood guard while visitors cooled their heels. Max did not cool his. The secretary moved right across to another door, turned the knob, and pushed the door open.

"Mr. Klemperer," she said. "Mr. Berg."

Max walked past her. The secretary pulled the door shut behind him. The man at the desk gave him a long, hard look.

"You're not Gerhardt Berg," he said.

"Who would want to be?"

"Who are you?" Mr. Klemperer said.

Max said, "I'm the boy who made your cousin Governor of Minnesota."

"I don't understand," Mr. Klemperer said.

Max said, "My name is Lessing."

"Oh," Mr. Klemperer said.

His glance dropped to the desk top. It was piled with papers and bound documents neatly stacked.

"What you've got sitting there on your desk," Max said. "Those three small green books. They look like some passports I've seen before."

Mr. Klemperer said again, "Oh."

"Yes or no?" Max said.

Mr. Klemperer seemed to come awake. He looked younger than Gerhardt Berg, but he had the same kind of face. Plump yet hard, as though the excessive amount of meat packed in under the skin were trying to shove its way out. This created folds of fat with narrow slits in between. These, on closer examination, appeared to contain peering eyes. What had made the little blue veins laced across the plum-colored cheeks was not hard to guess. Not for a man who for twelve years had been distributing to the American public vast quantities of bootlegged Kirkbean. The owner of the face stood up quickly.

"Sorry," Klemperer said. "I didn't mean to be rude."

Max said, "Here's your chance to correct that."

He stuck out his hand. Hastily, nervously, Klemperer reached across the desk. The hands met. Mr. Klemperer's hand felt like the expensive side of a lox-and-cream-cheese bagel.

"For a moment I was confused," he said. "I didn't know Gerhardt was in London. We don't keep in touch that much. I mean we're not all that close, you see. The two branches of the family is what I mean. Perfectly friendly, of course. My mother and Gerhard's mother are sisters."

Max said, "I know."

"You do?" Mr. Klemperer said.

"If you go around getting people elected governors of states," Max said, "it helps to remember things they tell you about themselves. Gerry once told me his mother's sister had a son in the State Department who was stationed in London."

"Clever of you to remember a thing like that," Mr. Klemperer said.

Max said, "Gerry never told me his cousin doesn't invite visitors from back home to sit down."

The thick, red, fleshy face seemed to swell.

"Sorry," Klemperer said. "Do sit down, please, Mr. Lessing." He waved to the chair under the American flag. It hung limply from the pole in a rack to his right.

Max sat down. "Where do you get these chairs?" he said.

"I beg your pardon?" Mr. Klemperer said. He sounded like Trimmer.

"Don't worry about it now," Max said. "You seem to be juggling more in your mind than office furniture."

"What's confusing me is I thought I had a lunch date with you and Sir Digby Locksmoor at one-thirty."

Using both hands, like an awkward but desperate swimmer trying to get his breaststroke going, Mr. Klemperer pushed around some of the papers and documents on his desk. He stopped at what Max guessed was a date calendar.

"Yes, here it is," Klemperer said. "One-thirty."

Max said, "At the Bath Club."

"Right, yes," Mr. Klemperer said with relief. "So you see—" His voice ground to a halt.

"Don't let it upset you," Max said. He glanced at his Patek Philippe. "It's only twenty minutes after twelve. We have more than an hour. We can still make it."

"I don't understand," Mr. Klemperer said.

"I've been living for a week in Sir Digby's house," Max said. "I've got to know a lot about him. I don't know anything about you. I thought I could find worse ways to pass my time than picking up a few facts about Orville Klemperer right from the source."

"What sort of facts?" Klemperer said.

"Like why Orville Klemperer didn't just validate my passport and my wife's passport and my secretary's passport and hand them back to Sir Digby's secretary, the way Orville

Klemperer always does," Max said. "I wanted to find out why a busy State Department official wanted to have lunch with an unimportant American citizen and talk about such a small, routine matter."

"The lunch was Sir Digby's idea," Klemperer said.

"This visit was mine," Max said. "Commence with the explanation, Buster."

Startled, Mr. Klemperer said, "Whuh?"

Max said, "Start talking."

"About what?"

"Your cousin's future," Max said. "And yours. Governors come up for reelection. State Department career men come up for promotion. I come up here in the best interests of the two branches of your family. Your mother's and Gerry's mother's. Don't let them down. I am listening, Orville."

39

The listening process did not take long. When Max came out onto the sidewalk, Hymie Shantz and the Locksmoor chauffeur were leaning against the maroon Bentley smoking cigarettes.

Max said, "How many?"

"My second," Hymie Shantz said.

Max said, "Don't light your third until we get back to Park Lane."

The chauffeur said, "I thought, sir, you were going on to lunch from here." He pulled open the door.

Max said, "What makes you think that?"

He ducked low so that his hat would clear the top of the door. The more these English cars cost, the closer you had to get to going down on your knees in order to find your seat.

"I don't really know, sir," the chauffeur said. "The hour, I suppose."

Max glanced at his watch. A quarter to one. The meeting with Orville Klemperer had taken twenty-five minutes, door to door.

Hymie Shantz ducked into the car and scuttled like a crab across Max's knees to the far seat. While Slote walked around the front to get to the driver's seat, Max said, "How come this boy knows so much about where I'm supposed to go at what time, and what I'm supposed to do when I get there?"

"I've been trying to figure that one out," Hymie Shantz said.

"While you're working up your case of T.B. with all those cigarettes," Max said, "what do you two talk about?"

"Norma Shearer," Hymie Shantz said. "He's got a thing for her."

The front door opened. Slote slid in behind the wheel.

"Back to Park Lane is it, sir?" he said across his shoulder.

Max said, "Please."

He made a small bet with himself about what Bryce would say when the butler opened the front door.

"You've changed your mind about lunching out, sir?" Bryce said.

Max wished he had made the bet bigger. It was borrowing from Peter to pay Peter, but when you were on a winning streak who cared?

"I'll know in a few minutes," Max said. "After I talk with Mrs. Lessing."

The butler said, "She's in the business room, sir."

She was also on her knees.

"Come out into the open," Max said. "I have something to tell you."

Ida stood up and came out from behind the desk.

"I was just checking the signature," she said. "Susie Shale was right. There are two Ps in Hepplewhite."

Max said, "Sit down."

Ida dropped into the chair beside the fireplace. Max took a few steps up and down the room.

"Stop gathering any more thoughts," Ida said. "Whatever it is you have to tell me, do it with the thoughts you've already managed to pull into the net."

"All I know is the facts," Max said. "The few they let me have."

"Who is they?" Ida said.

"A man named Klemperer," Max said.

He explained what had happened at the Embassy.

"That's all they dealt me," Max said. "It doesn't have the feel of a full hand."

"You keep saying 'they,' " Ida said. "But the only one you talked with is this Klemperer."

Max said, "He couldn't have been talking for himself."

He went around behind the desk, sat down, and pulled the telephone forward.

Ida said, "What are you going to do?"

"Call Coley in Minneapolis," Max said. "I'll get him started on finding the missing cards."

"Not on that telephone," Ida said.

"What are you talking about?"

"Stand up," Ida said.

Max got out of the chair. Ida came around behind the desk. She pushed Max aside, pulled the chair out of the way, and dropped to the carpet. She crawled far enough into the kneehole to conceal her shoulders. From the way she moved back and forth it seemed to Max she was tugging at something. After a few moments it seemed to come free. Ida backed out from under the desk and stood up. She was holding a three-pronged electric plug attached to a four-or-five-foot length of wire.

"What the hell is that?" Max said.

"What Hymie Shantz calls I believe a wiretap."

"How did you find out?" Max said.

"I'll tell you later," Ida said. "Right now let's get some place where you can call Coley without an audience."

"I can't stand out on a street corner in one of those red boxes and talk to Minneapolis," Max said. "Even in this brand-new Savile Row number I haven't got enough pockets to hold that many coins."

Ida said, "We can do better than that."

She dropped back to her knees and crawled under the desk. This time she made shoving motions. They ended in a small, muted click. Ida backed out of the kneehole and stood up. Minus the three-pronged plug and the wire.

She said, "Where's Hymie?"

"Out on the sidewalk," Max said. "Working on the balance of his left lung with the help of Slote."

"Go out and get Slote to stop smoking and run the Bentley over to the Bath Club," Ida said. "Tell him to give Sir Digby the message you won't be able to have lunch with him and that Klemperer because an unexpected business matter has come up."

"Like what?"

"I'll explain as soon as we're in the clear," Ida said. "God knows who else in this place is listening, and how they're doing it. After Slote drives away, you tell Hymie to get us a taxi."

"Us?" Max said.

Ida said, "You're not wandering around in London for one more minute unattended." She started for the door.

"Where you going?" Max said.

"My hat and coat," Ida said. "You get yours on the way out. I'll meet you on the sidewalk."

"What about Bryce?"

"I'll take care of him," Ida said. "Give me a minute before you go out to talk to Slote and Hymie."

Max gave her a couple of minutes. When he opened the business-room door, nobody was in the hall. Moving swiftly to the front door, Max scooped up his hat and coat from the settee near the umbrella stand. Out on the sidewalk, Hymie Shantz and Slote were discussing Norma Shearer in *A Free Soul*. The chauffeur did not think Norma showed to best advantage opposite Clark Gable.

"If it won't interfere with your smoking," Max said, "do me a favor, Slote, will you?"

"Certainly, sir," the chauffeur said.

Max repeated what Ida had told him.

"Yes, sir," Slote said.

The Bentley rolled away.

"Whistle up a taxi," Max said to Hymie Shantz.

The bodyguard stepped off the curb. He put the touching tips of a thumb and forefinger into his mouth. Through them he released a sound that brought the wild screeching of several sets of brakes from as far north as Hampstead Heath. Hymie jumped back onto the curb. A taxi rolled up. Hymie opened the taxi door. Ida came down the steps of Sir Digby's house and climbed into the taxi. Max followed. Hymie leaned around the meter and said something to the driver. The driver nodded. Hymie pulled his head back and pushed it along with the rest of his body into the rear of the cab. As though he were squirming his way into a pair of pants while standing in a phone booth, he worked his way down into the jump seat, facing Max and Ida.

"I hate to interrupt this vaudeville act while the two of you are going good," Max said. "But would you mind telling me where this safari is heading?"

Ida said, "To an untapped telephone."

"While we're en route," Max said, "you could fill me in on how you found out about the one in Sir Digby's business room."

"The entire week we've been living in that house," Ida said, "I felt uncomfortable."

Max said, "You've been sleeping like a log."

"I don't mean that way," Ida said. "I mean a house that big, a rich man's house, four floors, eight servants, a maroon Bentley for weekdays and a silver Rolls for bank holidays, things like that, but only one telephone? You're upstairs in the guest room on the fourth floor, you get a call, one of the maids has to climb all the way up three floors to tell you about it, and then you have to climb all the way down three floors to answer it. Would you and I treat a guest like that on Columbia Heights?"

Max said, "They talk different here in London. Why shouldn't they do things different?"

"No reason that's any of my business," Ida said. "My business is to think the way we do on Columbia Heights. So this morning I told Trimmer I wanted to write some letters in the business room. When I got in there, I locked the door and got down on my knees under the desk. Here we are."

"Where?" Max said.

Ida said, "I thought by this time you knew your way around the West End."

Max peered across her hat. "The Ritz?" he said.

"You and I, Max, we don't stay in places like the Nokomis on Anoka Avenue anymore," Ida said. "Hymie, pay the driver, please."

The bodyguard said, "You bet, Mrs. L."

He unwound himself from the jump seat, opened the taxi door, and climbed out. With his left hand he fed a pound note across the front seat to the driver. With his right he helped Ida out of the taxi. Max followed.

"We calling on someone?" he said.

Ida said, "Just this once, Max, till we get to that phone, try not to interrupt." She took Hymie's arm and started across the sidewalk.

"How about me?" Max said.

"Follow," Ida said.

Max followed her and Hymie to the desk. The bodyguard lifted a forefinger to the clerk. Not imperiously, but with enough authority to command attention.

"Seven-oh-nine, please," Hymie said.

"Right, sir." The clerk took down a key and handed it to Hymie.

"Thanks," the bodyguard said.

He wheeled Ida in the direction of the elevators. Max followed. On the seventh floor, when they started down the corridor, Max tried to move up beside Ida.

"Not yet," she said.

Max dropped back.

At the door marked 709, Ida and Hymie stopped. So did Max. Hymie used the key, pushed in the door, and stepped aside. He said, "It's all yours, Mr. Max."

"What is?" Max said.

"Two rooms, one bath, and two telephones," Ida said. "You go call Coley from this one here in the sitting room. I'll listen on the extension in the bedroom."

"You haven't written in a part for Hymie," Max said.

"I'll wait in the hall," Hymie said. He went out.

Max said, "When did this happen?"

"Yesterday," Ida said. "I wasn't sure about the wiretap, because I didn't have a chance until this morning to crawl under that desk in the business room, but between Bryce and his questions, and Trimmer with that black lace pulled down over her cap in front, I was sure what you needed was a place where you can make a telephone call without Sir Digby's team taking notes. So yesterday I told Bryce I was going for a walk in the park. Hymie came with me, of course, and I walked with him over to the Ritz and rented this little hideaway. It's not the Nokomis Hotel on Anoka Avenue, but it has enough privacy for calling Coley."

Max gave her a look.

"What's Hymie got to do with it?" he said.

"He signed the register," Ida said. "Mr. and Mrs. Hyman Shantz."

Max didn't like the way the Nokomis Hotel kept surfacing in Ida's explanations, but this didn't seem the appropriate moment to check that out. He threw his hat and coat on the couch and crossed to the desk. Max sat down and picked up the phone.

"Transatlantic operator, please." He put the mouthpiece to his shoulder and said to Ida, "Get on the extension, but don't talk unless I bring you in."

"All right," Ida said.

She went into the bedroom, sat down on the bed, and picked up the phone from the night table. She didn't listen very carefully to the talk between Max and the operator. The opening clicks and clacks and roars, she had learned, could be disregarded. Ida concentrated on what Max had told her about his meeting with Mr. Klemperer.

There was something about it that bothered her. Not because it was a threat. Ida was accustomed to threats. Or rather, she was accustomed to the way Max conducted his business and, as a result, to the climate in which she lived.

She had grown accustomed to it long ago, on Minnehaha Avenue, soon after she had started making Passover wine for Max to sell from the pushcart.

Ida had learned to live with the feeling that always, somewhere out beyond the circle of her immediate existence, there were people who begrudged her her pleasure in it, people who were waiting patiently, watching without pause for the proper moment when they felt they could move in and with impunity interrupt or even terminate that existence. What bothered Ida was the fact that Mr. Klemperer's threat was different. It didn't seem to belong to anything she had ever before experienced with Max.

"That you, Coley?"

Max's words, crackling in her ear, brought Ida out of her thoughts.

"Yes," Coley Scudder said. "Listen, Max, are you calling me or am I calling you?"

"I just put in this call to you," Max said.

"When?"

"A few minutes ago," Max said.

"That explains it," Coley said.

"That explains what?"

"A few minutes ago I put in a call to you," Coley said.

"Where?" Max said.

"Where I've been putting them through all week," Coley said. "Sir Digby's house. We got the butler—you know who I mean."

"Bryce," Max said.

"That's the boy," Coley Scudder said. "He said you were out, could he take a message. We said yes, it's important, and Myra no sooner hangs up than you're on the blower asking for me. You couldn't be returning my call that fast."

"I'm not," Max said. "I'm making my own."

"From where?"

"There are a lot of telephones in this town," Max said. "You tell me why you were calling me, and why you told Bryce it's important."

"That's his name, yes," Coley Scudder said. "Sir Digby's butler."

"Forget Sir Digby's goddamn butler," Max said. "Tell me why you called."

"Max, is something wrong?" Scudder said.

"Are you going to stop this and tell me why you called?" Max said. "Or do I have to hire me a new lawyer?"

"Calm down, will you?" Coley Scudder said. "What the hell is going on over there?"

"I'll be glad to tell you as soon as you tell me what's going on in Minneapolis," Max said. "Begin by telling me why you put in a call to me a few minutes ago."

"After we talked this morning," Scudder said. "After you told me about wrapping up the deal last night with Sir Digby, I had a call from Washington."

"The whole city?" Max said.

"Jesus, you're wound up tight this morning," Coley Scudder said.

"Who called you from Washington?" Max said.

"Somebody I know in the State Department," Scudder said.

In the bedroom, the extension at her ear, Ida could tell from Max's breathing he was making an effort to control his temper.

"All right," he said. "I understand, Coley. Skip the name. What did he say?"

"It's a she," Coley Scudder said. "She's in the Passport Division. She told me she'd just learned, and don't ask me how, Max, please, she'd just learned a cable had gone out to London ordering the Embassy to lift your passport. Yours and Ida's and Hymie's."

"She say why?"

"I don't pay out good money to her or to anybody else for waving loose threads at me," Coley Scudder said. "They don't call me until they've got all the answers they can give me when I start asking questions."

"Your questions are my questions," Max said. "What were her answers?"

"She said the best she could, find out is they, and she doesn't know who they are," Coley Scudder said, "they are trying to prevent you from coming back into the United States."

In the pause that followed, Ida, sitting in the bedroom, clapped her hand over the mouthpiece of the extension phone. A moment later she realized this was silly. Even on a good connection Coley Scudder in Minneapolis couldn't possibly hear her heart hammering in a bedroom at the Ritz in London.

"For how long?" Max said.

"Permanently," Scudder said.

Max said, "How can they do that to an American citizen?"

"If they can prove he's not an American citizen," Coley Scudder said.

"Coley," Max Lessing said. "In my safe-deposit box in the Minneapolis Bankers Trust there is a document. At the top, in the left-hand corner, there is printed a red number. It is 1610204. In the upper right-hand corner, in beautiful engraved script, it says, and I quote: *to be given to the person naturalized* unquote. Under this, in even more beautiful engraved lettering over the Seal of the United States, complete with eagle and shield, it says *The United States of America, Certificate of Naturalization*. Then underneath it says *Petition Volume 154, Number 3829*. You got that, Coley?"

"Yes, of course, Max, but—"

"Shut up, Coley. With that document in my safe-deposit box," Max said, "I would like to know how any sons of bitches in Washington, with their cables to the Embassy here in London, you just tell me how those bastards can prevent me and Ida from returning to our home."

"There's only one way," Scudder said.

Max said, "What way?"

"If when you took your oath as a naturalized citizen you swore to an untruth," Coley Scudder said.

"Such as?"

"Such as that you entered the country legally," Scudder said, "when in fact you entered illegally."

Max said, "How can anybody do that?"

"Never mind about how can anybody," Coley Scudder said. "You and I, Max, we're just interested in you."

"I'm interested in more," Max said. "As a good American citizen I'd like to know how anybody can enter my country illegally."

"Max, stop wasting time," Coley said. "There are a million ways."

Max said, "Name one."

"There's the most common way, Max. Up around here where you and I live, here in Minneapolis near the Canadian border, it's as common as dandruff, Max, as I'm sure you must know."

"Maybe I must," Max said. "But if it's so common, Coley, how come I don't?"

"Max, please," Coley Scudder said. "You've heard of people who can't enter the country because of quota restrictions, so they sneak across from Canada with forged papers."

"Oh, that," Max said. "Sure, yes, Coley. I thought this girl you were talking to in Washington had come up with something fancy. But Coley, listen. The only thing those bastards can have on me is tax stuff, and you've been handling that for years, so I'm not worried about that."

"Quite properly," Scudder said. "Your tax apparatus is in my hands. In that area you have nothing to worry about."

"Then here's something I want you to do," Max said. "I want you to call what's his name, the Secretary of State."

"Henry Stimson?" Coley Scudder said.

"Henry *Lewis* Stimson," Max said. "You get Lew Stimson on the blower and you tell him I called you from London and I told you to tell him to find out which clown it was in that circus he's running down there in Washington who thought up this stupid joke."

Coley Scudder said, "Max—"

"Shut up, Coley, this is an order," Max said. "And you

tell Stimson I want him to do two things and I want them done fast. You listening?"

Scudder said, "Of course."

"One," Max said. "I want my passport and Ida's passport and Hymie Shantz's passport, I want all three of those passports validated in time for us to sail for New York on the *Leviathan* tomorrow. Got that, Coley?"

"Yes, sure," Coley Scudder said. "But—"

"And two," Max said. "You tell Lew Stimson the son of a bitch in the State Department who thought up this wrinkle, I want Lew to fire that bastard immediately. Got that, Coley?"

"Max, yes," Coley said. "But—"

"One other thing," Max Lessing said.

"What?"

Max said, "You tell Lew Stimson those two things I want him to do immediately have a two-word time bomb ticking under them."

"A two-word time bomb?" Coley Scudder said.

"He does those things at once, immediately, today," Max said, "*or else!*"

He slammed down the receiver. In the bedroom Ida jumped. She held the receiver at her ear for several moments. She stared across the room at the gold-framed picture over the cream-and-yellow fireplace. It was a reproduction of Susie Shale's favorite painting: *The Age of Innocence* by Sir Joshua Reynolds. Finally, Ida returned the receiver to the hook. She stood up, hesitated, then walked out into the sitting room.

Max was standing at the window, staring down into Piccadilly. He turned. There was nothing in his face or manner to indicate that he had just been snarling orders to his lawyer at the other side of the world. Max did not look like a man of thirty who had just slammed down a receiver. Max looked like the copper-haired boy in corduroy pants and a flannel shirt who thirteen years ago had stopped at a barn door in Klein Berezna to beg a cup of milk.

"Ida," he said quietly.

"I know," she said.

"We have to get out of here," Max said.

"I know."

Max came across the room. He touched her arm. "Good girl," he said.

Everything inside her settled down. It was going to be all right.

"What do you want me to do?" Ida said.

"Get Hymie in here," Max Lessing said. "I'll lay out an A, B, C how we'll handle this."

40

Eleven days later, Ida was getting dressed in a bedroom of the Bannockburn Suite in the Duncansly Head Hotel at John o' Groats, on the northern tip of Scotland. She was not exactly wondering how she had got there, but the hint of a not too dissimilar thought was crossing her mind when she heard Max's shout from the living room.

"Hey, Ida!"

She came out of the bedroom. Max was standing in the bay window on the north side of the sitting room.

"Anything yet?" Ida said.

"Come look and tell me."

She came up beside him. The bay window looked out on Pentland Firth. It was like looking out on all the lentil soup in the world gathered in one enormous plate. Mr. McKenzie, the proprietor of the Duncansly Head Hotel, said it was fog. He also said the stuff always lifted by noon. When it did, he maintained, the view of Scapa Flow and the Orkney Islands was worth waiting for.

Ida had been waiting for two days. Her third noon on the shore of Pentland Firth was less than an hour ahead of her, but she had yet to see an Orkney Island or a spoonful of Scapa Flow.

"Stop looking at the ocean," Max said. "He won't show

up in a submarine. Down the hill there, to the left."

Down the hill there, to the left was the turn where the narrow, single-track road from the railroad station emerged out of the fog. At the lowest point of the hill the road bellied out into a shallow lay-by. This gave head-on traffic enough time to decide which vehicle would get out of the way first. The traffic that passed the Duncansly Head Hotel did not exactly deserve to be called that. So far as Ida had been able to judge, it consisted of two or three donkey-drawn peat wagons between dawn and dusk. In her two and a half days at the hotel Ida had never yet seen an automobile. Now she did, or something that looked like an automobile. It was parked in the lay-by at the foot of the hill.

"What is it?" Ida said.

"A dry cleaner's delivery truck," Max said. "It must have been making a pickup here at the hotel while I was on the blower with Coley's office. When I came back to look, the thing was just pulling out from right under this window. I saw the sign on the side. Rob Roy Cleaners & Dyers, Ltd. Castletown, Caithness."

"What's it doing down there?"

"Getting out of the way of something coming up the hill toward us, it looks like," Max said. "I called you when I saw it pull into the lay-by."

Ida said, "You get anything on the phone?"

"The same set of lyrics," Max said. "Every time I call she goes into her song. Coley left Minneapolis eleven days ago, a few hours after I talked to him from the Ritz. He was in Washington for two full days. A week ago today he sailed from New York on the *United States*. She docked at Southampton Monday. Coley called Myra from London Tuesday afternoon. She told him I'd been in touch with her every day, but I didn't give her my number because I didn't want anybody to try to reach me by phone. I just wanted him to hustle up to Scotland as fast as he could. Coley called her back in Minneapolis a couple of hours later. He had his transportation fixed. He told her the next call she got from me to say he'd be here in Castletown today about noon, depending on how the trains were running."

Ida said, "That could be him."

A vehicle had emerged from the fog below the lay-by. It was the ancient taxi that two mornings ago had carried Ida and Max and Hymie Shantz from the Castletown railroad station up the hill to the Duncansly Head Hotel. No matter how much luggage Coley Scudder had brought with him, it was obvious that the taxi would now be carrying less weight than it had carried when it brought the Lessing party up the hill. Hymie Shantz alone, fresh out of a steam room, came in at 205 pounds. The taxi, however, was not moving any faster. Not nearly so fast as the van of the Rob Roy Cleaners & Dyers, Ltd. The moment the taxi cleared the lay-by, the van shot out into the road and disappeared down the hill into the fog.

"That's Coley, all right," Max said.

"You going down to say hello?" Ida said.

"Not with that McKenzie sniffing around."

"Coley knows we're waiting for him," Ida said. "If you don't go down to say hello it might hurt his feelings."

"The only way to hurt Coley's feelings is to be late with his annual retainer check," Max said. "We'll say our hellos to him up here."

There was a tap on the door.

Ida called, "All right, Hymie."

The bodyguard came in. He looked strange in the Shetland cardigan Ida had bought for him in The Thurso Gentleman's Apparel Shoppe. It kept him warm, Hymie said, but nobody had to say what anybody could see: it was not the sort of garment that had been fashioned to go with Hymie's Minneapolis snap-brim black felt number.

He said, "Mr. Scudder's taxi is coming up the hill."

"We've been watching it," Max said.

"How do you want to play this?" Hymie said.

Max said to Ida, "What do you think?"

"How angry are you at Coley?" Ida said.

Max gave her an irritated look. "No angrier than you are," he said.

"That's not the point."

"Eleven days ago I called him," Max said. "He's been in Washington two days. He's been on the ship five days. He's been in England two more days. With all that time, what the hell do I know now that I didn't know eleven days ago when I called him from the Ritz?"

Ida said, "That's not the point either."

"What do you see is the point?" Max said.

"If you're really sore at him, Hymie should wait in the bedroom," Ida said. "If you're not so sore that you'll start screaming, Hymie could wait out in the hall."

Irritably Max chopped his hand down hard, slicing air, and he made an angry sound.

"Hymie," he said, "wait out in the hall."

"Right," the bodyguard said. He left the room.

Max said, "What about you?"

"What do you think?" Ida said.

Max said, "If I had any thoughts, would I be asking you?"

"For this thing," Ida said, "I think we have to hear it direct from Coley."

"Whatever direct is," Max said.

"It could be we can't go home to America."

"So?" Max said.

"So we're back where we started from thirteen years ago," Ida said.

Max said, "Suppose we are?"

"Then we're immigrants again."

"We did it once," Max said. "Why can't we do it again?"

"We can," Ida said.

"Good girl," Max said.

Without a smile or a touch. But that made twice he'd said it in eleven days. He wasn't exactly garrulous. But when he spoke he said the right things. The sort of things a girl kept going on. There was a knock on the door.

Max called, "Come on in, Coley."

The door opened. Joe Catalini came in.

"Where's Coley?" Max said.

"I don't know," Joe Catalini said. "Hello, Mrs. L."

For a moment, perhaps longer, Ida didn't answer. She stared at the tall, slender, handsome boy. Boy? He was twenty-four years old. All at once Ida wasn't sure what was going on inside her head. It seemed sensible to make an effort to find out. She worked backward. The last time she had seen him. Almost a month ago, at the railroad station in Minneapolis, when he came to the train to say goodbye to her and Max and tell them not to worry about Norman and Claire or the house, he would take care of everything. Then before that? At Ganyi's Gardens. The graduation party. When she had watched him dancing with Mayor Nagel's daughter, and Ida had become aware of a funny little feeling in her heart. And the time before that, on the platform in the Sanders Theatre, after taking his diploma, gracefully returning his mortarboard to his head with the tassel on the left side.

"Ida," Max said. "When did you give up saying hello to people?"

"Joe," she said.

She stepped toward him, and he stepped toward her. He kissed her on the cheek, the way he had kissed her a thousand times in the ten years since as a boy of fourteen he had come to live with them. Except that now, this time, the thousand-and-first time, something happened. It took her by surprise.

"Norman and Claire are fine," Joe said. "Mrs. Schiff is in the house taking care of them. Everything is fine, Mrs. L."

"Never mind the house," Max said. "What we're waiting to hear is what's not fine."

"Yes, Mr. Max," Joe Catalini said.

Max said, "Start with why we're expecting Coley and who shows up is you."

"I think, Mr. Max," Joe said, "you better hear first what's important."

Ida wondered about his voice. It was like the touch of his

lips on her cheek. It had a quality she had not noticed before. Somewhere on the way from Minneapolis to John o' Groats, something had changed.

Max said, "Are we in trouble?"

"Bad trouble," Joe Catalini said.

"Okay," Max said. "Let's have it."

"The papers you had when you got to Minneapolis thirteen years ago," Joe said. "The papers you filed with your application for citizenship in 1925. They can prove they're false."

"How?"

"They dug up the man who wrote them."

"What man?" Max said.

"Sumeg," Joe Catalini said. "First name Saul."

Max went to the bay window. He looked out at Pentland Firth. All the lentil soup in the world gathered in one enormous plate was still hanging in there, motionless, a solid mass. For the third day in a row the sun had refused to obey Mr. McKenzie's orders. Scapa Flow and the Orkney Islands remained no more than a promise. Max turned back from the window.

"There's a key," he said.

"Yes," Joe said.

"It's what?" Max said.

"Sumeg. Without him they've got nothing," Joe Catalini said.

"They're not stupid," Max said. "Whatever Sumeg has to say, they've got it down on paper in front of witnesses."

"True."

Watching Max's face, Ida saw something to which she had grown accustomed long ago. The eyes were changing color. He was pulling it all together.

"True what?" Max said.

"Anybody can get anything on paper," Joe Catalini said. "And witnesses, you can buy them in Woolworth's. A thing like this, against a man like you, Mr. Max, to make it stick they'll have to do more than that."

311

"Like what?" Max said.

"They'll have to walk him into court and sit him down in a witness chair," Joe said.

"Sumeg," Max Lessing said.

Joe Catalini said, "Yes, Mr. Max."

"Ten years ago I promised your father I'd send you to law school," Max said. "Looks like I sent you to a good one."

"Yes, Mr. Max."

"This mysterious 'they,' " Max said. "The boys who dug up Sumeg. They have names."

"Sir Digby Locksmoor," Joe said. "The memorandum he signed with you eleven days ago in his London house is just a front. He put together his own setup behind you in Chicago. All he has to do now is keep you out of the United States and they've got the whole ball park to themselves."

Max Lessing said, "He is not they."

"He's got friends in Chicago," Joe Catalini said.

"The boys who feel sure this Roosevelt is going to make it in November."

"Plus one other friend," Joe said.

"Who?"

"Mr. Max," Joe Catalini said, "how did your passports get into the hands of this Mr. Klemperer at the Embassy?"

"Why do you ask?" Max said.

"American citizens," Joe said, "do not need visas to enter or leave England. The U.S. Embassy has no control over the right of an American citizen to enter or leave this country. There is no such thing as validating the passport of an American citizen who wants to leave England. Getting out of England is under the control of British immigration authorities, not the U.S. Embassy. If a person wants to speed up his exit from England he has to go to the Foreign Office, but such a person would never be an American citizen. Americans can leave as they please."

"I know that," Max said.

Joe said, "Yet your passports ended up on the desk of

312

Mr. Klemperer at the U.S. Embassy, Mr. Max. How did they get there?"

"Sir Digby carried them," Max said.

"He didn't steal them from you."

"No," Max said.

Joe Catalini said, "Somebody must have got you to turn them over to Sir Digby."

Max's face cracked in a quick grin. He put his hands together and gave them a brisk scrub with invisible soap and water. Like a boy bent over a checkerboard who has just moved his king into striking position.

"Sir Digby's friend in Minneapolis," Max said.

"Coley Scudder," Joe Catalini said.

Max Lessing moved out of the bay window. Coming across the room he said, "You have any thoughts about how to handle this?"

"Only one," Joe said.

For Ida it was as though the sun had reached a sudden decision to keep Mr. McKenzie's promise. The lentil soup broke up. Light came pouring through. She could see Scapa Flow and the Orkney Islands. All at once Ida understood that quality she had never before noticed in Joe's voice. She took a step toward him and said, "You know how to do it?"

"Yes, Mrs. L," Joe Catalini said.

"You will do it?" Ida said.

"If Mr. Max tells me to," Joe said.

"He can't do that," Ida said. "Mr. Max hasn't heard anything."

"That's true," Max Lessing said.

He crossed the room and walked out into the hall. To the closing door Joe Catalini said, "I understand, Mr. Max."

"Mr. Max is not in this room," Ida said.

Joe said, "I understand, Mrs. L."

Ida said, "You will do what you think is right."

"Yes, Mrs. L."

"You won't tell me what you did," Ida Lessing said.

Joe Catalini said, "Never, Mrs. L."

PART V
1934

41

The Chicago friends of Sir Digby Locksmoor proved to be
right. This Roosevelt made it in November. Exactly fourteen
months after he took office in Washington, Ida Lessing took
the train from Minneapolis to New York. She had an appointment with Jake Blau. The appointment was Ida's idea.
Jake Blau was God's idea. Anybody who didn't believe this
was free to ask Jake. Many people did.

Jake published the questions in a daily column called
"Ask Me and I'll Tell You." Jake also published the answers.

It was generally held in American journalistic circles that
Jake Blau's editing of *The Jewish Daily Watchword* was a
model of what an ethnically oriented newspaper should be.
Carl Ackerman, dean of the Columbia School of Journalism,
had stated publicly that it was the best Yiddish daily in the
United States. Simon Guggenheim and Louis Marshall did
not disagree. It was their task, through banking and legal
connections in New York Jewish society, to wet-nurse the
fragile financial structure on which the life of *The Jewish
Daily Watchword* had managed, somewhat improbably, to
stumble sturdily along for forty years.

"It's a good paper, nobody says not," Louis Marshall stated
in his speech to the guests of the New York Bar Association
at the dinner given in honor of Jake Blau's fortieth an-

niversary as founder and editor of *The Jewish Watchword*. "But let's face it, my friends," Marshall added. "Without Jake's 'Ask Me and I'll Tell You' column the paper would be like a circuit court without a docket."

It was certainly true that Jake Blau's daily column of advice to the Jewish immigrant community was the first thing to which Jewish readers of the *Daily Watchword* turned. The paper had no other kind of readers. It was printed in Yiddish.

For the immigrant who had arrived in New York at approximately the same time Saul Sumeg dropped Max and Ida Lessing at the foot of the hill that led up into South St. Stephen, Maine, the *Daily Watchword* was indispensable. It was more than a gazette. It was a practical guide, written in the immigrant's own language, on how to cope with the bewildering, difficult, often terrifying daily round of a startlingly new existence as confusing to the non-English-speaking, often unskilled, and frequently penniless Jew from Central Europe as Brobdingnag had been to Lemuel Gulliver.

"The paper functions successfully for its dedicated readers because the paper is the dedicated passion of one man," Louis Marshall said. "And the man with that passion functions successfully because Jake Blau never hesitates. He never says maybe. He never uses the word perhaps. Above all, he never says he doesn't know. Jake Blau knows everything. Absolutely everything!"

This certainly seemed true to even a casual reader of his "Ask Me and I'll Tell You" column. Jake Blau had very few casual readers. The men and women who bought *The Jewish Daily Watchword* turned to Jake Blau's daily printed words as on Saturday in the synagogue they turned to the Ark of the Covenant.

"My wife lost on the street somewhere the book we have from the Dry Dock Savings Bank. Every penny we have saved up since we came to America it's in that bankbook. What should we do?"

"My boss on Allen Street he says I and all the other

workers in our shop we have to pay him a nickel a day every day out of our wages to use the toilet on our floor in the factory, and if we don't pay we have to go down to use the toilet in the yard, and the time it takes to go up and down, the boss takes it out of our pay. Is this right."

"I am nineteen years old and very tall, and I am in love with a girl sixteen years old who is beautiful and she loves me back, but she is very short. I am afraid if we get married in this country where I have learned people laugh for reasons I don't always understand, maybe they will laugh at me or at her as we walk down the street because side by side we look like these two American heroes in the papers Mutt and Jeff. What should I do?"

"What you should do is think the way I am thinking," Jake Blau's "Ask Me and I'll Tell You" column thunders. "What I am thinking is that this small girl is in danger of marrying a big dope. If you love this girl, are you not man enough to walk down the street with her? Who cares about the laughter of fools? In this country a man learns that the way to earn respect is not by being afraid but by holding his head high. Love conquers all, you dumbbell. In this country as well as in *da heim*. Grab this girl and marry her and live happily ever after, you damn fool, and stop sending letters with stupid questions to Your Friend Jake Blau."

Entering Jake Blau's office on the third floor of the *Jewish Daily Watchword Building* on East Broadway, Ida Lessing had a moment of shock. The man behind the untidy desk did not look like a friend.

"You are Mrs. Max Lessing from Minneapolis," Jake Blau said.

"Yes," Ida said. "It's a great honor for me that you agreed to let me come and see you, Mr. Blau."

"We'll find out in a few minutes if it's a great honor for me," Jake Blau said. "Sit over there where I can see you."

Ida eased the skirt of her two-hundred-dollar custom-tailored Marshall Field tweed suit down on the straight-backed kitchen chair that stood in a cleared space directly in front of Jake Blau's desk. It was not unlike, Ida thought, lowering yourself into a witness chair.

"You'll excuse me a minute," Jake Blau said. "I have to finish this letter."

"Of course," Ida said. "I have plenty of time, Mr. Blau."

"I don't," the editor said. "I have to be at a meeting in Coney Island in less than an hour."

He bent back over the pad of yellow foolscap on which he had been writing when Ida came in. Blau put the end of the pencil into his mouth, rolled it around until the point was thoroughly soaked with saliva, and went back to setting down words on the pad. He did it as though the pencil were a hammer and he were driving nails.

After a few moments of watching the scowling old man at the desk Ida realized what it was about Jake Blau that made her feel uncomfortable. It was Ida's recollection of a picture that hung on the wall of the room in Rabbi Jobsky's house in Klein Berezna where he made up the medicines and ointments with which he healed the members of his congregation when they asked for his medical help.

The picture showed Moses receiving the Ten Commandments on Mt. Sinai. Moses was depicted very clearly in several gaudy colors. The source from which Moses' outstretched hands were taking the stone tablet was not clear at all. There was no more than the hint of an aged, deeply lined, extremely grave, very stern face, fiercely bright eyes, and a naked skull from which, over both ears, sprouted what looked like enormous powder puffs of snow-white hair.

Ida had seen the picture every day for several weeks at a time when she was sent to the rabbi's house regularly to fetch the herb tea and radish salve he prepared for her mother's use in treating Ida's father. He had been badly hurt in a fall from his horse. Ida did not remember registering the conscious impression that the head in the picture, sketched vaguely over the hands holding out the tablet to the very clearly delineated Moses, was supposed to represent God.

Now, fifteen years later, seated in front of Jake Blau's desk, Ida understood why she felt uneasy. The editor of *The Jewish Daily Watchword*, bent down fiercely, relentlessly, implacably over his foolscap pad, was a precise reproduction of the face on which Moses in the picture had gazed with such rapture.

"*Nu*, all right," the man at the desk snarled.

Ida jumped slightly in the chair. Then she realized Jake Blau's words had been directed at the foolscap pad. The editor stuck the end of the pencil back into his mouth and rolled it around. He pulled out the pencil, stabbed the wet point at the pad in a gesture of unalterable finality, and flung down the pencil.

"Frieda!" he bellowed.

The door opened. Through it came the short, fat, dark-faced, white-haired woman in the shapeless black dress who had led Ida into the room. She could have been bringing an extra order of pickles to a table in a crowded delicatessen.

"Yes, Mr. Blau," she said.

The editor ripped the top sheet from the pad as though he were flailing at a buzzing mosquito.

"Here it is, and I don't want any more arguments from you know who about more changes," Jake Blau said. "If they don't like this draft they can write their own letter but Jake Blau is not signing it. The top copy goes to the Mayor, of course—Dear Fiorello. Carbons to the Governor with personal notes from me Dear Herbert, the President Dear Franklin, Mr. Guggenheim Dear Simon, Mr. Marshall Dear Louis. If I'm still out there at this Coney Island meeting when you get these all typed, you sign my name for me, Frieda, and send them out. I want these letters in the mail as fast as possible."

"Yes, Mr. Blau."

The short, fat woman took the sheet of yellow foolscap as though it were indeed the flat stone Moses took from the vaguely defined fierce old man in the Rabbi Jobsky picture. The fat woman left the room. From a plate on his cluttered desk Jake Blau picked up what was left of a badly oxidized apple. He took a bite.

"All right," he said. "Tell me what you want."

"First," Ida Lessing said, "I think I'd better tell you a little about myself."

"Don't waste time," Jake Blau said around his mouthful of apple. "Everything about you that I want to know I know already."

Surprised, Ida said, "You do?"

"If I didn't" Jake Blau said, "I wouldn't say so. Tell me what you want, Mrs. Lessing. What I have waiting for me at this meeting in Coney Island it's not going to be easier to handle if I'm late."

"It's a little embarrassing for me to say this to a man like you," Ida Lessing said, "but what I've come to talk to you about must be kept in strict confidence."

"You're asking me to keep my mouth shut," Jake Blau said.

"Not exactly," Ida Lessing said.

"I don't know how to keep my mouth shut not exactly," Jake Blau said. "A mouth you keep it shut or you don't keep it shut. How do you want mine?"

Opening it wide, the editor pushed in the apple.

Ida said, "Why don't I let you decide that, Mr. Blau, after I tell you what I came to see you about?"

"Better start while I'm still thinking about you," Jake Blau said. "When I start thinking about that landlords' association in Coney Island and what I'm going to have to tell those bastards, I won't even remember your name, Mrs. Lessing."

"All right," Ida Lessing said. "What I came to talk to you about, Mr. Blau, is Hitler."

Jake Blau said, "Mrs. Lessing, I don't believe you."

Startled, Ida said, "I beg your pardon?"

"That today, in 1934, a woman would come all the way from Minneapolis to East Broadway to talk to me about Hitler," Jake Blau said, "I don't believe it."

"When I say talk I didn't come to chat," Ida Lessing said. "I came here with a program."

"The only program I'd be interested in," Jake Blau said, "I'd like to kill the dirty rotten son of a bitch, if you'll excuse my language, Mrs. Lessing; that's all I'd be interested in."

His teeth snipped off the last edible fragment from what was left of the apple. He swung the core gracefully back across the desk toward the plate.

Ida said, "That's precisely what I came to see you about, Mr. Blau."

Jake Blau's hand, holding the apple core, stopped moving. It hung over the plate.

"You just said something," he said. "I'm going to repeat it."

"Please do."

Jake Blau said, "You said you came here with a program to tell me how you plan to kill Hitler?"

Ida Lessing said, "Not I, Mr. Blau. It's not my program. I have been authorized by people who are in a position to execute such a program to come here and ask your permission, to obtain your blessing, so to speak, for such a program to be set in motion."

The apple core plopped down on the plate. Jake Blau pulled back his hand and with the palm rubbed the area of bald skull between the powder puffs of white hair.

"Why?" he said.

"What do you mean why?" Ida Lessing said.

Jake Blau said, "Why do you want to kill Hitler, Mrs. Lessing?"

"The same reason you want to kill him."

"Never mind my reasons," Jake Blau said. "You came here all the way from Minneapolis to tell me your reasons, Mrs. Lessing."

"I'm a Jew," Ida said. "Unless this creature is destroyed, Mr. Blau, anybody who knows what's going on over there is aware he'll end up murdering every Jew in Germany."

"God forgive me for even saying this as a for instance," Jake Blau said. "But let's say a for instance for the sake of

argument you're right, Mrs. Lessing. How do you propose to
do this? This killing Hitler?''

Ida said, "I can't give you the details, because I don't
know them. I don't want to know the details. I know only
from my connections that what they have sent me here to
see you about is not a vague hope or an indignant protest.
What we want your sanction for, Mr. Blau, is a practical
matter. It can be done.''

"By gangsters," Jake Blau said.

"Isn't that irrelevant?" Ida Lessing said. "You just told
me the only program you'd be interested in is a discussion
of how to kill what you correctly called this son of a bitch.''

"We'll come to me later," Jake Blau said. "You asked for
this appointment. You came to see me. We'll stick to you,
if you don't mind, Mrs. Lessing. Why do you want to kill
Hitler?''

Ida Lessing said, "How can you ask such a question?''

"I'm a newspaperman," Jake Blau said. "A good one.
According to Carl Ackerman up at Columbia I'm the best
in the business. I do my business by asking questions. Now
you make it your business to answer this one, Mrs. Lessing,
or I'm going to be early for those landlords in Coney Island.''

"I've just told you I'm a Jew," Ida said. "My family are
Jews. Isn't it natural for us to want to destroy the man who
has embarked on a program to destroy us?''

Jake Blau said, "You got people in Germany?''

"No.''

"You got people anywhere in Europe?''

"Not anymore," Ida Lessing said. "My family is all gone,
and my husband's mother died six years ago in Austria
before we could complete the arrangements to bring her
over here.''

"So this passion you have to kill Hitler," Jake Blau said.
"It's only because you're a Jewish lady who doesn't like to
see other Jews killed?''

"What other reason does a good Jew have to have?''

"I'm still asking the questions, Mrs. Lessing," Jake Blau said. "My next one deals with these gangsters you say you have connections with."

"I did not say that," Ida Lessing said.

"I'm saying it for you," Jake Blau said. "While I'm talking, you please shut up and listen, Mrs. Lessing. We have come to these gangsters you and your family you've got what you call connections with. The killings they've done for your family in the past, Mrs. Lessing, were any of those people Jews?"

Ida said, "Mr. Blau, I wish I knew what you're talking about."

"Zalman Fruchter," Jake Blau said. "A brother he had, Jekuthiel? Then a man named Sumeg. You want to hear more, Mrs. Lessing? Or you want to answer only about those three?"

Ida Lessing said, "I repeat, Mr. Blau, I have no idea what you're talking about."

"Listen and you will be enlightened," Jake Blau said. "I'm talking about a new series of articles I have written for the paper. They deal with the morality of the American businessman. It is no secret that the first article, which is scheduled for next Sunday, deals with Max Lessing. It was a secret until yesterday, but yesterday it was in Walter Winchell's column, and today you are here in my office. People have tried to buy me off before, Mrs. Lessing. You have a unique distinction. You are the first person who has tried to buy me off with a promise to have Hitler assassinated by your family gangsters."

Ida said, "I am not a gangster, Mr. Blau. Neither is my husband."

"Of course not," Jake Blau said. "And me I'm not a barber. We have people we hire to do these things for us. A successful bootlegger, how successful would he be if he didn't have the kind of connections who do things for him?"

Ida Lessing said, "I am afraid you have been misinformed

325

about the Lessing family, Mr. Blau. We are not what you say in your article we are."

Jake Blau said, "Maybe we could save time here so I can get to these bastards in Coney Island on time if instead of telling me all the things you are not, Mrs. Lessing, you could maybe just tell me the things you are?"

"My husband is an American businessman who happens to be a Jew and wants to do something to prevent the extermination of our people," Ida said. "Isn't that enough for any decent man?"

"For a decent man, maybe," Jake Blau said. "For your husband, this visit from you is going into my article when it appears in the paper on Sunday. For your contribution I will give you a piece of advice that you can carry back to your husband. You can tell Max Lessing from me and for no charge that there's only one way to stop an honest newspaperman from telling his readers you are a crook, and that's to stop being a crook."

"Mr. Blau, I think you owe my husband an apology, and I demand it," Ida Lessing said. "Nobody talks that way about Max Lessing in my presence."

"Nobody except Jake Blau," the editor said. "And Jake Blau is finished talking, so now will you please get out of this office, wife of Mr. Legitimate Businessman Max Lessing."

The door opened. The fat, white-haired woman came in. "Mr. Blau," she said.

The editor snarled, "What do you want?"

Imperturbably the white-haired woman said, "Harry is downstairs with the car to take you to Coney Island."

"You tell Harry to take the car and go uptown and watch how the Yanks make out today, they're three games behind, the stupid clumsy butterfingered fools," Jake Blau said. "Me, I'll take the subway. I want to get the stink of this room out of my nose."

"You're late already, Mr. Blau," the secretary said. "You'll never make it."

"I'm a Jew," Jake Blau said. "We've been making it for

326

three thousand years. We're not stopping today because of some fancy talk from the bleached-blonde wife of a dime-a-dozen gangster from Minneapolis in a two-hundred-dollar Marshall Field custom-made tweed suit."

42

Within the month Ida Lessing's skirts were being made by Hattie Carnegie, and Max's pants were being tailored in Dunhill's on Fifty-seventh Street in New York.

Two months later the seat of those pants was being planted in a variety of Hepplewhite chairs. None was signed but, according to Susie Shale, all were authentic. Ida supervised Max's testing of each one on the different levels of the five-story town house on Fifth Avenue between Eighty-first and Eighty-second Streets. It was now their new home.

"The house was designed by Stanford White for Samuel J. Tilden," Susie Shale said.

"What was the J for?" Max Lessing said.

"Max, please shut up," Ida said. "Susie, who was Stanford White?"

"Don't skip Tilden," Max said.

Susie provided Max and Ida with background sketches on Stanford White and Samuel J. Tilden. She did it, as she did everything, with a kind of boop-boop-a-doop charm that was already a bit dated in 1934. Susie Shale was the sort of girl over whom the word "cute" hung like the odor of musk over a houri.

Blond hair. Pageboy bob. Snub nose. Saucer eyes. Silk

stockings no longer, in 1934, rolled beneath the knee, of course. You could, however, bet your bright yellow slicker and your floppy unbuckled galoshes that that was where they had been rolled when Susie met John Quincy Adams Shale in the freshman class at the University of Minnesota.

They were both at the time trying out for the staff of *Ski-U-Mah*, the college humor magazine. John Quincy Adams Shale did not make it. Susie did. Since then she had never stopped making bad jokes, or been able to see the point of a good one.

She was, however, five feet two, eyes of blue. Her husband was heard to ask not infrequently, once she entered the employ of the Lessing family, "Has anybody seen my gal?" Many people did. The move to New York changed Susie Shale's life.

"Wow," she said to her husband the day after they were settled in their own Lessing Enterprises–paid-for apartment on Madison Avenue, around the corner from the Lessing town house on Fifth. "Back home in Minneapolis all I had to worry about was teaching them not to split infinitives and how many Ps in Hepplewhite. You know what I learned yesterday?"

"What was yesterday?" John Shale said.

"Organization Day," Susie Shale said. "The relaxed, catch-as-catch-can methods of Minneapolis are a thing of the past. Queen Ida is tackling New York the way her husband tackles a new project for Lessing Enterprises. Yesterday she set in motion the project that I can see no other way of identifying except with the phrase Getting Organized for Luxury. On Columbia Heights I was an English teacher who came in when called to give a lesson in syntax, or answered the phone to solve a problem in pronunciation that had come up unexpectedly. Here in New York I am a social secretary. It says so on Mrs. Lessing's organization chart."

"Does that chart say anything about my appointment?" said the ex-scoutmaster of Minneapolis Troop 24. "I'm beginning to feel like a gigolo."

"You're on the agenda for this morning's staff meeting," Susie Shale said.

"You're kidding," John Shale said.

"Word of honor," his wife said. "From now on there will be a meeting every morning in the oval sitting room on the fourth floor at nine-thirty sharp. Queen Ida and her executive staff: Ellis, Miss Liddy, and yours truly."

"That's pretty late in the morning for a staff meeting in an efficiently run organization," John Shale said.

"Mrs. Lessing explained that no plans for her day can be made until she learns what her husband's plans for the day are," Susie Shale said. "And she never knows that until they've finished breakfast and the car arrives to take him down to the office at nine-fifteen."

"For an efficient organization," John Shale said, "it looks to me like an inefficient waste of fifteen minutes between the time Mr. Max gets out and the time Mrs. Lessing gets started."

Susie Shale said, "After she finishes with her husband, Mrs. Lessing explained, she needs fifteen minutes to catch her breath and go to the bathroom. I need five to get around the corner into that oval study, so I'd better run."

She did, and as a result she ran into Max Lessing on the sidewalk in front of his new home. He was coming down the steps of the town house toward the Duesenberg waiting at the curb.

"Susie, I've got news for your husband," Mr. Lessing said. "I can't stop now to tell you, but Mrs. Lessing has all the dope, and she'll pass it on."

Other things came first, however, and Susie Shale was pleased that they did. She preferred not to discuss John's problems in front of the rest of the staff. The first thing that came first was the meat situation.

"I've done some checking with friends I've made in the neighborhood," Ellis reported. "I think I've found the top butcher in the area, maybe even in the whole city, my friends say."

330

"Who's that?" Mrs. Lessing said.

"Place called Schaefer's on the corner of Madison and Eighty-first," Ellis said.

"What makes them the best?"

"They've got dead birds with feathers hanging upside down in the windows," Ellis said. "And they shut up shop every day for a solid hour from one to two. Draw down the window shades and everything, so the help can have a quiet rest along with their lunch."

"Until we have a chance to check out the meat," Mrs. Lessing said, "I wouldn't mention that to Mr. Lessing."

She made a check mark on the list fastened to the clipboard in her lap and said, "Mary?"

Mary was Miss Liddy, and the fact that it had become Mary was a tribute, Susie Shale felt, to Mrs. Lessing's talents as a diplomat. The nurse clearly felt the fourteen-year-old Claire was her own flesh and blood, or its equivalent. The rivalry between her and Mrs. Lessing for the little girl's affections had eased considerably after Norman was born; but easing, Susie Shale knew, would not have been enough to get the aging Miss Liddy to join the family move to New York. Something extra had gone into the persuasion brew, and while Susie Shale knew exactly what it was, she had never been able to feel she could identify it accurately with words. It was something you felt or didn't feel about the small, beautiful blond woman with the vestigial traces of a Hungarian accent that added a good deal to the quality Susie and her husband, English teachers both, could not nail down in the language of Shakespeare and Milton.

"You've got it or you haven't got it" was the closest John Shale would venture in the direction of a definition. "The lady has got it. According to Herodotus, so did Cleopatra. With a different accent, of course. It moves mountains."

Susie Shale didn't know about mountains, but she knew about Miss Liddy. It had moved her to uproot herself from the place of her birth, come to New York, and break her back for a month finding the institution into whose hands the light of her life could with safety be deposited for the acquisition of the foundation on which an appropriate education could be built.

"It's still probably a little early to say definitely," she said now. "I think, though, Miss Claire is going to be happy at this Brearley. She told me yesterday—"

Queen Ida cut in with a smile and "What's important, Mary, is: are you happy?"

The heavy, solid Irish face untouched by either makeup or guile took on very slowly a dark red hue that only someone who knew it intimately, as Susie Shale did, would have known meant the owner had been nudged into a glow of pleasure.

"I am, Mrs. Lessing," the nurse said. "Miss Claire will do well there. I feel it in my bones."

"That's what I've been waiting to hear," Mrs. Lessing said. "Thank you, Mary. Can you say the same about Norman and this school—" She glanced at her list. "Yes, Collegiate is it?"

"It is," Miss Liddy said. "And I wish I could say the same, but it's too early yet. With Norman we have—"

"I know," Mrs. Lessing said. "I also know you know more about handling it than Mr. Lessing and I do, so I'll say no more for the same reason, Mary."

"Thank you," Miss Liddy said.

"I see everything else I've got on this list is for Susie," Mrs. Lessing said. "So Mary and Ellis, thank you very much."

She stared at the list until the butler and the nurse were out of the room. Then she put the clipboard aside on the couch and she moved into what Susie Shale had long ago described to her husband as Queen Ida's Posing for Epstein's Egyptian Goddess Act. Mrs. Lessing sat back, keeping her spine as straight as a bayonet, and she put her small hands on her knees very delicately, palms down.

"Now, Susie," she said. "About your husband. Mr. Max tells me Joe Catalini has at last spoken to the right people.

It took him some time to catch on to the machiney here in New York, but finally he's done it and everything is fixed."

"That's wonderful," Susie Shale said. "He's been feeling sort of—you know."

"I do," Mrs. Lessing said. "Now he can stop, because Joe says he can have an appointment as an English teacher, with seniority and pensions and whatever else goes with it, and he can have it in any high school in the city. All he has to do is pick the one that's most convenient for both of you."

Late that afternoon, when Susie Shale got back to their Madison Avenue apartment, she repeated all this to her husband.

"That's all there's to it?" John Shale said.

"Except for one thing."

"What's that?" John Shale said.

"How would you like to be a college president?" Susie Shale said.

The ex-scoutmaster laughed. John Shale assumed he was being treated to another sample of the native wit his cute wife had honed to a cutting edge during her tour of duty as a *Ski-U-Mah* staff member at the University of Minnesota. This assumption vanished as soon as Susie conveyed to her husband the instructions she had received from Queen Ida.

John Shale followed these instructions to the letter. He had learned from Susie it was the only safe way to follow a set of Lessing instructions. As a result, John Shale found himself the next day emerging from an elevator on the 26th floor of 120 Broadway into an area that reminded him of the Minneapolis railroad station.

The high ceiling was arched and gilded. From the center hung an enormous tiered chandelier. The walls were constructed of white marble slabs. On these, in large block letters followed by arrows, were expensively made functional signs not unlike the directional instructions at a busy traffic intersection.

Under the central, dominating sign LESSING ENTER-

PRISES, LTD., John Shale ticked off swiftly the words AUDITING, LEGAL, GREAT BRITAIN, DOMESTIC, ELECTRONICS, KIRKBEAN AUSTRALIA, COAL, REAL PROPERTY, MEDIA, CASHIER, TRANSPORTATION, SHIPPING, VENDING EQUIPMENT, PAYROLL, MINING—and then the ticking-off process stopped. A girl had appeared in front of him.

"This way, Mr. Shale, please."

He said, "Yes, ma'am."

Then John Shale realized he had not spoken his name to anybody. He had not been announced. How did this girl know who he was? Or that her "This way, Mr. Shale, please" was the way he wanted to go? There was no time to ask questions. This girl was on her way.

She went swiftly, smoothly, with long-legged strides. These reminded John Shale but did not actually convince him that he was following a girl. She could have been one of those Rockettes he and Susie had gone to see at Radio City during their first week in New York. Girls obviously, but not girls really. No faces. Handsomely sketched outlines, clearly feminine, but curiously sexless.

The girl stopped her long, swift march down a long, high corridor and said, "You are expected."

Not quite sure how he had managed to set himself into such swift motion, John Shale swept past her. He was entering a room. He heard the door click shut behind him.

"This is a great pleasure for me, Mr. Shale."

Staring at the tall, slender figure in the double-breasted blue suit standing behind the desk, the ex-scoutmaster found himself wondering what had happened to his senior patrol leader's uniform.

"Joe," Mr. Shale said, and then he came out of it. "I mean Mr. Catalini."

The handsome young man smiled and said, "No, not Mr. Catalini."

He came with firm, purposeful steps from behind the desk. He took John Shale's hand. Then he put his other hand

334

on the ex-scoutmaster's elbow. The young man shook both the Shale hand and the Shale elbow in a gentle rocking motion of welcome that was not quite but felt to John Shale almost embarrassingly tender. He could have been watching John Barrymore, playing the lead in Elmer Rice's *Counsellor-at-Law*, having just destroyed for a six-figure fee the D.A.'s attempt to send the guilty Dutch Schultz to the chair, as he turned to greet his doting illiterate immigrant mother who for years had scrubbed floors to send him through law school.

Joe said, "It's been a long time since Whampoa's Open."

The voice matched the physical setting. Joe Catalini's ex-scoutmaster remembered neither. Aside from the clothes, and an overall more carefully barbered look, the young man of twenty-six in the double-breasted suit was easily recognizable as a taller, somewhat but not very much heavier version of the skinny fourteen-year-old kid in Scout uniform. The voice, though. The voice was something new.

"Twelve years," John Shale said. "I was a twenty-four-year-old scoutmaster with the best fourteen-year-old senior patrol leader in Minneapolis. Now I'm a thirty-six-year-old high school teacher with a twenty-six-year-old boss in New York."

"Ah, now, Mr. Shale," Joe said. "Don't call me your boss."

"Okay," John Shale said. "If you stop calling me Mr. Shale."

The handsome young man laughed. That too was new. As well as a surprise. Inside John Shale's neat, filing-cabinet mind a sight card written long ago popped up: SENIOR PATROL CATALINI: EFFICIENT, COMPETENT, RELIABLE, NEVER LAUGHS.

"You've got a deal," Joe Catalini said. "Sit down, John."

John Shale said, "Thanks, Joe."

The room was scaled to the marble grandeur of the intersection into which John Shale had been spilled from the elevator. The room was part of the plan that had brought into being the intimidating corridors along which he had loped in the wake of the long-legged girl. The desk, however, the chair behind it, and the chair beside it—these three things formed a sensible, efficient little island in the puzzling vastness.

Sitting down, John Shale was aware that he was putting his body into the sort of inexpensive golden oak office chair to which he had grown accustomed in Minneapolis. That Joe Catalini was pleasantly accustomed to his own chair, which was not unlike the somewhat cheesy number allotted to visitors like John Shale, was clear from the ex-senior patrol leader's relaxed, pleasurable squirm as he settled into the scooped seat.

"I've kept tabs on you," Joe said. "Just before my father died and I went to live with Mr. and Mrs. Lessing on Columbia Heights, my father introduced them to Mrs. Shale. They were new to America, and they needed some help with their English."

John Shale said, "When Mr. and Mrs. Lessing gained their English teacher, I lost my senior patrol leader."

Joe laughed. The sound was pleasant and effective, John Shale noticed, but controlled. As though it had been brought out of a pillbox whose contents were severely rationed by a prescribing doctor.

"Living with the Lessings," Joe said, "is a full-time job."

John Shale said, "Working for them, too, according to my wife."

A crease of concern, like a small primitive cloud on the horizon in a child's painting, appeared neatly in the middle of the young man's forehead.

"I hope she doesn't mind," Joe said. "The Lessings are absolutely crazy about her, you know."

"You bet I know," John Shale said. "So does she. Please relax, Senior Patrol Leader Catalini."

The crease vanished. Another dose of laughter came out of the pillbox.

"Now they've got your wife nailed down, they're beginning to have designs on you," Joe Catalini said. "In a perfectly nice way, of course."

"Barkis is willing."

"Anybody I ought to know?" Joe Catalini said.

This did not seem the moment for explanatory footnotes about Dickensian humor, so John Shale said, "I told Susie this morning that all the designs the Lessings have had on us so far have made a very attractive pattern, except for the fact that up to now only Susie has been the beneficiary of their attentions, and I'm getting jealous."

"That's what I want to hear," Joe said. "Because Mr. Max said more or less the same thing only yesterday. He was pleased, of course, when Mrs. Shale agreed to come with the family to New York. There was so much involved in making the move, however, as you can imagine, that Mr. Max said he didn't have time to give much thought to Mrs. Shale's husband. What Mr. Max doesn't give much thought to, Mrs. L does."

"Susie told me," John Shale said, "Mrs. L was the one who got after you to find out about getting me geared up again as a teacher."

"She was the one, all right," Joe Catalini said. "The way it worked, though, is typical of the way the Lessings work as a Mr.-and-Mrs. team. It was Mrs. Lessing who asked me to look into the Board of Education setup here in New York. By the time I had it worked out, Mr. Max's attention was attracted. Mr. Max is an improver. If somebody comes along and says it would be highly profitable for us to buy into, let's say, some bauxite mines in Chile, by the time I've done the legwork and checked it out and come up with an arrangement that's profitable to Lessing Enterprises, Ltd., Mr. Max says if it's profitable for us to buy a corner of Chile that has bauxite on it, it stands to reason it must be more profitable to buy Chile."

"Do you?" John Shale said.

Joe said, "Not infrequently."

This time the laugh was John Shale's, and it was not rationed. He was beginning to enjoy this weird, slightly pompous, yet curiously appealing marionette that, or who, had once been his senior patrol leader. To the sight card in his filing-cabinet mind where a dozen years ago he had noted SENIOR PATROL LEADER CATALINI: EFFICIENT, COMPETENT, NEVER LAUGHS, John Shale now scrawled a hasty addition: *Infrequently used but occasionally apparent: a sharp sardonic touch. Watch for it. Here lies maybe the real whatever-it-is now known to the world as Mr. Max's right-hand man Joe Catalini.*

John Shale said, "That explains Susie's joke last night."

"Growing up on Columbia Heights," Joe said, "I can tell you Mrs. Shale's jokes were certainly a pleasant thing to have around the house."

"They're not bad on Madison Avenue either," John Shale said.

"I hope the apartment is all right?"

"Perfect," John Shale said.

"I'm glad," Joe Catalini said. "I knew it was large enough, because Mrs. L told me before I started hunting what your needs would be. Before I signed the lease, though, I worried about the fact that only the living room and the kitchen faced Madison Avenue, so I asked Mrs. L to come over and have a look. She said immediately a bedroom on Madison Avenue was not very desirable because of the traffic noises, but in this case the bedrooms, both of them, as well as the study looked out on this very pretty garden out back, so having them at the rear of the apartment meant not only a nice view of trees and flowers but also it would be quiet at night for sleeping, and she was sure Mrs. Shale would prefer that."

"She does," John Shale said. "So do I. I didn't realize you and Mrs. Lessing had handled this apartment thing for us personally, so among all the other things I have to thank you for, I want to thank you for that, too."

"Nonsense," Joe said. "You know the Third Scout Law."

"A Scout Is Helpful," John Shale said.

"We hope you will be too."

"If I can," John Shale said.

"This joke Mrs. Shale made last night," Joe said. "Did it

338

have anything to do with your job as an English teacher here in New York?"

"It came out of that," John Shale said. "Susie said something about when Mr. Max heard the job was all arranged, he suddenly became interested and, as you just said, he started improving it. Or so I gather, because Susie's joke was, she asked me how would I like to be a college president."

"How would you?" Joe said.

Surprised, but on second thought not very much surprised, John Shale said, "Mr. Max is buying Chile?"

"Not quite," Joe Catalini said. "The problem is different."

"What problem?" John Shale said.

"Norman."

"I see," John Shale said.

He supposed he did, but he wasn't sure. All he knew about the Lessings' son had come from Susie, but it had been coming for twelve years. The two very bright Lessings had apparently spawned an egregious nonscholar.

"Mrs. Shale has known the boy as long as I have," Joe said. "He was an infant when I came to live on Columbia Heights and Mrs. Shale came to teach Mrs. L how many Ps in Hepplewhite."

The sight card flipped again. To it, scribbling hastily, John Shale addressed a stern admonition: *Watch this ex—senior patrol leader. How come he knows at eleven o'clock today down at 120 Broadway a remark Susie made kiddingly to me late yesterday afternoon? In the sanctity of our own, Lessing-paid-for home?*

John Shale said, "I gather he's not a very good student."

"Mrs. Shale is putting it with her customary discretion," Joe said.

"I didn't mean to suggest that Susie has in any way said anything that—"

"If she hasn't," Joe said, "I would not have the high regard for her intelligence I've developed during the past twelve years. Mrs. Shale has watched Norman Lessing grow up. She has tried to arouse his interest in studying everything from clay modeling to how to answer correctly for despairing classroom teachers complicated questions like What was George Washington's first name?"

The former senior patrol leader had clearly stepped into an area where he did not feel it necessary to exercise his customary circumspection. Joe Catalini had deliberately thrown a low pitch. John Shale had a feeling he was expected to step into it.

"Stupid?" he said.

"Far from it," Joe said. "Norman is as bright as his parents, and you know how bright that is. The trouble with Norman is that he's frivolous."

There was a pause. It was clearly created by Joe Catalini. John Shale decided to let his EFFICIENT, COMPETENT, RELIABLE ex–senior patrol leader work his way out of it. He did.

"If I sound tough about this," Joe said, "it's because I've been ordered to be. Up to now, the kid's refusal to study or make even a minimal effort at getting decent grades in school has been a sort of combination family joke and, let's say, minor nuisance. Now, though, Norman is twelve years old. To any other parents—well, let me, as we lawyers say, strike that. Mr. Max and Mrs. L are not any other parents, as I'm sure by now you've learned from Mrs. Shale if not from your own observation. They love the boy, of course, and they'll do anything in the world to indulge him, which is probably the root of the problem, but in addition to being indulgent parents these are also two very clear-eyed, tough-minded citizens. They see more than an adored child who happens to be a charmer but also a lazy student more interested in fun than in study. Mr. Max and Mrs. L see what must ultimately be the individual, who happens to be their son, into whose hands they will have to deliver the management of what is already today a not inconsiderable financial enterprise and, by the time Norman is old enough to be thought of seriously as playing a role in its management, will pretty certainly be an extremely big and complex international organization. Mr. Max and Mrs. L are doing something not many doting parents would be able to do. They are facing the hard facts about their son's not very great interest in the family business in a way that is characteristically Lessing."

"By making me a college president?" John Shale said.

This time, when the smile came out of the pillbox, it had a distinctly wintry look.

"The joke was premature," Joe Catalini said. "The provenance, however, is sound. Mrs. Shale has in abundance what Norman refuses to use—namely, brains. What it gets down to, John, is this. So far as schools for Norman are concerned, we've come to the end of the line. It's pointless to keep sending him to the schools that now exist and, when he inevitably flunks out, picking him up and carrying him to another. There is no other. We've gone the route. They like our money. But they won't take it twice. They have standards to maintain. So what we've done, taking my orders as always from Mr. Max and Mrs. L, I've located this school just outside Boston. It's private, of course, and it seems tailor-made for Norman. The place specializes in rich playboys, meaning mentally lazy slobs."

"Slobs?" John Shale said. "Or dumbbells?"

"Slobs."

"You're sure?" John Shale said.

"Pretty sure, yes," Joe Catalini said. "But in that field I'm no expert. Mr. Max and Mrs. L wondered if you'd check it out for us before we make an offer."

"You plan to buy the school?"

"Mr. Max," Joe Catalini said, "feels it's a good small investment that can be build into something very big."

"By educating mentally lazy slobs?" John Shale said.

"No," Joe said. "By educating Jews."

"I can't remember meeting many," John Shale said. "But I don't see why a man making an investment shouldn't put himself a little bit more over on the safe side by assuming there are just as many Jewish mentally lazy slobs as any other kind."

"After he gets Norman through the place where the boy is finally flogged into picking up his three Rs," Joe said, "Mr. Max's interest in the school as an investment will change."

"How does he know?" John Shale said.

"Mr. Max plans to arrange the change."

"How?" John Shale said.

Joe Catalini said, "By appointing you headmaster."

John Shale paused to hunt for the loose pieces. He could find only one. "My wife's joke," he said. "She asked how would I like to be a college president."

"You can give her this answer," Joe said. "After the school does its job for Norman, Mr. Max would like to do something for the Jews."

"The Jews as in the Old Testament?" John Shale said. "Or the Jews as in everybody is named Lessing?"

"Mr. Max takes a broad view of being a Jew, and he takes it seriously," Joe said. "He feels a Jew should do more than be a good citizen, meaning an honest, law-abiding business-man. Mr. Max believes a good Jew should devote part of his time and some of the fruits of his success to improving the condition of all the members of his race."

John Shale had the feeling his ex–senior patrol leader was reading from a prompt card somewhere over the ex-scout-master's head.

"By converting a school for mentally lazy slobs into a college?" John Shale said.

"A university," Joe Catalini said.

"For Jewish students only?"

"You're forgetting the most important point," Joe said.

"What's that?" John Shale said.

"Anti-Semitism."

"I didn't forget it," John Shale said. "I'm wondering how and why it all of a sudden got dragged into this conversation."

"Mr. Max feels it's the only point that matters," Joe said. "Anti-Semitism is a blight on our American way of life. Mr. Max feels he is charged with a responsibility, the responsi-

342

bility of helping to eliminate anti-Semitism. He feels he can do this by endowing with Jewish money a great institution of learning for which the whole world will have only one word."

"What word?" John Shale said.

Joe Catalini said, "The word for Lessing University will be 'nonsectarian.' "

43

Ida had another word for it. More accurately, two words.
"What are they?" Max said.
"Opening gun," Ida said.
"Who are we fighting?" Max said.
"Jake Blau."
Max put down his coffee cup. "You're taking that old *putz* too seriously," he said.
"Did you see Winchell this morning?" Ida said.
"Never on an empty stomach," Max said.
"Have another bite of bagel and take a look," Ida said.
She pushed the copy of the *New York Mirror* across the breakfast table.

Max read:
Guess what the whip-cracking mastermind at the helm in the conning tower of the mushrooming Lessing financial sheikdom has just added to his international holdings. Give up? The oh-so-swellegant, up-to-here-with-tradition, veddy lifted-pinky, oldest-in-America boys' private school, Aylmer Broughton Academy in Newton, Mass., which, according to the upper echelons of the Boston Brahmin set, was built with planks torn secretly by William Bradford in person in the dead of night from the decks of the just-anchored "Mayflower." Diamonds used to be a

girl's best friend, but it takes a Maecenas from Minneapolis to think up this kind of eyebrow-raising ornament to decorate the navel of his favorite stripteaser.

Max looked up from the newspaper. "What's this garbage got to do with Jake Blau?" he said.

Ida said, "You remember the first article in his *Jewish Daily Watchword* series on what's wrong with American businessmen?"

"What about it?"

"If you've forgotten, let me remind you," Ida said. "It was about you."

Max said, "That was three months ago."

"Yesterday when the last piece ran in the paper," Ida said, "Jake Blau announced the series had been just an opening gun. He's collecting material for what he calls his Crooks Revisited Series. Everybody who got a going-over in the first series is due for a second and more thorough treatment."

"He's a nut," Max said. "Forget him."

"I think he's dangerous," Ida said.

"I don't see why."

"His newspaper has been losing money for forty years but it keeps right on going."

"Because every year people like Louis Marshall pass the hat for him," Max said. "And rich Jews are afraid to say no to Louis Marshall."

"You know why?" Ida said.

"Because he's the big bug behind Temple Emanu-El," Max said.

"He's also a close friend of Judge Benjamin Cardozo," Ida said. "Who has written the Supreme Court's majority opinion in the last three antitrust cases. And in his article on you Jake Blau had two references to the Pacific Porcelain Corporation and Du Pont. Did you notice that?"

Max picked up his coffee cup and said, "Never mind what I noticed. Tell me what you noticed."

"It's the first time since we moved to New York that there's been anything about you in print except the usual stuff about Kirkbean and the Canadian real estate."

Max set the coffee cup back on the table. "Cardozo to Marshall to Blau," he said slowly.

"So far," Ida said.

"You see a next step?"

"Newspapermen," Ida said "don't write follow-up series to repeat what they said the first time."

Max said, "You have any ideas about the next step?"

"Only a guess," Ida said.

"Tell me."

"Justice Department," Ida said. "Antitrust Division."

Again Max started to reach for his coffee cup, but he seemed to change his mind. He pulled his hand back.

"Okay," he said. "What do you think?"

Ida said, "I think Jake Blau may be a nut, but he's got access to these big guns, and it seems to me the Lessing family would be making a mistake to pretend he's not getting our range."

"How do we get out of his range?" Max said.

"By joining Louis Marshall's club."

"Temple Emanu-El?" Max said.

"And anything else that will change our public image," Ida said.

"I've got Joe started on this Lessing University crap," Max said. "What more can I do for our image?"

"Get rid of Alma Pine," Ida said.

The breakfast table was always set up in the fourth-floor sitting room, the oval chamber between Ida's and Max's two bedroom suites. Max had never before realized how, in a room on which they had spent ten thousand dollars for soundproofing alone, it was possible to hear so clearly the sounds of Fifth Avenue traffic.

Finally he said, "Listen, Ida."

"Not much point in that," she said. "Nothing you say, Max, is going to do any good. What I say may help. So you listen."

346

"All right," he said.

When Ida finished, Max picked up the phone and punched the direct-wire button to Joe Catalini's desk at 120 Broadway.

"Morning, Mr. Max."

"Morning, Joe. What have you got on Slats Knorr?"

"In what area?" Joe said.

"His T.K.O. common stock," Max Lessing said.

"Hold it, Mr. Max."

While Max held it, Ida watched him steadily. Max returned her glance just as steadily. It was his only protection. If she suspected how badly she had hit him, she might be tempted to go deeper. He would have given a good deal to know just how long she had known about Alma, but a good deal in Ida's case meant everything, and Max knew he was not going to be fool enough to risk everything just to satisfy his curiosity. He had been leaning on Ida too long not to know her strength. If he started asking questions, he would be giving away something she still did not know: that Max was unaware of exactly how much she did know. It was better to give up without a struggle what he was pretty sure she was willing to take on the basis of her own assessment of what her knowledge was worth. No diamond expert in the De Beers combine could have made that assessment with greater accuracy. Max Lessing hoped he was managing to keep out of his steady glance the only thing that might tempt the prudent Ida in the direction of reckless adventure: her husband's reluctant admiration.

"Mr. Max?"

"Yes, Joe.

"Slats Knorr owns thirty-eight thousand seven hundred and fifty shares of T.K.O. Common," Joe Catalini said. "That's a controlling interest by a comfortable margin of twenty-two percent. Slats is willing to unload at this morning's market."

Max Lessing said, "Don't tell me what it comes to."

"Never, Mr. Max."

"Make the deal," Max said. He hung up and said to his wife, "All right, we own a studio."

347

"Give it to Alma Pine," Ida said.

"How?" Max said.

"Go out to the Coast and make the presentation in person."

"Anything else?" Max said.

"Yes," Ida said. "Make sure she understands it's a *cadeau de congé*."

"I see Susie Shale's got you deeper into French than she's got me," Max said. "What's a *cadeau de congé*?"

"On Minnehaha Avenue, a *moof tzettle*, or eviction notice," Ida said. "On Fifth Avenue, a farewell gift."

"All right," Max said.

44

Max Lessing did not like Southern California. It struck him as a place that had outgrown knee pants but was still struggling with a decision about what it wanted to be when it grew up. Like Alma Pine, who couldn't seem to make up her mind whether she was an ex-stripteaser or an about to be society lady. This, in 1934, made for a certain amount of confusion in the eye of the beholder. As well as the ear of the listener.

From Beverly Hills her voice on the phone said, "Okay, Max, tell a girl To what will I be owing the pleasure of looking forward to your arrival for this unexpected visit tomorrow?"

Oh, Jesus, Max thought. This was going to be tougher than it had seemed an hour ago when he made the promise to Ida across the breakfast table. Max could hardly blame her. It was not quite ten o'clock in his 120 Broadway office, which meant it was not quite seven o'clock in Alma Pine's Beverly Hills Hotel bungalow. Since she had started lying about her birthdays Max had begun to notice that Alma was not at her best when she was awakened by the telephone.

"I'll tell you when I see you," Max said. 'This call is just so you'll have time to warn Clark Gable and Dick Powell to

349

stay out of sight for a couple of days. You know how jealous I am of older men."

"All I'm jealous of is younger women," Alma said.

"I can't stand them either," Max said.

"That's not what I hear from the grapevine."

"Grapevines are no longer reliable," Max said. "You ought to start using this new thing everybody is switching to. It's called a heliograph. My plane gets in at a little after seven in the morning, it says here, but you know these airline schedules."

"Not as well as I know you, honey," Alma Pine said. "Anything I can do for you before you arrive?"

"Yes," Max said. "Take a bath."

What Max took, when the limo dropped him the next morning on the asphalt apron in front of the Beverly Hills Hotel, was the envelope the doorman handed him without a greeting. Max walked toward the front doors, but halfway up the slight incline he veered left and stepped into the shade of a palm cluster. He tore open the envelope and pulled out a small piece of paper. Printed at the top were the words FROM THE DESK OF HERNANDO COURTRIGHT.

Below, in the manager's handwriting: *Please come to my office as soon as you arrive. H.C.*

Max shoved the envelope and the note into his jacket pocket. He crossed the small palm-shaded oasis toward the flagstone walk that led around the main building and down toward the pool area. He passed two Filipino boys in white coats shoving a cart piled high with pool towels. Halfway down the path Max stepped off the flagstones. He moved through a narrow opening in the clipped hibiscus hedge and tapped on an unmarked green metal door. It was opened at once by a girl with a pageboy bob and a dazzling white-on-suntan smile.

"Flight okay, Mr. Lessing?" she said.

"Perfect," Max said.

"Mr. Courtright is waiting in his office," the girl said.

She led the way along a dimly lighted corridor. The cement floor had just been hosed down.

"Mind the wet, Mr. Lessing," the girl said.

She stepped daintily around the puddles. Max put his shoes down on the damp spots from which she lifted hers. At the end of the corridor she put a key into an unmarked gray metal door. She turned the key and twisted the knob. With a small frown she looked right and left, then gave the door a short shove. The key came out in her hand as the door moved in. The dazzling smile reappeared.

"There we are, Mr. Lessing," she said.

"Thanks," Max said.

He stepped past her, out of the cement-paved corridor into the handsome, not-quite-overdecorated, heavily carpeted room. The door closed behind Max with a click. Hernando Courtright looked up from his desk. He was holding a fountain pen. He smiled quickly and plugged the pen back into one of the golden tubes that rose like miniature flagpoles from a massive black onyx base in front of him. The manager stood up and came around the desk with his hand outstretched.

"Flight okay, Mr. Lessing?" he said.

"Perfect," Max said.

He pulled the note from his pocket. Courtright nodded and touched the small envelope with his forefinger.

"Call your office, Mr. Lessing," he said. "Urgent."

The manager was on his way across the wine-colored carpet before Max could start for the desk. At the other side of the room the manager took with both hands a bronze knob as big as a soup plate and pulled open a thick slab of redwood hinged with heavy bronze rectangles.

"The call is on hold," Courtright said. "The switchboard will put you through as soon as you pick up."

He went out. This redwood door at the other side of the room did not click. It closed with a sound not unlike the lid of a jewel box snapping shut on a diamond bracelet. Max sat down in Courtright's chair behind the desk and picked up the phone.

"Mr. Max?"

"Yes, Joe," Max said to the voice in New York.

Joe Catalini said, "Flight okay, Mr. Max?"

"I got here," Max said. "You want me."

"Yes, Mr. Max," Joe said. "George Jupiter called last night. After you took off."

"What's on his mind?" Max said.

"He wants to see you right away."

"About what?" Max said.

"He insists on telling you in person."

Max said, "That's going to take a little arranging, won't it? With me here in California and him out there in Australia?"

"He's not in Australia," Joe Catalini said.

"Where is he?" Max said.

"Where he called from last night."

"Where's that?" Max said.

"Suite 241," Joe said. "Beverly Hills Hotel."

"How did he know I'm here?"

Joe Catalini said, "He didn't and he doesn't, Mr. Max. He called last night to say he just got off the *Mariposa* at San Diego and he'd gone to the Beverly Hills for the night because he planned to fly out to see you here in New York tomorrow. That's today. I told him to stay put until I got back to him because you were out of town and I wouldn't be hearing from you until the morning, which is now."

Max said, "How long does it take for the *Mariposa* to make it from Sydney to San Diego?"

"Twenty-two days, Mr. Max."

Max Lessing stared at Hernando Courtright's desk set. The onyx base had a peculiar shape. Max's eyes remained fixed until the peculiarity made sense. The onyx was cut to represent a bas-relief map of California. Getting this straight freed the thought Max had been patting into shape in his mind.

"Three weeks on a ship," he said. "To see me in New

York about something he won't tell you about but he has to speak to me in person. Without a telephone call. Or a cable. Or even a goddamned postcard."

Joe said, "I thought it was peculiar, Mr. Max."

"You ever know George Jupiter to do anything peculiar?" Max said.

"I've never met him."

"You don't have to meet people who do peculiar things to know they do them," Max said. "Word spreads."

Joe said, "This word hasn't, Mr. Max."

"Not yet," Max said.

"I promised to call him back this morning and say when you'll be able to see him in New York," Joe Catalini said. "What shall I tell him, Mr. Max?"

"For twenty-one days he didn't let us know he was on his way," Max said. "Let's not make it twenty-two." Max glanced at his wristwatch. "Tell him to be in Bungalow J in ten minutes."

"That will be a quarter after eight, Mr. Max?"

"A quarter after eight," Max said.

He hung up and crossed the manager's office to the redwood door. He pulled the door open and stepped out into the lobby. The pace was picking up. Two clerks behind the desk were sorting mail. A chambermaid was pushing a cleaning cart toward the Polo Lounge. A bellman was standing knee deep in just-arrived luggage, reading the labels on the bags and making check marks on a slip of paper. Max skirted the hall porter's desk and moved toward the door that opened into the bungalow compound. Nobody had seen him. Anyway, Max had seen nobody who might recognize him. He went through the door and down the tree-shaded walk. He turned left, then right, then sharp left again. He had the key in his hand when he reached the door marked J.

"That you, honey?"

"It's me," Max called toward the bedroom.

He pulled out the key, shut the door, and slid the bolt across.

"Come on in," Alma called. "I've got a surprise for you."

Max crossed to the bedroom and looked in. She had indeed. He laughed and said, "Not now. Bury yourself in a good book until I finish."

"Finish what?"

"A meeting," Max said.

Alma punched the pillow and said, "Oh, Christ, don't you ever stop running?"

"Now and then," Max said. "At the moment, now will have to wait until then, which could be a half hour, maybe less. When it's over you'll get the present I brought you from New York."

"Give it to me now," Alma said.

Max said, "I don't want you oohing and ahing all during my meeting. For this deal I need total silence."

There was a sharp knock on the outside door.

Alma said, "How do you know I'll ooh and ah?"

"I know what I paid for it," Max said. "Now lie back and shut up. I'll do this as fast as I can."

He pulled the bedroom door closed and crossed the living room. He slid back the bolt, opened the door, and said, "Come on in, Pete."

Coming in, Pete MacPhail said, "What happened to George Jupiter?"

"I just liquidated him," Max said. "He'd served his purpose."

He closed the door and shoved the bolt back.

"I hope you got rid of Australia along with him," MacPhail said. "Telling myself I had to remember I was not Pete MacPhail but some character called George Jupiter was bad enough, but for a guy who has spent his entire life in the plumbing-fixtures business without ever setting foot outside the United States, this Australia bit was heavy going."

Max said, "Sit where you think you'll be comfortable and don't ask for coffee. You won't be here long enough to drink it, and I don't want anybody to know you've been in this bungalow—not even Room Service waiters."

"I figured that from the George Jupiter beard," MacPhail said. "Who we hiding from this time, Max?"

"With luck, nobody," Max said.

MacPhail was a big man both ways, but he was bigger horizontally than vertically. As a result, when he stopped moving toward the couch and sharply turned his six-foot-two-inch frame toward his host, the paunch that was part of the two hundred and fifty or more pounds hanging on the MacPhail frame was set aquiver.

"Jesus God," he said. "What have we done wrong now?"

"Nothing yet," Max said. "Better sit down, Pete. You look like a bowl of strawberry Jello-O caught in a high wind."

"You don't like this jacket?" MacPhail said. "The wife gave it to me for my birthday."

"It's a winner," Max said. "Except that when what you've got it covering starts jumping around like that, it's like a red light flashing on and off, and what that does is make me lose my trend of thought."

"That will be the day," MacPhail said. "Your thoughts, Max, they don't have trends. Only delayed fuses."

Like a parent soothing a hysterical child, MacPhail placed both palms gently on his strawberry-covered paunch. This stilled the quivering flesh. He lowered himself onto the couch. The springs released a gentle musical whine.

MacPhail said, "You bring me all the way down from Seattle like I'm about to get a part in a Mata Hari movie, and for a hello you tell me maybe we're in hiding and maybe we're not. Then, while I'm trying not to wet my underwear, your idea of calming a guy down is to give me the same kind of dialogue about my weight that I get all the time from my wife."

"Better start listening to her," Max said. "You're eating yourself into an early grave."

"Never mind my weight," MacPhail said. "As soon as I get back to Seattle I'm going on a high-protein diet. Right now just tell me, if we haven't done anything wrong yet, why could we be hiding from anybody?"

Max said, "Because in this room we are about to make a decision some people might not like. If they ever find out about it, I mean, which we will see to it they don't."

"Who is we?"

"You and me," Max said.

"Just us?" MacPhail said.

"For starters."

"Max, you better tell me what you're starting," MacPhail said.

"What we're starting," Max said.

MacPhail had a fat man's body but a thin man's face. It hardened. "I'm not starting anything," MacPhail said. "All I'm doing, Max, is listening."

"Ever since I bought my way into your Pacific Porcelain Corporation two years ago," Max said, "all I've got out of my investment is a deep interest in bathtubs and sinks and toilets. Not the way they work. I've known how a toilet works for a long time, long before I invested in Pacific Porcelain common. My new interest, my interest these last two years, is in the way toilets get sold to home builders."

"They get sold like anything else," MacPhail said. "For a profit."

"That's what I thought when I made my investment," Max said. "Since then I've made my discovery."

"What discovery?" McPhail said.

"The people who make toilets don't sell them for profits," Max said.

"What are you talking about?"

"They sell them for peanuts," Max said.

"Your Pacific Porcelain stock," MacPhail said. "Last quarter it paid a dollar ten a share. You call that peanuts?"

"Unshelled," Max said.

"What makes you think so?"

Max said, "For the same period Du Pont paid two twenty-five a share."

"We're not Du Pont," MacPhail said.

"As a decent, law-abiding American citizen you're entitled to be," Max said. "Did you know that in 1917, eight years before I became a decent, law-abiding American citizen, Du Pont bought twenty-three percent of the General Motors outstanding common stock?"

"What's wrong with that?" MacPhail said.

"Nothing," Max said. "Just the opposite. As soon as that stock sale went through, ninety-three percent of Du Pont's Duco paint production started being snapped up by General Motors. Do you have any idea what that meant in money?"

"I don't know a damn thing about automobiles or paint," MacPhail said. "All I know about is bathtubs, sinks, and toilets."

"Okay," Max said. "Do you have any idea how many bathtubs, sinks, and toilets were sold to American home builders this year?"

"I happen to be the president of the American Plumbing Fixtures Manufacturers Association, which I'm sure is no news to you, Max," Pete MacPhail said. "I can get the figures for you from the office by picking up this phone."

"Don't bother," Max said. "Joe Catalini's already got them. He's working on a memorandum. It will be ready next week. That's when I planned to call you and arrange a meeting place where nobody would know Pete MacPhail of Seattle and Max Lessing of New York any more than they'd know George Jupiter of Sydney, Australia. But something came up yesterday, a family thing that made me come out to the Coast last night. I figured as long as I'm here, I might as well push my date with you ahead, so I set the George Jupiter beard in motion, and here you are. Any questions?"

"Just one," Pete MacPhail said. "What do you want from me?"

"Not from you, I want it for you."

"From me or for me, frig that," Pete MacPhail said. "Tell me what you want."

"I want you to get in touch with every member of your A.P.F.M.A. on a confidential basis," Max said. "I want you to tell them that as of June first of this year the price of every

357

bathtub, sink, and toilet sold in this country at the whole-sale level will go up by five percent. On September first the price will go up by ten percent. On December first the price will go up by fifteen percent. At that point we will hold and see what the figures for the year look like. According to Joe Catalini's memo, when those figures come in, late in January of next year, they should indicate that the take for the last six-month period for all of us lucky A.P.F.M.A. members has increased by one billion dollars over the best six-month period in the history of the American plumbing-fixtures industry. If that figure is not met, as of February first of next year you and your executive board will increase the percentage in accordance with my instructions. In this way, Phil, you and I and all the membes of the A.P.F.M.A. will be in the happy position of other decent, law-abiding American citizens like Du Pont."

Max paused.

"I don't like this," Pete MacPhail said.

"I did not bring you down here from Seattle like a character in a Mata Hari movie," Max said, "to find out what you like or don't like. I flew out here to tell you what I want you to do. Do it."

"Price rigging is something the Justice Department doesn't fool around with. Count me out, Max."

"Too late," Max Lessing said. "I've counted you in."

"Max, this could mean prison," MacPhail said.

"Not for you," Max said.

"Why not?"

"By the time the Antitrust Division gets off its ass on this," Max said, "the money will be in the bank, and the Pacific Porcelain Corporation will be run by a new majority stockholder named Max Lessing."

Pete MacPhail blinked. His mouth opened, but for a minute he made no noise. Then he said, "For Christ's sake, Max, please listen."

Max Lessing said, "I have another date."

He went to the door and slid back the bolt. MacPhail used

both hands to push himself up out of the couch. On his feet he paused for breath. He opened his mouth, as though an important point had come to mind but he could not seem to get it into words. MacPhail very carefully set both palms high on the strawberry cloth that covered his belly. Then he set himself in motion. The paunch held firm as he came across the room slowly. MacPhail did not look at Max when he passed through the door into the blazing sushine. Max closed the door and shoved the bolt back into place. He crossed to the bedroom, taking off his jacket as he moved, and he opened the door.

"Where's my present?" Alma Pine said from the bed.

"T.K.O. is too big to carry around like a box of Cracker Jack," Max said. "I'll drive you over later and show you what you own."

"The movie studio?" Alma said. "That what you're talking about?"

Pulling free the knot of his tie, Max Lessing said, "Move over. We'll talk later."

45

"I like owning a movie studio," Alma said that night as she drove Max to the airport. "What I don't like is getting kissed off."

"Who's doing that to you?" Max said. "Clark or Bill?"

"I got the impression from this fast in-and-out visit today that it's a boy named Max."

"How do you get your impressions?" Max said.

"The way this George Gallup gets his," Alma said. "I read a piece in *Reader's Digest*, he calls it the sampling technique."

"This impression you got that you're being kissed off by someone named Max. How big a sample did you use?"

"One," Alma said. "This morning, when I was about to take a shower before we went out to look at the Studio, you said you had to see Mr. Courtright for a few minutes, and you'd be right back. You didn't see Mr. Courtright. You used his office to call Ida in New York and tell her you'd kept your promise to dump me."

"How do you know what I told Ida? Max said.

Alma Pine said, "After diamonds, a girl's best friend is a switchboard operator."

"I find them useful too," Max said. "That's why on an

open wire I never say anything I don't want the operator to be able to repeat to her friend."

Alma took her eyes from the road just long enough to give him a swift sidelong glance. Max made sure what she saw included the big, broad boyish grin that had proved its utility first with the farm girls in Vetzprem and had been honed to a cutting edge in Minneapolis for use in meetings where muscle was not quite enough. Swinging her glance back to the road, Alma Pine laughed. She did it in a way Max had not heard for a long time. Not since the days in the Nokomis Hotel on Anoka Avenue.

She said, "What did you leave out of your report to Ida on the phone this morning?"

"How all of a sudden my feelings about Southern California have changed," Max said. "Now that I've got a friend here who owns a movie studio, I've decided to pick up a shipyard I've been iffy about for a few weeks."

"What have shipyards got to do with movie studios?" Alma said.

"They're both on a coast," Max said.

Alma laughed again. She took one hand from the wheel and put it on his thigh. She said, "Do you have to fly back tonight?"

"Yes, but I don't have to do it alone," Max said. "I've got a double lower. In the morning, when we get to Idlewild, I'll go off to handle Ida. You fly back to handle your studio."

"I feel like a bride," Alma said. "What about Ida?"

Max said, "You keep your mouth off me and Ida."

"I just said three simple words," Alma said.

"They were three too many," Max said. "Don't do it again."

When Max got out of the plane at Idlewild, the sun was coming up behind the huge revolving KIRKBEAN electric sign that loomed high over the traffic-control tower. The limousine was waiting. It took him direct to the office. Before he finished taking off his coat, Joe Catalini was in Max's room with the papers.

361

"I don't want to read them," Max said. "All I want to know is what Ida will want to know: does the lady own the studio or doesn't she?"

Joe said, "It's all Miss Pine's."

"All right," Max said.

"It's not a bad deal, Mr. Max," Joe said. "Pretty good, in fact."

The words were words. The tone had something in it that Max had never noticed before. He kept the reaction out of his own voice as he said casually, "What's good about buying a movie studio just to give it away like a tip to a manicurist?"

"I'm thinking of the overall picture," Joe said. "This should make things easier."

Nothing wrong with that. It was Joe's job to think of the overall picture. Yet Max Lessing was aware of an odd curiosity as he said, "What things?"

Joe Catalini said, "The Court of St. James's, for one."

"That, yes," Max said. "Sure."

Yet he wasn't sure, so he wondered about it. Was the picture getting too big for him to see into all the corners without squinting? He had never thought of that before. Now that he was thinking of it, Max was aware of a sense of discomfort. It was not unlike the way years ago on the well deck of the *Friesland* he had felt uncomfortable during his first meeting with a little man with a Charlie Chaplin mustache named Saul Sumeg. A connection had been made. At that time Max knew immediately that all he had to do was wait. He sensed that when the little man was ready he would move in with whatever it was he had made the connection for. Max had been right that time.

Was it possible that he wasn't right this time? Or was he? The moment he had met the fourteen-year-old boy in the rain-soaked Scout uniform on Columbia Heights, Max Lessing knew an important connection had been made. Fourteen years later, Max Lessing felt he certainly should have known if he had made the right move. Joe Catalini's record as his

362

right-hand man spoke for itself. Joe Catalini himself never did any speaking for himself. It was a quality Max Lessing did not share but could not help admiring. Underlings who talked about their roles as underlings were trouble. What, then, was wrong?

The answer was: nothing. That answer came, however, from Max's head. The uneasiness was coming from his gut. It was an area over which Max Lessing had no control. It told him things he wished it would shut up about. It spoke a language Susie Shale had not got him very far into.

Max had no such difficulty with the language of Walter Winchell. Two days after Max got back from the coast, Ida pushed the *New York Mirror* across the breakfast table.

"Take a look at this," she said.

Hottest rumor in the B'nai B'rith Set is that youthful financial shogun Max Lessing has purchased the prestigious, tradition-drenched Aylmer Broughton Academy, a short Paul Revere-type ride from Boston Common, as the turning-up-the-first-spadeful in a campaign to establish America's first Ivy League institution of higher learning which will be funded entirely by Jewish money and called, you guessed it, Lessing University.

"This is certainly an improvement," Max said to Ida. "How did it happen?"

"I've been thinking for some time what we need is a press agent," Ida said. "So I went and found one."

"Congratulations," Max said. "Looks like you found a good one. While you're at it, congratulate him too, whatever his name is."

"Katz," Ida said. "Hector Katz. They say if Arnold Rothstein hadn't fired Katz because of some minor difference of opinion just before the Black Sox scandal broke, nobody would ever have caught on it was Rothstein who fixed the 1919 World Series."

"The boy's good," Max Lessing said. "Tell him I said so."

Ida said, "It would be more productive, Max, if you told him in person. He'll be in Joe's office this morning."

363

An hour later, Max said to Joe Catalini, "Bring him in."

Hector Katz was not the sort of man you brought in. On his first appearance in Max Lessing's life, the press agent gave Max the impression that on innumerable subsequent appearances was never altered: the impression that Katz had been leaning all his weight against the other side of the door when the knob was turned from the inside and, as a result, he had tumbled in to the room.

"Joe Catalini tells me you saw the Winchell item," Katz said. "The way to handle Winchell, you feed him stuff that has a future. He likes continuity. Like this feud he has going with Ben Bernie. It's as phony as a three-dollar bill. He and Bernie know it, not to mention the public, but it has a future. Bernie can always be counted on to make a crack about Winchell on the air, which is good publicity for Winchell, and that sets it up for Winchell to put a zinger into the column about Bernie, which is good publicity for Bernie and at the same time fills a couple of lines in a hungry column that never stops eating. You give Winchell a one-shot item, the only way he can get mileage out of it, he has to explode a bomb, which means an attack. When you explode a bomb, somebody is going to get hurt, and you can be sure it won't be Walter. But you feed him something that's more than a single item, something that has a future, Walter forgets the attack, he gives you the space, and he waits for more. After all, he's got seven columns a week to fill, and Rose says it's murder."

Max said, "Who is Rose?"

"Rose Bigman, his secretary," Hector Katz said. "To her face, though, you better call her his assistant."

"When I meet the lady," Max said, "I will remember that. Meantime, where's the future in this item about me?"

"I told Rose your next move," Katz said.

"Which is what?" Max said.

"The West Coast."

Max Lessing said, "How do you know my next move is the West Coast?"

"I don't," Hector Katz said. "I'm just guessing."

"Based on what?" Max said.

"Past experience," Katz said. "Everybody who asks for my services, Mr. Lessing, I don't take them on for a client. Most requests I turn down. I run a one-man show. It's all here under this hat."

He touched his hat, a black snap-brim felt not unlike the item Hymie Shantz had used to wear in Minneapolis. Max supposed Hector Katz had not removed the hat when he came into Max's office because the press agent did not want the ingredients of his one-man show to tumble out all over the floor.

"If I can't pull out of this hat the kind of stuff I enjoy doing," Katz said, "the guy who wants me to do it for him can't pay me enough money to get me off the dime. If when I meet a guy who wants me I get the feeling I can do it, I say Yes if you can meet my price. With you, the minute Joe Catalini came to me, he knew enough about me not even to mention price. He just said Write your own ticket."

It had not occurred to Max until this moment that Joe had helped Ida find the press agent.

"True enough," Joe said with a small nod and a small smile, like Talleyrand's secretary sprinkling sand over his chief's signature on a brand-new treaty.

"With me," Max said, "you had the feeling you can do it?"

"Based on, like I said, my past experience," Hector Katz said. "Yes."

"To my best recollection," Max Lessing said, "I don't think you and I have had any past experience."

"Like the lady said to the judge when she was defending herself in the divorce court on a charge of adultery," Katz said, "the corespondent slept with me, yes, but I did not sleep with him. You and I, this is our first meeting face to face, but I've had my eye on you for years, Mr. Lessing."

"Why?"

"You remind me of an old client of mine," Hector Katz said.

"Which one?"

"Arnold Rothstein," Katz said.

"In appearance?"

"No, you're younger and taller and better-looking," Hector Katz said. "In a feel for the action, I mean."

Max said, "What kind of action?"

"You could take Arnold and drop him by parachute from Mars into Samarkand," Katz said. "He'd pick himself up, dust off his pants, straighten his tie, and walk straight to the biggest game in town."

Max Lessing said, "You're talking to a man who doesn't even know how to make a two-dollar bet on a horse."

"When you get interested you'll learn," Hector Katz said. "When you do, I'll hand you back every nickel of my salary and ask you to take it to the track for me. All the time you were out there in Minneapolis you were just another one of those names a guy hears once in a while. You know when you got interesting to me, Mr. Lessing?"

"Tell me."

"When you got interesting to Jake Blau," Katz said. "When I read that blast about you in his first piece in that new series about the morality of American businessmen he just finished running in *The Daily Watchword*."

"You read Yiddish?" Max said.

"Napoleon read Yiddish."

"I've been wondering what the three of us had in common."

"I'm sure we'll find others," Hector Katz said. "The way I work, what makes me worth my money, I always put myself in the other guy's shoes. The minute I read the blast by Jake Blau, I said to myself, What would I do? The answer came back like a belch. I'll show this son of a bitch, that's what I'll do, I'll show him who's a good Jew and who isn't. The next time your name crosses my path, Mr. Lessing, you're settled here in New York and Walter is dumping on you in the column because you're buying this fancy boys' school up there in Boston and he's making cracks about stripteasers. This looks to me like he's taking off because of this Jake Blau blast, because one thing about us boys who read Yiddish, Mr. Lessing, anybody calls us a bad Jew, we don't take that shit from anybody. So I was not surprised when I got a call from Joe Catalini."

Joe said, "I'd been thinking for some time we could use a press agent."

"That's right," Max said. "I remember now."

He remembered also that Ida had told him the thought had been hers.

"I told Joe I felt you needed help," Katz said. "We made a deal, and here's the first result."

The press agent tapped the copy of the *Mirror* Max had been handed by Ida an hour ago at the breakfast table.

"Which Winchell ran because you told Rose Bigman my next move?" Max said.

"First I had to tell Joe Catalini," Hector Katz said.

"Why?"

"With Winchell, you give him one bum steer and it's curtains," Hector Katz said. "Before I told Rose about you and the West Coast, I had to make sure that was where you were going."

Max said, "And Joe told you that?"

Joe Catalini squeezed an inch of indulgent laughter out of the toothpaste tube and said, "It seemed an ideal way to prime the pump of Hector's talent."

"As a result of which I've got Rose on the hook," Katz said, tapping the copy of the *Mirror* on Max Lessing's desk. "When the Alaskan Pacific Shipbuilding Corporation starts firing up its boilers again, and when the smokestacks over the T.K.O. Studio start belching smoke that spells out Lessing Productions, you just tell me, and Hector will take it from there."

Max decided to take Hector to lunch instead.

"I'm doing this behind Joe Catalini's back," Max said two days later when they were settled on the first floor of "21" at the corner table facing the archway that led out to the landing and the kitchen. "He's very possessive about you."

367

"I guess Joe is about me the way you are about Joe," Hector Katz said. "You picked him out of the crowd because Joe had something that hit your eye, so now he's your special boy, and Joe picked me out of the crowd because I had something that hit his eye, so now I'm Joe's special boy."

Max said, "That's why I thought maybe it might be better if neither one of us told Joe we had this lunch."

Hector Katz moved in smoothly. "I like Joe. I'm grateful to Joe for putting me into your operation; but I'm also a boy who reads Yiddish. When you're in any danger of pissing upwind, it's the only language you can rely on to tell you which way the wind is blowing. The man I work for is Max Lessing. Joe Catalini just signs the checks."

"And don't you ever forget that," Max Lessing said in Yiddish.

"I forgot it once," Hector said, also in Yiddish. "As a result Arnold Rothstein fired me. The next thing you know they hung the rap on him for fixing the 1919 World Series."

"That sounds like a threat," Max said.

"Your remark was no invitation to a waltz."

The eyes of the two men locked. Max laughed first.

"Okay," he said. "Let's talk English."

"You start," Hector Katz said.

"Our two new West Coast operations," Max Lessing said. "Alaskan Pacific Shipbuilding and the T.K.O. Studio. Joe feels it will help with what he calls the Court of St. James's."

"Among other things," Hector said.

"What other things?"

"The things Jake Blau was rubbing your nose in," Hector Katz said. "For those things getting belly dancers out of town has got to help."

Max Lessing said, "She's not a belly dancer."

"There are some things for which I don't deal in euphemisms, Yiddish or English," Hector Katz said. "One of those things is a client's women. Charles Parnell, the great Irish statesman, was my boyhood hero. The poor son of a bitch was totaled because he had the hots for a girl named

Kitty O'Shea. Parnell's great misfortune was that Hector Katz was not handling his press relations. A youthful financial shogun mit a Cherman accent who happens to be a client of mine could get the same kind of *zetz* because he has what *Time* calls a Great and Good Friend named Alma Pine. Speaking purely in terms of my job, Mr. Lessing, I must tell you what I told Joe when he first came to me about taking you on as a client. These other places you want to go, this Court of St. James's thing, for a for-instance, you got a hell of a lot better chance of hanging your hat on Grosvenor Square if you move Miss Pine off camera."

Max said, "Anything else you think I ought to know or do?"

"There's one thing you've got to do," Hector said.

"What's that?"

"Here we go back to Yiddish," Hector Katz said.

"I am listening," Max said in Yiddish.

"You've got to do something about Joe Catalini," Hector said in Yiddish.

"Why?" Max said in Yiddish.

"The best right-hand men in the world," Hector Katz said in Yiddish, "sometimes at the wrong moment they turn out to be left-handed."

46

"You're left-handed!" Ida Lessing said.

The surprise in her voice caused Joe Catalini to look up from the head of the niblick.

"Mrs. L," he said with a smile, "I always have been."

It was one of the small, quiet smiles that he seemed to put together for her. He worked at it. That was clear. Yet it was never a finished product. It never failed to give Ida that odd little feeling in her heart. As though he were uneasily aware of a capacity to release so much radiance that he was shy about releasing too much of it at one time because he did not want to overwhelm her. He took a gentle, brushing swing at one of the pale pink roses in Susie Shale's needlepoint rug.

"But I don't understand that," Ida said.

Joe straightened up, holding the golf club in his left hand like a mace.

"Neither do I," he said. "It's just something you're born with. Like tall or short. Some people are born right-handed, some left."

"That's not what I mean," Ida said. "I mean all those years we were living together in the same house, I never noticed that."

Joe released the pressure of his palm on the club handle. The silver shaft slid down the tube of his cupped hand with a gentle hiss. The club head landed with a delicate thud on his circled thumb and forefinger.

"Maybe because you never before gave me a set of matched golf clubs as a birthday present," Joe Catalini said.

Ida stared at him. He was always saying things like that. Things that made sense in a way. And yet, in another way, they made no sense at all. Of course she had never before given him a set of matched clubs. She had never before given him a surprise birthday party, either.

For weeks, excited and troubled by the fact that he was about to turn twenty-six, Ida had worried about how to celebrate the event without being obvious. If she made too much fuss about his being twenty-six, she would merely be calling attention to the fact that she was thirty-one. Or would she? Who was aware of what she was aware of?

For Ida the exasperating thing about Joe Catalini was that she had never known what he was aware of. In spite of the way she had felt about him for twelve years, ever since as a boy of fourteen he had come to live with her and Max and the children in the house on Columbia Heights, the handsome, reserved youngster had made her uncomfortable. Part of the discomfort, of course, was the feeling that she was drawn to him.

It was not at all like the feeling that had come down on her like a landslide that day in Klein Berezna fifteen years ago when she had walked from her milking stool to the barn door and caught her first glimpse of the tall, copper-haired boy in the flannel shirt who begged a cup of milk. Ida knew all about that feeling. As well as what her response to it had been and still was. This feeling about Joe Catalini was totally different.

It was like being attracted to a statue. Or a marionette. Or a ventriloquist's dummy. You liked the way it looked. But once you got to see it move? Once you heard it make the sounds? Those sounds that seemed to be coming out of its mouth but you knew were actually being made by the skillful person on whose knee the dummy was sitting? Once you saw

371

that and once you heard that, what had you seen? Whom had you heard? What were you drawn to? What was giving you that funny little feeling in your heart?

Ida said, "I did it because I think you ought to take some exercise."

"Here?" Joe said. "In the Shale apartment?"

The blood came up into Ida's face with a hot rush.

She said, "No, of course not, you idiot."

He laughed. Ida remembered something Susie Shale had told her after her husband's first meeting with Joe Catalini down at 120 Broadway, the meeting that had led to the purchase of the school up in Newton. John Shale told his wife that when Joe Catalini laughed it was as though he was taking a pill out of a box, and as he did it he was trying to remember how many he had left in the box, to see if he could afford to make it a real belly laugh or limit himself to a restrained chuckle.

"I'm sorry," Joe said. "I was just teasing."

Ida stared at him. It was a funny word. It wouldn't have been funny if somebody else had spoken it.

Ida said, "Teasing about what?"

"You and me," he said. "Right now. Alone in this apartment in the middle of the day. You know what people would say."

"People don't say anything," Ida said, "about things they don't know anything about."

Joe said, "Susie Shale knows."

"No, she doesn't," Ida said.

"She gave you her key."

Ida said, "Susie, yes. Susie knows I'm here."

"Where does she think I am?" Joe Catalini said.

Ida said, "Where the whole world thinks you are twenty-four hours a day, three hundred and sixty-five days a year. On the twenty-sixth floor of 120 Broadway talking into four telephones and dictating to three stenographers, running what this Winchell calls Mr. Max's mushrooming international financial sheikdom, whatever that means in English."

"How did you get Susie's key?"

"I told her for your birthday," Ida said, "I wanted to bake a surprise, one of those *lekachs* Shotzie Schiff used to make when you were a boy on Columbia Heights, because I remembered how much you used to like honey cake. Here in New York, when people have a birthday party, they order a cake from Sherry's, and what they get tastes exactly like one of the twenty-dollar bills it cost. I told Susie I wanted this to be special, and I wanted to bake it myself, without all those servants watching me around the corner in the house on Fifth Avenue. I told Susie to take the day off and drive up to Newton with her husband. John was going up today to check on Norman's schoolwork anyway, and Mr. Max is out in California pretending he's a movie producer, so nobody knows you're here. Not even the man from Abercrombie & Fitch who delivered the golf clubs personally. I promised to meet him downstairs in the hall to let him in, and I did, because he knew it was a surprise. I ordered the clubs nearly three months ago, they were made specially, I gave them all your measurements, because I wanted it to be something special, just from me, and—and—"

Ida did not realize she had been babbling, so she did not know she was sobbing until he dropped the niblick and he stepped across Susie Shale's pale pink needlepoint rose and he put his arms around her.

"Mrs. L," Joe Catalini said. "For God's sake, Mrs. L—"

"They're no good," Ida sobbed. "You're left-handed. How could that be? All these years, twelve years, I thought I knew everything, and I prepared so carefully, and then like a fool I didn't even know you were left-handed, and now it's all—"

Her voice stopped. Ida realized he was holding her very hard. The realization must have come to him at the same moment. She could hear his heart stop or thump or do something. She didn't know what it was but Ida was sure she heard it. The sound came from inside his chest. Ida pushed herself away, to get a clear view of his face, and then she saw he too was sobbing.

"Joe," she said. "Joe, darling, for heaven's sake."

He said, "It's no good."

She was holding a stranger. Ida had never heard that voice before.

"It's—it's no good."

Ida pulled him back. She held him tight. She rocked him gently in her arms. She put her mouth to his ear.

"Honey, don't," she whispered. "It doesn't matter. I'll have them make another set, left-handed. Please, honey, don't."

"It's not that."

"Then what is it?"

The moment she asked the question, Ida Lessing knew the answer. The pause did it. Into the small gap of time something leaped with a message. She could hear what she had not been listening for. The sounds her own heart was making. They told Ida Lessing why all these years it had been different from the feeling that had come down on her like a landslide that day fifteen years ago at Klein Berezna in the barn doorway. Why it was different, and why it would never be anything but different, for Ida Lessing or for any other woman.

"Me," Joe Catalini said. "I'm not like other men. I'm—"

She put her hand on his lips. She did not want to hear.

"Don't worry about it, darling," Ida said. "It's nothing, honey. It won't make any difference."

Mixed with the regret, cutting through the sadness in her own voice, she could hear what nobody else would ever hear: the unhappy but clean sound of relief. Now she was safe. She would never again have to worry about the possibility of betraying Max.

PART VI
1939

47

The movements of Mr. Max inside the Lessing Enterprises offices at 120 Broadway were as predictable as the tides.

When he arrived, he went as directly as the complicated network of corridors permitted from the elevator to his private suite. When he left the office, he followed the same route in reverse. Members of the organization and visitors who had occasion to see him face to face came to Mr. Max's private suite. He never went to the offices of other people in the organization. Almost never, anyway. When he did, it was an occasion that did not go unnoticed.

On the day in 1939 when Mr. Max walked from his private suite to Joe Catalini's office, news of the event spread through the organization as rapidly as a few years earlier the news had spread through Wall Street that Richard Whitney had been booked on charges of grand larceny at the Elizabeth Street police station.

"Mr. Max," Joe said when the door opened.

He must have been surprised. Max had intended to surprise him. That was why Max had come all the way across the office from his own suite on his own two feet. The only surprise Joe showed, however, was in the way he came up onto his own two feet. He didn't exactly jump. The word, if used to describe the performance, however, would not have been inaccurate.

"This is a surprise," he said.

Max said, "What else does a man do for a member of his family on a boy's thirty-first birthday?"

"Oh, that," Joe said. He smiled shyly, with relief. "My birthday was yesterday," he said.

"It looks like for me your birthday is always yesterday," Max said. "Remember five years ago? When Ida gave you that set of golf clubs on your twenty-sixth birthday? And I didn't wake up until the next day that you'd even had a birthday?"

"That's a little incident it would be hard to forget," Joe said. "Mrs. L had some things to say about your memory that linger in the mind."

Max started to laugh. "Mind if I sit down?" he said.

"Of course not," Joe said. He gestured to the chair beside his desk. "Please."

Max sat down, still laughing. Joe dropped back into his own chair behind the desk.

"What's funny?" he said.

"The way I found out today is your birthday," Max said.

"How did it happen?" Joe said.

"I was lunching with Rube Messerschmidt of the Bank of New York and he mentioned it," Max said.

"Rube Messerschmidt told you it was my birthday?"

The hike across the office had not been wasted. This time there was no doubt about the surprise in Joe's voice. No doubt so far as Max Lessing was concerned, anyway. He'd had seventeen years of experience with Joe Catalini's voice.

"These bankers are sneaky," Max said. "They do a lot more than read *The Wall Street Journal* and take their good customers to lunch at the New York Yacht Club."

"How did my birthday come into the conversation?" Joe said.

"Just as I got out of the car to meet him inside," Max said, "I saw him coming up the street from the bank, so I waited, and the first thing he said after we said hello and shook hands, he pointed to the Harvard Club next door, and he said, 'Is it true Joe Catalini lives there?' I said Yes, it is, and we went inside, and there was all that crap about taking our coats, and the headwaiter This way, Mr. Messerschmidt, and You're looking well, Mr. Lessing, and What will you have to drink, gentlemen, and then when all that was out of the way and we were alone at the table, the first thing Messerschmidt said was 'Don't you think that's funny?' "

"Don't you think what's funny?" Joe said.

"Exactly what I said to Rube Messerschmidt," Max said. "And he said 'That Joe Catalini should live at the Harvard Club.'

" 'What's funny about it?' I said. 'He's a graduate of Harvard Law.'

" 'He's also thirty-one years old,' Rube Messerschmidt said.

"I said What's that got to do with it," Max Lessing said. " 'In the Harvard Club,' Rube said, 'they don't let you bring women to your room.' "

There was a pause. Joe Catalini filled it by picking up a pencil. He never used the solid-gold writing implements he had accumulated at his law-school graduation and on previous birthdays. Joe liked yellow octagonal wooden Eagles with rubber tips. One of his secretaries kept a leather cup full of them, needle-point sharp, within ready reach of his hand. Examining the one he had just picked up, Joe was apparently dissatisfied with the condition of the point. He dropped it on the green desk blotter and plucked a fresh Eagle from the leather cup.

"They don't," he said.

Max said, "Where do you take your women, Joe?"

The pause could have been no more than an inaudible clearing of his throat, but Max Lessing's seventeen years of experience also included Joe Catalini's throat. He never cleared it. Joe ended the short silence with "Doesn't that come under the head of private business?"

"Ordinarily, yes," Max said. "But you and me, Joe, it's

not ordinarily. The whole world knows we're in business together."

"By the whole world," Joe said, "you mean Rube Messerschmidt?"

"Plus the other banks we do business with," Max said.

"The Chase," Joe Catalini said. "Morgan Guaranty. National City. Have any of them told you they think it's funny I live at the Harvard Club?"

"Not yet," Max Lessing said.

"You expect them to?"

"Rube does."

"Do you?" Joe Catalini said.

"Bankers are no different from bootleggers or shoemakers," Max said. "They're in business. People in business talk to other people in the same business. It's a way of keeping posted on what's playing that day at the Roxy, you could say, so you won't be too far off base when a surprise comes along. You and I, Joe, we can't afford to be surprised by the banks we do business with."

"What did Rube suggest?" Joe Catalini said.

"A man your age should be married," Max Lessing said. "Rube feels it stops the wrong kind of talk."

"Getting married isn't easy," Joe said.

"It's easier than you think," Max said. "And you better start your thinking right now."

He stood up and went to the door. He opened it and looked out at the girls bent over their desks in Joe Catalini's outer office. The girl nearest the door had soft brown hair, a nice profile, and from what was visible in a sitting position a neat little figure.

"Miss?" Max called.

She looked up, startled. She was pretty.

"Me?" she said.

"Yes," Max said. "What's your name?"

"Blanche," the girl said. "Blanche Berkowitz."

Max smiled and said, "Are you married?"

Nervously, the girl started to smile and said, "No, Mr. Lessing, I'm not."

"Would you mind coming in here, Blanche?"

"Shall I bring my notebook?" she said.

"A very good idea," Max said.

The girl stood up, took a steno notebook and a pencil from her desk, and came toward Max.

"Don't be afraid," Max said. "Mr. Catalini has something he wants to discuss with you."

He pulled the door wide and motioned the girl in. Joe Catalini came to his feet.

"I have to get back to my office," Max Lessing said. "I'll leave you both now to complete the arrangements."

48

As it worked out, Joe Catalini and Blanche Berkowitz had nothing to do with the arrangements. Mrs. Lessing took care of everything, including the decoration of the five-room apartment on Gramercy Park into which the young couple were scheduled to move when they came home from their European honeymoon.

We're coming home earlier than we planned, Blanche wrote from the Savoy in London to her brother, Sid, in the Bronx. *Not that Joe is really worried, but he feels just in case there should be something more than the usual hot air to this Danzig business, and Hitler should really start something, Joe feels if and when it starts he'll be happier to have it start when we're back home in New York than wandering around Europe. Not that what we've been doing over here this last month could be called wandering. It's like one of those Grand Tours we used to read about in Edith Wharton back in high school, deluxe all the way, meaning up to here, and seven-course meals three times a day, with wine, naturally and of course. You wouldn't believe what Joe is paying, for instance, just for our suite here at the Savoy, not counting meals or anything. He must be even richer than I thought when he first asked me to marry him. The postcards that are all I've had time to send you and Yetta don't tell the half of it. I can't wait until we get back and I come up to Vyse Avenue with my snapshots to tell you all about it.*

Sid Berkowitz and his kid sister, Blanche, were orphans who had continued to share a home after their parents died. Later, when Sid and Yetta met and decided to get married, it was Sid and not Blanche who had insisted that she move into the spare bedroom of the attractive, airy five-roomer Sid and Yetta rented at the corner of Vyse Avenue and Bronx Park South with its lovely view from the kitchen window of the Bronx Park Zoo and the rose gardens on the north side of the Small Mammals House.

This made it easier for Blanche, of course, because while she earned a perfectly good salary as a stenographer down at Lessing Enterprises, and there was no question about her ability to support herself, Blanche still had two years to go in the evening session at C.C.N.Y. toward her B.A. Aside from the convenience of not having to worry about running a home for herself and preparing meals, the most important thing about the arrangement was that Sid Berkowitz and his kid sister, Blanche, were more than just brother and sister. They had always been good friends, a fact that Yetta had understood from the beginning, so there never had been any awkwardness about Blanche's moving in with them.

What it got down to, as Yetta herself put it, was that instead of two good friends living together, now there were three. And when out of the blue came this astonishing thing, without warning, a man like Joe Catalini confessing to Blanche he'd fallen in love with her the moment he saw her in the steno pool outside his office, and would she marry him, it was Blanche's turn to assure her brother, Sid, and his wife, Yetta, that the astonishing change in her fortunes would not in any way interfere with the friendship between Blanche and Sid and Yetta.

Blanche expected to see them as often down on Gramercy Park as they would continue to see her up on Vyse Avenue. Not to mention Joe, who was a wonderful person, and they were not to be put off by his position in something as big and important as Lessing Enterprises with a capital E, if you please, or his money or his shyness, which a lot of people took for standoffishness or something. That was just not true, as nobody knew better than the former Blanche Berkowitz, now proudly Mrs. Joseph Catalini. Blanche remembered how when she had first come to work at 120 Broadway she was so scared of the man all the girls in the office never called anything but Here Comes Mr. Catalini that she had been afraid to look up from her typewriter when he walked by. Boy, had she been wrong. Far from being standoffish, Joe was the nicest, warmest, kindest human being Blanche had ever met, and she considered herself darn lucky to find herself married to such a superior person.

Which doesn't change the fact, she wrote to Sid and Yetta from the Savoy, *that I'm glad we're coming home earlier than we planned. Lessing Enterprises has a lot of representatives all over here in Europe, and all kinds of important contacts in government circles in every capital. We've been entertained until I'm ready to drop, but Joe, in addition to being entertained, gets himself informed, if you know what I mean, and from what he's learned he thinks it's wise for us to get home early. He's booked passage for us on the* United States *for August 28th, which means we'll be steaming into the Lower Bay, as we world travelers say, on September 3rd, which works out just beautifully because my classes at C.C.N.Y. start on September 10th, especially that all-important three-credit course I told you about in Freud and Marx: Concatenations and Contradictions, which gives me a whole week to register and get my curriculum set. Not to mention settle myself and my brand-new husband into our brand-new apartment on Gramercy Park, which I'm dying to see, because. I have no idea what it's like, not even the colors, because the whole thing has been done from top to bottom and A to Z by Mrs. Max Lessing personally, no less. I don't really know her at all, because the wedding was such a fast thing I hardly had time to get to know even my husband, but I hear some of the servants call her Queen Ida, so I'm going to play it cautious*

384

*and keep my little trap shut, and I'm not opening it until
I hear what Joe has to say.*

What Joe had to say on September 3, 1939, ten minutes
after Mrs. Lessing had conducted the newlyweds from the
ship into their new home, was "I like it, Mrs. L."

At once Blanche knew there was one thing she did not
like: that "Mrs. L" business. Or rather, she didn't like the
way her husband pronounced the words. Blanche had not
liked it from the moment she first heard Joe do it a month
ago, during the first few moments she had spent in Mrs.
Lessing's presence. Blanche had forgotten her dislike, and
she could not remember now if she had figured out then the
reason for her dislike, but she decided now it was something
to which she would have to give some serious time.

There was something about this Mrs. Max Lessing that
brought back feelings Blanche's parents had made plain to
her and Sid when they were kids. Mr. and Mrs. Berkowitz
had been Litvaks—immigrants from Lithuania. They had
a whole string of jokes, some not very funny, about "those
rich German Jews." Joe had told Blanche that Mr. Lessing
had come to America from Austria and Mrs. Lessing was a
native of Hungary. This did not seem to make them part of
the group at which Mr. and Mrs. Berkowitz used to direct
their bitter humor.

And yet Mr. and Mrs. Lessing aroused in Blanche the
same feelings she remembered having as a little girl when her
parents were driven to playing their roles in an ancient feud
Blanche and Sid did not understand but accepted as something they had no right to question. To the editors of *Vogue*
who photographed Mrs. Lessing in her Fifth Avenue oval
drawing room, she might have been the entrancingly chic
wife of the hottest young conglomerate tycoon since Howard
Hughes. To the former Blanche Berkowitz, Ida Lessing was
a Galitzianer *yenta* who had achieved the detestable state
known contemptuously to Mr. and Mrs. Berkowitz as "a Jew
with a Dollar."

"I know you like it," Mrs. Lessing said to Joe. She turned

to Blanche. "Joe likes everything," she said. "Anyway, he's so polite he always says he likes everything. What counts, Blanche darling, is Do you like it?"

"Oh, yes, Mrs. Lessing," the brand-new bride said. "It's simply beautiful."

Which was exactly what Sid and Yetta would have said.

Mrs. Lessing said, "When you tell that to the decorator, who should be here any minute now, you'll be doing me a great big favor, Blanche darling, if you leave out the word 'simply.' She says it simply sets her teeth on edge."

Isn't that too bad! Blanche thought icily, but in an appropriately warm, nervous voice she said, "I'm sorry."

"Who is the decorator?" Joe said.

"My foster daughter, Claire," Mrs. Lessing said. Then she caught the small, frightened look Blanche, out of long experience with Galitzianer *yentas*, had hung up as a background for her fraudulent apology, and Mrs. Lessing put her hand lightly on the bride's arm as she said through the charming smile that the lens of Cecil Beaton had for a stiff fee on a number of occasions made more charming, "That was a joke. Claire makes them all the time. You'll like her, and she'll like you. Won't she, Joe?"

"Of course she will," Joe Catalini said. "What's Claire doing decorating apartments? When we sailed for Europe she was sharpening her pencils and her tongue for handling her second year at Sarah Lawrence."

"Girls who go to Sarah Lawrence don't just sit down after they matriculate," Mrs. Lessing said. "Most of them do other things besides go to Sarah Lawrence. Right now, for example, in addition to going to Sarah Lawrence our Claire is decorating apartments and making jokes."

"Does she get credit toward her B.A. for doing it?" Joe said.

Mrs. Lessing dropped another friendly tap on Blanche's arm and said, "In addition to the things all brides learn on their honeymoons, did you also learn that your husband has a tendency to make jokes too?"

386

"Not very good ones."

Blanche turned toward the new voice. What she saw first was two parallel slashes of color. Straw yellow hair. Over white, white teeth. Then the leggy girl underneath who wore both like a badge. And Blanche's heart turned to water with instant recognition and ancient envy. At last, after twenty-six years of living, Blanche Berkowitz knew what all of her life she had wanted to look like.

"I'm Claire Boyle," the dazzler said. "You must be Joe's wife."

Then Blanche seemed to sink into the enchanting mixture of bold colors and faintly hoarse voice and even fainter odor of lilac, and she realized Mrs. Lessing's foster daughter had thrown her arms around her. For Blanche it all came right in a flash. With Claire Boyle she would have no trouble. This was no Galitzianer *yenta*. This was good goods.

"Disregard your husband's jokes," the golden girl said. "He has other qualities that compensate. And disregard this whole apartment. I did it from a sketch in my head of what a girl who would marry Joe would look like."

She made in the air the motions of tearing a blueprint to shreds and scattering them to the winds that had appeared on schedule out of nowhere to do her bidding.

"You're not like that at all," Claire said. "You're a nice person. Clearly human. Don't answer my unspoken question, quote, How in God's name did someone like you come to marry someone like Joe?"

"Claire, dear," Ida Lessing said. "You're overdoing it."

"Am I?" said Claire to Blanche. "Don't answer that either, until you know what I'm doing. I'm forming a whole new concept for this apartment, building it around a real you, and I want you to know that I know just from looking at you, I can tell you are the kind of person who can tell me exactly what it must have felt like to be aboard a luxury liner on the high seas last Thursday night."

"What happened last Thursday night?" Ida said.

"Prime Minister Neville Chamberlain," her foster daughter said, "told a shocked world on the radio that Hitler had not responded to his ultimatum and so it was with regret that he had to announce that a state of war exists between Great Britain and Germany."

"Oh, for heaven's sake," Ida said. "I thought you were talking about something in the family."

A telephone bell rang. Nobody seemed to know where the sound was coming from.

Claire Boyle said, "Mother, behind you."

Ida turned and picked up a white telephone.

"Hello? . . . Yes, she is. One moment, please. For you, Claire. Canada."

Claire took the phone. The effortless grace with which she transported the piece of machinery to her ear put another crack into Blanche Berkowitz Catalini's already splintered heart.

"Hello? Yes, this is— Darling! Oh, yes, of course it's me. I'm—"

Pause. Not the sort of pause to which Blanche was accustomed to applying that word. This was a whole new idea in the concept of pauses. It was a total cessation of life.

"Yes, darling," Claire said finally. "I've got it all. Every syllable. And I'll do exactly as you said. Go with God, and with my love. With that umbrella, you are out of destruction's reach. Remember that."

She replaced the phone and then, as though she were replacing the top on a box of candy from which she had carefully extracted a choice piece, Claire Boyle replaced the hand with which she had held the instrument. It came to rest at her side like a corsage.

"Everybody listen, please," she said, enunciating very clearly in the slightly hoarse voice that to Blanche had suddenly become a favorite piece of music. "Don't ask any questions, because I have no answers," Claire said. "Only the facts as he just gave them to me."

"He," Ida Lessing said, as though she were making a check mark on a list of chores. "It was Norman."

"Yes, Mother, it was Norman," Claire Boyle said. "He wants us all to know, quote, that he is through with the Aylmer Broughton Academy and all schools forevermore. He was talking from Halifax. He has enlisted in the R.A.F. and is being sent to England for training. He's sailing in convoy."

"When?" Joe said.

"He said, quote, Tell Joe and Father not to try to stop me," Claire said. "There's a war on. I'm still quoting. Forces are at work that even Lessing Enterprises, Ltd., cannot bend to its will. I am going to be a fighter pilot. Unquote."

Ida Lessing said, "Claire, I know Norman. He must have told you when he's sailing."

"Yes, of course you know Norman," Claire said. "But perhaps not well enough. As he hung up he was whistling a tune he and I are both very fond of."

"What tune?" Joe Catalini said.

"Put away your pencil, Joe," Claire Boyle said. "It will tell you nothing you will understand or be able to use to stop Norman. The tune was 'Will You Remember?' "

PART VII
1976

49

Almost forty years later, in 1976, while Hurricane Carla was threatening South Florida, two men were waiting out a phone call in a bowling alley north of Pompano Beach. Neither of them had been born on the day Joe Catalini had brought his bride to Gramercy Park and Norman Lessing had enlisted in the R.A.F. Both events, however, had affected the lives of Chick Rosen and Abe Shantz, and both were aware of it. Not because they understood the connection, but because they were aware of the tensions that were a part of being born into the Lessing apparatus. At the moment, for example, Chick Rosen's own words seemed to astonish him. He paused with both hands in the air, supporting the bowling ball against his right shoulder.

"I'm betraying Mr. Max?" he said, staring at the pilot from New York.

"You heard me," Abe Shantz said.

"How the hell," Chick said, "do you figure that?"

All around him the gusting winds of Hurricane Carla were slapping at the tall storm-shuttered windows of the Deerfield Bowling Lanes.

Abe said, "You just told me you didn't believe all that crap Mr. Max is lying in bed up there in that penthouse on top of The Frontenac recovering from a stroke. You just told me you believe Mr. Max is dead."

"All you airplane drivers suffer from defective hearing," Chick said. "It must be on account of spending so much of your life listening to jet engines."

He dropped his left hand in a graceful arc. Dipping low, he allowed his right hand to swing the ball down and back. With an easy, twisting motion he brought the neatly balanced weight forward and pulled his hand free.

Chick said, "I never said any such damn-fool thing." He brought his body back smoothly into standing position. "What I said was, I said there's a lot of talk all of a sudden down in Miami how Mr. Max actually died two years ago, but Joe Catalini, who everybody knows runs the Lessing show, for business reasons Mr. Catalini gave it out that Mr. Max had a stroke and these two years he's been up there in that penthouse recuperating with nurses around the clock, a fact which is, according to all this new talk I hear, strictly a lot of shit."

Abe said, "Why would Joe Catalini do a thing like that? And don't call me a driver. Pilots are *pilots*."

"How would I know?" Chick said. "Do I ever see Joe Catalini? All I know and all I passed on to you is what I hear."

"You hear anything else?" Abe Shantz said. "Like detail? Don't be shy. Tell me all."

"I hear that a lot of people the Lessing organization is into," Chick said, "the Lessings were able to get into them because these people couldn't help themselves at the time. Now, though, these last few years, these people have been getting restless, and the only reason they've been hanging in there is because it was Mr. Max who slapped them into the operation in the first place. With him still around and keeping an eye on things, they've been scared even to try to get out. If it gets around Mr. Max is dead, though, these jokers won't waste much time going over the fence."

At the far end of the lane the ball hit. The clicking flurry

394

of pins brought Chick Rosen's head out of the sullen argument with Abe Shantz and around to where he had aimed the ball.

"Strike," he said.

Abe grunted acknowledgment, but the words with which he continued the argument were "And where do you hear this crap?"

"You want an answer?" Chick said. "Or you want me to chew some taffy that will come out in such a way you won't be able to start screaming I'm betraying Mr. Max?"

Abe said, "I asked the question."

"Okay," Chick said. "Where I hear this crap, I hear it in lots of places up and down the coast from here to Miami, but mainly I hear it in the gay spots."

"What are you doing in the gay spots?"

"My family, we run a limo service," Chick Rosen said. "We pick up people at things like airports. They tell us to take them places. They pay us? We take them."

"A college man like you," Abe Shantz said. "In that cashmere blazer with real gold buttons, and your hair all fixed so manly and casual by a twenty-bucks-a-throw hairstylist, I thought now your old man is taking it easy, you've taken over the show, now you're the snappy new head man in the office, Joe Executive, keeping an eye on the computers and goosing the bikini-clad secretaries. I thought the only time you get behind the wheel yourself anymore it's when you're picking up a member of the family that put your old man in business and you through college."

"Your thinking is right on," Chick said. "You have got the situation taped exactly right, Mr. Shantz."

Abe Shantz hesitated, then dipped down and picked up his ball. He stepped across to the line, and he brought the ball with both hands up to his right shoulder. He sighted down the gleaming alley and started down into his swing, then stopped. Abe brought the ball back up with both hands. He held it against his chest like a bride cradling her bouquet.

"All right," Abe Shantz said. "Which member of the Lessing family?"

Chick Rosen said, "The kid from Harvard."

"Stevie?" Abe said.

"So far as I know," Chick Rosen said, "Stevie Lessing is the only kid the family's got at Harvard or any other place."

Abe said, "Tell me something."

"You ask it, Mr. Shantz."

"Are you working on seeing how big a pile of trouble you can put together for the Rosen family?"

"If that's how you interpret my getting good and tired of being treated like a lousy broom pusher," Chick said, "I guess you could say maybe I am."

"Could it be you're one of those people who put in with the Lessings long ago," Abe Shantz said, "and for some time now you've been getting sort of restless, but with Mr. Max around, keeping his eye on the store, you've been scared to make a move? But if all this talk you hear is true, and Mr. Max is dead, you're getting ready to go over the fence?"

Chick Rosen said, "This cashmere jacket, and the tab for cutting my hair, and my right to goose those bikini-clad secretaries, Mr. Airplane Driver, I earned that money myself. Nobody handed it to me. I don't see why the hell every time somebody in the Lessing organization opens his mouth I have to dig my toe into the hot sand and start tugging my forelock. All I did, I told you something I've been hearing around. Something my common sense tells me you should be interested in hearing because maybe you could make yourself a score with Joe Catalini by passing it on to him, so what happens? I get a dumb-dumb remark that I'm betraying Mr. Max."

Abe said, "You're overlooking the important point."

"Which is what?" Chick said.

"Stuff like that," Abe Shantz said, "it's poison."

"What stuff?" Chick Rosen said. "That the organization is covering up the fact Mr. Max is dead? Or that the grandson and heir apparent keeps flying down here practically every weekend to relax from the Harvard grind by living it up as a mover and shaker in the Gay Lib movement?"

"You've been picking him up?" Abe said.

"When he calls from Cambridge he asks for me personally," Chick said. "A Lessing asks, a Rosen answers."

"How's he been getting down here?" Abe Shantz said.

"As a means of transportation the Lessing family gave up using the Conestoga wagon a long time ago," Chick Rosen said. "You don't serve the Lessings as a manicurist, Mr. Shantz."

"It's a four-jet fleet," Abe said.

"Which means you got a lot of other *pilots* you can ask that last question," Chick said.

Abe Shantz turned back to the lane and brought the ball up to his shoulder. He sighted down toward the pins, dropped into his swing, and let the ball go. He turned back to Chick Rosen.

"What I meant about betraying Mr. Max," Abe said. "I don't mean Benedict Arnold. I meant only this kind of poison, you repeat it you spread it. You spread it, it's not exactly loyal."

"Loyal," Chick said. "You're like all the rest of them. You got this thing when you hear those words 'Mr. Max,' you act like it's the voice from the head of the table at the Last Supper. What is it with you guys?"

Abe Shantz said, "You ever hear of Hymie Shantz?"

"You kidding?" Chick Rosen said. "Everybody knows he's your father. Everybody knows he was Mr. Max's first bodyguard all the way back there in Minneapolis. So what? He's like my father. My father knew Mr. Max when the family first hit New York and my old man was driving a cab."

"When you ask What is it with you guys," Abe said, "I think maybe the best place for you to get your answer is ask your own father."

At Abe's elbow appeared a skinny man in tight blue-and-white-checked double-knit slacks topped by a cherry red sport shirt with a little green crocodile embroidered over the breast pocket.

"One of you gentlemen named Shantz?" he said.

"Me," Abe said.

"Telephone," the man said.

Abe followed him across to the cash desk. The man nodded toward a row of hanging telephone slots next to the cash desk.

"In there," he said.

Abe Shantz hunched his head and shoulders into the slot and picked up the dangling receiver.

"Hello?"

"Abe?"

"Yes, Mr. Catalini."

"How's the weather up there?" Joe Catalini said.

"Just about the same as it was when I put down at Miami a couple of hours ago," Abe said. "A lot of wind and rain, but the TV reports keep saying there's no immediate danger."

"Then driving won't be any problem?"

"We had no trouble getting here," Abe Shantz said. "No reason we should have any trouble getting back."

"Can a plane take off?"

"If you want it to."

"I want you to make a stop before you get back," Catalini said.

Abe said, "Yes, Mr. Catalini."

"I'm calling you from The Frontenac," Joe Catalini said. "I'm downstairs in the manager's apartment. There's been a change in plans."

"Yes, Mr. Catalini," Abe said.

"Please listen carefully," Joe Catalini said.

"Yes, Mr. Catalini," Abe said.

Joe Catalini said, "Here's what I want you to do."

50

The way Abe Shantz did it changed Blanche Catalini's plans for what was left of the night.

Her nights were long. Getting through them required careful planning. They began at approximately three o'clock in the afternoon.

Blanche could always tell the exact moment by the electric clock on the table next to her bed. No matter how bad things became, she always managed somehow to pull the plug of the electric clock from the socket just before she passed out. On this day Blanche Catalini's night began at 2:48 in the afternoon. She learned this when the telephone bell blasted her awake.

It was a special bell. Joe had ordered it installed three years ago, a few days after he had made half a dozen unsuccessful attempts to reach her from Hong Kong through the New York switchboard between the hours of 4:00 P.M. and 8:00 P.M., Massachusetts time. He said nothing about this to Blanche. Joe Catalini never said much to Blanche. He certainly never criticized her. After thirty-seven years of marriage, however, Blanche knew pretty much everything about her husband. Everything she wanted to know, anyway.

Blanche knew, therefore, that the Hong Kong experience was the point at which Joe had decided the normal bell provided by the telephone company could no longer be counted on to bring her to consciousness. The next day a young man from the Lessing electronics division in New York had come up to Newton and installed a new bell on the night table next to Blanche's bed. When she was asleep it sat about eight inches from her ear.

"You sure this is okay?" the young man had said after he finished the installation and the first test blast exploded in the bedroom.

Blanche said, "Who told you to install this thing?"

"The job order came out of Mr. Catalini's office."

"Then it's okay," Blanche said.

It was. For things like summoning the appropriate equipment to extinguish a four-alarm fire, or for waking the dead. Which these days was what Blanche felt like whenever or however she came awake. Sometimes the revival came about because nature had decided it had gone about as far as it could with sleep to repair the damage of the day before. Sometimes because Joe had decided to call her from wherever he happened to be.

It was unlikely that Blanche, at sixty-three with an arthritic hip, would be summoned by anybody to help put out a four-alarm fire. When it was the bell that slammed her into consciousness, therefore, Blanche knew before she knew anything else that the voice at the other end of the phone belonged to her husband.

He said, "Blanche?"

"Yes," she said.

Occasionally, but not often, Blanche wondered how he would answer if she said no.

"You all right?" Joe said.

He always said that, so she was okay so far.

"Sure, fine," Blanche said.

Still okay. Actually, even a little better than okay, because that was what she always said too. The process of surfacing into the land of the living, therefore, was on course. Or seemed to be.

"Where are you?" she said.

"Logan."

"The airport?" Blanche said.

She didn't always say that, of course. Most times, when he called, Joe was half a world away from Boston's Logan Airport.

"Yes," he said. "Honey, look, I just flew in. I'm driving up. I should be there in about an hour. Less."

"Oh," Blanche said.

Off track, that. She concentrated. The sequence came back to her.

"Anything I can do for you?" Blanche said.

"Coffee, if it's not too much trouble," Joe said. "See you in a little while, honey."

The phone went dead. The realization that she was not came as a nice little bonus.

Cautiously, she moved the receiver back to the hook. On the way there, it rattled a little. But it got there. Any way you looked at it, that was a plus.

Blanche pulled on the light. She squinted the face of her watch into focus. Ten minutes after five. Then she looked at the electric clock. It had stopped at 2:48. She couldn't, of course, do the arithmetic with accuracy, but she could manage a rough calculation. A matter of practice.

So: 2:48 was not far from three, never mind which way, and ten minutes after five was not far from five. That came to what? Two hours. Only two hours? It didn't seem possible. On only two hours of sleep she couldn't possibly have made it to where she was now.

Blanche snapped off the light and turned her head toward the window. It was dark outside—but wait a minute, not totally dark. In fact, Blanche thought she could make out a sort of hazy gray smear beyond the glass. Yes, she could. Morning was definitely on its way to Lowell Lane in Newton, Mass.

Which meant Blanche had been out for, let's see. From not far from three in the afternoon to, what was it? Yes, to around five in the morning, that meant, let's see, three to midnight, that's nine. Plus midnight to five, that's another five. Five plus nine? Right. She'd been out fourteen hours.

Fourteen hours? Blanche squeezed her eyes tight and concentrated. She shoved things around inside her head. It was like moving furniture in the dark. Yes, why not? Fourteen hours sounded normal. With fourteen hours of oblivion under her belt, she shouldn't be feeling too bad.

"Let's put it to the test," Blanche said to her friend the electric clock.

She eased her legs over the side of the bed. A searing gash of lightning ripped across the inside of her skull. Nothing serious, however. She put both palms down on the mattress and pushed. A howling scream of pain twisted through the bad hip, but so what? Her one hundred and sixty-two pounds did move upward, didn't they?

"Test passed," Blanche Catalini said to the only friend she had in the world. She gave the electric clock a small pat. It deserved more, but at this stage that was all the clock's devoted friend could manage.

Once she was on her feet, the first few minutes of the regular daily performance were automatic. She didn't even have to open her eyes, but she did. A tiny gesture of defiance. A small nose thumb at the demons. She moved across to the bathroom. From under the soiled clothes in the hamper Blanche pulled the bottle of vodka.

The first dose went down without jolting the stomach muscles in the wrong direction. Blanche steadied her heavy body by resting her free hand on the cool porcelain of the basin. She waited. Not long. Just long enough to feel her insides begin to firm up.

At which point it was safe to lift the bottle and take down the second phase of the treatment. Blanche did this and then, to avoid breaking the routine of revival with damaging temptation, she rapidly screwed the top onto the bottle, buried it under the soiled clothes in the hamper, and went back to the bed.

She sat down, gave herself a couple of moments to gather strength, then put the plug of the electric clock into the socket. The sweep second hand began its endless journey. Another couple of moments, another couple of deep breaths, and she was ready for the tough one: synchronizing the hands of the revived electric clock with the time on the face of her wristwatch.

Not knowing how, as she never quite did know how, she managed to do it. She was ready to utter the opening words of the ritual with which she began what for everybody else was morning but for Blanche Catalini was evening.

She asked aloud, "How in the world did I get here?"

It was such a small question, it never failed to take her by surprise. Because she knew the dimensions of the answer, it never failed to make her feel inadequately prepared.

With more energy, and not a little anticipation, she went back into the bathroom. She fumbled the bottle from the bottom of the hamper. With a hand that was almost steady, she unscrewed the cap. Then she took down a couple of ounces with a hunger that was beginning to be tinged with pleasure.

It was the sort of pleasure that had once been a part of every morning of her life. Once, of course, was a long time ago, in 1939, when Blanche Berkowitz was twenty-six years old, living with her brother, Sid, and his wife, Yetta, in their attractive, airy five-roomer at the corner of Vyse Avenue and Bronx Park South with its lovely view from the kitchen window of the Bronx Park Zoo and the rose gardens on the north side of the Small Mammals House.

Now, in 1976, Blanche had trouble remembering just when that sort of pleasure had gone out of her mornings. Could it have been in that nice apartment on Gramercy Park? Or the nicer one she and her husband moved into on East Eighty-sixth Street? Or the lovely house in Riverdale? Or the even more lovely one later on in Scarsdale? Blanche had a feeling it might have been in another dale somewhere along the line. Perhaps there had been two dales. She wasn't sure, because none of these places in which she had lived since those happy days with Sid and Yetta on Bronx Park South was making much of an impression on her at this moment in 1976.

What was making an impression on her was the feeling that there was something odd about all these places where Blanche Berkowitz had lived after she became Blanche Catalini. The places always got nicer and more expensive, but they always seemed to get farther north, away from Bronx Park South. Until when Mr. Max founded this big university up here in Newton, and he installed Susie Shale's husband as the president, and you began to be reminded to call him not president but chancellor, Blanche Catalini also came to live in Newton.

She couldn't imagine how or why, because she didn't really care about this university. It wasn't anything at all like those wonderful days in the evening session at C.C.N.Y. when she was picking up those three crucial credits toward her B.A. by taking that marvelous course in Freud and Marx: Concatenations and Contradictions.

It was strange that out of all those thirty-seven years since 1939 when she became Mrs. Joseph Catalini only two things stood out clearly in the mind of the former Blanche Berkowitz. The first thing was that her husband was nice to her. He really was. A gentleman to his fingertips. Kindness itself. The soul of generosity. A model of consideration. A tower of thoughtfulness. Generous to a fault. And as loving as any woman could possibly—

The thought stopped in Blanche Catalini's mind. Loving? Stubbornly the stalled thought shouldered its way forward. Yes, loving. Fair is fair. No woman ever had a better husband than Joe Catalini. Blanche Berkowitz had to admit that. No, she insisted on admitting it. So why was it that the second thing that stood out clearly in her mind about those thirty-seven years was that every time she saw him, every time she even thought about her husband, even today, even right now, even this minute, when she so much as heard his voice on the telephone, it made her want to—to—

She did, and the thick body dropped forward at the lumpy waist with an unexpected jerk, like the blade of a pocket-knife snapping into its slot. When she stopped retching, Blanche Catalini straightened up. She stared down at the mess in her lap, then brushed it from the nightgown to the floor with the side of the vodka bottle.

"I'm sorry about that," she said in a clear, firm voice, addressing her brother, Sid, wherever he might be, because Sid knew the kind of person his kid sister was, and even if he was dead, wherever he was Sid Berkowitz still knew. Earnestly Sid's kid sister said to him, "If there's anything you know I can't stand, it's a sniveling drunken woman who feels sorry for herself and can't stop whining about—"

Blanche did stop. Her head came up. She listened. The sound was repeated.

"Oh, God," Blanche Catalini said helplessly. "Here comes the little prize package in person."

She came up off the bed smoothly enough. She staggered only slightly on her way out of the bedroom, and she slipped only once crossing the living room to the front door. As she reached for the knob, the vodka bottle intervened and clanked against the brass. Carefully she shifted the bottle to her other hand. Even more carefully, as though she were threading a needle, she made a second attempt at the door-knob. It was successful. The door came open.

"Excuse me," said the man at the other side of the thresh-old. "Mr. Catalini called me from Logan Airport about an hour ago and asked me to come up here to his home at once."

"Who are you?" Blanche Catalini said.

"I work for your husband," Lou Mangan said.

405

51

"I'm not saying I've solved this thing for you," Lou Mangan said. "All I'm saying, Mr. Catalini, I think I've come up with something helpful. I believe it's also going to surprise you."

Mr. Catalini opened his mouth, but whatever he was about to say was aborted by a splashing crash from the room beyond the fireplace. It sounded like the offstage noises heard in cafeterias during peak-load periods. Dishes and silverware hitting tile floor from a height of at least several feet.

"Excuse me," Mr. Catalini said.

His movements were unhurried, as always. Yet he was out of his high-backed wing chair and across the large living room before the retired policeman had a chance to turn in his own chair for a clean look at the door through which the noise had come.

By the time Lou Mangan had his clean look, the door was swinging back and forth in a series of strong, whining arcs. The shove it had received when Mr. Catalini straight-armed his way through the door had not looked powerful enough to cause that much commotion. It occurred to Mangan that like everything else about Mr. Catalini, his physical strength was deceptive. When he came back into the room he was carrying a loaded tray with one hand as though it were a cocktail-party wafer.

"Fortunately," Mr. Catalini said, "she didn't drop the percolator. I shouldn't have asked her to make coffee. I didn't realize when I arrived and found you both chatting out here in the living room that she'd had one too many."

Mr. Catalini had arrived almost immediately after his wife had opened the front door for Lou Mangan. The ex-policeman and Mrs. Catalini had not spent those brief moments chatting. What they were doing when Mr. Catalini came in was staring at each other. In entirely different ways, of course. The startled ex-policeman had been trying to find words with which to address this swaying creature. Her gross, shapeless body was more outside than inside a torn night-gown soiled with what looked like the results of recent retching. From the way she kept working her eyes it was obvious that what Mrs. Catalini had been doing was trying to get a grip on the basic but frequently elusive proposition Which end is up? The entry of her husband solved the problem of neither his wife nor the ex-policeman, but it did break the frozen tableau of confused uneasiness.

"Hi, honey," Mr. Catalini said. He kissed his wife's cheek and gave her a gentle push. "Be a sweetheart and make us some coffee, huh?"

The push, Lou Mangan saw, had not been all that gentle. It sent Mrs. Catalini through the swinging door in a direct, on-target manner of which in her present condition she would have been incapable without help. Her husband dropped his raincoat on the couch, took the policeman's arm, and led him to one of the two wing chairs flanking the fireplace.

"Sorry to drag you up here at this hour of the night," he said. "This one okay?"

"Sure," Lou Mangan said.

He sat down. Mr. Catalini took the other chair. He formed a tent with his fingers by touching the tips together and swung into a small series of affable remarks about the weather on the Atlantic Coast, from Florida, where a hurricane was threatening the Miami area, to New England, where it was as usual just average, normal, everyday, garden-variety rotten. The ex-policeman had not paid much attention to these opening remarks. They were like the opening bars of a piece of music. Getting-the-listener-into-it stuff, but not memorable. Besides, Lou Mangan's mind was in the other room, beyond the swinging door.

From it came a series of complicated noises. They sounded exactly the way Mangan would have imagined them if he had not been present to hear them: the erratic clatter of a pretty-far-gone drunk trying to make coffee in a kitchen that was probably in a state of disarray not unlike her own.

When Mr. Catalini finished with the weather, and he asked the first question that demanded Mangan's full attention, the ex-policeman's answer had been drowned out by the crash of china that sent the man from New York punching his way out through the swinging door. Now he was back, smiling imperturbably, holding the neatly loaded tray.

"How do you take it?" he said.

"Black, please," Lou Mangan said.

Mr. Catalini set the tray on a low table between the wing chairs. He sat down facing Mangan and started talking as he picked up the silver coffeepot.

"What I was saying before the kitchen fell apart out there," Mr. Catalini said, "I asked if there's anything you've been able to learn since I called you from Florida last night—or more accurately, early this morning."

Leaning forward to take the coffee cup Mr. Catalini was holding out, Lou Mangan said, "What I've found out, I'm not saying I've solved this thing for you, Mr. Catalini, but I've come up with something that I think is not only helpful but will also I think surprise you."

This time the crash from the kitchen had a different tone. This time it was not china hitting tiles. Still unhurried, Mr. Catalini moved from his chair toward the noise in a more restrained way. Across his shoulder he said, "Excuse me, please."

Inspector Mangan took a sip of coffee and watched the arcs of the swinging door grow narrower and narrower. Before the door stopped moving Mr. Catalini punched his way back into the room.

"Sorry," he said with a rueful smile. "She couldn't remember where she parked the vodka bottle."

Lou Mangan wondered what he was supposed to do with that remark. It was not the sort of thing most husbands would say in the circumstances. On the other hand, the ex-policeman wondered how many husbands ever found themselves in precisely these circumstances. Clearly the circumstances did not bother Mr. Catalini. On the contrary. Mangan had the feeling the man from New York enjoyed them.

Mr. Catalini said, "What is this thing you've come up with that you feel will be helpful and is also going to surprise me?"

"This Idwal Lurie?" Lou Mangan said.

"Steve Lessing's roommate, yes," Mr. Catalini said. "What about him?"

"He doesn't think Steve Lessing's been kidnapped," Mangan said.

"Is that an opinion?" Mr. Catalini said. "Or does he know what he's talking about?"

"Both," Lou Mangan said.

"How does that work?" Mr. Catalini said.

"Did you know Steve Lessing is queer?" Mangan said.

Mr. Catalini said with a shrug, "How does anybody know that about anybody?"

"If you're his roommate," Mangan said, "I would imagine you're one of those who do."

"Idwal Lurie told you he and Steve Lessing—?"

"He did," Lou Mangan said. "And that's not all he told me."

"You lead a more interesting life than I do," Mr. Catalini said. "I think you better tell me the rest."

"Lurie told me Steve's taken up with a new boyfriend," Lou Mangan said. "Somebody down in Florida, and the last two or three months he's been flying down regularly on weekends, sometimes in the middle of the week, too, cutting classes, and he thinks that's where Steve Lessing is right now. In Florida."

For several silent moments Mr. Catalini stared down into his coffee. Finally, he said, "Why would Idwal Lurie tell you something like that?"

"Two reasons," Mangan said.

"One?" Mr. Catalini said.

"I beat the shit out of him."

"Two?"

"He's jealous as hell," Lou Mangan said.

Clearly surprised, Mr. Catalini said, "He told you that?"

"He did."

"This new boyfriend of Steve Lessing's," Mr. Catalini said. "Who is he?"

"I don't know," Mangan said.

"Idwal Lurie didn't tell you?"

"He doesn't know."

"You believe that?" Mr. Catalini said.

"Yes, I do," Lou Mangan said.

"Why?"

"The kid's all busted up about it," Mangan said.

"Lurie?" Mr. Catalini said.

"That's right," Lou Mangan said. "That's why he spilled his guts to me. He thought I could tell him who the new boyfriend is."

"I thought he did it because you beat the shit out of him."

"So did I," Lou Mangan said. "Until he broke down."

"Lurie?" Mr. Catalini said.

"He cried like a baby."

Mr. Catalini tugged his lower lip for a couple of moments, then said, "That's an odd one."

"I don't know," Lou Mangan said.

Mr. Catalini said, "Don't know what?"

"I guess that's where the word 'queer' comes from," Lou Mangan said. "First time I've ever seen anything like it. I know it sounds funny, but watching the way this kid took on about it, when he was telling me, I mean, you couldn't doubt it for a minute."

"Doubt what?"

"He's crazy dead stuck on this Lessing boy," Mangan said. "In love with him, for Christ's sake." The ex-policeman hesitated, then said, "The feeling I had, it was like a guy's wife, I mean a woman, he's nuts about her, and he has been for a long time, she with him too, he thinks, and then all of a sudden she takes up with some other guy. It's like what my father used to say about booze. It turns a man."

"Even a man who is not a man," Mr. Catalini said. "If you know what I mean."

"I don't think I would have known if I hadn't seen this Lurie kid tonight," Lou Mangan said. "Now I sure as hell do know what you mean."

Mr. Catalini's coffee cup absorbed his silent attention for another few minutes. He broke the silence with a single word.

"Florida," he said.

He said it to nobody in particular, Lou Mangan grasped after a moment. Mr. Catalini did not even say it, Mangan suspected, to himself. The man in the blue pin-striped suit had merely uttered a few sounds. To Lou Mangan he now uttered words: "You said this should be helpful to me."

"Isn't it?"

"Not unless you can think of something I haven't thought of," Mr. Catalini said.

Mangan said, "If the boy's been kidnapped, the kidnappers would get in touch with you or his family and tell you what they want. If the boy's just shacked up with someone he's stuck on, he'll come home the way according to Lurie he's been coming home these last two or three months every time he's gone off on one of these dates."

Mr. Catalini nodded. "Yes," he said. "Yes, that would be helpful." He took a sip and studied the amount of liquid left in his cup. After a while he said, "You mentioned something else about what you learned from Idwal Lurie. Yes. You said what you'd discovered would surprise me."

"Doesn't it?" Lou Mangan said.

"How does it surprise you?"

"Well, like everybody else who reads the papers," Lou Mangan said, "I've picked up a lot of stuff about the Lessing family, but I never heard any of them is queer."

Mr. Catalini said, "I would guess a lot of that sort of thing doesn't get into the papers."

Lou Mangan had been pretending for some time that he was not sitting on a feeling of disappointment. Now he stopped pretending. He'd come to this house with the sense of a job well done. He'd earned his pay. Mr. Catalini, however, didn't seem to think so. Lou Mangan couldn't understand why. He found himself wondering why the man in the pin-striped suit had asked him to come out here to Newton in the first place. Mr. Catalini could have asked the ex-policeman to give him on the phone whatever information Mangan had picked up.

"I apologize for bringing you out here at this hour," Mr. Catalini said.

Mangan shrugged and said, "You're paying me."

"True," Mr. Catalini said.

Mangan said, "Is there anything else I can do?"

"There is," Mr. Catalini said. "My wife, as you may have noticed, is not in what might be described as the pink of condition at the moment. She rarely is at this hour. I must get her signature on a business document at once. Considering her physical state, it may not look like much of a signature. I may be fortunate if I get so much as an X out of her. It would help me a good deal if you would watch the performance and then sign the document as a witness."

52

"Are you talking to me?" Alma Pine said.

"Yes, please, madam," said the young man in the red tailcoat. "Whom do you wish to see, please?"

Abe Shantz, who had just flown over from Florida, was a few feet behind Alma Pine when the young man said it. As he came in from the street, it had not occurred to Abe that he might know anybody in this crowded hotel lobby. Now that he saw he did, Abe put the brakes on his progress toward the elevators. It was not the moment for distracting encounters.

Abe Shantz had known all about Alma Pine even in the days when he was a boy in Minneapolis and Abe's father, Hymie, had been Mr. Max's bodyguard. Abe knew better than to mention the subject at home, but he remembered enjoying at school a not unpleasant notoriety from the knowledge common among his classmates that Abe's father worked for a man who was keeping a burlesque stripper in a suite at the Nokomis Hotel on Anoka Avenue.

Years later, when young Abe was in the Air Force, it seemed sensible to keep his mouth shut among his colleagues about what his father did for a living. Abe read the papers, however. Even during his tour of duty in Korea it was not difficult to keep up with the Lessings and their social

activities. Mr. Max's purchase of the T.K.O. Studio in Hollywood, and the six million he added to the purchase price in
his disastrous attempt to make a movie star out of his aging
doxy, could not exactly be identified as social activities. The
fighter pilot in Korea, however, could not avoid keeping
up with them.

Soon after Abe came home from Korea, and Joe Catalini
brought him into the organization as chief of the Lessing jet
fleet, Abe's father retired to Florida. The old man's interest
in the Lessing family did not diminish. On the contrary.
Now that his son was a member of the organization, the old
man's interest intensified. He clipped from the newspapers
and sent to his son every scrap about the Lessings that came
his way.

Thus, even though Alma Pine had long ago dropped out
of public sight, in Abe Shantz's areas of awareness her memory
had been kept, if not green, at least watered.

From these he had a very clear picture—fully clothed, of
course—of the now seventy-four-year-old ecdysiast. The picture in his mind was so clear that Abe Shantz, who had never
seen Alma Pine in person, now recognized her strong, coarse,
attention-gathering voice in the lobby of the Hotel Värmland
in Stockholm.

"I don't wish to see the creature," Alma said to the young
man in the red tailcoat. "But she has a huge suite that over-
looks this thing called Shleppers Home Island—"

"Skeppsholmen Island, madam," the young man said.

"—and she invited me to come watch the fun from her
balcony as the King and Queen come sweeping out of the
palace, climb into the royal barge, and start dodging the
shells from their twenty-one-gun salute."

"You are a guest, then, madam, of Mr. and Mrs. Norman
Lessing," the young man said. "Yes?"

"I'd better be," Alma Pine said. "I flew all the way over
here from London just to see this cookout."

"And the name, then, madam, please?"

Alma Pine told him. From the way she pronounced it,

414

Abe Shantz could tell she hoped it would be recognized. It wasn't, of course, which was no surprise to Abe. The kid in the red getup looked about eighteen. Which meant he had been born just about the same number of years after Alma had made her last picture. From the flow of intelligence directed at him by his father in Florida, nobody knew better than Abe Shantz that Alma Pine's last picture, which was also her first, had made neither money nor history.

"Ah, yes," the young man said, looking up from his list. "If you will be so good, madam?"

He made a mark on his list with a tiny gold pencil from the top of which a red-and-blue tassel bounced perkily.

"The elevator on your right, madam, please?"

The elevator on the right was full of pink camellias and the kind of people Abe Shantz had been seeing for years in Claire and Norman Lessing's penthouse at 689 Fifth and their many temporary homes all over Europe. As Abe squeezed into the elevator, one of these, a woman wearing a monocle, said to Alma Pine, "Are you Gloria Swanson?"

"No," Alma said. "Are you?"

The man beside the woman with the monocle said, "Careful, pet. This one bites."

The elevator stopped with a clunk. In the service of the jet-minded and -propelled Lessings, Abe Shantz got around. This was not the first time he had noticed that the Swedes wasted very little money on machinery that functioned below street level. A white glove followed by a red sleeve slid smoothly out of the massed camellias and pulled the elevator door open.

It brought to Abe's mind at once the feeling he'd had the first time, years ago, when he had been sent on an errand to one of those places in Europe where Claire and Norman Lessing had for a while come to rest. The opening of any front door behind which Claire and Norman Lessing had settled always reminded Abe of what he remembered thinking as a kid in school was meant by the opening of Pandora's box. It involved a sound of buzzing.

Abe hung back until the guests in the elevator had poured themselves into the buzzing. The sound seemed to push against the walls and the high ceiling of the vast room like an overloaded pot of boiling rice pushing against the lid. A waiter appeared at Abe's elbow.

"Drink, sir?"

Abe turned and said, "Thanks, no."

By the time he turned back, all the people with whom he had shared the elevator had lost their identities. Even Alma Pine had merged into the buzzing. That was all right with Abe. He had not come here to satisfy his curiosity about one of the legends of his youth. Abe Shantz was on assignment.

He knew what to do. He had been doing it for years. His work for the Lessings had brought him to Stockholm many times. This was the first time it had brought him to the Hotel Värmland. Abe stood quietly at his point of entry, doing what Alma Pine had done to the monocled slob in the elevator before she let her have it. Abe Shantz was quartering the terrain.

The wall facing him at the other side of the room was almost all window. The density of the buzzing was concentrated along the glass. What the guests had come to see would be seen from that side of the room. Abe had not come to see the royal procession. What he wanted would be either to his left or to his right, on the side of the room where he had entered from the elevator.

He glanced casually to the right. Nothing. He turned to the left. Nothing except possibly the top of Alma Pine's head. She had been wearing a yellow hat. He would have to make a move.

"I knew it, I knew it, I knew it."

The familiar voice, Abe grasped at once, had made the move for him. He turned back to the right and said, "Hello, Mrs. Lessing. You knew what?"

Claire Lessing said, "If Joe Catalini comes, can Abe Shantz be far behind?"

"I have a message for Mr. Catalini."

"The years I've known you, Abe," Claire said, "you've carried so many messages for Joe Catalini, in my heart of hearts I think of you as Western Union."

The notion that she thought of him at all was a surprise Abe was not sure he welcomed. Claire Lessing had always been a problem to him. She was the only Lessing who made Abe uneasy about that deep sense of loyalty to the family he had been goaded into defending in his argument with Chick Rosen in the Deerfield Bowling Lanes in Florida the night before.

Claire Lessing and Abe Shantz were just about the same age. Once, long ago, Abe had made it a point to check. She was exactly six weeks and four days older. Soon after he came out of Korea to take over the Lessing jet fleet, Abe had flown the orchids from Kenya to The Plaza for Claire's wedding to her foster brother. She had been at her peak then, although at the time Abe had not thought of it that way. He wouldn't have allowed himself to think such thoughts about the girl who was marrying Mr. Max's son.

Abe Shantz wouldn't have allowed himself, but he did. How could he not? Claire Boyle at thirty had been a dead ringer for the first movie star with whom Abe Shantz at twelve had fallen in love. Miss Claire was, of course, as unattainable as the movie star had been. Abe could not, however, help how he felt. All he could do was conceal it, even from himself. Anyway, he could try. Nobody had to tell him, not even Abe Shantz, that the attempt was a failure.

"I have a job," he said. "I do it."

"Everybody has a job," Claire Lessing said. "Of one kind or another, and everybody does his job, in one way or another. But everybody does something else, too. What's your something else, Abe?"

Abe Shantz said, "I think about Mr. Catalini's next assignment."

Claire gave him a long look. She was no longer at her peak, but for Abe that didn't matter. When she looked at him that way, directly, her gray eyes unblinking, it was like

417

staring into a flashlight beam. Abe had to look away. The way years ago, in a darkened movie theater, when the camera came in close on that now forgotten actress and he found himself staring directly into those incredible eyes, young Abe Shantz had been forced to look away. The direct, head-on contemplation of beauty made his heart go so hard it hurt.

Claire Lessing said slowly, "I wonder—?"

The sound of her voice, all at once so utterly and unexpectedly different from the way Abe had ever before heard it sound, brought his glance up again. There was a funny little look in those wide, wide, unbelievably wide gray eyes. It didn't remain long.

"No, I guess not," Claire said in that same slow way. Then she laughed, and whatever it had been for that brief moment, it was gone. She sounded the way she always sounded when she said, "How's your family, Abe?"

It took him a couple of moments to come back from where, now that it was over, he realized he had briefly been.

"Great, thanks" Abe Shantz said. "Come September, Abe Junior starts his freshman year at Lessing U."

Claire Lessing said, "Why don't you send the boy to a decent college?"

Shocked, Abe said, "Miss Claire!"

"Miss Claire my foot," Claire Lessing said. "You don't see me and Norman sending our Stevie to that preposterous tax write-off, do you? If you're going to ask a kid to spend four years of his life at college, it seems to me he has the right to expect you to send him to a place where he's going to get what colleges are supposed to be about. I mean an education. A son of yours is bound to have the brains for some place like Yale or Harvard. If you haven't got the money, I'll be glad to underwrite it."

"Anybody who works for Mr. Max," Abe Shantz said, "has the money to send his children to college."

Claire Lessing laughed. The movie actress used to laugh like that. When she laughed it did something to the way her face was arranged in repose, and the arrangement did something to Abe's heart. Claire Lessing's face now did the same thing. It didn't have quite the same effect. After all, Abe Shantz was past his prime too. But in a way that was not really painful, it still never failed to touch, not unpleasantly, the old painful but welcome bruise.

"What's funny?" he said.

"You," Claire said. "You and Joe Catalini and your father and all the rest of them. Your feelings about Mr. Max. He's not only my father-in-law, Abe; he was my foster father. My own father died when I was two months old. I grew up in the same house with Mr. Max. I know him a lot better than most people do, and I love him as much as you love your father, but I have news for you. Mr. Max, believe it or not, is not a reincarnation of the Seeing Eye Dog who made it possible for Moses to lead your people out of Egypt. Mr. Max is a cheap little gangster who moved up from nickel-and-dime bootlegging to the point where when there's a war on, he gets appointed by the President to things called the War Production Board. When Mr. Max got there, he had enough brains to start covering his tracks by building solid things like universities on the places where the murdered bodies are buried. Nobody in 1976 is going to start digging up fifteen story dormitories to find the skeleton of a small-town crook who was erased half a century ago by a more skillful crook on his way up. That doesn't mean you have to send your boy to the place. Loyalty to Mr. Max won't get Abe Junior what bright kids are supposed to get out of college."

Abe Shantz said, "Mr. Shale says Lessing University ranks with the best in the country."

"What else can he say?" Claire Lessing said. "He's the chancellor of the damn thing. John Shale has made a very successful career out of holding Mr. Max's coat in public."

Abe said, "I guess you could say the same thing about me."

Again that funny little look appeared in the cool, wide gray eyes. For its second appearance it did not stick around much longer than for its first.

"Yes, I guess I could," Claire said quietly. "But I'm not going to. Because then you'd have the right to say that about me."

"I'd never say that," Abe said.

"I didn't say you would," Claire Lessing said. "I said you'd have the right to say it. What else can you say about a woman who has spent twenty years of her life as a buffer between the image of himself Mr. Max wants the world to see and the truth about the gin-soaked playboy who is his only offspring?"

"I don't know Mr. Norman very well," Abe said.

"Count your blessings," Claire said. "And don't waste your time trying to add to your fund of knowledge. Getting to the bottom of Norman Lessing is about as difficult as getting to the bottom of a soup plate. I ought to know. I've loved him since I was a kid. I tried not to. There were other men. But in the end you do what you have to do. Or should. You marry the man you love. Even when there's only one word for him. Shallow. I don't think in all the years since he got out of the R.A.F. Norman has given a moment's thought to anything more mentally taxing than his golf handicap or what flower to put in the lapel of the jacket he plans to wear at his next party.

"Mr. Max's brain is in there somewhere, of course, and there are enough traces of Mrs. L's character to make you regret at times that they're so effectively hidden under an almost childish lust for amusement. Luckily there's enough money on hand to keep the business running smoothly without interfering with Norman's real interests, and a wife who has signed on to see that the smoothness remains smooth. Which is why I've spent twenty years doing what you see me doing now. Inviting the more newsworthy bums of Europe to come watch one of their kind who happens to be a king get married to a girl who probably has something of what my foster mother must have had when she was the same age. The sweepstakes ticket came in for both of them. How is she, by the way?"

"Fine, according to Mr. Catalini," Abe Shantz said. "He saw her last night."

"Didn't you?" Claire Lessing said.

"One of the other men flew Mr. Catalini to Florida," Abe said. "I picked him up in New York this morning and brought him over here."

"You boys can't seem to stay away from each other very long," Claire said. "Joe got here only twenty minutes ago."

"Could you tell me where he is?" Abe said.

"If you tell me why you have a message for him so soon after you both arrived in Stockholm."

"Mr. Catalini asked me to keep an eye on the weather in Florida," Abe Shantz said. "He may want to fly back there after he finishes with Mr. Norman here. I just got a report out at the airport I thought I'd better bring in person. Where can I find him?"

"He's with Norman in the study," Claire Lessing said. "Come."

Moving along beside her, Abe Shantz caught a glimpse through the windows of the crowd moving down the palace steps to the royal barge. The sun chipped sparks of light from the decorations on the uniforms and the brass scabbards of the ranked guards. They held their drawn swords stiffly upright, hilts at the chin. It reminded Abe Shantz of newsreel shots he used to see as a boy of the graduation ceremonies at Annapolis.

"It's that door next to the bronze lion," Claire said. "Knock twice, just to make sure the boys are decent, then wait for the order to advance and give the countersign."

"Thanks," Abe said.

He started for the door, but he didn't get very far. At that moment, from the crowded scene outside the window came a roaring sound to which Abe Shantz had grown accustomed in Korea: an artillery piece had let one go.

"Twenty more to come," Claire Lessing said. "I'd better go have a look."

She turned toward the windows, but she didn't get very

far either. At that moment the door next to the bronze lion opened and a woman emerged. She did it like a watermelon seed coming out of a good hard squeeze between thumb and forefinger.

"My God," she gasped to nobody in particular, "all I was doing, I was looking for the loo, and then—"

The rest of her words were lost in the roar of the second artillery piece. Astonished, Abe Shantz saw that it was the woman with the monocle.

"Nineteen to go," Claire said.

"For God's sake," the woman with the monocle gasped. "Somebody stop them!"

Abe Shantz did not realize the woman's gasp was actually a scream until he saw, framed in the doorway, the two men flailing away at each other on the floor of the study. Just as Abe grasped that the battling men were Norman Lessing and Joe Catalini, a woman in a yellow hat appeared from somewhere behind them. She stepped fastidiously across the writhing bodies and came out into the drawing room.

"My money is on Joe Catalini," Alma Pine said. "He had all that unarmed-combat training as a Boy Scout in Minneapolis."

She said more, or started to, but the words were lost in the third explosion outside.

"Eighteen to go," Claire Lessing said.

Imperturbably she stepped through the open study door, pushed the door shut behind her, and said, "All right, you two, cut it out."

The men on the floor stopped moving. For a few moments they lay motionless, arms and legs frozen. They looked like actors in a blowup of a single frame snipped from a movie fight scene. Then they pushed themselves away from each other. Joe Catalini stood up first. He brushed back his hair, tugged down the double-breasted blue pinstripe jacket, and muttered to a far corner of the room, "I'm sorry, Miss Claire."

"For what?" she said. Then, as her husband came to his feet: "How about you?"

"I'm not sorry," Norman Lessing said. Then: "No, I'll correct that. I'm sorry as hell. If you hadn't come butting in, I could have fulfilled my lifelong ambition to kill this little bastard."

"I think we can do without the Sam Spade bit," Claire said. "It's becoming a bit frayed at the edges. Which one of you is going to tell me what this is all about?"

"You'd better let him do it," Norman said. "If I hear the stuff he just told me coming out of my own mouth, even your presence in this room won't be able to stop me from tearing the son of a bitch into bite-size pieces."

Claire Lessing saw at once that her husband had stepped into one of the several roles that served him as platforms from which he faced the daily round. At the moment Norman was being the far-seeing, firm-jawed, strong-willed, taciturn commander, the field marshal who wielded power from afar, missing nothing as he remained carefully above the sweaty battle while with quiet, unruffled brilliance he directed every move of his cowering but dedicated underlings. It was a role that Norman Lessing performed with surprising conviction.

Much of the success of the performance was due to the fact that while he had probably not inherited all of his father's brains, Norman Lessing had undoubtedly come out on stage with most of his father's looks. Years ago, when Claire had finally accepted the fact that other men would not do, and she had to marry the man she had loved all her life, Norman Lessing had been the younger member of the handsomest father-and-son team she had ever encountered. From the pictures her foster mother had shown her over the years, Claire knew that Norman at the time of their marriage had looked very much like the boy who in 1919 had stopped at the barn door in Klein Berezna to beg the famous cup of milk from the second actor in the most durable anecdote of the Lessing family legend.

Now, at fifty-four, Norman had lost his dew, but he still had Mr. Max's tall, powerful frame, and he had kept his trim physique, and the gray that streaked through the Lessing copper-colored hair made him more photogenic than Mr. Max had ever been. Perhaps because Mr. Max had never been vain about his appearance. Norman, however, gave the impression that he had very little more than his appearance to be vain about. It made him popular with people who carried cameras to cocktail parties. For this reason Norman was fussy about his clothes. Right now, for example, he was wearing the pale blue velour jump suit Claire had tried to talk him out of buying the week before in Paris. She had to admit, if only to herself, that she had probably been wrong. On anybody else the thing would have been embarrassing. On Claire Lessing's husband it looked just right.

An observer would have had to know Norman Lessing very well indeed before he or she grasped that this powerful, impressive, bizarrely but attractively costumed figure, whose tanned, intelligent features were fixed in a thoughtful frown, was actually a dedicated playboy whose mind, no matter what else might at the moment have plodded into it, was primarily concerned with the question: if the door should open suddenly to admit Lord Snowdon and his Leica, would Norman be offering the better of his profiles to the royal lens?

"All right, Joe," Claire Lessing said. "Your turn."

Joe Catalini said, "Could we all sit down?"

"If you think it will help," Claire said.

She dropped into the chair at the right of the fireplace. Joe took the chair on the left. Norman walked around behind the desk, where he remained on his feet, his body arranged in a manner that Claire had come to identify as her husband's Churchillian stance. Norman had copied it from the famous photograph of the prime minister taken by Karsh in his Ottawa studio. Left fist on hip, right palm on desk, bulldog scowl on camera. The blue velour jump suit added something, but Claire Lessing was not sure what.

"Please listen carefully," Joe Catalini said. "Please don't interrupt until I'm finished."

Norman Lessing said, "Don't you tell me what to do and what not to do."

"Shut up, please, Norman," his wife said. "Go ahead, Joe."

Joe said, "A few minutes after ten last night, I was working late in the office. The phone rang. I picked it up expecting Miss Carey, the night secretary, but it wasn't. It was a man's voice, a voice I'd never heard before. He said, *Mr. Catalini, we've got Steve Lessing. Don't ask any questions. Don't call the cops. Don't do anything. Just stand by. We'll call later and tell you what it will cost to get him back alive.*"

Joe Catalini paused. He scowled down at his pin-striped knees, as though running through in his mind the words he had just spoken to make sure he had quoted them correctly. Claire Lessing came to her feet as though she had been kicked.

"For God's sake," she said, "what are you saying?"

"He's saying Stevie has been kidnapped," her husband said. "Now stop screaming and calm down. Wait till you hear the rest of this."

"I am not screaming," Claire said. "And if I am, it's my son you're babbling on about, God damn it." She turned and said, "Joe, this is for real?"

"No question about it," Joe Catalini said.

"I have a coal scuttle full of questions about it," Norman Lessing said.

"Please, darling," his wife said. "Please let Joe tell us before we—" She must have heard the sounds her own voice was making. She caught her lower lip in her teeth and dropped back into the chair. "Sorry, Joe," Claire Lessing said. "Please go on."

"I tried to trace the call at once," Joe said. "I couldn't. The call had not gone through the switchboard, so it wasn't on the tapes. I called Communications, and they said they didn't know how any call could get through to my desk without going through the switchboard, and could I give them any more details. I didn't want to make any waves, so I told them it was not important and to forget it."

"Not important," Norman Lessing said. "My son gets kidnapped, and to this son of a bitch it's not important."

425

Joe Catalini devoted several moments to the silent study of his knees, then said, "Miss Cláire, when I told Communications to forget it, I meant—"

"I know what you meant," Claire Lessing said. "And I'm sure my husband has intelligence enough to know it too. It's just that the news is a shocker, and we're both understandably—"

"I have something better than intelligence," Norman Lessing said. "I have instinct."

Claire drew a long, deep breath and said, "Then you must understand what I understand—namely, when Joe said Forget it, he meant he didn't want the Communications center putting on a full-dress hunt, which would have been just what the kidnappers warned Joe not to do."

"If they are kidnappers," Norman said.

His wife gave him a sharp glance and said, "Norman, what—" Then she stopped and, more quietly, she said, "Go on, Joe."

Joe said, "I flew to Florida at once to tell Mrs. L."

"Why not me?" Norman said. "I'm his father."

"Or me?" Claire said. "I'm his mother."

"I didn't want to do any of this by phone," Joe Catalini said. "It's quicker to get to Florida than to Stockholm. Also, there's the element of shock. You're the parents, yes. But you're young and, so far as I know, healthy. Mrs. L is seventy-three. These last two years, locked away down there with Mr. Max, she's been under all kinds of strain. Most important, though, the kidnappers had come to me. Not to Stevie's parents. They told me to shut up and sit tight and wait. Calling you could be dangerous. Flying down to see Mrs. L could be helpful. I wanted her advice."

"Did you get it?" Claire Lessing said.

"Yes," Joe said. "She said I was doing the right thing by following the kidnappers' instructions. She said that was the way she would have handled it. She told me not to worry about her but to fly right back to New York and wait for the message from the kidnappers."

"Then what the hell are you doing here?" Norman Lessing said.

"Yes, Joe, what?" Claire Lessing said.

"Bringing the news to Stevie's parents," Joe Catalini said.

"But you just said that was the one thing you didn't want to do," Claire said. "Because it was the thing the kidnappers had warned you not to do. By doing it, Joe, this very minute you could be endangering Stevie's life."

Norman said, "Answer that one, you slippery, forked-tongued, double-talking—"

"Norman, please," Claire Lessing said.

"Norman please my ass," he said. "Wait till you hear this one. Go ahead, Mr. Catalini."

Claire said, "What happened, Joe?"

"It turned out I didn't have to go to New York to get the message from the kidnappers," Joe Catalini said. "The message was waiting for me in the lobby of The Frontenac."

"By arrangement perhaps?" Norman Lessing said.

Joe stared down at his knees like a man counting ten, then shook his head.

"No," he said in a tired voice. "Not by arrangement, but very much by surprise."

"You just told me it's this son of a bitch Ohmstetter," Norman said. "The building manager. You hired him, didn't you? You and your great big intelligence network. How come he could turn out to be a surprise?"

Addressing Claire Lessing, Joe Catalini said patiently, "When I hired him two years ago I did not know Paavo Ohmstetter was going to be involved in the kidnapping of your son, Stevie."

"He did it?" Claire said. "That dark, weird little man Ida once pointed out to me when Norman and I were visiting?"

"He may have," Joe said. "I don't know. All I know is he stopped me when I was leaving the building after my visit with Mrs. L. He took me into his apartment and he told me the kidnappers had appointed him the intermediary to negotiate with me and the family for Stevie's release."

"Which you of course believed," Norman Lessing said.

Joe Catalini turned from Claire Lessing to look directly at her husband.

"Wouldn't you?" Joe said.

"You bet your ass I wouldn't," Norman said.

Claire scowled at her husband for a moment or two, then said quietly, "Norman, why wouldn't you believe what Ohmstetter told Joe?"

"Because I'm the fool of the family," Norman Lessing said. "The nitwit playboy. I don't have Mr. Max's brains. I'm just a great big round zero who has to be tolerated. So the whole bunch of you—my father, my mother, you, the whole team— you let this little wop here run everything and all I get to do is sign papers. It's what you all want, and who am I to fight three tough guys like my old man and my old lady and the watchdog they signed on as my wife? I'll tell you who I am. I'm a father with a father's instincts, and they tell me I don't have to believe everything this bastard says. The way he operates, he calls in the F.B.I. and the C.I.A. to run a check on the kid who delivers the pastrami sandwiches from the delicatessen to the typists' pool when they're working late. How come he hires a manager for The Frontenac without knowing anything about his background to show that two years later the bastard is capable of kidnapping our son?"

In a voice as troubled as the look on her face, Claire Lessing said quietly, "That seems a fair enough question under the circumstances. Before I go crazy, Joe, please answer it."

"Ohmstetter was checked out as thoroughly as anybody we've ever hired for anything," Joe Catalini said. "I don't know any more than I've just told you."

Claire shook her head. It was as though she did not like her suddenly troubled thoughts and she wanted to shake them loose. She said, "You must know more, Joe. You must know what Ohmstetter told you the kidnappers want."

"That's what I flew here to tell you," Joe said.

"Bullshit," Norman said. "You didn't fly to Stockholm to tell my wife anything. You flew here to tell it to me. To the hind tit of the Lessing family. The asshole who signs anything you put in front of him because that's the way you've got my father and mother hooked into believing is the only way to make things work. The only reason Claire is in this room now is because when I heard what you wanted me to sign this time, I started to tear your fucking head off, you son of a bitch. It's the best idea I ever had."

The Churchillian stance ended with the right palm shoving the blue-velour-clad body up from the desk. Norman Lessing came around the desk with his fists beginning to punch air. His wife came up out of her chair, met him head on, and shoved her husband back with a sharp thrust of both palms against the chest pockets of his jump suit. She turned her back on Norman Lessing, both her arms spread wide as though she were a riot-squad policeman trying to restrain an unruly crowd, and said, "Tell it to me, Joe."

Joe Catalini said, "Ohmstetter told me the kidnappers will return Stevie alive in exchange for fifty-one percent of the stock of Lessing Enterprises, Ltd."

Across his wife's shoulder Norman Lessing said, "Did you ever hear anything as crazy a that?"

Without turning, Claire said, "No, but our son has never before been kidnapped. Joe, what does that mean in practical terms?"

Joe said, "In practical terms, it means if we want Stevie back alive we'd better begin the process of getting him back by meeting what may at first glance seem the kidnappers' impractical terms. For the time being, anyway."

"How can we do that?" Claire Lessing said.

"By giving me powers of attorney from enough stockholders to add up to fifty-one percent of our stock," Joe Catalini said. "Which I can then convey to the kidnappers by whatever means Ohmstetter directs. He made it plain that that would be the second stage of his directions to me.

429

On my way over here to Stockholm I stopped off in Newton to pick up my wife's power of attorney to cover her holdings. Hers plus mine add up to—"

Norman Lessing's voice, from at least eight inches above his wife's blond head, came booming in with "A power squeeze that even the family fool can see is a shakedown. This is one time the family fool is not playing the part the family has cast him in. I ain't signing nothing, Mr. Catalini."

In the pause that followed, Claire had the strange feeling that Joe Catalini had suddenly developed a toothache and was probing its source with his tongue. When he seemed to locate the pain, he pursed his lips and blew out his breath very slowly.

"Miss Claire," Joe said quietly. "I have to fly back to Florida to face Ohmstetter. What shall I tell him?"

Just as quietly, Claire Lessing said, "Is Stevie's life in danger?"

Joe said, "Yes."

Norman said, "How about your life, Mr. Catalini?"

Claire Lessing turned to look up at her husband. "Norman," she said, "what does that mean?"

"Ask him," Norman Lessing said. "What I'm asking, the dumb playboy you all think I am, I'm asking myself Why is this little wop falling all over himself to get us all to give in to this creepy little stupid janitor down there in Florida? How do we know this stupid little janitor down there in Florida has anything to do with this? How the hell do we know what in God's name 'this' is? How do we know the smartest thing to do isn't to stop listening to this slimy little weirdo who has been running our lives all these years and do what any normal parents would do? Why the hell don't we call the cops? How the hell do we know anything except what anybody, even a dope, can see, which is that this little jerk sitting here in front of us is scared shitless?"

Claire Lessing said, "Joe, are you?"

Joe Catalini shook his head as though the toothache had resurfaced and he was trying to pretend it did not exist.

"I don't know what Norman is talking about," he said.

"Norman," his wife said, "do you?"

"I'm talking about him," Norman Lessing said. "Can't you see it, for Christ's sake? It's not Stevie. It's him. Whoever these guys are that Ohmstetter has behind him, they've got something on our friend here, and it doesn't take a genius to figure out what it is. This great big stone face behind the Lessing Enterprises scenes, Mr. Joseph Catalini, the whole world knows what he is. So do you. But nobody's ever been able to nail him for anything, even though plenty have tried. Now they've done it. He's slipped up somewhere, God knows how—maybe in a public toilet, for Christ's sake, where everything from knights on the London stage to Bible Belt congressmen seem to get caught these days—and all those boys who were watching and waiting, at last they've got the goods on him. So naturally he wants us to buy him out of it. I may be dumb, but I'm not that dumb. If all that was involved here was some cash these bastards want in exchange for Stevie, they'd come to Stevie's father and mother. They'd come to you and me. Or they'd go to his grandmother. Everybody knows she's always handled the old man's rough stuff. She'd be the logical person to approach. So why didn't the kidnappers go to Ida or come to us?"

"Why?" Claire Lessing said.

Her husband said, "Because it's not Stevie who's in danger."

Joe Catalini said, "Yes, it is, Norman."

Coming in under Norman Lessing's fury, Joe's quiet voice had the impact of an explosion. He stood up and came across the room toward Norman Lessing. As he came, Joe pulled a sheet of paper from his breast pocket.

"You're right," he said. "I'm the one they're after, which is why you'd better sign, Norman. Because that's exactly what they've got on me," Joe Catalini said: "Stevie."

Norman Lessing made a roaring noise deep in his chest.

With a sweep of both arms, he shoved his wife aside. He moved forward to meet Joe Catalini, struggling, as he came, to pull something from a side pocket of the blue velour jump suit.

Out in the drawing room, Abe Shantz became aware of a sound that was separate and distinct from the roar of the guns saluting the wedding of the king on the palace grounds outside the window. Abe had no trouble identifying the surprising sound.

One thing you learned from a tour of duty in Korea: the difference between the noise made by an artillery shell hurling itself from a field piece and the sound made by a 9 mm. automatic pistol.

PART VIII
1976

53

Max Lessing was checking a list. He had been doing it for hours. Ever since Ida had come to him with the news Joe Catalini had brought down from New York about Stevie.

The news had done something unexpected to the contents of the sealed-off four-wall handball court in which Max Lessing had for two years been kept alive. The entrance to the handball court was, of course, a moment in time. The day they dedicated the Lessing Tower to Max as a seventy-second-birthday present. The day Max was hit by what Herb Zlotkin and the other doctors called a stroke.

Until a few hours ago, when Ida had brought Joe Catalini's news about Stevie's kidnapping, Max had forgotten his first reaction to that stroke. Until a few hours ago he had forgotten what it had been like to accept the knowledge that he would never again use his vocal cords, or both legs, or his right arm. The moment when Max Lessing had finally grasped he had nothing left inside him with which even to pretend he could put up a fight for his hearing.

Astonished by the total defeat, Max had stared in amazement as his mind filled with images of losers he had forgotten long ago. Men who had lost all sorts of battles because Max Lessing had won them.

Suddenly, after two years, all those losers had come tumbling and elbowing and shoving their way back into his consciousness. As though they had just heard of some tremendously important event, something for which they had long waited without ever really daring to hope it would actually come, and now that it had arrived they could not contain their furious eagerness to capture the best seats up front.

For a while, puzzled by this array of clamoring spectators, Max had not given them much thought. Then he began to notice their faces, and the puzzlement turned to shock. He lost what remained of his already slipping interest in *The Vampire's Two-Headed Daughter*. Max Lessing's interest in his unexpected visitors turned to total absorption.

He saw something he had at first glance missed: they were not spectators. They were creditors. They had not shoved their way into his sealed-off cell to watch a spectacle. They had come to claim credit.

"I did it," they said. "To pay you back for what you once did to me."

Yes, but who was "me"?

There were so many shouting voices, so many waving hands, that Max Lessing could not tell them apart. Which he suddenly realized was the only thing that mattered. Telling them apart. Cutting the culprit out of the herd. It was the only way to fight these things. Max Lessing had done it before. Many times to get what he wanted he had been forced to weed out the crazy bastards who always showed up on the scene of a crime and claimed credit for the murder or the rape or the bombing.

Max Lessing knew all about the creeps. They didn't care what they confessed to, so long as the confession brought them what they had never had: stage center. Max couldn't waste time on them now. Time was the key to saving Stevie's life. Because whoever the son of a bitch was who had snatched Stevie, Max Lessing knew he would not hold Stevie for long. He couldn't. Revenge didn't become revenge until it paid off, and Max Lessing knew in what was left of his damaged brain that whoever the man was, for him the payoff would not take the form of money.

Who? In the noisy crowd clamoring for Max's attention, which one should he choose?

The fierce question, hammering away inside what was left of Max's brain, turned the sealed-off cell into a list. The piece of Max Lessing's brain that still functioned forced itself to throttle down, to shove aside time-wasting emotions, to examine the list with the precision he had more than half a century ago brought to examining the motives of Ober-feldwebel Sauerlich.

The thought of Sauerlich led to Colonel Eyquardt. Max could see the bastard again, on the floor of the orderly room in the Fürstenfeld barracks. Max was about to wipe this scrap of ancient history impatiently from the list when the piece of his brain, now working in high gear, leaped forward eighteen years, from 1919 in Fürstenfeld, to 1937 in Washington. The year Ida had decided he should have the ambassadorship to England.

Joe Catalini had worked on it. Joe had given it everything he had. But the answer from Washington was no. England was committed to Joe Kennedy. Austria, however, was free. Max Lessing could have Austria. The President felt it was a good idea for Max to take Austria. The President said after all, the great Max Lessing had been born in Austria.

"No," Max Lessing said.

Joe Catalini said, "Why not, Mr. Max?"

Max told him.

"I'll take care of it," Joe said.

He took care of it. Washington cleared the appointment. It was never announced. The clearance came through on the day Hitler marched into Austria and annexed it.

Years later Max learned how Joe Catalini had taken care of it. Max was a little surprised by what he learned. The job lacked the surgeon's precision of the Saul Sumeg settlement. Max sensed that Joe had left loose ends behind him. Max was right. Some of the people Joe had taken care of in 1937 showed up in 1947 in the community of escaped Nazis living in Argentina.

The knowledge had not troubled Max Lessing at the time. It was the time of his life when it was all blowing his way. Now, however, the knowledge did trouble him. Those loose ends Joe Catalini had left behind? Could they have been left deliberately? Now that he was locked away in this cell, and Stevie was old enough to attract the attention of ex-Nazi vengeance, had Joe all those years ago taken the precaution, as personal-liability insurance, to set up the machinery for that vengeance to flow from the figure with the crushed skull on the stone floor of the orderly room in the Fürstenfeld barracks? It was the sort of careful advance preparation that was Joe Catalini's trademark.

Which made Max Lessing suddenly wonder about Rabbi Fruchter. The bearded old bastard who in early 1920 had forced Max to marry Ida in Rivière du Cojot before he would put them on the train to Winnipeg. The rabbi was dead. By the numbers he had to be. This was 1976. His brothers were even deader. Zalman in a bathtub on the top floor of the tenement on Minnehaha Avenue. Jekuthiel behind the woodpile in Whampoa's Open.

They could have left kids, though. And the kids could have done likewise. Besides, there was always that son of the original son of a bitch up in Rivière du Cojot. The young man in the *shtrahmel* and alpaca coat who had been bending over his broken-down Ford when Max and Ida came out of the woods on the day they stole Mrs. Perlmutter's Model T for the escape from South St. Stephen across the Canadian border.

On that day in 1920, that young man had been about Max's age. If he was still alive, therefore, he would be Max's age today. Which was only seventy-four. Even if he wasn't alive, he could have left kids who would pass on the story of the immigrant boy from the S.S. *Friesland* who half a century ago had helped Saul Sumeg unload the booze on a lonely beach in Maine and then had gone on, with the help of all those Fruchters, to become the great Mr. Max of Lessing Enterprises, Ltd.

Which one of those little bastards, broke and bitter in some cockamamy corner of nowhere—which one had worked out this scheme to get a little of his own back? His own and his family's? By going after what they knew Mr. Max would give anything he owned to keep from getting hurt.

Working down the list of possibilities, Max grasped, you didn't even have to go back half a century. Or make guesses about the location of cockamamy holes in nowhere. All you had to do was look out your window. Assuming you were able to move your vegetable body out of this goddamn bed to do any looking out of any windows. If you were able, you could practically spit on the Rosen Limousine Service, Inc., down in Miami.

The old taxi driver who had been coughing out his lungs in New York when Max set him up in business in Miami had been smart enough to keep his trap shut in public about the reasons for Max Lessing's generosity. Maybe he hadn't kept it shut at home, though. From Ida's bedside gossip, Max knew that Rosen's son Chick had graduated from Penn State a year ago and had taken over running the family business.

The kid would be almost exactly Stevie's age. When Stevie flew down from Harvard to visit on weekends with his sick grandfather, it was a Rosen limo that met the Lessing jet at Miami International. Maybe the meeter was even Chick Rosen himself, taking a turn at the wheel for the chance to double-O the great Mr. Max's grandson and heir. It wouldn't be hard to figure out young Chick Rosen's thoughts on the dollar gap between what he was going to inherit and what Stevie Lessing was going to end up with.

In his pushcart days in Minneapolis, Max Lessing had learned what happens to a man's thinking when he starts looking at the gap between the buttered bagel that is all he can afford with his eleven o'clock cup of coffee and the cream-cheese-and-lox bagel his more prosperous colleagues can afford. It was the kind of thinking that had put Zalman Fruchter fully clothed into the bathtub on the top floor of the tenement on Minnehaha Avenue. What was to prevent Chick Rosen's similar thinking from putting Stevie Lessing wherever it was the bastards were at this moment holding Mr. Max's grandson for ransom?

It had not prevented Gerhardt Berg from trying to pay Max back for getting Berg's cousin Orville Klemperer fired from the U.S. Embassy in London after the 1932 passport-lifting incident. Berg had chosen the wrong way to do it. The wrong way from the standpoint of his health, that was.

By trying to cut Max's Canadian delivery lines through Washington intervention, Berg had forced Max to do more than cut into Berg's vote at the next election. Max had been forced to order Joe Catalini to take what Joe called definitive steps. With the result that Gerhardt Berg became the first Minnesota governor to end his term by falling from the roof of Ganyi's Gardens to the pavement of Hennepin Avenue.

The Berg family had not been pleased. The displeasure had undoubtedly been passed on to the next generation. Who could say whether or not it was a member of this generation that was at the moment holding Stevie Lessing for whatever the pot-smoking weirdos with hair and Indian beads nowadays called ransom?

Jake Blau could have said it, of course. Because Jake Blau, in his *Jewish Daily Watchword* office on East Broadway in New York, had known everything there was to know about every Jewish family of any prominence in America. Jake Blau, however, was dead.

Besides, when you got right down to it, which was where Max Lessing on the list in his mind was relentlessly getting, it could be Jake Blau himself who was responsible for the danger Stevie Lessing was in at this very moment. Max had

440

never forgotten Ida's report of Jake Blau's rage when she had gone to the editor in 1934 with the offer to arrange the assassination of Hitler.

It had come back to Max over the years that Jake Blau had never forgotten it either. The Lessing family's offer had become for the fiery old editor a symbol of the double standard by which the American businessman conducted his life.

"Under the umbrella of a piety that would embarrass Isaiah, to make a buck he will stoop to practices that would shame Daniel Quilp."

Without mentioning Ida's name, Jake Blau had for years used the dramatic incident in his editorial columns and in his lectures. Max Lessing did not know how many people in addition to Max and Ida knew the name of the anonymous woman visitor to Jake Blau's office who figured so prominently in Jake's endless retelling of the anecdote. Max Lessing did not doubt, however, that one of those people could have set in motion the chain of events that had resulted in what at this very moment had placed his grandson's life in jeopardy.

In fact, it began to come clear to Max, the trouble was that he could not with safety strike anybody from the list.

Sir Digby Locksmoor, to whom he had tied the can on the Kirkbean deal, was just as good a possibility as any one of the Hollywood characters Max had left holding the T.K.O. bag when he decided the cost of the studio plus six million big ones for the movie Alma produced personally was enough to convince even the head of Lessing Enterprises, Ltd., that the public was never going to accept Alma Pine as the successor to Mary Pickford.

Speaking of which, what made Max think Alma herself was not a possibility?

Nobody knew better than Max Lessing of what she was capable in the revenge department. Since he had dumped her, even though Norman and Claire kept inviting her to their parties all over Europe, why wouldn't Alma Pine plan a thing like this to get back at the man to whom, she kept telling all those interviewers, she had given the best years of her life?

So had Blanche Catalini—except that Blanche had given those years to Max indirectly, when he ordered her to marry Joe Catalini so the bankers wouldn't listen too hard to all those stories about Max's right-hand man's being queer.

The only thing that might get Blanche off the list was the fact that she was locked away all the time up there in Massachusetts with a vodka bottle. Too drunk to cook up any sort of feasible plan about anything, including how to get the morning paper in off the front steps without breaking her neck.

She might, however, get some help from Hector Katz. When Max had fired him because of the stuff that got into the papers at the time he cut loose from Alma, Max stated in a taped interview with Mike Wallace that it was all a bunch of lies invented to embarrass him by a disgruntled ex–press agent. Hector Katz had sent Max a wire: YOU HAVE MADE A BAD MISTAKE.

Max had not taken the threat seriously. Now, however, locked away in the prison cell of his mind, he saw something terrifying. In terms of the vengeful human wreckage he had left in his wake, Max Lessing's whole life loomed as a very bad mistake.

His one attempt to correct the mistake had been made too late. On that day in 1974 when Ida had decided to celebrate his seventy-second birthday by dedicating the Lessing Tower in his honor. Max had not attended the dedication ceremonies. He had explained to Ida that an important piece of business was coming up. She had asked no questions. Max was sure she knew what the important piece of business was. When he came into Max's office, Joe Catalini seemed to know it too.

"I see it's true," he said.

"What's true?" Max Lessing said.

Joe said, "My new girl, the one I stole last week from

Ari Onassis, she said you were watching the dedication ceremonies on the TV screen."

Max pressed the OFF button on his remote-control switch. The TV set went dead.

"I was also listening," he said. "But now I want to listen to you."

"Could I do it sitting down?"

"On your feet," Max Lessing said, "I wouldn't know how to talk to you in this room."

Joe Catalini walked across the large room to the chair in which he always sat when he came in to see Max. He sat down and crossed his legs. The blue pinstripe was, as always, double-breasted. It was also new. Max could tell by the gaps between the stripes. This fall Joe was into one-inch gaps. He undid the jacket buttons and spread the wings of the coat away from his neat little belly. There was about that belly an element of pride, as though it were meant to advertise to the world in a modest way how many prime steaks and four-dollar servings of strawberry shortcake topped with Devonshire cream had gone into creating the discreetly impressive, beautifully tailored little bulge.

Joe said, "What you have to say to me must be very important, Mr. Max. Or it could have waited until after the dedication ceremonies."

Max had what he had come to identify as one of his book-end moments. As he got older he found these moments came with increasing frequency. He welcomed them. They saved time. They showed him a beginning and an end.

Now, with vivid clarity, Max could see a naked boy of fourteen in 1922 wrapped in a blanket on the couch in the old Minneapolis living room on Columbia Heights, and a short distance away, at the other end of the bookshelf so to speak, Max Lessing could see the 1974 portly, good-looking, gray-at-the-temples banker sitting in the Billy Baldwin chair beside Max's desk. The hysterical half century in between suddenly made sense.

"Kiss me," Max Lessing said.

443

Unstartled, Joe Catalini said, "Why?"

Max had not expected Joe to be startled. Just the same, Max was aware of something he disliked: disappointment.

"When I get screwed," Max Lessing said, "I like to get kissed."

Joe Catalini uncrossed his legs. He did it slowly, as though the creases in the pin-striped pants were part of a carefully baked cake and he were afraid to ruin the frosting. Then, with care, Joe contemplated the result. He did not seem to find it satisfactory. He recrossed his legs the other way. Another moment of contemplation, and Joe Catalini was ready. Max could tell from the way the solid body settled into the solid chair. With an I'm-ready-to-stay-the-distance finality: *You may fire when ready, Gridley.*

Joe Catalini said, "You'd better begin at the beginning, Mr. Max."

"This building they're dedicating to me today," Max Lessing said. "How much did it cost, Joe?"

Joe Catalini's body did not move. The shrug was in his voice: "A hundred million, give or take ten or twenty."

"Given to whom?" Max Lessing said. "Taken by whom?"

"You know what's involved," Joe said, "when you buy a hole in the ground on Park Avenue and Forty-eighth and you fill it with something at which a couple of thousand human beings arrive every morning to do their daily jobs."

Max said, "I know a lot of things. The reason I asked you to come in for a talk is that I wanted to add to my fund of knowledge. Add to it, Joe."

"In what way?" Joe Catalini said.

"The hundred million give or take twenty," Max Lessing said. "All the money that went into building this Mount Everest here on Park Avenue at the top of which we're sitting right now and having this friendly chat? Who got all the money, Joe?"

Quietly Joe said, "Starting with A for architects, moving on through P for plumbers, and going up to whatever it is that gets listed on cost sheets and paid for under Z, I'd have

444

to go back to my office and dig up all the details from the books. If you want me to, I can put my whole staff on it, Mr. Max."

"Including this new girl you stole from Ari Onassis?" Max said.

Joe said, "She's just my appointments secretary. If you're in a hurry for your answer, though, she'll be willing to lend a hand, I'm sure."

"So am I," Max Lessing said. "It's been my experience, though, that the answers you get from brand-new people, especially if you steal them from Greeks, are not always reliable. Brand-new people pick up surface stuff, what's on the books. You know as well as I do, Joe, what's on the books is what you and I put there. We put it there so it can be picked up by people who are satisfied with surface stuff. People like the I.R.S., for example. I'm not interested in surface stuff. I'm interested in what's under the surface, because that's where the hard money sits. Or should be sitting, Joe, if you know what I mean."

Joe Catalini studied the crease in the pin-striped cloth that sliced up over and then down the top knee of his crossed legs. He said, "No, Mr. Max, I don't know what you mean."

"That's strange," Max said. "From the day back in 1922 when you showed up on my doorstep in Columbia Heights in a soaking-wet Boy Scout uniform with the news that you'd just found a dead man named Jekuthiel Fruchter out in the woodshed at Whampoa's Open—that's fifty-two years ago, Joe—all those years you've always known what I mean."

Joe said, "Things change."

"When did they start to change for you and me?" Max Lessing said.

"I can't remember," Joe Catalini said.

"Make an effort," Max Lessing said. "I'm about to do what Coley Scudder used to describe as refresh your recollection."

"You do that, Mr. Max."

"How about your twenty-sixth birthday?" Max Lessing

445

said. "In John and Susie Shale's apartment on Madison Avenue? When Ida gave you a secret birthday party? Just the two of you? And your birthday present was a set of matched golf clubs? Except they were for a right-handed player? And it turned out you're a southpaw? So you couldn't use them?"

Joe said, "The golf clubs were not the only things I couldn't use."

"Is that the only reason Ida never cheated on me?"

"So far as I am concerned, yes," Joe Catalini said.

"How about where other men are concerned?" Max said.

"You'll have to ask the other men."

"You're the only threat I ever had," Max Lessing said.

"In that area threats don't count," Joe said. "It's the only area you ever had to worry about."

"Until we built the Lessing Tower," Max Lessing said. "There are rumors all over this town that the graft and the payoffs and the under-the-counter deals on this building ran to ten or twenty million dollars, maybe more. Joe, how much did you get away with?"

Evenly, without inflection or hesitation, as though he had lifted his head to tell a secretary who had just poked her head into the room that he would be along in a minute, Joe Catalini said, "Personally, not a dime."

"How about Blanche?"

"My wife's financial affairs," Joe said, "I don't have to tell you, Mr. Max, I know nothing about them. She has her own accountants and her own lawyers. They take care of everything for her. I never ask."

"If you did," Max Lessing said, "how much would the soaked-in-vodka former Blanche Berkowitz be worth, Joe?"

"I can't set a figure yet," Joe Catalini said.

"Why not?"

"There's still some I haven't taken away from you," Joe said.

Pause. Max Lessing broke it with "You want it all?"

"Every dime," Joe Catalini said.

"Why?"

"I don't have anything else," Joe said.

Max shook his head.

"The reason isn't good enough," he said. "I'm sorry, Joe. You've taken all you're going to get, and what you've got you're not going to keep. I'm taking it all back. Every nickel as well as every dime. The game is finished, Joe."

"Not for me," Joe Catalini said.

"When I bought you from your old man back in Minneapolis in 1922," Max Lessing said, "it was because I thought I'd run into a youngster who didn't know how to say anything stupid. It took fifty years for me to learn I'd made a mistake. You just said something very stupid, Joe. When it comes to mistakes, though, I'm like my old friend Fiorello LaGuardia. When I make a mistake, he once said, it's a beaut. The difference between me and Fiorello is he's dead. I'm not. I can correct my mistake."

Joe said, "Too late, Mr. Max."

"Not for the major stockholder in Alaskan Pacific Shipbuilding," Max Lessing said.

Joe Catalini's total absorption in the way the crease in his pin-striped trousers angled up and over his crossed knees suddenly became less total. For a moment he looked startled, as though something had come bursting in through the window, but it was a brief moment. As though he were correcting a child, Joe said quietly:

"Mr. Max, there are no more stockholders in the Alaskan Pacific Shipbuilding Corporation, major or minor. We dissolved A.P.S.C. in 1947, when with the end of the war the demand for its products vanished overnight, as one might have predicted. By 1947 there wasn't much demand for assault landing craft. I don't expect you to remember the details of everything we've been into and out of, especially things like the Alaskan Pacific Shipbuilding Corporation, which went out of business thirty years ago, but I did think you'd remember that one because of the size of the capital loss the I.R.S. allowed us because the company's enormous expansion was due almost entirely to war contracts."

"I remembered it very clearly, Joe," Max said. "That's why I was so surprised when I realized A.P.S.C. wasn't dead at all. It had just been hibernating. Frankly, Joe, it was quite a jolt when I made the discovery."

"Discovery?"

"Yes, Joe," Max Lessing said. "Discovery."

Joe Catalini did not look startled during the next pause. Perhaps that was why this one lasted longer. Joe looked puzzled, as though for his next statement several choices were available to him, all equally serviceable, but none better or worse than its fellows, so he was finding it difficult to make a decision. Finally, as though abandoning the process of decision making, he seemed to decide on taking a stab.

"What kind of discovery?" he said.

"After thirty years in mothballs," Max said, "the Alaskan Pacific Shipbuilding Corporation is full of piss and vinegar. It's no longer making assault landing craft, but what it's making today turns out to be a lot more profitable than the war ever was even for Lessing Enterprises."

"What is A.P.S.C. making these days?" Joe said.

"Gravy."

This word did not seem to provide Joe Catalini with quite so wide a choice of interchangeably serviceable alternatives. Perhaps that was why he abandoned the obvious question and asked instead, "When did you make this discovery, Mr. Max?"

"Almost two years ago," Max Lessing said. "Just about the time you started putting together the real estate parcel at Park Avenue and Forty-eighth where today they are dedicating the Lessing Tower to me as a birthday present and on top of which right now you and I are having this heart-to-heart talk."

Joe nodded, as though this answer checked with some computation he had been working out in his head, and he

448

said, "When people make a discovery they usually do something about it, Mr. Max. What did you do?"

Max said, "What would you have done, Joe?"

Joe Catalini's small, tired sigh did not interfere with the clarity of his enunciation as he said, "I'd have called in Price Waterhouse to do a secret audit for me."

Max Lessing said, "That's the difference between a top man and a right-hand man. I did that, Joe. But I also called in S. D. Leidesdorf. The way we used to call in scriptwriters when we were trying to make Alma a movie star out at T.K.O. One behind the other, both working secretly."

Dryly Joe said, "I take it from the way you're handling this heart-to-heart talk, Mr. Max, that you had better luck with A.P.S.C. than you had with Alma."

"Much better," Max said. "That hundred million give or take twenty that went into building this Mount Everest on Park Avenue at the top of which I am laying cards on the table, Joe, it was closer to twenty-two million, and I know where every penny of it is sitting right now. It's time for you to go, Joe."

"I'm not going," Joe Catalini said.

"Yes, you are."

"How?"

"The way Saul Sumeg went," Max said.

Joe said, "You don't know how Saul Sumeg went."

"Because Ida ordered you not to tell me," Max Lessing said. "Now I'm the one giving the order."

He opened the top drawer of his desk. He pulled out a small plastic vial. Max worked off the cap and shook out into his palm a small white pill. He pushed the pill across the green desk blotter until it was directly in front of Joe Catalini.

"One will do it," Max Lessing said.

He shook another pill from the vial. He pushed the pill across the green desk blotter until it touched the first.

"So you better take two," Max said.

Joe Catalini did not move. Max did, but not the way he

wanted to go. Max wanted to come around the desk, to do with his fists what he had failed to do with his words, but he did not make it. His legs refused to obey. Then everything inside him seemed to join the rebellion. Max felt a short, sharp, stabbing pain. For several moments he did not realize he was unable to locate it. Then the pain became total, and through it the terror struck.

"Ida!" he cried.

Miss Farragut pulled her glance from the problem facing The Vampire's Two-Headed Daughter on the TV screen over the orthopedic bed. Astonished, the nurse saw something she had never seen before. Her patient's hand was moving.

Fascinated, Miss Farragut watched the hand on the bed hump itself up, like a diver pulling himself together at the end of the board for takeoff. The bunched knuckles inched forward, toward the electric typewriter. The pinky came down on the keyboard. The ON button clicked. The motor began to whirr.

Mr. Max's pinky crawled, dragging itself from key to key like what in Miss Farragut's mind suddenly resembled a tiny bird she had once seen on the beach trying to move with a broken leg. Slowly, in erratic little spasms, single letter by single letter, the night nurse watched her patient begin to tap out a word, then another, and another, and another. The door opened. Mrs. Lessing came into the room.

"Wouldn't you like a cup of coffee?" she said.

"Thanks very much," Miss Farragut said. "I had one just a little while ago."

"Why don't you go out to the kitchen and make yourself another," Ida Lessing said. "I'll stay with Mr. Max for a while."

"All right," the nurse said. "Would you like me to make a cup for you, Mrs. Lessing?"

"Thanks, no," Ida Lessing said.

She waited until the door clicked shut before she walked across to the window. For a while Ida stood there, staring down at the wild surf. It was sending up to her in the penthouse a new moaning sound. The strange noise seemed to be coming from the south. It was like a deep bass chord being struck again and again on the world's biggest organ. Then Ida Lessing returned to her chair beside the bed.

Max's eyes provided a moment of shock. Something had happened during her absence. She was not looking into the eyes of the boy who had come to the barn door in Klein Berezna fifty-six years ago to beg a cup of milk. Ida Lessing was looking into the eyes of the Jew in all those Gestapo movies at the moment in the middle of the night when he hears the dreaded knock on the door. As casually as she could manage, Ida said, "I just had a call from Claire in Stockholm."

The eyes flicked wildly. Nothing in what Ida could see happening to Max's eyes suggested she would gain anything by delay. Swiftly but with care, the way hours ago she had explained to Max what Joe Catalini had revealed in her sitting room across "The Bridge at Argenteuil Under Attack by Caesar's Fifth Legion," Ida Lessing now told her husband what their daughter-in-law had just told her on the phone from Stockholm. She took another look at Max's eyes.

They were flicking wildly in the sunken sockets. After a few moments it occurred to Ida that what Max was attempting to do was use his eyes as a pointer. He seemed to be trying to direct her attention. A moment later she became aware of the direction. Max's eyes were pointing downward.

Astonished, Ida saw the sheet of paper in the typewriter. Across the top of the sheet marched a single line of letters.

nvr wrk 4 2 spoilers

The question Ida had been wanting to ask all night now abruptly clamored for attention.

"Why not?" she said.

The hand on the bed humped itself up in the familiar crouching movement. The diver pulling himself together at the end of the board for takeoff. The bunched knuckles inched forward, toward the electric typewriter. Ida leaned across to press the ON button, but the motor was already whirring. Slowly, in erratic little spasms, single letter by single letter, Ida Lessing watched her husband tap out:

```
they always trn on each othr
when they do we be cawt in middle
joe cat ded good news
means only 1 left 2 handle
must get him fast
no more wait
bring in cops
fast fast fast
```

Ida Lessing nodded. He had always known more than she knew. Her problem for half a century had been simple: how to contain her impatience until Max was ready to tell her what he wanted her to do with his greater knowledge. He had never let her down. After a while she saw from his eyes that he was not going to start now.

"Consider it done," Ida Lessing said to her husband.

She stood up and went slowly toward the door. With her hand on the switch she turned for a final look at the room in which, after fifty-six years in other rooms, they had together hung up their last DO NOT DISTURB sign. Then Ida Lessing snapped off the light. She went out, and she closed the door quietly, and she walked back to her sitting room.

The time had come to call Hymie Shantz.

54

Hymie Shantz had been her own idea. Something Ida had kept from Max as well as from Joe Catalini. The one defection of a lifetime.

Soon after Max was settled into the complicated nursing apparatus of the penthouse, Ida realized what she had undertaken: the job of serving as communications center between the world in which the rest of the world lived and the world in which Max Lessing's illness now forced him to live. The realization brought with it an unsettling discovery. Ida had overlooked a third world. The world in which for almost six decades she had lived with Max. She had left that world behind. More accurately, Ida sensed that that world had left her behind. She felt a chill.

Being with Max had always been enough. From that first day in Klein Berezna when he had begged for a cup of milk to the day on Park Avenue when the Lessing Tower was dedicated, Max had always created the world in which she functioned. Now somebody else was creating it. The difference was unsettling. Soon Ida found it intolerable.

The Lessing communications network was no solution. Neither were Joe Catalini's innumerable telephone calls and frequent visits. With Max she had spent her life making history. Now she was reduced to reading reports from the field where somebody else was making it. The bulletins she read were marked, of course, FIRST COPY FOR MR. M. A carbon, however, was a carbon, even when it was a Xerox. Considerably less than that to a person accustomed to receiving the top copy. At this troubled point in her new life Ida Lessing had received a note from Hymie Shantz.

She had known for years that the old bodyguard from Minneapolis had been pensioned off. Ida knew also that he had retired to Florida. Occasionally, after Abe Shantz took over the Lessing jet fleet, whenever Ida ran into the pilot she would ask about his father. Perhaps as was the way with most sons, perhaps because Abe was Abe, his replies had been pleasant but unrevealing. The old man was fine. So was his wife. They were enjoying retirement. By the time Ida came to live in The Frontenac, Hymie Shantz had long ago slipped from her mind. He reappeared in the form of a birthday card postmarked COCONUT GROVE STATION.

He had been going through his old logbooks, Hymie wrote around the edges of the joke cartoon on the Hallmark greeting card. Sort of getting his papers in order. And he came across a reference to a birthday party that had been given for Mrs. Lessing in Washington during the war. Mr. Max had been unable to attend. He was at Yalta with the President. Mr. Max had called Joe Catalini in New York, however, to make sure that Hymie and nobody else from the security staff was assigned to accompany Mrs. Lessing and her group of friends to Washington.

Hymie had never forgotten the date, and now that he was living in retirement not too far from where Mrs. Lessing and Mr. Max had come to live, Hymie had felt the urge to wish her a happy birthday and many more of them. For Mr. Max too. Hymie would never forget the years he had spent with them, and it made him feel proud that his son Abe was now a member of the organization. So, as he'd said, *Happy Birthday, Mrs. Lessing, and God bless you both.*

Ida told Max about it, but got no reaction. It was the time when Max was beginning to slide from casual interest into total absorption by Creature Features. Ida sent Hymie a note inviting him and Mrs. Shantz to come to The Frontenac for lunch. Hymie came alone. His wife had died several months ago.

Ida remembered Max's telling her in Minneapolis that Hymie Shantz was almost exactly Max's age. Which meant that when he sent Ida the birthday card he was seventy-three. Not a good age to have a good wife die on a man. Ida was sure Hymie was lonely. The only thing Ida was not sure about was whether Hymie had got himself into costume for the visit.

Under a sharp, plum-colored Italian silk sports jacket he had worn the Shetland cardigan Ida had bought for him in the Thurso Gentlemen's Apparel Shoppe when in 1932 he was holed up with her and Max in the Duncansly Head Hotel at John o' Groats. And when he came through the penthouse door, what Hymie removed from his head was either the black snap-brim felt number he had always worn in those days, or an exact replica. For Ida the sight took some of the edge off the growing feeling of being on the sidelines.

"When you're not going through your old logbooks," Ida said over the coffee cups in her sitting room, "how do you keep busy?"

"I wait for the bell," Hymie Shantz said.

"What bell?"

"I'm an old firehorse," Hymie said. "Once a security guard always a security guard. I may have racked up too many numbers on the statistical tables to be useful to the operation the way Mr. Catalini is running it now, but the time I'm supposed to be retired down here with all this grapefruit, what I've picked up about the area, the way they work things down here, the police and all, you'd be surprised, Mrs. L."

Ida was, but not by the extent of Hymie Shantz's knowledge about the Gold Coast and how it worked. Ida Lessing was surprised into an idea. Over a second cup of coffee she outlined it to Hymie. He did not exactly snap at it. The

Shantz family were not snappers. But Hymie Shantz took the idea to his bosom with what for him could be construed as fervor.

"Mrs. L," he said solemnly, "I think the arrangement could do us both a lot of good."

It was doing Ida a lot of good right now.

"Consider it done," she had told Max a few minutes ago before she pulled out the light in his room. Now, as she sat in her own room, the process of considering it was made easier by the knowledge that Hymie Shantz was about to call. The phone rang.

"Hymie?"

"Yes, Mrs. L."

"How does it look?" Ida said.

"The cops picked up Ohmstetter and his wife a few minutes ago," Hymie Shantz said.

"You sure?"

"Lieutenant Ritter of the Pompano force is a personal friend of mine," Hymie said. "When he climbed into the paddy wagon behind the Ohmstetters, I was out on the driveway and I slammed the door behind Lieutenant Ritter myself. Okay?"

"That leaves two to go," Ida said.

"One of those two has gone," Hymie Shantz said. "I just hung up on an old friend in Boston. He checked me out on this kid Lurie."

"Idwal Lurie, yes," Ida said.

"Mr. Catalini's had a private tag on that boy for two days," Hymie Shantz said. "A retired Boston cop named Lou Mangan. Lou just told me a half hour ago he got the word to start earning his pension. This Lurie kid is what in my day was described as talking freely to the authorities."

"That leaves only one," Ida said.

"Yes, Mrs. L," Hymie said. "With that one we have a problem."

"Bad?"

Hymie Shantz said, "Not if you cooperate, Mrs. L."

456

"Tell me what you want me to do," Ida Lessing said.

"You dressed?"

"Except for going out in this weather," Ida said. "But if you want me to, that won't take a minute."

"Not necessary," Hymie said. "Where we're going it ain't cold."

"Where's that?"

"Do like this," Hymie Shantz said. "Don't tell anybody you're going. The nurses or Mrs. Schiff or anybody. You're taking this call in your sitting room?"

"Yes."

"Just walk out and go down the hall and out into the foyer," Hymie said. "The elevator on the penthouse bank is working. I just sent it up, so it's waiting. You get in, but don't hit the Lobby button. Punch G. I'll be waiting for you in the garage."

He was, wearing the black snap-brim felt and the Thurso Men's Apparel Shoppe cardigan.

"There's been a few leaks because of this heavy rain," Hymie Shantz said. "So just watch the puddles." He took Ida's arm.

"Where are we going?" she said.

"Not far."

He led her carefully around the puddles, across the brightly lighted cement apron covered with Cadillacs ranked side by side in numbered parking slots. At the south end, Hymie stopped in front of a gray metal door. From behind it came a low, steady, roaring hum. On it in black stencil letters appeared four words: AUXILIARY GENERATOR KEEP OUT.

"It's like this," Hymie said. "You can have until Lieutenant Ritter comes back."

"How long will that be?"

"Let's figure," Hymie Shantz said. He looked at his wristwatch. "He took the Ohmstetters down to the slammer in Pompano. Ordinarily, normal weather, that's a ten-minute ride from here. Round trip, twenty. This weather, Mrs. L, I can't say exactly."

457

"I can," Ida said. "I won't need twenty minutes."

"Good," Hymie said. "The Lieutenant is doing this for me as a personal favor. Twenty minutes, okay. Longer, it might be noticed. I wouldn't want him to get in any trouble."

"He won't."

"Thanks, Mrs. L," Hymie Shantz said.

He took a ball-point from his breast pocket. With the blunt end he rapped out some sort of signal on the metal door. It opened from the inside. A policeman wearing a transparent rain cape over his uniform looked out at them.

"Oh, hi, Mr. Shantz," he said.

"It's okay," Hymie said.

The policeman pulled the door wide and stepped out. "You know about the time frame," he said.

"We'll be finished before the Lieutenant gets back," Hymie Shantz said.

"Okay," the policeman said.

He stepped aside. Hymie Shantz held the door for Ida. "You first, Mrs. L," he said.

She stepped inside. Hymie Shantz came in behind her. He pushed the door shut.

Ida had never been in this part of the building, but the room held no surprises for her. Gray cement floor. White-washed walls. Large unshaded electric bulbs screwed into ceiling sockets. Asbestos-covered pipes laced in a complicated network around an enormous piece of machinery. From somewhere deep in the machine's metal gut came the smooth, purring hum Ida had heard at the other side of the door. Even her grandson was no surprise.

Stevie looked exactly the way he had looked the last time she had seen him. In April, when Claire and Norman had flown over for her birthday, and Stevie had come down from Cambridge. There was one difference. Instead of on the couch in her sitting room, Stevie was now sitting on one of the many fat asbestos-wrapped pipes that connected the humming machine with a series of heavy metal wall outlets.

458

Then Ida saw another difference. Stevie's wrists were handcuffed. She sent a quick look at Hymie Shantz.

He said, "I'm sorry, Mrs. L. That was Lieutenant Ritter's idea."

"Why?" Ida said.

Shantz said to Stevie, "You want to tell your grandmother?"

"It's your party," the handcuffed boy said. "You perform the introductions."

The voice surprised her. It was not the voice Ida had known for eighteen years. She wondered when she had last heard a voice that sounded like that.

"After you called me and gave me the tip," Hymie Shantz said, "I got with Lieutenant Ritter, and he and his men had no trouble collecting both Ohmstetters in their apartment upstairs. It didn't take the Lieutenant long to knock out of them where they were holding Stevie."

Hymie nodded toward a closed door behind the enormous piece of machinery on which the handcuffed boy was sitting.

"It's a toolroom," Hymie Shantz said. "We got Stevie out here and cut him loose. After they took the tape off his mouth, I asked the Lieutenant if I could take the boy upstairs to see his grandmother for a few minutes before they all drove to headquarters for his statement. The Lieutenant said Sure, if we didn't take too long, but your grandson, Mrs. L, he said no, he didn't want to go upstairs to see you."

Hymie's voice stopped. He had clearly reached the end of a denunciation to which his command of the language made it impossible for him to add anything more that would indicate the depth of his contempt for such conduct on the part of a grandson who had the incredible good fortune to have Ida Lessing for a grandmother.

Ida helped Hymie across the hump with "So you asked the Lieutenant to keep Stevie under guard down here while you went upstairs to fetch me."

"Correct," Hymie Shantz said. "The bracelets were the Lieutenant's idea."

It was clear that with this new glimpse of Stevie Lessing's character, the bracelets would also have been Hymie's idea.

Ida said, "Is there any way out of this room except through that door you and I just came in by?"

"No, Mrs. L," Hymie Shantz said.

"Then it's safe to leave us alone in here for a few minutes," Ida said.

With a forefinger Hymie touched the brim of his black snap-brim felt hat. "I'll be outside," he said.

At the door he turned and pointed the same forefinger at the handcuffed boy.

"Don't try anything funny," Hymie Shantz said. "Your grandmother is an old friend of mine."

He went out and pulled the door shut with a click that was not quite a slam. There was no doubt, however, that the sound was meant as a statement.

"If I could say the same," Stevie said, "I would have come up to see you."

Ida remembered when she had last heard a voice like the one coming out of her grandson. It was Max's voice, in the sitting room of the Bannockburn Suite in the Duncansly Head Hotel at John o' Groats in 1932, when Ida told the twenty-four-year old Joe Catalini that her husband could not hear her instructions about handling the Saul Sumeg problem because Mr. Max was not in the room, and Max, walking out of the room, had said, "That's true."

"Maybe it's just as well that you didn't come up to see me," Ida said. "It's a small room, and very personal. I've never had anybody but friends in it."

Stevie said, "Skip the lectures, Grandma."

"I don't have one on the agenda," Ida said.

Stevie said, "I'm glad to be sprung, but it was bound to happen. Those Ohmstetters are clearly nuts. A retarded kindergarten kid could have outmaneuvered them, and Joe Catalini is no retarded kindergarten kid. So you can scratch all requests for tearful expressions of gratitude. I'm not playing."

"Good," Ida said. "It's been a long night. I wouldn't want it to end on a tiresome note."

The boy gave her at sharp glance. To do it he had to move his head. The movement shifted the pattern of harsh brightness that fell on him from the big naked bulbs. Ida's heart turned over. It was going to be more difficult than she'd thought. In the new light pattern, the boy in blue jeans sitting on the asbestos-covered pipe looked exactly the way, fifty-six years ago, the blond girl who rose from the milking stool had looked as she went across the barn to the door. Looking at her grandson, Ida Lessing could have been looking at herself.

"You're not a rubbernecking tourist just passing through the Sunshine State," the boy in blue jeans said. "You must have a reason for wanting this private session, Grandma."

"I want a couple of Is dotted and Ts crossed," Ida said. "I knew you'd been kidnapped. I assumed it happened up at Harvard. I was surprised to learn a little bit ago that it happened down here in Florida."

"I flew down to keep a date," Stevie said. "I didn't expect to be sidetracked by kidnappers."

"A date with whom?" Ida said.

"Cut it out, Grandma," the boy said. "Your grandson is a gentleman."

"Your grandmother is not a lady," Ida said. "Your date was with someone you didn't want me and your grandfather to know about?"

"That's right," the handcuffed boy said.

"A man or a woman?"

"What difference does that make?" Stevie said.

"If that's your answer," Ida said, "none at all."

Surprised, the boy said, "Then why do you ask?"

"I wondered why when Joe came down to see me last night he didn't use one of the family jets to Miami International," Ida said. "It seemed strange he should fly Delta to Palm Beach."

"Is it still strange?" Stevie said.

461

"Not anymore," Ida said.

"Great," Stevie said. "Now call in your man and get this hardware off my wrists. These Ohmstetters have upset my schedule. I have to get back up North."

"There's no rush."

"Not at your age, perhaps," the boy said.

The sarcasm was well done. Ida was not pleased by her feeling of pride, but she felt it only fair to acknowledge it to herself. She had always liked style. Max had it. It was right that his grandson should have it too.

"Your mother and father just talked to me from Stockholm," Ida said. "They told me as much as a person my age wants to know."

"Good," Stevie said. "Then I'll be on my way."

"North is the wrong direction," Ida said.

For the first time since Hymie Shantz had led her into the room, the boy looked scared.

"All right, Grandma," he said. "Let's have it, whatever it is."

Staring at the handcuffed boy, Ida wondered if she could do what Stevie asked. She knew what "it" was. She had always known what "it" was, once Max laid it out for her. But could she pass it on to this boy?

nvr wrk 4 2 spoilers

Stevie obviously did not see himself as a spoiler. Just as Joe Catalini hadn't and, now that Joe was gone, as Stevie's father obviously didn't. Yet there they were. The end of the line. The inevitable occupants of what Winchell had once called "the conning tower of the mushrooming Lessing financial sheikdom." Norman the Fool and Stevie the What?

Ida and Max had not planned it that way. Ida and Max had not planned anything. Maybe that was the trouble. From that cup of milk in Klein Berezna to this basement half a century later in Florida, Ida and Max had just lived from day to day, enjoying each other, doing whatever seemed at the moment the best way to keep that mutual pleasure functioning successfully. Ida and Max had planned absolutely nothing, and here facing her after fifty-six years was what their unplanned lives had come to.

"I understand," Ida Lessing said.

"Understand what?" her grandson said.

"I wasn't talking to you," Ida Lessing said to the handcuffed boy.

She was talking, Ida realized with astonishment, to somebody about whom she had not thought for years. She was talking to Jake Blau in his office on East Broadway. She was replying to something the old man was saying to her. Something Ida had forgotten long ago. Now, forty years later, it suddenly seemed very important. Something Ida wished she could remember, but it was like trying to remember a dream out of which you had just come awake. Some pieces were clear and solid. Others were vague and shapeless. Without these vague and shapeless pieces the clear and solid pieces remained unconnected, so that the dream made no sense.

What was clear and solid was the sound of Jake Blau's voice. After all these years Ida could still hear the old man's fury. What she could not hear, what Ida could not pull back into her consciousness, was the details of the denunciation. Ida sensed that Jake Blau's rage was directed at the things she and Max had done together. They had done all of it in such a way that both of them could later disclaim under oath any knowledge of things to which it was better for neither of them to be able to testify. It was a way of life. When you'd lived it for half a century, it was too late to pretend you hadn't.

Jake Blau's voice faded into another. Ida concentrated. This voice was more familiar and more welcome. Ida forced herself to reach toward it. The effort brought Susie Shale out of the Minneapolis past into the Florida present. The cute little boop-boop-a-doop blonde was explaining to Ida and Max that the surest way to mastery of the English language was to study its masters, and Susie's favorite master was a poet. She read him aloud to Max and Ida. She quoted him from memory. Now, in this basement room in the middle of a hurricane, facing her handcuffed grandson, Ida could hear Susie Shale quoting:

> I've paid for your sickest fancies;
> I've humored your crackedest whim—
> Dick, it's your daddy, dying;
> You've got to listen to him!

Ida could hear it clearly, the way she had heard it when she was a girl and her life was beginning. Now that she was old, and her life was over, Ida knew something else. Susie's poet was wrong. Stevie did not have to listen. Nobody did. You worked it out for yourself. And the way you worked it out was your responsibility. What you started, only you could finish.

"All right," Ida said.

"No, wait!"

It was Susie's voice. Louder now, and more urgent, as though she were sending a plea. Or was it a final warning? Quoting again the words Susie Shale had loved:

> Never seen death yet, Dickie?
> Well, now is your time to learn,
> And you'll wish you held my record
> Before it comes your turn.
> Not counting the Line and the Foundry
> The Yards and the village, too,
> I've made myself and a million;
> But I'm damned if I made you!

Ida shook her head. The poet was still wrong. Susie's warning came too late. Ida Lessing had made Stevie. Ida Lessing and Mr. Max. The boy was their responsibility.

"Grandma," Stevie said.

Ida came up out of her thoughts. "Sorry," she said. "There's one thing I forgot to tell you."

"What's that?" the boy said.

"Your father won't be coming back to America," Ida said.

"Why not?"

"Your mother just called me from Stockholm," Ida said. "An hour ago your father shot and killed Joe Catalini."

It was not easy for her to get the words out. She had been carrying them locked tight inside her from the moment an hour ago when Claire in Stockholm had sent the message halfway across the world into the ear of the woman who forty years ago in Susie and John Shale's apartment on Madison Avenue had held in her arms a sobbing young man to whom, along with a set of matched golf clubs, Ida Lessing had given her heart. She had never taken it back. Nor had Joe Catalini ever returned it. Not even now, now that he was dead.

Carrying the awareness of that death away from Claire's voice on the telephone, into Max's bedroom, and then down to this basement, had been for Ida Lessing like carrying a wound with both hands clamped tight over the oozing blood, aware that only disregarding the pain, pretending she had not been hit would make it possible for her to keep going and reach her destination. Ida Lessing had reached it, and only now, now that she had got there, had she been able to think the words again.

What they did to her did not come as a surprise. Ida Lessing was prepared. When she had said the words aloud to Max, she had been in shock; she knew that only when she heard herself say them again would the reality of Claire's message strike. Now it had struck. The blow brought with it the inexorable demand for accepting the unacceptable: the rest of her life was now emptied of the knowledge that Joe's voice was always there, ready and waiting, at the end of a telephone wire. In the moment of accepting the unacceptable, Ida saw something that astonished her. She had not been prepared for what speaking the words would do to Stevie.

"Oh, my God," she said. "Oh, my God, honey, don't."

Ida Lessing took her sobbing grandson in her arms as

once, forty years ago in Susie and John Shale's apartment on Madison Avenue, she had taken the only rival Max Lessing had ever had.

"Stevie," Ida Lessing said to the only rival she had ever had. "Stevie, darling, don't."

Into her shoulder the boy's despairing voice rasped, "No, oh, my God, no."

"Honey, don't," Ida whispered in the ear of the boy who she now realized had stolen Joe Catalini from her. "Please don't, darling. I know how you feel, but—"

The shove was like a blow. It slammed her against the asbestos pipe. Ida put out her hand and steadied herself. Looking at her grandson, watching the transformation in that face which only moments ago had evoked a memory of herself as a girl in Klein Berezna, Ida Lessing closed her eyes.

"You stupid old bitch," the boy said, spitting out the words. "Who the hell are you to know how I feel? Did you ever love Joe? Did Joe ever love you back? Not until that happens to you or anybody else can you or anybody else have the remotest idea how I feel, and it's never going to happen to you or to anybody else. Because Joe is dead. You just told me so. All right, now I'll tell you something."

Ida was not sure that she heard it all. She was sure, however, that when she had listened to as much as she could, she had heard enough. She pushed herself away from the asbestos pipe. She crossed to the door and she pulled it open. Hymie Shantz looked in at her. The policeman in the transparent rain cape looked at her across Hymie's head.

"Everything all right?" Hymie said.

Not yet, Ida thought, but it still could be.

"You'd better go back in with Stevie," she said to Hymie Shantz and the policeman. "I have to go upstairs for a few moments and talk to Mr. Max."

55

The conversation was, of course, one-sided, as for two years all Ida's conversations with Max had been. Yet this time, as she told him what she had learned from Stevie in the basement, Ida had the feeling Max was listening harder. The fiercely restless eyes, burning up out of the motionless figure on the bed, gave her the impression of a man leaning forward on the seat of a bicycle.

"I now know exactly what happened," Ida said to the motionless figure on the bed. "Not what Joe Catalini told me when he flew down here last night. Joe lied to me."

Ida stopped. The fingers of Max Lessing's good hand had started their painful, dancing crawl toward the typewriter. Ida leaned over and pressed the ON button. The fingers carried their painful, dancing crawl up onto the keyboard. Ida waited. The hand dropped back to the bedsheet. Ida leaned forward and read:

```
            always lied
            bin trying tell u 4 2 yrs
```

Ida nodded. To herself more than to Max. Ever since that bad day two years ago when the Lessing Tower was dedicated, the day Max had collapsed in his office while in a meeting with Joe, Max had been peppering his typewriter pages with insulting remarks about Joe Catalini. Ida had pretended she had not noticed. In discussing with Herb Zlotkin the way Max had turned on Joe, she had suggested frustration as the reason.

"No doubt about it," Herb Zlotkin had agreed. "It's been his show from the beginning. He invented it, he built it, he's been controlling it for half a century, and now, all of a sudden, without warning and for no reason that makes sense to a bundle of restless energy like Max Lessing, he can't control anything, not even his bladder. No matter how he's felt about Joe Catalini all these years, none of that matters now. All that matters now to Max Lessing is that now he's out of it, and Joe is in charge, and it could drive him crazy. If you pay any attention to it, Ida, you might contribute toward driving him there. Whenever one of these outbreaks occurs, I would suggest that you pretend it has not happened."

For Ida the pretense had been easy. It eased the low-key, out-of-sight but ceaselessly pulsing sense of guilt about her feelings for Joe Catalini. She had carried that sense of guilt as part of her daily baggage every moment of her life since that day in 1932 in the Duncansly Head Hotel in John o' Groats when she realized what the then twenty-four-year-old young man had come to mean to her. Now that he was dead, that meaning was more alive than ever, but now it was a secret that Ida need no longer fear. Now she could control it. There was no longer any chance it might spill over and leave a stain that Max could notice.

"I know," Ida Lessing said to the motionless figure on the bed. "It was stupid of me not to listen to your warnings, Max, but I didn't know what to do about them. Stevie apparently did. He just told me down in the basement that Joe moved in on him as soon as you got sick. The day after you were taken from your office to the hospital, Joe Catalini went up to Boston to see Stevie. They must have been more friendly than I ever suspected. Anyway, it didn't seem to take Joe very long to get Stevie to join him in a plan. He made Stevie the president of one of our old corporations. I'd forgotten about it. I thought we dissolved it after the war because it was the umbrella under which we'd been building tankers and landing craft for the government. When the war was over I remember we figured out the capital-loss write-off was so enormous, it seemed sensible to—"

Again Ida stopped. Again the fingers of Max Lessing's good hand had started their painful, dancing crawl toward the typewriter. Again Ida leaned over and pressed the ON button. This time the process was short. When it ended, and Ida pressed the OFF button, only four letters had been added to the page in the typewriter:

apsc

"That's right," Ida said. "The Alaskan Pacific Shipbuilding Corporation. Stevie just told me downstairs—"

She paused. Those letters came back to her. They had figured prominently in the attacks Max had been painfully pecking out against Joe Catalini on the electric typewriter for two years. The attacks Ida had found it so convenient to disregard.

"Joe revived the old corporation legally but kept it under wraps," Ida said. "For two years he's been funneling into it everything he could divert from Lessing Enterprises. According to Stevie, what it comes to would shock us both. A week ago they were ready for the final phase of the plan. A fake kidnapping to scare us into making terms with the kidnappers. They got it going, and everything seemed to be working, until Ohmstetter took them by surprise. Stevie and Joe did not know what Ohmstetter knew. He knew that Stevie and Joe had been meeting regularly down here at a motel near Hallandale. When Joe flew back to New York from their last meeting two nights ago, Stevie remained in Hallandale, hiding out as planned in the motel. When Joe flew down last night to tell us Stevie had been kidnapped, Joe was telling us the lie on which the plan was based.

469

"After Joe finished telling me that lie, he found out from Ohmstetter in the lobby that the fake kidnapping had suddenly become real. Stevie was not where Joe had left him, in the motel in Hallandale. Stevie had been picked up there and was being kept somewhere else by the people Ohmstetter claimed had appointed him their intermediary. Now Joe had to do something to save Stevie. What he did was hire a policeman in Boston to check on whether Stevie was being held in Cambridge, and then Joe flew to Stockholm to see Norman. What I did, after I learned what happened in Stockholm and reported it to you, was follow your instructions about the police. They had no trouble. They caught the Ohmstetters and they freed Stevie."

The fingers of Max's good hand, Ida saw, were back in motion. She pressed the ON button and waited. When she pressed the OFF button Ida read:

y stv not here

Ida said, "I didn't want the kidnapper personally presenting his ranson terms to his own grandfather."

In the pause that followed, Max Lessing's eyes seemed to lose control. They began to dart about in their sockets, like prisoners trapped in adjoining cells that were slowly filling with rising floodwaters. When the fingers of the good hand started again on their painful crawl to the typewriter, Ida did not reach across to the ON button. She reached across to Max's crawling fingers and stopped them with her hand.

Ida said, "Stevie told me he intends to go ahead with the plan without Joe. He's demanding that we meet the terms Joe presented to Norman a few hours ago in Stockholm. I told him he was crazy if he thought we would agree to such a thing. He said we'd better, or he would go to the Attorney General with evidence that would destroy us. He says Joe Catalini gave him all the information on Saul Sumeg and Zalman and Jekuthiel Fruchter. The boy has papers, Max. He can prove everything. I asked him why he was doing this. All he has to do is wait, and Lessing Enterprises—everything, the whole thing—will come to him. I didn't understand what could have happened to make the boy threaten his own grandfather and grandmother. I told him you and I never planned to leave a penny to anybody except him and his father. Stevie said—"

Ida paused. She was not sure that the pause was voluntary. What had caused it was her recollection of the boy's face when Stevie was speaking. Under her hand Ida felt the fingers of Max's wasted hand begin to struggle. Ida held them firmly.

She said, "Stevie told me, 'I'm not waiting. My father is ahead of me in line and he's as healthy as you are, Grandma. So even if I outwait him, you'll still be there, Grandma. With both hands and both feet on the controls. So far as I can see you've made one of those grand-opera pacts with the devil to live as long as Mr. Max does. Judging by what I've learned from a lifetime of watching you and my grandfather operate as a team, that adds up to what the dictionary calls forever. That's too long for me. So I'm doing it all myself. You take that message up to Mr. Max, and don't come back without his X on the dotted line.' "

Hearing Stevie hammer the demands at her, Ida had been reminded of herself as a girl in Klein Berezna hammering her own demands at Rabbi Jobsky. The girl in Klein Berezna had in the end got what she wanted. Ida knew in her heart that the boy facing her in this Florida basement would in the end get what he wanted. Nothing had been able to stop Ida Wawrth. Nothing would be able to stop Stevie Lessing. Making that clear to Max had not been easy. The task had required a certain amount of concentration.

When it was finished, Ida became aware of two things. First, Max's eyes. The struggling fury had vanished. The eyes were quiet and cold, the way they had been in 1932 at John o' Groats when Max Lessing ordered his wife to tell Joe Catalini how to handle the Saul Sumeg situation. The second thing Ida became aware of was the struggle under her hand. It had become a desperate fight for escape. Ida took her hand away. The freed fingers started the agonizing crawl toward the typewriter keys. Ida pressed the ON button and waited. In between the muted clacks of the keys she could hear her own heartbeats. When at last she pressed the OFF button, Ida Lessing read:

```
this a repeat of sumeg situation
requires same treatment
now
fast
if stv allowed 2 move we sunk
tuf thng hav 2 do
cant b hlped
do it now
before 2 late
do it do it do it
dont disobey me
```

She didn't. Without hesitation Ida Lessing opened the elegantly unobtrusive carryall that always hung from her wrist. She checked the .38 special. A distant sound brought her head up. It was the sound she had heard earlier at the window in this room as she stared down at the boiling surf.

Ida stood up and went back to the window. The surf was boiling more wildly. The moaning sound was louder. It was still like a deep bass chord being struck again and again on the world's biggest organ. There was, however, a change. The realization came as a short, sharp thrust of shock. When she had first heard it, the sound had frightened her. Now she found it soothing. It eased her feelings about what she now knew she could not avoid doing.

There were people who had disobeyed Max Lessing. They had paid for their disobedience. Now that he was incapacitated there were people who disobeyed him all the time. Ida had made sure their payment was collected. She herself, however, had never been one of those from whom payment was required. She never would be.

She turned from the window. She crossed the room, and

she went out, and she closed the door. In the elevator she punched the G button. When she got out at the garage level, with her hand on the .38 in the carryall, Ida Lessing was met by the most important discovery of her long life. It was just as possible for her as it was for anybody else to disobey Max Lessing.

All that was required was a little help from what Jake Blau would have called the Right Quarter.

Unlike Abe Shantz, Ida Lessing had not served a tour of duty in Korea. She did not know the difference between the noise produced by an artillery piece and the sound made by a Smith & Wesson .38. Now she would never know.

Neither would the newscaster in the studio down in Miami who was saying into his microphone:

"—the details about this storm surge. It seems to have come up without warning. Our cameras are in the air over the area. Please stand by while we try to—"

The studio door slammed open behind him. The newscaster whipped around from the microphone. It was his assistant. The young man ran toward him, waving a yellow strip from the teleprinter. The newscaster shot a glance up to the control booth, where the director was on his feet. He gave a fast order to the technician hunched over the instrument panel and, with both arms, wigwagged a signal down to the newscaster.

"Wait!" the newscaster said into the microphone. "Here's something that looks—"

The monitor seemed to explode with a confused scene of turbulence that had no shape. The airborne camera, itself obviously taking a beating, caught ragged, terrifying snatches that moved into and out of focus. Huge walls of roaring, foam-topped water. Palm trees bent over like inverted Us. A flying pickup truck whipped across the monitor screen and smashed itself to splinters against what looked like the side of an apartment house. The newscaster snatched the yellow teleprinter strip from his assistant.

"Yes," he said into the microphone, his voice shaking. "The storm surge came up without warning. You are seeing it hit the beach. The estimates are about thirty feet, in some places reaching forty and fifty. The basements and the lower floors of many Gold Coast structures are being completely flooded, drowning all living creatures trapped in these lower areas. Among those already reported are The Chiswick West, in Fort Lauderdale; Ce Esta Village, in Pompano Beach; The Frontenac, just north of—"

The screen went black. The assistant tugged the newscaster's rolled-up shirt sleeve.

"Jesus, Chief," he said. "Listen to this. *A rumor has just swept New York that Stephen Lessing, the young heir to the huge Lessing Enterprises conglomerate fortune, has been kidnapped.* Looks like nobody else picked it up down here. If we put it on the air we got ourselves a scoop, Chief. We'll be talking about a Lessing."

The newscaster said, "A who?"